THE FIRST MAN ON THE SUN

ALSO BY R. H. W. DILLARD

Poetry

The Day I Stopped Dreaming About Barbara Steele (1966)
News of the Nile (1971)
After Borges (1972)
The Greeting: New and Selected Poems (1981)

Novel

The Book of Changes (1974)

Criticism

Horror Films (1976)

THE FIRST MAN ON THE SUN

*

A NOVEL BY R. H. W. DILLARD

Dillard, Richard H. W.
III

LOUISIANA STATE UNIVERSITY PRESS

BATON ROUGE AND LONDON

1983

Library of Congress Cataloging in Publication Data

Dillard, R. H. W. (Richard H. W.), 1937–
  The first man on the sun.

  I. Title.
PS3554.I4F57 1983   813'.54   82-18649
ISBN 0-8071-1090-6
ISBN 0-8071-1098-1 (pbk.)

Portions of this book were first published in *Black Warrior Review*; *Jeopardy*; *Ploughshares*; *Window*; the anthology *Into the Round Air*, edited by Raymond Roseliep; and Sean Siobhan's "Talking to Trees" as the Palaemon Broadside Number Thirteen. Grateful acknowledgment is made to the publishers for permission to quote from the following works: From "The Song of a Man Who Has Come Through" from *Complete Poems of D. H. Lawrence*, collected and edited by Vivian de Sola Pinto and F. Warren Roberts, Copyright © 1964, 1971 by Angelo Ravagli and C. M. Weekly, executors of the estate of Frieda Lawrence Ravagli. Reprinted by Permission of Viking Penguin, Inc. From "Notes toward a Supreme Fiction," from *The Collected Poems of Wallace Stevens*, Copyright 1954 by Wallace Stevens. Reprinted by permission of Alfred A. Knopf, Inc. From "Pale Fire," from *Pale Fire* by Vladimir Nabokov, Copyright © 1962 by G. P. Putnam's Sons. Reprinted by permission of G. P. Putnam's Sons. From "The Closing of the Rodeo" from *The Traveler's Tree: New and Selected Poems* by William Jay Smith, Copyright © 1980 by William Jay Smith. Reprinted by permission of Persea Books.

for Cathy
with a love unfeigned

and
to the memory of
Leigh Brackett
*"I look up at the stars
and wonder which one is hers."*

THE FIRST MAN ON THE SUN

A LIST

Lo ministro maggior della natura,
   che del valor del cielo il mondo imprenta
   e col suo lume il tempo ne misura. . . .

              —Dante Alighieri
              Paradiso (1321)

The yeer of oure Lord 1391, the 12 day of March at
midday, I wolde knowe the degre of the sonne.

              —Geoffrey Chaucer
              A Treatise on the Astrolabe (1391)

I wish to fire the trees of all those forests;
I give the sun a last farewell each evening. . . .

              —Sir Philip Sidney
              Arcadia (1593)

Our graves that hide us from the searching sun
Are like drawn curtains when the play is done.

              —Sir Walter Ralegh
              (1612)

Of Light by far the greater part he took,
Transplanted from her cloudy Shrine, and plac'd
In the Sun's Orb, made porous to receive
And drink the liquid Light, firm to retain
Her gather'd beams, great Palace now of Light.

—John Milton
Paradise Lost (1674)

Half his beams Apollo sheds
On the yellow mountain-heads!
Gilds the fleeces of the flocks:
And glitters on the broken rocks!
　Below me trees unnumber'd rise,
Beautiful in various dyes:
The gloomy pines, the poplar blue,
The yellow beech, the sable yew,
The slender fir, that taper grows,
The sturdy oak with broad-spread boughs.

—John Dyer
Grongar Hill (1726)

Who comes from the land of strangers, with his
　thousands around him?
The sunbeam pours its bright stream before him; his
　hair meets the wind of his hills.

—Ossian (James Macpherson)
*Fragments of Ancient Poetry, Collected
in the Highlands of Scotland* (1760)

Whether I did or did not see a flying fish, catch a
dolphin or observe a black whirling cloud called a
water-spout, is of very little importance to the world.

—Captain Adam Seaborn (John Cleaves Symmes)
Symzonia: Voyage of Discovery (1820)

We might try our lives by a thousand simple tests; as
for instance, that the same sun which ripens my beans

illumines at once a system of earths like ours. If I
had remembered this it would have prevented some
mistakes.

—Henry D. Thoreau
Walden (1854)

Once upon a time there came to this earth a visitor
from a neighboring planet. And he was met at the
place of his descent by a great philosopher, who was to
show him everything.

First of all they came through a wood, and the
stranger looked upon the trees. "Whom have we here?"
said he.

"These are only vegetables," said the philosopher.
"They are alive, but not at all interesting."

"I don't know about that," said the stranger. "They
seem to have very good manners. Do they never
speak?"

"They lack the gift," said the philosopher.

"Yet I think I hear them sing," said the other.

"That is only the wind among the leaves," said the
philosopher. "I will explain to you the theory of winds:
it is very interesting."

"Well," said the stranger, "I wish I knew what they
are thinking."

"They cannot think," said the philosopher.

"I don't know about that," returned the stranger,
and then laying his hand upon a trunk: "I like these
people," said he.

"They are not people at all," said the philosopher.
"Come along."

Next they came through a meadow where there
were cows.

"These are very dirty people," said the stranger.

"They are not people at all," said the philosopher;
and he explained what a cow is in scientific words
which I have forgotten.

"That is all one to me," said the stranger. "But why do they never look up?"

"Because they are graminivorous," said the philosopher; "and to live upon grass, which is not highly nutritious, requires so close an attention to business that they have no time to think, or speak, or look at the scenery, or keep themselves clean."

"Well," said the stranger, "that is one way to live, no doubt. But I prefer the people with the green heads."

—Robert Louis Stevenson
Fables (1896)

What is the knocking?
What is the knocking at the door in the night?
It is somebody wants to do us harm.

No, no, it is the three strange angels.
Admit them, admit them.

—D. H. Lawrence
Look! We Have Come Through! (1917)

For all action, even the ultimate act of faith, must issue in contemplation; and this is the law of life, that what we contemplate, *that* we become. He who contemplates malice becomes malicious. He who contemplates hideousness becomes hideous. He who contemplates unreality becomes unreal.

—John Cowper Powys
The Complex Vision (1920)

And then perhaps, who knows, together they would some day venture out and find a new Sun, a new world, one that had trees and flowing waters, a radiant warmth, and mayhap a moon or two to light their night!

—Leslie F. Stone
When the Sun Went Out (1929)

I ask then that we face the literary product, rich in meaning, potent to heal and save, a life-giving sun.

> —G. Wilson Knight
> *The Christian Renaissance* (1933)

If it is with outer seriousness, it must be with inner humor. If it is with outer humor, it must be with inner seriousness. Neither one alone without the other under it will do.

> —Robert Frost
> "Introduction to *King Jasper*" (1935)

Excellent, remarked Mr. Furriskey with that quiet smile which endeared him to everyone who happened to come his way, but do not overlook this, that the velocity of light *in vacuo* is 186,325 miles per second.

> —Flann O'Brien
> *At Swim-Two Birds* (1939)

There is a project for the sun. The sun
Must bear no name, gold flourisher, but be
In the difficulty of what it is to be.

> —Wallace Stevens
> *Notes toward a Supreme Fiction*
> (1942)

Good-by, says the rain on the iron roofs.
  Good-by, say the barber poles.

> —William Jay Smith
> *Poems* (1947)

Everybody's everywhere, so far as I can make out, and I'm beginning to not be sure where I am, myself—and I don't believe you know.

> —William Goyen
> *Ghost and Flesh* (1952)

lovers alone wear sunlight.

—e. e. cummings
95 Poems (1958)

All the atoms emitting light inside wavehood, there is no personal separation of any of it. A hummingbird can come into a house and a hawk will not: so rest and be assured. While looking for the light, you may suddenly be devoured by the darkness and find the true light.

—Jack Kerouac
The Scripture of the Golden Eternity (1960)

The journey of rays from that central core to the outposts of blackness is the adventure and drama of light.

—Josef von Sternberg
Fun in a Chinese Laundry (1965)

Here, we're very warm; on the sun everything is warm. But if we're late, lunch will be cold.

—Eugene Ionesco
Story Number 3 (1971)

So, whether the world is going to pieces or not, whether you are on the side of the angels or the devil himself, take life for what it is, have fun, spread joy and confusion.

—Henry Miller
"Foreword to *The Angel Is My Watermark*" (1972)

Many things are not worth doing, but almost anything is worth telling.

—Ursula K. Le Guin
"Schrödinger's Cat" (1974)

And off they went,
  feet pounding,
    wings beating,
      legs scurrying,
        feathers flying,
          with a flippity flap and a
          flutter.

—Ruth A. Sonneborn
Someone Is Eating the Sun
(1974)

Old Sun watched it with a dull, uncomprehending eye
until it disappeared.

—Leigh Brackett
The Book of Skaith (1976)

GALILEO

Galileo's birthday. Galileo Galilei, his four hundred and thirteenth birthday, four hundred and thirteen spinning years. Galileo Galilei knocking at the door.

Lucette has fallen down and broken her hip. The pins are in it now, and she is swinging on crutches, delicately down stairs, easing across the treacherous earth. Everyone I know has fallen down at least once in the last month. We are like a silent movie, slapping down left and right. And in the newspaper, an old man, one hundred and four years old, whose pipes burst and flooded his freezing kitchen, who mopped and struggled until his feet froze solid, walking on death like an awful dream, disconnected flesh and flesh until finally the doctors amputated the feet that once were his, mopping away at a floor he did not even own, the weather teaching him, teaching us, that we never own anything for long, feet or floor, day or long winter's night.

This is the great winter, the worst in two centuries. Perhaps *worst* is wrong; say, rather, the coldest, the fiercest. The ground hard underfoot and iced. When you fall, you shatter. Or the bruise in your hip is so deep and dark that it never even surfaces, and you limp on a cane for weeks, and when you turn in your sleep you wake with a start and a cry. You know you are alive. You never forget, for all the steaming baths and heating pads, the patriotic thermostat turned back, and the day bright and rigid outside the whistling door, the humming window.

And still it is not the coldest, not the fiercest. Nothing like the seventy years from 1645 to 1715 when the sun relaxed, when no sun spots (or few) were seen, the sun's corona faded away, famine and harsh winters, when the aurora borealis failed, the northern lights winked out. H. H. Lamb's "Little Ice Age." The sun, that golden godly lover, proved inconstant, and the ponds and streams and rivers froze, the ground froze, trees cracked in the woods like small arms fire, the whole earth froze.

John Donne, some years before, wrote these prophetic lines upon S. Lucies Day:

> The Sunne is spent, and now his flasks
> Send forth light squibs, no constant rayes;
> The worlds whole sap is sunke. . . .

The sun, roaring in silent space, a solar wind rushing from coronal holes, and the earth, sailing on that solar wind. And when the wind falls, the world's whole sap is sunk indeed. And we shiver and bundle, stumble and fall, hold to each other, huddle and hold on.

It seems today as though the sun were turning its bright face away again, or, at least, growing pale and cool and distant. The wind knocks at my window, and I stop work to answer, to put on a sweater, my duffle coat, to step outside and squint carefully at the sky where the sun edges along the blue mountains to the south. The wind tugs at my sleeve, and I turn away. A few ragged white clouds disturb the blank blue sky, and the dog, Oliver, shakes almost apart with cold, by my feet. The winter is here to stay; even the groundhog got the word from the sun. The shadow knows. If winter comes. Ice is in the pipes; I can almost hear them popping like some new era's celebration around the neighborhood. And the sun, pure and unblemished and aloof, is cooling toward us, looks across the hills to me with a former lover's lucid scorn.

Galileo watched the sun with a lover's eye and sketched the sun's pocked face, not that perfect orb of Aristotle and the church, nor the one I imagine in the sky today, but a turning, tilting ball of fire, marked by moving spots and rolling in the indefinite sky. And he suffered for all his attentions, his weak eyes ruined finally by the sun's steady (or unsteady) gaze. He went blind and saw the sun no more, the stars and planets, the moon swaying slowly in earthshine, the Galilean satellites sketching their even arcs around Jupiter. But he saw the sun.

The spots on the sun. Galileo knocking on the door. Let him in, he has much to say. Wrap him in a blanket or the patched quilt; persuade the dog to curl up at his side; talk with him deep into the cold night. Of the multitude of forces that guide each simple move, of the rhythms of the wheeling sky, of the turbulent sun, warming us with its unease, chilling us with its calm. His blank eyes course the room. His voice goes on. His voice wavers. "Eppur si muove!"

It is Galileo's birthday in the great winter of 1977.

IN AN OWL BAR

*

Call me what you will, I like to picture it this way.

They will be in an Owl Bar. Not the Owl Bar, though I can't really be sure about that. But an Owl Bar for sure. The usual decorations: the long curving oak bar; the lights shaped of blown brown glass, brown owls with red glowing eyes; the huge neon red owl perched at the rear of the narrow room, the whole room cast in a dull red glow; the high-backed wooden booths along the right wall as you enter from the swinging door, no slats but a carved owl split down the center by your entrance or hurried exit; the large mirror behind the bar to your left, reflecting the red room, red booths, red patrons leaning on the dark wooden tables in the booths, the red rear of the barman's head, the tufts of his own ears wavering in the red light as he moves as though they were hovering above rather than attached to the top of his owl uniform, the dark red feathers of his owly back, and the three evenly spaced tables down the center of the room, humped around their circumferences with the carved curves of nests, owls' nests, the chair backs woven wicker, the tangles of an owl's wood; and, at that time, the campaign posters, Owls running for governor, for senator, for attorney general, for commissioner of public lands, and, for the first time, for president and vice-president of the United States.

And around the third, the innermost of the three round center tables, leaning soddenly on the nest rim, the center of the table ringed with the wet echoes of some dozen drinks, will sit three men peering at each other dimly in the owl light.

A Russian. An American. An Irishman.

I don't know how they will have gotten there, how they will happen to be there, only that there they will be. The Russian will be a heavyset man, close-cropped dark hair, a jowly face, the spreading stubble of his blunt chin almost maroon in the dim red light. He will be in a dark, pinstriped suit with wide lapels, the coat unbuttoned and lolling open, the tie wide and rumpled and apparently dark red, though who could say for sure. His name is Prostranstvo, Piotr Prostranstvo. He is a functionary of the Soviet government, although I do not know in what exact capacity. He will have been tossing back vodkas for some time, and his face will have a damp, somewhat unfocused quality, red and blurred.

The American will be an engineer, sturdy, clean-shaven even at the late hour, dressed in denim, purple in the light of the bar, pens and pencils in a plastic pouch in and lapping over the lip of his bulging shirt pocket. I am sure that he will be wearing boots of some kind, and his fawn Stetson will lie on its crown, the careful shape of its curled brim protected, in the empty fourth seat of the table. His name is Welser, Mark Welser. He is a dam builder, a searcher of canyons, rock hefter, and earth shaker. He will have been drinking bourbon on the rocks ("That means they pour it over little chunks of ice," he will have explained to his foreign companions), and the stiff poise with which he will be sitting offers some evidence as to just how many.

The third man, the Irishman, will have a smooth, plump, almost babyish face, his overcoat collar turned up around it, nestling it like a precious smooth egg in a dark cup. His eyes will burn in that innocent face like the glowing owls' eyes all around the murky room. His pug nose will have a reddish glow to it, too, and his whole face will gleam out of his collar and from under his dark slouched hat like an impish beacon, his lip curled in perpetual mockery or some foolish inner delight, selfish and unshared. His name is O'Ertel, Sawel O'Ertel, and he will have been putting down Paddy's, neat and tidy as you like, for hours and possibly days. He is a happy man.

This unlikely trio will have been sitting around that avian table for some hours. They will have come in, one by one, dripping and shaking, seeking shelter from the growling rainstorm that will have been rushing at the windows and doors of the bar all day, a storm that will have clearly settled in to stay. First, the Russian, out of place in an Owl Bar, in any American bar, beating his astrakhan cap against his thigh, water flashing from its curls all over the floor, grumbling to himself, demanding a table, a glass and a bottle of vodka. The barman will rustle about, comply and then set about mopping at the wet floor, his long tail feathers dashing about in the damp dust. Then the American, beating his Stetson carefully against his thigh, settling next to the Russian, ordering bourbon, rocks, branch water. The barman will again comply and again mop at the dark floor. And, of course, the Irishman, who will emerge from the shadowy men's room door under the neon owl, carrying his own bottle and glass, plopping down, after wavering for a bleak moment over the chair with the upturned Stetson in it, in the empty fourth chair. A string of accidental arrivals or a planned meeting; who could say, but, as I said, there they will be.

A few other bedraggled customers will come in and settle at the bar or in booths, none at the other tables. The barman will finally give up struggling with the floor and will perch behind the long bar permanently. A young waiter will arrive and begin handling the sparse booth and table business. The day will drain into night, the only perceptible difference, aside from the different position of the hands of the clock nestled in the neon owl's belly, a reddening of the light in the room as all outside light ceased filtering in. The three men will continue to drink steadily and to talk.

The barman will listen. Occasionally he will hear a whole sentence or a phrase. Mainly he will hear words, disconnected and random. Some of these he will write down on an Owl Bar order pad which he will keep out of sight behind the bar's raised edge. Some of the words he will hear and note are:

> Wandering Angus
> Shqiperia
> tacky ones
> Hanrahan
> silo
> Kolozsvar
> line stir
> magnetosphere
> McCormack
> poshlost
> election
> Dublin
> Owl (owl?)
> Pete

He will tuck the pad into some hidden feathery pocket in his uniform whenever one of the three drinkers and talkers weaves his way to the bar to order additional liquor, water, or ice. He will make change quietly and never speak. But he will watch with his eyes wide, and he will listen, cocking his head from time to time so that the tufted owl ears tilt like directional antennae, which perhaps they will be. The red light will never waver, and the three faces will glow damply around the round table.

When the neon owl hoots twelve, the hour of midnight, the lone waiter will disappear in the gloom beneath the owl, and the last patrons of booth and bar will wander away into the still roaring and raining night, bidding their good nights, Bill to Lou to May, and splashing out through the owl's split and swinging back.

The three men at the table, Prostranstvo, Welser, and O'Ertel, will have decided to part as well, for suddenly their voices will raise as they rear back in their wicker chairs and loft their glasses in a toast. The barman's pencil will scratch across his pad.

"To the Soviet Union," Prostranstvo's voice will blurt, his heavy hand squeezing his small glass high, "who put the first man in space!"

The three glasses will clink over the table, and three gulps swell the red air of the room. Bottles will be tilted, and the three men will rear back again.

This time the American will speak, slurring slightly but still distinct enough, "To America, who put the first man on the moon!"

Again the glasses will clink, throats bulge and bob, and the glasses will be refilled. The Russian and the American will peer across the table to the Irishman's pale face. They will wait as he licks his lips, then raises his glass.

"To Ireland, green and glowing Ireland," he will say, his voice low and musical, "to Ireland, who'll put the first man on the sun!"

He will toss his whiskey down, but his partners' glasses will hang in the air.

"The sun?" the American will say.

"You cannot put a man on the sun," the Russian will say.

A pause. A silence.

"And," O'Ertel will say, "I'd like to know why not?"

"Why, man," Welser will say, a laugh cracking at the edge of his voice, "it's too damn hot!"

"Well, what," O'Ertel will say, tugging his coat down over his back, coat, and overcoat, bunching at his elbows, as he rises leaning over the table, looking up at the barman, saying to him, "Hold me back, man; hold me back, or I'll have to teach these lads a thing or two." But then before anyone can move, he goes on, "Well, what do you think we are, stupid or something? Do you? Do you think we're stupid?"

The room will stand still like a red dim dream.

"Do you think we're stupid? Well, no, we're not. We're not, I say. We're sending him, you know, at night!"

A DAY WITHOUT SURPRISES

✳

This morning the snow began falling at about ten o'clock. I had been up for some time, ever since Oliver had stretched himself out of bed, alert to the rhythms of my breath, and flapped his ears soundly to wake up. It always wakes me up, too, that flailing of ears, this time out of a winter's sleep as deep and sound as fallen snow. The day was gray and even, not so cold as yesterday but, in that diffuse colorless sunlight, seeming colder. Silent and empty, not a sound, a day without surprises, and then the snow.

It had already covered the old lingering snow and the bare patches on the ground and edged the tree limbs and tangles of dormant honeysuckle before I even noticed it. It defined and gave structure to the flat day, sets of new lines and curves sharp in this white shimmer of motion.

Oliver stands by the door, his black and white tail wagging, looking me eye to eye, more eager hound now than protective terrier. He knows the uses of new snow, and I accept the definition, tie my red bandanna around my throat, bundle up, step out the door into the white noon light.

And the day is full of surprises. That is, of course, the point of surprises, the point I always seem to forget, that they surprise you. Surprises: the footprints that stagger slew-footed behind you, the first ones in a smooth field of snow, not even a sparrow's skittering hieroglyphs there first today; a song sparrow sounding its notes from a dark hemlock, from one of a row of tall hemlocks across the road, hemlocks in which I can't find the bird who is singing as though a February snow were the surest sign of spring; the echoing cry of a blue jay, "Thief! Thief!" the cry you've known since you were a child, and you are a thief, stealing something, you're not sure yet what, as you track across this new day, and the bird is right to complain; the sifting snow wetting your glasses so that you have to pull the bill of your blue sail-cloth cap down and look only at the white ground before your feet as you climb the hill and leave the birds behind.

The road turns as it goes up the hill. No tracks, no dogs barking the way they often do, Bandit and Wally and Beau, nothing moving but the snow and Oliver wig-wagging back and forth across the road, writing his name in the new snow, sniffing old signatures at the feet of bushes and trees. Up the hill on an easy slope, the snow so new and soft and light that you move silently, cushioned, even the squeak and crunch of the old snow muffled and hidden, no icy crust now to shatter and tinkle underfoot like flimsy glass. Down the hill to the left through the dark tree trunks, there is no sign of life at Tom and Mary Ellen's new house, not a mark or shadow. Oliver disappears into the woods ahead at the road's end, and I follow to where I know a narrow path begins.

I have no idea whose woods these are. I've met people in them before—boys, young men on trail bikes, leathered and helmeted with opaque visors like cosmonauts or moon walkers; some teenagers, sometimes with small rifles, once five boys and one girl sprawled around a branching of the path, who stopped talking, said hello, but looked stiff and worried until I passed (you could feel the relief like a sudden breeze on the back of your neck); once, Mary with her long Rosetti hair picking blackberries, her hands stained and dripping red like those of the maddest of murderers—no one who showed any signs of ownership.

There is a gate on the path, but it is rusted, bent, and long broken, being drawn by tough vines into the soil below it. And there is a dump, one growing like a summer weed patch, two upended arm chairs, a shattered commode, one grainy vinyl-covered sofa with its cushions tidily in place sitting under a bent sumac in a posture of absurd invitation, a thick litter of cans and cheap glass bottles (Bud and Blue, Iron and Pearl), a tatter of wire and stuffing and porcelain and plastic. It must still belong to someone even after it's been thrown away, a lesson in ownership, that no matter how difficult it is to own things, it is hard, too, to throw some things finally away, for long, for good.

But who the owner is, I do not know.

The trees filter the snow, censor it, so that you may raise your head and see darkly around you. Green leaves on the low bushes, some on the twining underbrush, but mainly the dry brown and brittle texture of the winter woods, the grays and blacks of the bare branches and trunks of trees, the dark brown of the earth stippled with snow, the drifting silence. The world's whole sap is sunk indeed. Oliver crashes through a barrier of vines and lost leaves, snow tunnels down through the net of shadowy branches, and we reach a clearing where the path splits in three.

We are on the ridge of the hill, out in the open and the snow again. To the right the path burrows through a field high in brown chickweed and broom-sedge until it reaches a rail fence and the flank of a new housing development, brick ranchers and splanchers, and owners who squint at you suspiciously if you walk across the clipped grass; we seldom walk that way these days. To the left, the path winds downhill through shoulder-high jewelweed and tall hardwoods, past the broken remnants of a fine tree house, steeply down the hill past the quarry to pivot just before plunging into Tinker Creek; a cool summer walk, but today too dark and sheltered. We came for snow, and Oliver waits inquisitively and then darts straight ahead at a nod of my head, his black spots bouncing in the white air.

The path leads past the dump, where Oliver steps gingerly and precariously among the slivers and slices of glass and curled tin, until the path splits again by a maze of berry bushes and young locusts and sumacs. The path to the right coils around to join the main path again, so we head on, watching the snow fill and disguise the bike ruts, alert for cats. There is a farmhouse at the end of the path, and cats often stray out this way looking for prey with which to dawdle away the day. They don't mix with Oliver too well, and I am happy enough when he chooses to turn away from the path into a large open field. We pick our way through bushes and briars to it, past the thin shell of a long dead groundhog, the snow arching delicately along the ribs, the yellow curved teeth still standing clear of the dwindling mound of skull. Oliver does not stop; I always do.

When I look up he is a distant series of bounds, tracing an obscure message, a puzzle on the snowy field for low-flying aviators. The field lies on a low rolling hillside, a silent rollercoaster of low grass bounded by walls of blackberries and honeysuckle and kudzu. Directly across, the woods lead to the edge of the quarry, the sharp drop to the creek. In the summer the twine and weave of the underbrush with its promise of invisible copperheads and tricky, spongy footing makes it an unpleasant place for walking, but today it seems to open through the whirl of light snow. Oliver heads into it without a sign from me.

In the woods again, you pause, undo your bandanna, rub your glasses clear with it, tie it back around your throat which is just beginning to feel, without it, the sharp edge of the cold air. You look around in the new dark woods, pick your way from branch to mound of vines to crackling twigs to flat sure soil; you follow the dog's wise way. But even he falters and doubles back, testing ways, leaping with his front paws tucked tight against his chest and his hind legs taut and straight like a diver's, stepping tentatively on a mound of snow and then pressing on. The quarry should be just ahead, and you can see where the ground begins to slope away to its rough edge.

But I am wrong. My summer eyes have misjudged these winter ways. The ground does drop away, but not into a quarry. Rather, into a low bowl, no more than fifty yards across, a wasted land of fallen trees and vines and snow patches, the new snow caught and scattered by vine leaves and circling air. But there is a path, an animal track, a groundhog's ramble from field to quarry, no more than six inches wide, but used, pressed and open. We follow it down the steep bank, by a broken and battered oak, and there is his door, a hole by the path, its lip fur smooth and brushed clean. Oliver pays it no mind, seems drawn on, and I follow.

No one ever comes here. It is near a variety of human lives, but it is utterly alone. At the center, its lowest point, you feel suddenly much smaller, the trees along the rim too high, the tangle of its path and briery underbrush too complex, the wind and falling snow too silent and too steady. If you fell, as I did a few weeks before, and could not stand, no one would find you in this silence, cracked and splintered only by the dog's worried barking, his eagerness to go, to go on. Snow gusts in your face. You shiver once all over, like a dog shaking the snow from his back into the snow-filled air. Even the groundhog's hole you passed seems empty now, a cold and silent tunnel where nothing lurks or even sleeps.

Then you see just ahead of you a splash of orange, of orange and red, white mounds too even to be snow, another hole, a larger one with three white lumps, one orange and red, around it. The dog trots up to it, no hackles raised, so you must go, too.

It is an animal hole, a large one, dug into the side of a low bank, a ridge that runs the width of the bowl, and by its open mouth, as smooth and well used as the other one, three white paper packages and, opened and its contents gone, the flat orange and red cardboard of a package of sliced bacon. The three white packages are clearly also meat, wrapped in tidy butcher's paper, one of them marked in black grease pencil, SHORT RIBS.

You are no longer alone. You look around you and call the dog away from the meat. He walks back to the animal track and bounds up the rim of the bowl and out of sight. It is the hiding place of a hobo; you think foolishly, irrationally, of some fleeing Jack the Ripper, blood staining his hands like the red juice of fresh berries. It is just a dump, you answer. A dump where no one can easily come. It is a mystery. It is a dream; it has the rational absurdity of a good dream. It is someone trying to poison the inhabitant of the hole. With tightly wrapped packs of butcher's meat, short ribs, fine bacon. It is a groundhog or badger whose butcher gives him home delivery.

You pick up a stick, a stout club of fallen wood. You look around you at the quiet snow, the silent woods in the pale gray sun. You climb the bank, pushing at the hard soil with the crooked tip of the stick. You smash through a web of undergrowth, twigs snapping underfoot, and come out on the curving path by the quarry, the bowl now invisible behind you, on familiar ground, the dog circling the quarry's rim, the snow settling easily through the still air down into the rocky quarry walls, down onto the solid layer of ice and cold deep water of its measureless bottom.

I cannot find a suitable rock in the mounded dirt and packed snow at the quarry's edge to toss down into the pit, to watch and hear its rattle and hop across the echoing ice, so I whirl the stick out into the sliding air, and it does bounce and shatter on the solid ice and scurry in a dozen directions across its surface and out of sight. But the bowl is still near behind me, and Oliver is already far below, probably dipping into the creek, showering the bank with his shaking, and something has changed in this familiar place and even day.

I whistle him up, clapping my hands to carry the message where the whistle won't go, and here he comes, a darting flash of black and white through the gray woods.

You climb the steep hill from the creek and quarry on the path you did not take earlier. The day is grayer, dimmer, and your legs feel the climb in their winter weakness, your left hip beginning to ache with a faint memory of the fall. The stalks of the jewelweeds lean on each other around you; a tree creaks above you, and the snow has begun to cover even the floor of this thick wood. It is still early afternoon, but it has a twilight feel, a waning edge to it. You turn back onto the path the way you came at the top of the hill, and the dog begins circling wide around your course to avoid repetitious examinations. You walk out of the woods into the steady snow.

Down the hill to your right you see a light through the trees where Tom has probably returned home from class and is settling down to write. He is nearing the end of his novel, and you silently wish him luck. The road slopes down to your house, and you pause by the mailbox, pop its hinged door open, and rap its empty floor with your fist. No mail, just the letters and messages formed on the familiar landscape by the snow. You go in by the back way where you can rub the dog down with his large orange towel, so you can dump your snowy boots on the covered floor where they won't stain wood or rug. You go in and settle down for late lunch at the kitchen table.

Just as your soup comes to a proper boil, the doorbell begins a desperate clamor, a ding-a-ling-a-ding-a-ling of such fury that you shove the soup pot onto a cool eye and pad to the door in your sock feet. The dog is barking by the door, his hackles raised, bunched at the shoulder and ruffling a clean ridge down the length of his spine. You grab him by the collar and open the door, expecting another surprise, almost expecting the worst, and you find the postman. "I've brought you a record," he says and hands you the mail, a record sure enough and a letter. You thank him and shut the door. The dog stops being a terrier and subsides again to easy hound.

This afternoon the mail came at three o'clock. It was a record, Twiggy, and a red and white crossword maze from Alice and Dorothy: "A puzzle from *A Game of Arcana*. One player began by forming a word, any word in the world, put it down on a graph paper board and named it number one, named it QUESTION. The next player touched QUESTION with REASON and defined the game as Reasons for Questions (or things that come before questions). The players played into the night, then decided upon a puzzle gift for a certain friend."

Silent and empty, the day filled with snow, a day without surprises, a day full of surprises, puzzles, thefts, gray light and swirling snow, ribs and twigs, sticks and hieroglyphs, tracks across the day. That is, of course, the point of days, the point I always seem to forget, that they surprise you. A February day, and it is cold and snowing, Oliver is asleep, and I am puzzled and surprised.

WHEN LILACS BLOOM

✳

Ash Wednesday, a day of ashes and dust, and today the air has warmed to spring, a February thaw in full force. The sky is bright and clear, touched with a white etching of clouds. I am out checking on the sun, dipping in radiation, when a handsome bug walks by my foot, a small milkweed bug, a rich orange and black, a strong and beautiful bug through hibernating for the day, checking out the new sun himself.

"It's still winter," I say, bending over his small parade, careful not to cast a real shadow in his path, but he pays me no mind, walks steadily on in his purposeful six-legged stride. There is a pod of splayed-out silky milkweed on the table by the door, an autumnal explosion, quiet like the sun, that Alice gave me last October, a feast for this fine Hallowe'en fellow, but I remember it too late to offer. When I return with it, he has wandered away into the day.

Henry Vaughan described this day, writing just at the beginning of the Little Ice Age:

> The Sun doth shake
> Light from his locks, and all the way
> Breathing Perfumes, doth spice the day.

And the day is spiced, the mourning doves by the cherry tree puffing out their throats and eyeing each other's strut and peck, a gray squirrel poised in the tree, nut in hand, eyeing me warily, no spring blossoms, not even a tentative crocus prying out through the loosening ground by the mailbox, but spiced with the sun's perfume, the sweet rhythm of solar radiance, whiz of neutrinos through flesh and cold bone, the monopole's secret passage, dance of wave and particle across the skin. A girl walks by on the road, wearing knee socks with blue-jean shorts, a loose white blouse. Her loafers are puffing dust that floats around her feet, dust from the road that last week was stiff and snowbound, that has moved from ice to mud to drifting dust in days, dust that we are, dust to which we shall return. I watch her walk on down the road, Ash Wednesday in the sun, dust settling in the road, windows opening all down the way and up the hill, the groundhog proven a liar, the dog asleep and content in a patch of dry yellow grass, the sun shaking light from its locks, unlocking light.

A day like today can make you forget the hard winter surrounding you past and future, makes you remember that this century has been a time of bright suns, of warm weather, high water and quick winters, of an active sun. John Eddy has noted an increase during these years of sunspots on the sun, and Wes Lockwood has charted a steady brightening of the planets, of the sunlight they reflect. They have no way of proving that the sun has grown brighter or warmer, but it is Eddy's feeling that the flow of energy from the sun has been increasing during this century, that the solar constant, that steady and unvarying flow of energy reaching us at the rate of five million horsepower per square mile, has proved itself inconstant, a misunderstanding, a dream.

Galileo charted sunspots and showed the sun to be imperfect, to the displeasure of the Church. Eddy has charted sunspots and shown the sun to be inconstant. Stability and constancy waver and fade even in the circling solar system and the silent roaring sun, but today the sky is open and blue, and the sun swings across the blue ridge, sweeping out winter like a spring broom. The inconstant sun will warm us as our ancient fuels fail. If winter comes, the sun will warm the numb ground and puff it into swirling eddies of living dust.

It is Ash Wednesday, when the sign of the cross is made in damp ashes on the foreheads of the kneeling faithful, sketched as symbol of the insecurity of human life. "Remember, man, that thou art dust, and unto dust thou shalt return." That dark smudge, a reminder, ash without hint of fire, cold ash, world whose whole sap is sunk.

We stir the ashes to free ourselves from time, to reach the city where there is no need of the sun, neither of the moon, to find worlds within worlds and life within life. But today we need the sun and have it, the day is warm and the sun is warmer, and winter is in full retreat.

I settle down in the early afternoon to read the newspaper and find there, in Dr. John A. Eddy, a synchronous event, a sign. It is February, and the American Association for the Advancement of Science is meeting in Denver, and Eddy has been talking again of the variable sun. We are at the low point of the eleven-year sunspot cycle, but the ebb has stretched out for a year and a half beyond its regular time, the swing back to normal activity delayed, ignored. The sun has proved itself not only imperfect and inconstant, but irregular. Drought and fierce winter settle in around us.

"We have lived our lives," Dr. Eddy said in Denver, "and built our explanations of the sun during solar conditions that have applied but ten percent of the time, or less, in the longer run of history. Moreover, although it is hard to evaluate the present period of solar activity, the general long-term level appears to be falling again, after an unusual peak that was reached in the late 1950's."

What goes up, even the vast roil and flow of solar energy, must, it seems, come down. The sun that warmed to us all our lives has become somewhat aloof, has cooled, emptied its face of all expression, combed back its light locks. The air is now thoroughly small and dry, winter under every bush and shrub, snow pressed against the north banks, gritty with dust, ashen and gray. False spring is in the air. Clouds build and mass in the west. Tornadoes touch down in the dry midwest with a rush and blast. Static begins to rattle in the radio, mingle with the primordial hiss of television snow, the Big Bang's minatory daily echo. Thunder and lightning expected tonight with high spring winds. False spring elbowing its rough way through the dead of winter, twisting the still air into spirals and corkscrews and fiery explosions.

If winter comes. The still sun settles into the darkening west. "If the spots don't come back by the time the lilacs bloom," said John Eddy, "we're in big trouble." Ash Wednesday, a warm day before the season of repentence, the wintry stretch into the days of lilacs, time of retreat and mortification.

I whistle up the dog as the day drops down into night and shut the door. The wind begins to thump against the western wall. The sun is down. A day of signs, of ashes and dust, a milkweed bug that woke too soon, a flaw on the face of inconstant winter. The slumber of lilac and lily is deep and sound. It is a time to lie low and listen to the wind.

DUBLIN

*

It is simple enough to say how it will begin, and where.

The old Volkswagen, still shiny and well kept but some twenty years old, once jade green but now only a rather vegetal beige, will be bouncing and buzzing down the one-lane dirt road leading from Route 11 around behind the town on the side opposite the interstate. A plume of high wavering dust will mark its progress to any interested eyes across the rolling meadows or flat fields of dry corn stubble, and interested eyes there will no doubt be. The driver of the small old car, Padraic Estaban, will be intent on maintaining speed without losing stability on the rutty road and will say little, but his passenger, a rugged man in his late forties, dark-haired and dark-eyed, will be watching every detail of the passing countryside with nervous interest. He will refrain from asking questions, both because he is unsure and somewhat ashamed of his English and because he comes from a race of traditionally stolid and silent people. He is Xhavid Shehu, and this will be his first day in Dublin.

What he will be seeing:

The dry winter-burned meadows, patches of snow tucked in banksides and under clumps of evergreen trees, the flat plowed fields, the stubble of harvested crops, the bright morning sun glaring and glancing off the snow or occasional slick of ice, a brown rabbit skittering across one field with its white tail flashing like a heliograph, a farmer leaning in his denim garb on a fence post, a long shotgun reclining in his arms, how he nods stiffly to Estaban's wave, a large circling bird almost directly overhead, its tattered

26

wings spread, sailing on the sunlight, the cold bright air, a raw red and bare head incongruously jutting from those magnificent wings, the nearly hypnotic wave motion of the passing electric lines, dipping and dipping and dipping, another poised farmer, another shotgun, this one returning Estaban's wave, this one beginning to stamp his boots and smack his gloved hands together as the car passes on, bright green helicopter that rises up from behind a stand of pines like a jack-in-the-box, hovers for a moment, darts toward the car, then retreats again behind the trees, a dog, a black and white hound, running hard, head low and nose alert, that darts across the road and swerves out of sight in a weedy field, the way Estaban's speed does not waver for a second as they flash toward and by the dog, a house, whitewashed walls, a rounded thatched roof, tidily tied in place, two chimneys puckering out of the curved top of the roof, a thin tendril of gray smoke stretching up into the icy blue air from one of the chimneys, the tiny rectangular recessed windows, the almost Egyptic extended doorway, flat posts and narrow flat lentil, a huddle of woolly and dust-stained sheep in the narrow fenced-in meadow behind the house, the low walls of piled stone that parallel the road for some distance beyond the house, another slouched farmer, this one with a wide-brimmed black hat pulled down over his ears and tied under his chin with a red bandana, another shotgun, a cold nod or quick tossing up of the chin, distant grain silos, white and clean in the clear winter air, an approaching low hilltop, the whole top planted thickly with spruce and pine, the distant blue mountains, etched hard against the sky yet remaining soft in their folds and contours, two more armed farmers on either side of the road, more nods as Estaban waves, the road's beginning to climb the low hill curving and coiling, a glance back across the way they've come, the fields and thatched cottages, the cluster of the town, the flat line of the far interstate, the entrance of the road into the evergreens, almost invisible until the small car actually follows it through, the startling surprise of the hill, how its top is actually concave, a bowl, surrounded by a high chain-link fence, barbwired along the upper rim and spaced with guard posts, each of them manned as far as Xhavid can see, two men in dark green coveralls and fur-lined green caps who open the wide fence gates at Estaban's wave, as the car starts forward again the way Estaban pulls the gearshift lever back into second before popping it into first, then the whole of the bowl's contents, a ring of white cottages, these with steeply sloped and pointed thatched roofs, low interconnecting gray stone walls, smoke rising almost invisibly from the curious chimneys, and in the center of the large ring, an enormous metal building, a huge bright cube with a large round tube rising from its center some meters above the flat roof, a low barracks-type building extending from it, two huge coppery tan disks leaning back to face the sky, both slowly turning from side to side, a tall chimney beyond the disks, no smoke rising from this one, four identical dark green buildings with no windows visible, a smaller tan disk that remains motionless, no windows visible in any of the buildings except for the cottages, enclosed aerial walkways connecting the buildings, white concrete walks weaving around and among the buildings and towers and disks, a tall (but not tall enough to extend above the rim of the bowl) flagpole flying a green, white, and orange tricolor, the smoothly paved road that circled down the walls of the bowl, through the cottages, into an evenly marked off but nearly empty parking area near the enormous metal cube, the curious lilt of Estaban's voice as he announces their arrival and shuts off the car, tugging its parking brake handle up and into place, the engine's ragged sputter into silence, the emblem at the center of the car's green metal dashboard:

They will rush across the paved lot, Padraic Estaban and Xhavid Shehu, ducking their heads into their collars, the bitterly cold air numbing their faces, their hands tucked deeply out of sight in their coat pockets. They will follow a concrete walk along the front of the huge metal building to a doorway in the smaller green building alongside it. The door will snick open as they approach, triggered by an electric eye that Xhavid will be unable to find along the walk or in the walls, and it will snap shut behind them as they enter the building.

"Come right along this way," Estaban will say as they proceed along a gleaming hall, their heels popping and rattling along the slick walls ahead of them. "I'll introduce you to the director, and then we'll see about getting some hot tea."

Xhavid will nod to him and follow him down the deserted corridor, past closed metal doors, turning into a corridor to the right, passing one or two men in green coveralls who will nod and speak, and ending up finally before a smoothly burnished metal door exactly like all the others except for the emblem of a harp painted on its bright surface and the single word, DIRECTOR. Estaban will knock on the door, and as he does so, Xhavid will notice that the green harp is centered not in a simple red-orange circle as he has first supposed but is rather superimposed on a blazing solar disk.

The door will slide open suddenly and quickly, revealing a plain and bare room, a room with a single desk, three small wood chairs, no windows, a single decoration—a large photograph of the sun, red-orange and spilling out from itself, a loop of high fire swirling out and back from its boiling surface on one side, this photograph nearly filling the wall behind the desk, and also behind the desk, rising from a swivel chair also made of wood, a tall, strong, red-haired man, saying, "Padraic, welcome and do come in, and this must be Xhavid Shehu of whom I've been hearing so much. Come in. Come in."

Xhavid and Estaban will step into the room, the door slipping closed in its groove behind them, and Estaban will introduce Xhavid formally to the red-haired man, saying to Xhavid, "This gentleman, Mr. Shehu, is our director, Mr. Owen Hanrahan."

"And you must, for sure, be calling me Red," Hanrahan will say, and the three will seat themselves in the plain room, Hanrahan back in his swivel chair before the blazing wall, his hair blending and blurring with the raging solar surface, and his two guests scuffing two plain chairs into place before the desk.

"We know a good deal about you, Xhavid," Hanrahan will begin, "most of it, as you know, garnered from O'Ertel's reports about you, and we've done a bit of gathering up on our own."

Xhavid will feel a flush of shame gather and spill into his face, will duck his head, will find it difficult to look the director directly in the eye, but Hanrahan will press on, putting his flustered guest at ease, "And, I might add and will, that we're very impressed with you, with your abilities, with your discipline and dedication."

Xhavid will try to conceal his surprise, but he probably won't succeed.

"Oh, yes," Hanrahan will continue, "and we're also pleased that you're Albanian."

"Yes, and why, sir, is that?" Xhavid will ask, daring to speak if only to cover his confusion, to keep Hanrahan talking.

"Well, and it's two reasons," Hanrahan will reply, "the first being that this project is the combined effort of peoples from the world over, all of them, ethnical, products of small nations, subcultures among the larger nations and cultures of this world, Irish and Welsh, Kurdish and Eritrean, Basque and Khmer. That the Illyrian should be a part of this mighty effort would and does seem to me singularly appropriate. And second, a more immediately practical reason is that among us here is a small group of Albanians . . ."

"No one I know?" Xhavid will ask suddenly, asking this time with serious concern, not just trying to fill the potential silence.

"I doubt it," Hanrahan will say. "No, for these are Albanians who left the Illyrian shore long before the long labors both by land and sea you bore began."

"They wouldn't, then, know of me either?"

"By no way that I can comprehend."

Xhavid will not literally heave a sigh of relief, but he will slump in his stiff chair, relax, and allow Owen Hanrahan to make the necessary explanations:

How Dublin was founded in the eighteenth century by genuine Irish immigrants, not the so-called Scotch-Irish who filled the upper Great Valley with stone Presbyterian churches and tight-fisted businesses—

How these Irish settlers succeeded in re-creating the best aspects of the land they left behind them, the green agriculture, the winding walls and simple cottages, the snug pubs and wayside altars—

How the success of their settlement attracted other groups from other small, abused lands in the nineteenth and early twentieth centuries, the ones Hanrahan mentioned earlier, Welsh and Kurds, Eritreans, Basques, and Khmers, irredentists from Deseret and Texas, and others, Lithuanians, Estonians, Latvians, Tibetans, Serbs, and Croats, all of them settling in separate groups, establishing in the fertile valley lands around the Irish town their own enclaves with their own languages, customs, and ways, among these the small group of Albanians—

How these groups have remained somehow pure, intermarrying to be sure, as in the case of Padraic Estaban's Irish mother and Basque father, but maintaining a cultural identity, and respecting always the Irish right of precedence—

How the community of Dublin laid, in essence, low, staying out of public view, farming and living, avoiding for many years the temptation to lure in tourists and their money and becoming in that foul bargain the costumed unreality that the Amish have become in eastern Pennsylvania—

How the pressures of global politics and global war increased with technological advances, creating the global village that threatened to swallow their small but sacred identities as it had swallowed or was swallowing the identities of their long lost mother- or fatherlands—

How they had attracted, without particularly intending to, not only the tourists who do appear now in the town in the summers, but also a body of brilliant artists and scientists who fled the power and hungers of the global world to the peaceful pursuits of learning and expression available to them in this refuge—

How, in a last and desperate effort to preserve themselves and the world on which they live, in which they live, they have decided to make a gesture so large and so significant that it will stun the world, teach it a lesson of humility that it must learn in order to survive—

How, with monies begged and borrowed, with funds secretly acquired from certain elements of the Irish government for the privilege of naming their project an Irish one, flying the tricolor, and picking a crew that is exclusively Irish, they have been pooling their talents, pressing their science beyond that of the global village and all its suspicious, greedy, warring, and wasteful "neighborhoods"—

How with those funds and that knowledge, they are going to send a man, three men, actually, in a spaceship of their own designing and building, to the very heart of the larger village in which all these villages lie, to the roaring source of all immediate energy in this energy-starved and energy-gobbling time—

How this small community of Dublin, Virginia, is going to set the first man on the sun.

Xhavid will sit silently, partially stunned by the tale he is being told, partially relieved that his shameful past is either unknown here or does not matter. He will not really believe what this strong and forceful man is saying, for all his scholarly tone, for all his power of conviction, but he will realize how much superior life in this cold, rural land would be to the life he will have been leading in the Milanese slum in which Sawel O'Ertel found him.

"We need a man of your experience, a military or naval man capable of leadership, a man able to quell the fiery tempers and quarrels of our Albanian colleagues and lead them into productive cooperation with the rest of our group," Hanrahan will say, adding, "We believe, in fact we know you to be such a man."

"I shall do my best," Xhavid will answer, unsure really what is being asked of him, only knowing that he will soon be among his countrymen again, not freed of the shame that clings to his name, for it will live in his own heart until the debt is paid, but at least freed of its constant reminders, freed of seeing it in every face around him.

"And I know that you must be tired from your long trip," Hanrahan will say, and he will dismiss them gently but surely from his presence, guiding them to the door, standing silhouetted in that door before the blazing wall behind him until they have walked down the bare white corridor and away.

"Does he mean that about the sun?" Xhavid will ask Estaban, once they are around a corner and in another corridor.

"He says what he means," Estaban will answer.

"But how . . . ?"

"Why, don't you know the answer to that one?" Estaban will say, then add, clapping him on the back, "We're sending them at night!"

And, pointing out the way and laughing now, he will lead Xhavid through a maze of identical corridors, windowless and white and clean, to a tearoom, a snack bar, a lounge, call it what you will. It will be low ceilinged and dim, paneled in dark woods, rough beams up the walls and across the roof, lantern-lit and wavering in the lanterns' light. Two sturdy red-haired young women in white aprons over green dresses, their bright hair pulled back in large buns, will be moving through the room, lasses with freckled faces and long hands and solid haunches which are poked and pinched and pounded by men in the familiar green coveralls at the various tables scattered throughout the dim room.

"Ah," Estaban will say, apparently surprised but most probably not surprised at all, "there are your former countrymen now, all together at that table by the bar."

The two men will make their way across the room, swerving from table to table, stepping aside once to allow one of the fine large waitresses to pass them by, until they reach a large table with five men leaning on its polished wood, seated in the wood chairs with their curving spoked backs.

"Gentlemen," Estaban will say, "how fortunate to find you here, for I wish to present you to your fellow countryman, just arrived in Dublin today, Captain Xhavid Shehu of the Albanian Navy, Retired."

The men, all roughly Xhavid's age, all in the neighborhood of fifty years, will nod their heads, no looks of suspicion among them, no glances back and forth, just open greeting, nodding their heads as Estaban calls their names: Ismail Alia, Mehmet Xoxe, Enver Szende, Velimir Noli, Koci Peza.

"Hot tea," Estaban will suggest. "I still haven't thawed myself properly from this frigid day."

The men will nod and speak, ask the appropriate polite questions, put Xhavid at his ease. Tears will spring to his dark eyes as he hears his mother tongue spoken for the first time in nearly fifteen years. Estaban will wave down a serving lass and order a large pot of Irish tea, a set of mugs. The past will swirl around Xhavid, a confusion of images, Albanian, Italian, the new images of this day. The huge black bird, ragged and soaring in the freezing air, its naked red head, will circle once through his thoughts, its shadow splashing for a passing second over his happiness. He will shiver, look at the faces around him, and allow the bird to sail on out of his thoughts and back into his memory from whence it will have come unbidden.

The tea will arrive at the table. Estaban will see to the pouring, but Peza will insist that he take over, that Estaban settle back and enjoy a rest at the end of a busy morning and afternoon. Xhavid will watch Peza, a squat dark man with a thick curling moustache, pour the tea carefully into the seven white mugs and then pass the mugs one by steaming one across and around the table to each man until finally only Xhavid will remain unserved.

"Xhavid Shehu," Peza will say as he sets the pot back onto the serving tray and lifts Xhavid's cup in his hand, rising to his feet as he does so, "we recognize you, we, your countrymen, as one of us."

Peza will raise his booted right foot to his chair, the chair right next to Xhavid's, and, looking Xhavid directly eye to eye, he will lower his hand bearing the white cup of hot tea down past his knee and will offer the cup to Xhavid from under his propped leg. Estaban's face will open with wonder, and Xhavid will stand up suddenly, his chair scraping back noisily across the floor, and will shout, "No! No!"

Everyone in the dim room, waitresses and customers alike, will be watching the scene, the five seated men, the one man holding the cup of tea under his leg, the stranger standing there as if dumbstruck in the silence following his initial outcry. Then they will see Xhavid, a cold sweat slick on his face, his trembling hands, step one step forward and take the cup in his hands, take it from Peza's hand and set it on the table before him. Peza will sit down immediately, looking away from Xhavid's face, and after a moment Xhavid will pull his chair back into place and settle his weary body down heavily into it.

DUST TO DUST

The ashes are gone, washed away on Wednesday night, but the dust has come to dust, the dust storm that blew up in Colorado has come across the country, raining mud in Minnesota, soaring across the Alleghenies, across McAfee's Knob and Green Ridge, to hang high above the swirls of dust in my road, to tint the air brown in Friday's dawn, to sting my eyes and tease the membranes of my nose, to wake me up to a dry and rolling day, high winds, and gusting air.

The dust storm, sweeping from mountains of Colorado east, Florida's sunny air filled with Texas topsoil, Oklahoma and eastern Colorado and Kansas blown my way. Forty-four years after the great dust storm of 1933 filled these same skies with the earth of the Dust Bowl, four sun spot cycles ago. The smooth and spotless sun continues to have its way with us, tossing the surface of our planet around, causing its soil to whirl in patterns like its drifting beautiful clouds. Two Soviet cosmonauts came down through all the turmoil today, sunstruck and safe, but not back on solid ground, back instead on turning earth. We swing through the cosmos, sun and twirling planets, nine and possibly ten, Neptune and Pluto preparing to change places in a solar dos-a-dos, circled with our own swirling air and watery clouds, and now joined by this large and spreading cloud of dust, brown at dawn, hazy gray by day, and glowing pale green at sunset.

Winter stays in hiding. The wind brought dust instead of cold. Today four small milkweed bugs strolled together by my open door, taking the weather, ignoring my Wednesday's warning. A small tornado or desperate dust devil did touch down briefly yesterday on Reserve Avenue, battering tin roofs and scattering trailers. The midwest coming our way in small, in dusty fact. Weather words and weather warnings, the photographs from weather satellites, cloudy fronts stepping and stepping and stepping across the continental floor from left to right. And the air today is filled with Kansas dust.

And everyone is moving, too. Lucette and Leslie and Marnie came to lunch today, a surprise. Dara and Michael drove off to Blacksburg, more to savor the winding way over Catawba and up the narrow valley than to be efficient. Allen stayed at home, having his way with words on the blank page, and I watched and watch the dusty moving day.

Gray clouds mixed with the dust at three, a damp speckle of quick rain, almost clear sky, and then the dust circling and flowing again into the green-gray sunset.

False spring, but the snow has finally gone, unless it is still lurking by the groundhog holes in that mysterious bowl of tangle and shrub by the quarry. I did not go to look. Instead I watched the sky, sniffed the soil of the Great Plains, thought of the blazing dust storms of late spring Mars, let four small milkweed bugs pass by before I ventured out, and washed the drifting dust out of my eyes.

The night chills down. The stars waver in dust. The half-moon hovers in a halo of haze.

THE EARTH MOVES

*

"Eppur si muove," grumbled Galileo to himself after rising from his knees to which he had been brought by the Inquisition. He recanted his beliefs but still insisted to himself that it moves, that the earth, that staple and stable of flawed medieval metaphysics, does move. It all moves, earth and sky, sun and stars, galaxy and condensing nebula, a cosmic dance and spin and whirl beyond conception, a dizzy mix that ought to be lesson to us all.

You get up in the morning to the same room in which you went to sleep, the same sun prying at the window, the same stiff journey down the stairs to let the dog out, the same leg in the same trouser leg, the same foot in the same shoe. You can be sure, and are, that the mountains will not have danced away over night, that the sun is standing over Read to the east, that it will later set over McAfee's Knob to the west. As sure as the sun sets. As sure as the sun will rise. The thing that hath been, it is that which shall be; and that which is done is that which shall be done: and there is no new thing under the sun. When you step out the door, now that the ice is gone, melted away in this false spring determined to stay and be true, the ground will stay still under your foot, step by same step. And yet it moves.

It rotates in nearly twenty-four hours at about the same speed as those cold planets in the outer dark, Uranus and Neptune. It takes its turn around the sun, revolves through the seasons, in 365.26 days. It sails with its eight or nine planetary fellows, its fellow prisoners of the sun, companions to the sun, through the turning of its galaxy. It moves with that galaxy toward the leery, fleeing limits of the universe, this flowing universe. You know all that.

You learned most of it in fifth (or was it fourth?) grade, learned it from a delicate, wind-up model of the solar system, little stamped-tin planets grinding with their tin moons around the bright yellow tin sun, gears whirring and sprocket chains rattling. I wonder what they will do with those little machines in 1987 when Pluto moves inside the orbit of Neptune to stay for some twenty years; maybe unscrew the little tin balls and switch them, or tell the children just to pretend. Those simpler schools with grapefruit suns and circling orange and lemon and apple planets will have an easier time of it; Polly will have to step in closer with her pear, and Ned will step to the outer edge with his nectarine. You know it moves. As sure as the sun.

And then one day it moves even more drastically as though to remind you just how small you are, to bring you to your knees in surprise and horror, to make you recant your smug belief that it will always stay still under your feet. Last week it moved in Romania. Sixty miles deep it twitched itself, and the ground rippled in Bucharest, buildings toppled like propped sticks, the roof fell in on hundreds of people, on thousands. The ground wrinkled and crumpled like stamped tin, and the mountains, the Transylvanian Alps to the north, seemed to dance away. You weep for your lost wife, lost in a rubble of stone. You tap your one free foot and cry out, lost in a rubble of stone and dusty mortar, hoping they'll hear you and not bury you deeper while looking for others. And the warnings are printed and posted that the ground may move again, soon.

The government responds. Governments respond. Ceausescu helps dig into the collapsed buildings himself. Medicine and food is flown in from around the world. Money and new clothes, two suits for the men, a dress and a suit for the women, will be given to the survivors. Those who suffered worst will receive a ten-day vacation by the sea. There they will be able to watch the sun rise and ripple across the waving Black Sea, and to feel the solid ground underfoot, and to wonder when the earth will move again. And it does move.

It sails in solar wind, through the ragged, saw-tooth winds rising from the choppy sea of the sun's chaotic surface. Solar wind, ionized coronal gas heated by the blazing fury of coronal temperature, amazingly much hotter than the sun's 5,700° C. surface, expanding out from the sun, breaking free of its gravity, rushing out into interplanetary space in an even flow. But within that flow are high-speed streams, streams flowing out from coronal holes, those gaping mouths of low-density gas that smack their lips across the whole face of the sun. These streams flash through the even flow, hiss and crackle in our radios, unlink us for a time from our connections around this world. But even that "even" flow rises and falls in waves, waves spiraling out from the sun's rotation, waves that roll over us day by unchanging day, waves that rise higher during sunspot activity, that ebb and splash lower from the sun's blank face. Unchanging like the sea, unchanging like motion itself, the very process of change.

"The line of beauty," Bronson Alcott said, "symbolizes motion." The spiral of the DNA, the Chambered Nautilus, the waving solar wind, this galaxy, the ultimate spiral of time and space, beauty and motion, the unceasing movement within and without. Physicists have discovered yet another particle in the nucleus of the atom, which leads them to believe that the number of such particles may well be infinite. The universe flows out to infinity, and as we explore within, the reach there is infinite, too. And all of it moving, moving, moving.

And where is the still point, the point where you may stand stock-still and secure to get your bearings, to focus on all that whirl? It is just there, where you are. And it is everywhere. Each point in that vertiginous and dazzling display of pulsing, circling motion is the still point around which it all moves, for which it all moves and displays its beauty still. As each point in time is in itself all of eternity. We turn and touch and turn and touch again, and we are never apart. "Life," Poe said in *Eureka*, his moving cosmic poem, "Life—Life—Life within Life—the less within the greater, and all within the *Spirit Divine.*"

There is no new thing under the sun, and yet all things are new. You step out the door, and the ground stays still under your foot. The air is clear and warm and bright. You feel the sun's sweet radiation tingle across your back, your face, your closed and wrinkling eyes. The slick crocus cups by your feet are clean and yellow. The ragged forsythia by the window is stretching itself into that same bright color. The first thick green blades of the tulips have sliced out of the loosening ground into the day. If winter remains, it comes out only at night, chilling you by surprise, skulking by the walls. March came in like a lion, roaring and spitting a quick sheet of snow over the dusty ground, and then, like a lion, it lay down and began to drowse in the sun, another content prisoner of the sun. Surprising spring, arriving ahead of time, heralded by parading milkweed bugs and new yellow blossoms.

It may well snow again. I'm sure it will, as sure as I am that I shall wake tomorrow on March the tenth, nineteen seventy-seven, and that the day will probably be fine. As sure as I am that I will awaken in the same room in which I went to sleep, the same sun prying at the window or sulking behind a passing wave of clouds. As sure as I am of surprise and how it always surprises. Secure and sure at this still point. And yet it moves. You know it moves. As sure as the sun.

A WALK

*

Despite the earth's wintry tilt, the day will be a warm one, a warm one for winter, warm enough that Sean Siobhan will be drawn out of the training complex in the two joined and identical green buildings, "Siamese Castor and Thaimese Pollux," having shed his green coveralls for brown corduroy trousers, stout boots, a bright red flannel shirt, a Donegal tweed cap, stout stick of ash—except for the absence of coursing hound, a gentleman farmer out for a stroll. He will walk through the complex, the nearly empty parking lots and wide walkways, and up the slope of the bowl to the gates, walking evenly and smoothly, breathing with no strain, for he will be fit, well trained physically and mentally alert, the product of months of study and active effort appropriate to one so closely involved in the mission, to a first and future solarnaut.

He will pass out through the gates, after being halted and properly recognized, and down the winding dirt road through the thick pines and spruce and high hemlocks, the red dust coiling and curling around the tips of his boots, the point of his swinging stick with its brass ferrule and tough tip. The winds will be high and moaning once he is out of the protective bowl, the sky brownish and shifting, dust in the air, high piles of dust to the west spreading over the Alleghenies.

"Dust in the air," he will think, "dust in the air from Kansas," as he wipes his soft red sleeve across his face, his eyes, stifling a sneeze, clearing his vision. Nearing the bottom of the steep hillside, he will pause, prop his stick against the rough bark of a pine, remove a small black notebook from his

40

shirt pocket, the stub of a green pencil tucked in the leaves, point snug in the spiral, and he will write down some fragmentary lines: "a dry day in February and now wind from the west . . . dust catching in your hair, dusting through each breath . . . the sun stammers in the south." He will stare vacantly at the page for a minute or two, then fold the pencil back in place, and replace pencil and pad in his pocket. He will pick up his stick and walk briskly on down the dusty way.

Sean Siobhan walks this way often and will do so until the day of the launch. He will be watching the dust in the air, the brown stubble of the fields, the swerving flock of motley starlings that will circle out from town where they winter on the ornate ledges of the town bank, the marquee of the Dublin movie theater, the freshly spotted top of the neon owl over the new Owl Bar. He will be startled by the voice that speaks abruptly just beside him.

"And where is it you'll be going this fine day, Sean Siobhan?"

It will be Patrick Magehee speaking to him, Patrick at his post, the long shotgun cradled in his arms, his fur-lined hat and woolly coat hanging from a nearby fencepost.

"Oh, Patrick, you startled me," Sean will say.

"Mind off somewhere?" Patrick will say with a brown-toothed grin, his red thumb pointing over his shoulder where the clouded sun swung across the southern sky. "Or maybe you'll be thinking of some sweet mavourneen you're off to visit in town?"

"No, Patrick," Sean will say, used to Patrick's teasing, Patrick who will have buried three wives already in his fifty odd years, whose seven fierce and freckled sons were and are the terrors of the Dublin public schools, "I'm just out for a stroll, stretching my legs and having a look at the day, maybe to take a turn by Syrtis Minor and curve through the village on my way around."

Sean never responds to Patrick's, or to anyone's references to the sun, preferring the awkwardness to the off chance that he might once speak loosely to the wrong person, say the one word that might give everything away, that might turn the whole dream into daydream or even nightmare.

He will chat with Patrick Magehee for a time, but not for a long time, and soon he will be off down the road, passing two other of the guards before he reaches the crossroads and turns off to the left toward the Syrtis Minor. The dust in the air will be irritating his eyes, but he will go on his way, blinking and sniffing, watching the fields, the trees, his mind on the words of the poem he is composing bit by bit in his head, pausing twice more to jot down phrases and fragments, and muttering to himself that he is not paying proper attention to the things around him, the tan field of shattered cornstalks to his right, the cluster of leafless maples that dot the banks of the thawing stream to his left, the bright red flash of a male cardinal flying into the bare branches of those trees, the dart and quick brown scatter of a rabbit across the road before him and into the dry cornfield, the way its flicking white tail disappears or becomes one of the few remaining patches of mottled snow left among the cracked stalks.

"I must watch closely," he will be thinking, "I must not retreat from this encounter with a world that may not be mine for long more, mustn't slip off into mind and away from world, must hold hard to world while I still have it."

He will stop for a time, watch the water moving under a skim and scum of ice in the small creek, then will start up suddenly, realizing that his attention has slipped back again to words and away from the water. He will move back into the road and walk on as it begins to slope gently down toward a huge depression ahead, boggy land, still soft and treacherous underfoot despite the hard freezes of the winter, punctuated with large bare trees and split by the built-up road on which he is walking, Syrtis Minor, as the men at the project have named it, a peat bog, one of the reasons that the nostalgic founders of the town planted Dublin just here in southwest Virginia.

Sean will follow the road along until he comes to the diggings where he usually stops to watch the men chop and slice and remove the long thick slabs of peat, peat for burning, peat for other more esoteric uses, but today the men will not be working, will be instead sprawled along the ridge of the road in the sun, their sleeves and trouser legs rolled up, sunning, leaning back with faces tilted up in the dusty air, their boots and wool socks off, their legs cocked in the red dirt, their toes spread wide, stretching the pale freckled webs wide to dry in the warm air and diffuse sunlight.

"And look it's Sean Siobhan," one of the men will announce, "come to visit the bog trotters on this grand day. Come join us, lad, for a touch of the Irish!"

Sean will be embarrassed that, although all these men know his name, he knows none of theirs, even though their faces are all familiar to him.

"A fine spring day it is," he will say to cover his awkwardness, "if a bit dusty."

Some of the idle workmen will nod and smile. One of them, an old man with ragged teeth and sparse gray hair who will have been carefully scraping the winter's accumulation of mold off the backs of his hands with his clasp knife, will look up at Sean and say, "False spring. That's all it is. Oh, we may take what advantage of it we may, but the winter's still here, lurking in the bog. Mark my words."

"Here, lad," the first man who spoke will say, extending as he speaks a thermos cup, "now will you be joining us in a touch of the Irish?"

Sean will not want to drink, to blur his perception or the clarity of the words forming in his mind, but his embarrassment and shyness will make him take the cup and gulp the burning, peaty liquid down, look up with wet, watering eyes, and smile his thanks.

The men will gesture for him to seat himself on the roadside, and he will join them as they fill and pass the cup again and again, talking as they do of the weather, the dust, the dust that blew this way "all the way from Oklahoma and the great dust bowl" in the thirties, the work, the justice of their choosing to take this afternoon off given the grueling nature of that work. None of them will mention directly or aslant the project or its goals. Sean has no idea what exactly these men think he does, nor will he learn anything on this warm afternoon. They work as their fathers before them worked. They talk and drink and take their ease when they will. You see them stooping and swinging their mattocks and axes and spades in the bog. They will stop and give you directions if you need them, will wave you on your way. They all do know Sean. I will have seen them call him by name either in the bog or on the streets of Dublin, but I have no more idea than he will that dusty day whether they do know just exactly who he is or what he does or will do.

After the cup has passed around the group a few times more than once, Sean will bound to his feet, his eyes and nose smarting in the dust, spin himself around dizzily trying to get his back to the swirling wind, and will sneeze mightily. The men will laugh and jeer and bid him noisy farewell as he walks on his way, through the wide bog on the narrow road, dust puffing up and racing away from his scuffling steps, his brain reeling as he goes.

He will walk on through the bog, scarcely noticing it, past it, along the road until it crosses a two-lane paved road. He will turn right onto that road and, his spirits rising with the wind at his back, a tune whispering on his lips in a half-whistle, stepping high, he will pace down that hard road toward the outskirts of Dublin.

As he comes round the long curve into town, he will see a figure ahead of him, a woman, also walking toward town, her long sandy hair sprawling thickly over her bare wide shoulders, her bright aqua shirt. She will be wearing dark blue denim shorts that will leave her long sturdy legs bare down to the white socks that rise out of her walking boots, a hiker out taking in the day, a young woman, a strong and healthy young woman, and from the back, a very handsome young woman.

Sean will begin walking more quickly, striving to catch up with this appealing vision before they actually enter the streets of Dublin, the curving roads that wind through the international enclaves that circle the town proper. Just as they are entering the Croatian section of town, passing between the two gray stone pillars marking the border of the Nova Zagreb subdivision, Sean will catch the young woman and realize, as she turns to see who is walking alongside her, that she is no stranger to him, that she is, in fact, Pegeen O'Rourke whom he will not have recognized out of the green coveralls in which he usually sees her, Pegeen O'Rourke who has long featured in his dreams, even anonymously in his poems, but Pegeen to whom he will have never spoken other than the obligatory hellos and thank yous of daily working transactions.

"Sean," she will say, showing no surprise, a slow smile beginning to open and brighten her face, "so it's you as has been following me for so long."

The whiskey will warm and blur Sean's vision, cause him to keep staring into her smiling face, her remarkable green eyes under the high arching heavy eyebrows, and, for once, instead of grinning or stammering and dashing away, he will speak to Pegeen, holding to the world, directly and with feeling.

"Not following you, Pegeen," he will say, "but drawn after you, caught up in your gravitational wake, if you know what I mean. And not following you anyway, Pegeen O'Rourke, for I've caught you up and am walking beside you, and a fine place I find that to be."

Again Pegeen will show no surprise, and again she will allow that slow smile to transform her face, causing something within Sean to stagger and fall even as they walk on together through the tile-roofed cottages of New Zagreb and into the Manchurian neighborhood where three small round-faced boys are amusing themselves by pitching loud, snapping firecrackers at each other's bare dusty feet.

They will walk on, Sean and Pegeen, by the Estonian fishmarket and the Nepalese drugstore, prayerwheels spinning gaudily all along the propped-out front windows, talking of this and that, Sean carefully not looking down at Pegeen's strong bare legs or her breasts through the thin aqua cloth of her shirt, looking often into her face, her green eyes, walking and talking of this and that all through the western edge of town and back finally to the narrow dirt road that leads directly to the project gates.

"Well, Sean Siobhan, it's been a pleasure talking to you," Pegeen will say, something amusing her, delighting her, dancing just behind her eyes, "but I'm leaving you here. I'm off into town to be seeing my aunt and staying with her the night. But come by my lab sometime soon, and we'll pick up where we left off. You will be doing that, won't you?" She will wink at him and then smile slowly again.

Sean will be suddenly speechless, will only grin and nod his head in abrupt assent, will wave and turn away up the dirt road, looking back once to see Pegeen walking quickly away into town, not swinging her hips loosely and self-consciously the way so many town girls do, but moving steadily along, striding, lifting her heavy boots, stepping away.

"Pegeen," Sean will say to himself, repeat it and repeat it, "Pegeen, Pegeen O'Rourke."

He will walk away, walk up the narrow road, dust zinging up in twisting small devils around his feet, shattering on his legs, snatching at his hair. He will pay them little mind, for once again he will have slipped away into himself, not into words this time, but into the past, into memory, blushing in this brusk and windy day for memory of an awkward night in his recent past, shy Sean Siobhan—"fool," he thinks, "buffoon."

It was, he will remember, a warm night, appropriately a spring night, no full moon, but a sliver of moon (whether new or old, he will not recall) hanging somewhere in the dark sky, light spilling from the curved lamp standard some meters down the walk, spreading around the pole but not far beyond. She, Pegeen O'Rourke, was walking from her laboratory office in Thiamese Pollux along the smooth walkway toward the snack bar, Snake Farm as they were calling it that year. She had only been at the project for a few weeks, not long enough for Sean to know much about her, long enough for him to cast her in his dreams, remove her from those green coveralls, imagine the touch of her fingers on his face, his fingers in her hair. He wrote her a poem about it, a poem with high wind in the encircling pines, a racing moon, a blue jay fighting to hold its place in the wind, hanging still overhead as its wings pounded and whirred in the fast air. He walked toward her down the walk, the poem neatly typed and signed, folded and held in his hand.

"Miss O'Rourke," he had said.

"Mister Siobhan, is it?" she had answered.

Struck dumb, he had thrust the poem toward her, trembled all over when her hand touched his as she took the folded paper, and then, unable to do anything else, to speak or stand or even faint silently away, he had run off into the night, down the pale walk and across the grass and blindly, desperately away. He had run home, had gotten immediately drunk, had talked to the walls for an hour or so, had thrown his glass across the room to smash in a dark corner, and had slewed off into a dizzy sleep.

He has never spoken to Pegeen of the event, will not have even as they did walk along the road this dusty day in Dublin. Seamus claimed the week after the event that Pegeen had allowed as how some desperately lovesick young man had peeled off his skin in front of her one night and that his white bones had clattered away across the lawn, but Sean did not let on, only laughed and commented on her imagination.

But now he will be remembering, his face red, waving his clenched fists into the air, muttering, "damn and damn and damn," saying aloud, "fool and buffoon," until he realizes that Mad Jack Pearse is staring at him from his post by the side of the road, the long shotgun dangling from the crook of his arm. His face will flush still brighter as he waves and speaks to Mad Jack, who will nod his head and pass him on down the road with a motion of the gun's slick barrel.

Sean will walk on up the road, his thoughts muddled, past and dreamy future mingling absurdly, his feet beginning to drag and wander, the whisky making its demands on his quiet system. A dark cloud will pile and build itself over the piney hill before him, swirl out of the dusty west. Sean will try to walk faster, thinking possibly to sit out the storm at the Harritys' cottage just a mile up the road on the left, but the cloud will mount and move too quickly, and before he will have covered half that distance, the rain will begin.

It will be a light, spraying rain, nearer to a mist than to a downpour, spattering on the dusty ground in quick muddy blots, flicking Sean's face and hair, almost too light to dot his shirt. He will duck his head and walk on. The cool rush of the damp air will begin to clear his thoughts, and by the time he reaches Willy Mahon's guardpost, he will be feeling more himself again, able to speak to Willy about the odd weather and walk on in control of himself, put the past in a safe place (out of mind, out of sight), and try again to attach himself fully to the physical day through which he is passing.

And suddenly, even more quickly than it began, the rain will stop, the cloud swirling away to the north, the sun breaking through, drying the damp echoes of the rain's passing on the road's dirt and on Sean's brow. He will notice that a dusty shadow drop will linger where each rain drop dries, that the rain has brought the airy dust to earth in small, sparse points. He will stop again, pull out his handkerchief and wipe his face, tuck the handkerchief away again, and then stand staring at the ground for a minute or two. He will then remove the small notebook and its pencil from his shirt again and write a few more words in it: "gray cloud sprinkling mud then steering away." Then he will once again replace pencil and notebook, breathe deeply, shake his head like a dog in the morning, and steer himself away on up the narrow road.

He will walk on through the early afternoon, the sun swinging across the south to his left, wavering in the dust that swirls in the air despite the rain, but still bright and warm. Sean thinks of the sun day and night, measures its temperatures, and examines its busy face in the shielded telescope at the project, writes of it in his notes and in his poems, but on this day, on this walk, despite its bright presence, he thinks in other directions, watches the slow approach of the Harrity house with its rounded thatched roof, the black and white hound lying by the front doorway, barking from the ground, thumping its tail in the dust, not even trying to get up. Sean will pass along the road by the low stone wall, will wave at Mrs. Harrity, rehanging the day's wash on the swaying line beside the house from which she will have hurriedly plucked it when the rain blew up, will walk on toward the next outpost, the flanks of the hillside, the distant blurred blue mountains.

And he will still be thinking of Pegeen O'Rourke, not the remembered Pegeen of his shameful memory nor the smiling Pegeen of today's walking, but another Pegeen, one who comes unbidden into his thoughts at odd and unpredictable times, one who is always lying down, motionless, hair spread around her head, unapproachable, distant, cool, perfect, beautiful. The image will have been entering his thoughts for months, possibly even years, Pegeen lying down. And even more oddly he is never sure what she is wearing, even whether she is naked or clothed. He is able, as he will do this day, to focus on the image, to clothe or unclothe her as he will, but the true unbidden image is, for all its clarity and force, never somehow just one way or the other.

He will walk on past Jamie O'Donnel's post and, shifting his weight and pace, drawing out his steps longer, up the steep and curving hill road. The hemlocks and pines will soon close around him, blocking him from the south and the sun, and he will suddenly feel, as he hears the wind soughing and sighing in the needly boughs, terribly alone, terribly unreal. He will stop in the road, dig his boot toe into the gravel and ruts, grind it around and stomp then flat on the ground.

On the way to the sun? On the way up a hill in Virginia? On the way, know it or not, through warped and wavering space and time? On the way at all? Sean will feel the rocky ground wobble and disappear. He will be no more substantial than the wind in the trees. Pegeen, his poems, his work, the very flesh and bones in which he lives and thrives, all will wink and go out like a shielded light.

Sean will stand there alone and lost, and then the dust will whirl down through the trees, whirl along the graveled road, whirl stinging and grating into his face. He will turn and duck his head, turn and reenter the world, Sean Siobhan, fighting a sneeze, his eyes watering, feet flat on the ground, desperately in love, soon to be off to the sun, alive again and, having this day walked out with Pegeen O'Rourke, ready to climb on up the hill and go home.

SOLAR SAILING

※

The Ides of March. A spring day, Oliver's eleventh birthday, almost eleven years since that fat black and white puppy strolled into my office wearing a maroon and black striped Wembley tie, very Ivy, and sat on my foot. Love at first sit. We've been together ever since, and this giddy spring day seems right for a birthday.

The willows are already pale green. All of the smaller trees are stippled with swollen buds, tender buttons waiting to swell in the heat and open to the day. Grackles startled me at the feeder today, the feeder almost lost in the growing Chinese cherry tree, its red buds edging out, a sly peek, a tentative sniff at the spring air. Grackles, enormous and iridescent, the purple and green flowing through their black feathers, their eyes that astonishingly bright yellow, gazing, the black pupil at their center black and wide. Not really such a large bird, but these three huge in the tree, huge in my surprise.

A warm, bright day, this Ides of March, full of life daring to open out and test the air, bathe in the sun. The life is moving in the ground again, too. Grass greening noticeably in bold patches. Two nights ago it rained—a hard, steady rain. The creek is still high, an even rolling undercurrent to the ear's explorations. That night the earthworms, drowning in their slim tunnels, crawled up and under my back door, slid in onto the dry floor, dried out and drained, and died there. I found a dozen brittle coils and curls littered around the door, clinging stubbornly to the floor with their dried life's juice when I tried to sweep them out. Oliver tip-toed through the shards with no concern on his way out. A nine-spotted ladybug walked gingerly

49

across the window ledge by the door. I slid a card under her and escorted her to the door, out to life, away from this small dry killing ground.

Oliver and I take a birthday turn, a walk around the neighborhood, not into the woods away from the sun, staying out in it. I cut down a small wild cherry that chose the wrong place to grow and punch the rusty point of a strand of barbed wire lying low by the tree trunk into my knee for my troubles. An ordinary day, a new spring day, a birthday, a day expanding in the sun, filling with life like the bubble and strain of a hot-air balloon wrinkling and swelling on the grass and beginning to rise. No death in sight today, the worms safely swept away, the tree sawed down and up and stored, and the sun opening the east and spilling across the day, the west not yet in sight.

And I find the news that the Jet Propulsion Laboratory in Pasadena is planning to sail an unmanned spacecraft out to meet Halley's comet when it swings by in 1986, sail it with a huge sail of plastic film, five times thinner than Saran Wrap, a sail of 6,760,000 square feet, the whole ship to be ferried up to orbit by space shuttle and the sail unfurled there. Sailing on solar wind, steadily accelerating, sailing freely out to check on that famous comet's dirty nose, sending postcards home, jettisoning its sail finally and sailing along without it just above the comet's head, telling all and sweeping away.

Of course, Cordwainer Smith wrote of solar sailing years ago in "The Lady Who Sailed *The Soul*," of "the great sails, tissue-metal wings with which the bodies of people finally fluttered out among the stars," and Arthur C. Clarke wrote about it, too, in a story called "Sunjammer," published in, of all places, *Boy's Life*, over a decade ago. His sailors were yachtsmen, cruising out beyond the world, racing to the moon, but the sails are the same, the dream's the same, the fact's the same, sailing through flowing space on solar wind. Louis Friedman, of the Jet Propulsion Laboratory, thinks that perhaps a flotilla of sunjammers could sail off to Mars, carrying men to that dusty red planet by the end of the century. We are all sailing on solar wind, sailing around in solar wind, but men may soon enough sail out on it, risk their lives on it, out to Mars and farther, maybe to distant thin-ringed Uranus, like Saturn circled with sheets of light, named for Uranus the father of rain, of grass, flowers and trees, of birds and beasts, of lakes and seas, and farther still, shimmering plastic sheets spread to the sun, tacking elegantly across the solar system, making a way, our way.

But first to Halley's comet in 1986, the year of the comet. Comets have always drawn us, given our days an edge of wonder, given us open gossamer dreams at night. I remember the comet Arend-Roland that held my mind and eye in the spring of 1957, flaring out and streaming, punctuating the northern evening sky day after day, no sputtering dim Kohoutek that even my inquisitive telescope couldn't find, but a great pale glowing wonder, the universe come to call and finding us out every evening, out staring at the sky, at the calling comet. I remember my hair standing on end when I first saw it, trying to stream out like a comet's wispy trail, electrical and luminous and long. And soon we may sail out to meet another comet, not just wait to answer its knock at the door.

The sun has begun to slip down toward the west by now, yellow and round and smooth as a grackle's glowing eye, and I think of Allen's dream, his dream of two nights ago when the rain was raising Carvin's Creek to rush by his house and stirring the soil to coils and curls of earth and earthworm.

Allen's dream:

You are traveling down a narrow road, high banks, perhaps in a car, moving to the east, moving along eastward. Then ahead of you, filling the sky and rising steadily up into the roadway is the bright orange and blazing ball of the sun. But it is not round; it is bulging out on one side, lopsided, ragged and raging. Then you are able to see that the sun is resting in a gypsy cart. But it is not resting in the cart, for it continues to rise, to rise up and out of the cart, slung crookedly by ropes that stretch above it into the sky, ropes pulling at it, pulling it, fiery and orange, up into the sky, ropes that stretch up and over the swollen top of the enormous hot-air balloon. They rise, balloon and dangling fireball, floating on solar wind, until they light the sky, light up the sky. And it is full day.

But the sun is moving down here and now, nearing the far blue ridge, touching the sky with iridescence above those western mountains. Oliver is barking outside the door. I make a loop with forefinger and cocked thumb, thrust it into the light slanting across the room and throw the sun's smooth face, round and bright, glimmering onto the wall. The force of that clear circle could sail us off to Mars.

Soon the sun will settle like an orange balloon into the mountains, the pine trees igniting and silhouetting themselves with dark blue and precise clarity across the miles. It is time to furl sails, stow gear, and feed the dog his birthday dinner.

The light is waning. The west is a green-gray haze. The spring is here to stay. For a time, for a circling, sailing time.

VERNAL EQUINOX

*

Spring has officially arrived. Last Sunday was the vernal equinox, the earth in precious balance, holding its breath at that certain moment, the new cycle under way. A lady at the local Howard Johnson's asked Lewis if it were true that if conditions were right, you could see the vernal equinox. No, he told her gently, but he could have added that you do feel it, a pause in the blood, some stirring of the inner tides about to swell, an urging in the air. He wouldn't have been stretching it too much.

You could see, can see, the signs of sure spring everywhere. The Chinese cherry tree has loosened itself out into a spray of delicate pink and red, its own precise cherry color, the grass greening around it, sliced with the familiar tangs of wild onion making their regular appearance all over the ragged front yard. Tom has finished his novel. Lucette is already limping tentatively around, her crutches propped in the corner or held by some friend holding his breath as well, as she wobbles across the room. Bird song begins to fill the daily calm; Ross told me that he watched two flickers step out an early mating dance just yesterday. The moon, only an arc now, its dark bulk hovering over that luminous curve, crosses the clear night sky following the smaller bright crescent of Venus. And the sun moves higher across the day, lingering longer, shortening all the long winter shadows, driving them under the bushes and trees, making them stick close to the walls.

But all this is too easy, stretches it too much. On the Monday following the equinox, the winds tore through the valley, flapping my shingles and scattering them over the yard, knocking people down, cars veering abruptly across the highway, the willows writhing in a desperate pale dance, the cherry tree holding onto its blossoms for dear life, but losing many that swirl up the road, a flutter of pink grace across the twisting landscape. Not the high winds that often lift the spirit and clean out the drab closets of the soul by rushing steadily through the high trees and racing the clouds, but practical, down to earth, strong winds that bend the day from the ground up. Old trees creak and shatter, break over and fall. Tall signs raised on structural steel bend like summer taffy to the ground. At lunch the heavy metal tabletops, thirty-five pounds each, Edna says, lift and almost ripple, then two do take off, sail high, and slam into the wall of the building. We're under assault. The March lion stirs in his slumber, and everything darts away in terror.

Mike and Marcia's television antenna is bashed down onto their roof when I drive by to feed the sulking black cat. They won't be back from Florida for a week, so I drag out their ladder, prop it up and do my own spring dance across the roof, twisting at nuts, tugging the wires loose and lowering the whole delicate structure over the windy side and to the ground. I wobble on the ladder going down but never fall, do not blow away. The excitement of doing battle with the wind, the pleasure of bowing your head into it and making a way, the whole world whirling around you.

But across the rest of the country, winter has resurrected in snow and blizzard and ice. The cold has not gone yet, the equilibrium of the seasonal movement buried under the drifts, skidding away on the dazzling sheets of ice. And the human winter continues to howl unabated. In Birmingham, Michigan, whenever it snows, a tall, clean man continues to steal children, to keep them and abuse them, to wash and tidy them before smothering them, laying them out like an undertaker and throwing them away on the roadside among the gaudy food wrappers and bent beer cans. No vernal equinox there, no spring, just deadly rites, need beyond expression, the feast of death laid out and eaten again and again. And here the winds toss and bang across the day and night. A bird, a black grackle, hangs in the speeding air, his wings pounding furiously, getting nowhere, working for balance in this unbalanced world.

Today the winds have slowed. Oliver is out sniffing the air and snoozing in the sun, but he does stay close to the ground, curls up in a sheltered corner. Dara brought me an article from *Science*, which she had found last fall but forgotten until today. Three scientists, James Hays, John Imbrie, and Nicholas Shackelton (an icy echo in that name) are worried, like John Eddy, that our warm times are ending, that the ten percent of known time in which we've lived our lives is drawing to an end. They've studied the known cycles of changes in the earth's orbital tilt, shape, and wobble, matched them to the duration of the great ice ages, and determined that the trend of climate over the next twenty thousand years will be toward extensive northern hemisphere glaciation and cooler climates, a new ice age, accelerating over the next thousand years. Between an inconstant sun and a wobbling planet, what chance does spring have? Cold days ahead, cold years, cold centuries.

But the sun is out and high today, and the winds are falling. I hear a bird call from the towering, still-bare tulip tree across the way. The sun's light falls steadily through the window, ignoring what wind remains, wavering only as slim clouds are blown across its face. The lilacs are not yet in bloom, but I decide to examine the sun again for spots. Set up my cardboard square in the window, with its pencil-punched hole that casts the sun's round face, inverted and real, across the room and through the door and finally down the hall and onto the smooth white wall. It is round and bright and clear. A cloud knifes through the image, an enormous disturbance that would warm us all if it were on the sun and not sailing in our own windy air. Not a spot, none anyway that I can find with my uselessly crude apparatus, but I'll wait for the lilacs.

So the vernal equinox is past, and the weather signs are mixed. But spring is here, windy and wobbling like the world itself, and the light is lengthening day by day. A fierce spring, the lamb, like the dog, lying low. I walk out the front door and look to the cherry tree, usually alive with birds. A gray cat, his head suddenly caught and fixed by my appearance, looms in the branches, hanging out over the bird feeder. The birds are scattered, their chatter shrilling along the phone lines and out of the hemlocks. No corpses in sight, only this frustrated, worried cat. I pick up a stone and zing it his way; he disappears, a flurry in the underbrush, only an echo that alerted Oliver chases in the wind, a scent that causes him to scamper back and forth, nose to the ground.

The birds circle and settle. I walk around the house, collecting torn shingles, then turn back indoors to stack them up. Fierce spring and a day of mixed signs. The cherry wrinkles in the sunlight and slow wind outside the window, its branches filling again with small birds, brown sparrows and a lingering junco, a last snowbird. I settle myself to await what will come, think ahead to the summer, to the long slow days on the other side of the lilac's sure blooming.

A NIGHT ON THE TOWN

*

It will be an early and mild spring night, the kind that will draw people out of the houses to stroll up and down the lanes until sunset, cool enough to make the girls carry their shawls or light sweaters draped across their shoulders, warm enough to increase business at the pubs and bars that stand on a few neighborhood street corners but cluster mainly along Parnell Street down the center of town. Men and women, scientists and technicians and even solarnauts, will not be tempted to stay on late at the project, to work extra hours in the labs and shops in the concave hilltop as they do so often in the winter months. They will drive or hitch rides or ride the project bus (green and unmarked) down the steep hillside and across the fields into town. The sidewalks of Parnell Street will be full and busy, the boys and girls walking out, the loafers by the storefronts whistling and elbowing each other when unescorted girls step by, the married couples trying to herd their gangs of children home before the dark is too deep, and the serious drinkers crowding into the pubs and bars, maneuvering for seats on the long benches or around the small tables, propping themselves along the damp bars, throwing darts across the room, shouting and complaining, singing, and above all talking, a steady roar of storytelling and lying and unceasing commentary on the events of the day.

The new Owl Bar will have been open long enough to have attracted a reasonably loyal clientele of its own, built from the early curiosity seekers and loners, the outcasts from the other bars and crowds, random Tibetans, quarrelsome Lithuanians, a lonely and troubled Albanian, the few faithful Owl Party members who live in this area where the party is, so far, so weak.

It will be an Owl Bar like all the others scattered across the country, the same birdy decor, the same round "nest" tables down the center, the same booths along the right wall, the same long bar along the left, the same large red neon owl looming at the rear. The manager, Kevin Shanahan, who will have joined the party during a stint on the West Coast in the navy, will have pled with the national headquarters to have the bird etched for once in green neon, perhaps with a shillelagh in one claw or leprechaun's hat tilted cleverly over one winking eye, at least a shamrock suspended over its tufted ears, but he will have been rudely rebuffed and told to consult his operations manual carefully again.

This mild spring night, Seamus Heanus will make his first appearance in the Owl Bar, having just been told bluntly that if he ever appears in his favorite pub, the Up the Rebels, again, drunk or sober, he will be beaten about the head with a stout club and thrown out back among the garbage cans where the cats may come and lick him clean or clatter and howl on the tiles above his broken head. Offended, hurt, puzzled at their behavior but convinced for once of their sincerity, Seamus will have left the pub with only a few complaints and one loud speech and not a blow swung nor landed, and made his way down Parnell past the Banshee's Wail, the Last Snake in Eire, and the nearly empty, noisy Disco Drake, to the red-litten Owl Bar and its swinging carved-owl doors.

He will bump those doors open with his stout belly and swagger into the dim interior like one to the bar born, his fists rolled on his hips and ready, a sneer on his lips, and a sharpness to his roving blue eyes. Seamus Heanus is a man always ready for trouble, eager for it, and he will walk into the bar with his muscles tense, looking for trouble and disappointed when he sees the quiet drinkers bent over their tables who do not even look up to see who has made such an abrupt entrance.

But he will not pause. He will make his swaggering way through the first of the tables and up to the bar, where the owl-garbed barman, Kevin Shanahan himself this busy night, will ask him what he requires.

"I'll have a Black and Tan," he'll say in a booming voice designed to ring around the room, "and fuck the begrudgers!"

The barman will soon supply the pint mug and its foaming contents to Seamus, who will have noticed by the time he does that the room apparently contains no begrudgers, no one who seems especially interested in him at all. No one, that is, but a single middle-aged man, dark skinned and black haired, his dark eyes staring directly at Seamus, not challenging him, just looking at him steadily. Seamus will heft his pint, drain off the top quarter of the mug in a long draw, wipe his mouth with the back of his other hand, and walk directly across the red room to the dark man.

"I'll be recognizing you now, won't I," Seamus will say to the seated man as he stands at last over him. "From a place where we both work?"

"That could be," the man will answer in a voice scented with the powerful smell of anise and an accent that Seamus has never heard before, but that is not unusual in a town like Dublin.

"Well, then," Seamus will say, "you won't be minding if I join you at this fine round table."

"Suit yourself," the man will say, or maybe, "Seat yourself." Seamus will not be able to tell which, what with the way the man talks. In either case, he will seat himself at the table, banging his heavy mug down on it, and that will be exactly, at the moment, what suits him.

"And what'll you have?" he will say to his new companion. "What may Seamus Heanus offer you to drink on this odd occasion?"

"I already have what I already have," the man will reply, nodding at the careful line of small glasses reaching across the table before him, "and that is what I shall have, too."

Seamus will not quite know how to take these remarks, but he will appreciate the man's apparent capacity, which bodes well for the long night ahead.

"And I've told you my name," he will say, "and what might yours be?"

"I knew your name," the man will reply, his voice low and steady and alien, "but my name is . . . Xhavid Shehu . . . and perhaps you've heard it yourself."

Seamus will have heard the pauses with which the man surrounded his name, but he will not have heard the name before, and he will tell the man so immediately and bluntly.

"Well, then," the man, Xhavid Shehu, will say, "then it appears that you are much the more famous of the two of us, and that is fine with me. Yes, I do say, that is much fine with me."

The two men will sit facing each other as the day disappears outside the bar, matching pint and shot, leaning on their elbows and looking eye to eye, telling tentative tales, then wilder ones, grand extravagant tales of old countries and the new, of Seamus's adventures in the U.S. Marines, of Xhavid's in the Albanian Navy. Most of these stories will be lies. Some of them will be true, true enough for the men to come to know each other a bit, to draw together with a bond stronger than the one of a shared taste for spirits.

As they talk and come to know each other, the company in the bar will wax and wane with shouted greetings and quiet farewells. A fervent Owl Party member will come in and greet the barman with the party salute, a handshake in which they link thumbs and flutter their extended fingers as they move their joined hands up and down like a wounded bird.

"What's bred in the bone, eh?" Seamus will say with a wink and nod of his head toward the saluting pair, and Xhavid will nod and laugh, though he will have no idea what Seamus means.

A tall, clean-shaven man in denims will come into the bar out of the gathering dark and will seat himself, after carefully inspecting the layout of the room, in a narrow booth near the two men's table. He will lay his fawn Stetson brim up on the seat beside him and order a double Wild Turkey neat. Neither Seamus nor Xhavid will pay him any mind, but he will watch them closely from the dark booth while he slowly sips his drink.

Finally, long after nightfall, his eyes drifting in and pleasantly out of focus, Seamus will have had enough to drink to give him a proper sense of well-being. This man Shehu, he will think, might be a Patagonian for all I care, but what a fine fellow he is, best friend I have in the world, as close as Dickie Dumphries was to me once, as close as my sainted mother, and as he thinks of his mother, he will put his hand into his right coat pocket and touch the small stone he always carries there, the stone he picked up from the mounded soil of her grave the day she was laid to proper rest.

"Xhavid," he will say, his eyes welling now with tears, "Xhavid, my boy, my brother, you're a fine man, and I mean it, I do."

Xhavid, whose mind will not have been functioning at all well for at least an hour, will grasp Seamus's extended hand across the table, and the two will hold their hands together and have a good cry, oblivious to the attention they will be drawing from the room around them.

"You're a right fine fellow," Seamus will say, "and I'm glad they let you into this country, let you come be with us, for you're a fine man. Not like that scummy Russian that showed up today out of nowhere, demanding, do you hear, demanding to be let see certain things he has no right to see, demanding to be an 'observer' of things he's got no right to observe under God's heaven, no right at all."

Xhavid will nod heavily, then manage to ask, confusion and interest rising in his shaky consciousness together, "What Russian is that?"

"Oh, don't you know?" Seamus will say. "Well, maybe I'm not supposed to say."

He will look suspiciously around the room, glare for a moment at Shanahan, who will be greeting the late night replacement barman with obvious pleasure, the two big birds rustling their embarrassing feathers and nodding their wobbling ears, and scan the rest of the crowd, not noticing as he does so anything particularly important about the lone silent drinker in the booth next to their table.

"But look," he will say, apparently satisfied with his examination of their surroundings, "since you're such a fine fellow and all, I'll tell you. He's some Russian bigwig who found out, the Good Lord knows how, about . . . well, about something . . . you know of what I'm speaking. Well, he's shown up, saying he'll ruin everything if he's not allowed in. We're getting so near the time that Red was apparently forced to let him stay, though me, I would have said, me, I did say, I said, 'Let's put this man where he won't be of no harm at all, stick him in the peat bog or concrete him into a wall, and fuck the begrudgers!' But Red is the boss, and Red has ways of his own, and now this Russian is hanging all about, making a nuisance of himself and a quite general bother."

"Who is he?" Xhavid will ask. "His name?"

"Something incomprehensible," Seamus will answer, "something I can hardly remember, much less manage to say. His name is, I believe, Piotr Prostranstvo."

Xhavid will stare uncomprehending at Seamus for a moment, and then he will repeat, his voice hissing and low and cold, "Piotr Prostranstvo. Piotr Prostranstvo."

"That's it, laddy."

Xhavid's eyes will suddenly burn and glow like the neon eyes of the huge owl on the wall. He will grip the latest of his small glasses until his knuckles whiten and press nearly through his taut skin. He will lapse into a reverie, a silent and intense examination of years long past, of events that will still be moving in his blood like an unseen disease. Seamus will scarcely notice his silence or the brooding darkness that will cloud his already dark face, for he will be concerned with drinking the bad taste of the Russian's name out of his mouth and with attracting the attention of the new barman who will be bustling about behind the bar, checking Shanahan's log sheet, the levels of liquid in the bottles lined up along the wall, and the glasses of the various men staggered along the length of the bar.

Xhavid's reverie:

will be of his career in the navy, a career that brought him down from the rugged mountains and backward ways of his people, that freed him to the sea, that gave him a sense of external values completely contradictory to those with which he had been raised, the family clannishness, the Code by which all families lived, the rifles on every home's front wall, the fierce pride that burnt itself out in self-destruction, in ritualistic violence, in genocidal feuds that erased generations as though they were mere hills of insects or of earthworms—

will be of his training in submarines, of his delight in the dive, his absolute pleasure in the confinement within a craft that was speeding through a watery void, of the paradoxical sense of immense freedom which that moving confinement always gave him—

will be of his rise through the ranks, of his gaining the captaincy of his own submarine, the *Enver* itself, Russian-built and sleek and alive as a Mediterranean dolphin, of his astonishing promotion at the age of only thirty to command of the entire national fleet of six silent submarines—

will be of bright days in the sunlit Adriatic, the bridge splashed with salty spray, his heavy binoculars weighing against his chest as the small fleet deploys out of Durrës, spouting and diving together like whales, whirring underwater, bursting up through whitecaps into the surprise of a rising storm—

will be of that day in 1961 when he rushed down to dockside, his black shoes untied, his collar open, his face unshaved, leaping out of the battered ZIS staff car in time to see the fleet, his fleet, the entire Albanian submarine fleet, out to sea, westering into the Adriatic, their black hulls dark and distant in the morning sunlight dashing over the mountains after them, and, as he was soon to learn, with not an Albanian sailor aboard, not a one, only Soviet advisers, Russians stealing the entire fleet, all six, the *Enver* among them, taking them all to sea and away—

will be of the new Russian adviser who had arrived in Durrës only the week before, who had sailed out with him on the *Enver*, had observed maneuvers and complimented him on the skill of his captains and crews, a heavy-set man with close-cropped black hair, a jowly face, a heavy stubble of beard spreading over those jowls from his blunt chin, the new Russian adviser who manipulated the theft, who had sailed away with the fleet—

will be of his own shame, the shame that followed, the shame that will still linger, the shame that drove him away from Albania, that led him to defect, slip across the border, rowing his last command, an old flat-bottomed wooden boat, across the still flat water of Prespansko Jezero, landing in the rough Macedonian highlands of Greece, making his way finally to Milano where Sawel O'Ertel found him, recruited him, made it possible for him to come here to Dublin, to begin his life almost anew—

will be of his shame, the shame that caused his countrymen to revert to the Code, to look away from the shame in his face or stare at it without mercy, to serve him always under the knee, the terrible sign that he was a man without honor, the sign he will have thought to have left behind in the Illyrian mountains but which will have found him in the cupped complex of the "Irish" solar base in Dublin, Virginia—

will be of that Russian, of his heavy features, of his lying tongue, the man he must kill to regain his honor, the man he must kill to free himself of the shame of being served under the leg, the man he must kill, Piotr Prostranstvo.

He will be startled away from his reverie, his shame, his bitterness and his awe at the circumstance that will have placed his nemesis at his very doorstep, by Seamus's sudden loud bellow, "Blackie!"

Seamus will be waving his arms and beckoning as he shouts, and to Xhavid, by way of explanation, he will say, "Look, and it's Blackie O'Flynn, and what a surprise it is to be seeing him here of all places."

Xhavid will try to focus his bleary eyes, will peer through the red atmosphere, and will finally see Blackie, a handsome man, black slick hair, eyes that shine bright and dark even in that red light, dressed in a dark green double-knit leisure suit, the open collar of his pale green shirt laid out over the suit's collar. Blackie will acknowledge the greeting with a curt nod, will gesture with his thumb to the young woman with him, a slim girl with blond hair, large breasts under a white blouse, and an unchangingly open expression. He will then wink broadly to Seamus and steer the young woman away toward the swinging doors, whispering in her ear as they go, his green shiny arm encircling her slim white shoulders.

"That Blackie," Seamus will say to Xhavid, "as fine a crew-mate as a man could ask, but he does love his pussy," he will shake his head sadly. "He does that indeed."

Xhavid will not see whether Blackie and his lady friend have gone out the door or settled secretly into one of the booths at that end of the room, and he will soon forget that they were ever there at all, lost as he is in the blurred labyrinth of his thoughts.

Noticing, finally, Xhavid's silent and deep brown study, Seamus will wave his arms until he catches the new barman's eye and will order another round for the two of them. Xhavid will pay him no mind until the new barman wobbles across the floor in his awkward feathers, a heavy mug and small shot glass balanced on his small cork-lined tray. The man will set Seamus's full mug down on the wet-ringed table before him, will place a small mark on the check lying on the tabletop and another on the one before Xhavid, and then he will remove the small glass from the tray, prop his feathery leg on the twiggy edge of the table, and swing the glass under the propped leg onto the tabletop.

Xhavid will stare into the blank owl's face for a moment, not really comprehending what has just occurred, and then the truth will penetrate the foggy corridors of his wandering mind like a rattling smoking bomb, bouncing and bumping inward until it blasts into explosive recognition.

"You stinking whore suck dirty foreigner," he will shout, kicking himself back from the table, knocking his rustic chair over backwards. "You stinking refuse of a bitch," he will scream, "you have no rotten right."

He will smash the silent owl square in the curving plastic beak with his balled fist, bashing the beak back into the barman's nose, a gush of bright owl-red blood rushing out through the beak and down over his feathered chest. The barman will stagger back and fall over onto a table behind him around which four or five Mongolian welders will be sitting and drinking from rough goblets. The Mongolians will as a man leap up and crouch facing Xhavid, their hands held flat and hard like metal wedges. Xhavid will leap onto the fluttering barman on the tabletop, scattering goblets and plates around them, and the Mongolians will attack, pounding him with the honed blades of their hands, kicking at his legs with their booted feet.

"Holy Beloved, it's a brawl!" Seamus will shout with joy, and he will begin peeling Mongolians off his new friend and hurling them through the dim room.

And a brawl it will be. Soon the room will be full of fights and fighters, clots and knots of tumbling, punching men and women. Bleary shattered Xhavid will remember the pain of the blows, how he will be spun away from his bleeding prey and dashed across the floor, how his knee will connect with a Mongolian kneecap with a pop and snap as the man will topple like a small cut tree, and how a thrown chair will arc over his head, whirling leg over back over leg, will sail the length of the room and smash into the glowing neon owl with a gassy smash and electric sputter. He will remember little else, but Seamus will remember it all and will tell him all the bright details later, how they battled their way up and down the noisy, smashing room, back to brawling back, swinging and kicking, poking and gouging, donnybrooking and slugging away, how that womanizing Blackie O'Flynn popped of a sudden out of a booth with his wide-eyed lady and disappeared through the swinging doors with only a wave and a shout of good luck but without ever landing a single blow for right or wrong, and how the silent stranger who had been sitting near them in a booth had joined their cause and battled with them side by side by side until the three of them were the only ones left standing, male or female, in the whole broken room.

Xhavid will remember running down a wide street and then down a narrow alley with the sound of police sirens whooping and sneering in his ears, and he will remember standing in the darkness alongside a rough brick wall, panting and wheezing and licking the blood from all around his mouth, his flattened nose.

"Xhavid, darling," he will remember Seamus saying, "you're a real broth of a man. Oh, what a brawl, what a glorious brawl."

And he will remember Seamus' introducing him to the stranger, their ally in the fight.

And he will remember, will remember for a long time to come the man's reply, "It's really swell knowing you guys. My name's Mark Welser, and I'm new here in town."

A DAY FOR ALL FOOLS

✳

The first day of April, the world's sap rising, March having gamboled away like the lamb it was supposed to be, no more snow, fooled again, Palm Sunday tomorrow, Easter a week away, a day for us all and a day for all fools. And a spring day like today does fool us all. Every winter thing is changing shape and size and color. The tulips press out of the ground and grass in pale green clumps, rise on slender stalks and finally spread open in the April sunlight, a white curved cup, a surprising red. A black ant explores the new white blossom, examining its depths, its gleaming surfaces. The early spring world of yellow and palest green has opened on all sides into red and white, the dancing fountains of redbud and japonica, the white spray of bridal wreath and early apple, and the lush, multihued lobed blooms of the extravagant tulip trees. What has been down is coming up. The sluggish bumblebees are humming slow circles through the greening, tangling honeysuckle.

Spring fools the eye near and far. Where you could see last week, across the hilltop and on to Tinker Mountain or down the way and up the steep hill to the Lucas houses, now your vision is blurring with color. Like an eye misting with cataracts, you see around you at first clearer than ever, second sight, the day bright as it never was in clearest winter light, the sun on high shaking new light from its locks, but your sense of distances blurs and fades, blocked by trees and spreading, darkening leaves. And the air thickens, too, fills with the moist exhalation of spring, the humidity of new and renewing life. Where you could see each edge and crusty lip of the craters of the moon but a couple of nights ago, now the bright image glimmers and mists, hides itself in the coy soft focus of new spring air. The night shimmers, and though we still see—far Arcturus and the delicate sisters, the Pleiades—we see not so well. Winter held us low and in; now spring lures us out for a seven-veiled view of life, fooled again.

I often think, especially on days like today, of Christ's curing of the blind man, that astonishing miracle that is reported only in Mark. Jesus is in Bethsaida, and a blind man is brought to him. He takes the blind man by the hand and leads him out of town, into the bright countryside, and there he spits on the man's blank eyes, covers them with his hands, takes the man firmly in his grasp, and asks him whether he sees anything. The man looks up and says, "I see men as trees, walking." Then Christ puts his hands on his eyes again, and this time his sight is fully restored, he sees every man clearly. Jesus sends him home, asking him not to go into the town and, in some versions, not to tell anyone there what has happened.

Theologians have worried over this story for centuries. Is it not in Matthew and Luke because it was added much later and really shouldn't be there at all? Or, did Matthew and Luke omit it because Christ's spitting and pressing of his hands on the man's eyes was beneath him, too physical, too undignified? Or possibly because the two stages of the healing mean that Christ failed the first time and was not in all ways perfect? They scramble and worry, apply careful reason and arrive at explanations, carefully logical or enigmatically parabolic, that deal with the story but never solve it, never, fortunately for us all, rob it of its mystery or its wonder.

The 1560 Geneva Bible says the man, when finally and correctly given his new sight, "sawe everie man a farre of clearely." Nearby or far off, it is hard to learn to see, to see yourself and to see what is beyond yourself. The seasons, inner and outer, flow and change, and your vision flows and changes with them. Einstein told us that we are never separate from what we see, nor it from us. A hard saying. We are what we see, even as we see what we are. We circle and wheel within our seeing; our knowing and seeing chase in that vital circle like a pup that just caught sight of its tail. What's that? You wouldn't believe me if I told you.

"Neither go into the town, nor tell it to any in the town," Christ said to the once-blind man. In the town, men see and know as the town does. They wouldn't have believed him even had he told them. Go home, see every man clearly, know they are not walking trees but men, but do not tell it in the town. Over and over Christ speaks in parables and adds, "He that hath ears to hear, let him hear." Eyes to see and ears to hear. Without them you may see and not perceive, hear and not understand. Hard sayings. The Sufis call their knowledge the wisdom of the fools; it cannot be seen or heard in ordinary town ways. To the eye and ear of reason, it is foolishness. The QUESTION, I ought to tell Alice and Dorothy, should not be touched with REASON, but rather with SEEING or HEARING or KNOWING. Each point the still point, no point ever still. The men around you often seem like moving trees, look like walking trees. Spit and rub your eyes and look again. Look again.

Every day I feel at some point like an April fool. That's one on me. Ha, ha. And each day I know some new thing I never knew before. Ouch, help! The world circles and wheels. Uranus, we now can see, is circled with five fine bands, a ring of snowballs even on this fine spring day. The sun swings high across the sky. We can look at it by looking away. The shadow knows. The dry hard land bursts all around into bloom; the bloom fades away. The Chinese cherry is fully blown, the limp petals browning and filtering down into the straining grass. I walked by a strawberry the size of a large man's thumb, red and full and bright, lying by the side of the walk in the downtown market, a gray fur of mold chewing away at one side, edging out to cover the entire fruit. This much I know. The mystery of day to day of day to day.

April Fool's Day. All Fool's Day. Poised just before this holy week. Maybe this should always be the case. A reminder that we must see as a fool, hear as a fool. See and see and see. Trees blurred with a yellow-green haze. Trees breaking into bud and bloom. Trees filling with wide green leaves. Trees swaying and snarling in the wind. Trees black and bleak in long steady rain. Trees ringing out with each new spring. Trees moving. Trees walking. Men and women walking, the way of man and of us all.

To see and see and see. The joke's on me, on you, on each and every one. And especially it's on those who do have eyes to see and ears to hear. All fools.

A DREAM OF EASTER

*

The moon is full and hanging in the western sky, settling slowly down. I do not see the moon, but it is there. The night is cold and clear, the delicate petals of the fruit trees singed and curled by the cold. A week of rain and high water, floods that ate towns and chewed out the sides of mountains, and now a clear, cold night. Rebecca told me that she opens the curtains and raises the shades at night so that the sunrise will awaken her, be her rising, too. So she sleeps in moonlight. What dreams the moon must bring. Lunacy, the dreams of the mad, but what dreams are not the dreams of the mad, things as they never were, things as they never will be? I do not see the moon, but I know that it is there. In my own dark room I lie bundled against this lingering cold, cocooned and waiting for warmth, dreaming of Easter and an end to this inconstant weather.

I am at the foot of the dam. You are, as well. The moon is full and cold and pale. It hovers just above the lip of the dam, afloat on the flowing water, water kissing the moon in a cold, long, lingering, flowing embrace. We are standing on the concrete wall at the foot of the dam, the wall that juts out from the solid rock that roots out into the perimeter of the spillway. The water rushes straight at us, its roar so even and so loud that it has the effect of silence, motion without movement, noise without sound. The water rushes toward us, slides onto the barrier of stone, leaps high, a spray yearning for the moon's embrace that it has left behind, leaps up before us and dives down and to the left, dashes into the spillway's stream, and leaves us low and dry.

Carvin's Creek is rolling in a tortured rush. It snarls behind us, shakes the tops of the slim young trees that once grew safely on its banks, are growing and tossing now in its full bed, shakes them with a wind that we cannot feel, can only see in the blue moonlight. We are standing at the foot of the dam, the spray arching around us, shivering in the cold, safe and dry.

We follow the stream downstream, watching it tumble and soar where we walked last summer, where we could have walked last week. Last week it did bump and float a large white plastic elephant, an elephant decorated with pink and orange and yellow spots, down this way, past these houses we are coming to, all the way to the college, lodged it like an absurd, upside-down emblem just by the college gates. Tonight it rumbles and crushes, batters at the young trees and yielding rocks. We pass Allen and Dara's house in the moonlight. It is silent and dark. Even Schatz does not bark, the gentle gray cat Loco with the torn left ear nowhere to be seen. We pass on by, like the water move downstream.

This flood, or floods from this rain, tore through Grundy, smashing houses, uprooting walls and stones and trees alike, ripping men from bridges and balconies and sweeping them away, filling streets and stores and homes with mud and silt, as though it were determined to fill up the valley it carved itself so very long ago. This inhospitable world, earthquake- and flood-ridden, wobbling under the silent moon, its crust slipping and sliding, flowing across its beautiful surface like its constant marbling of clouds.

Somewhere, just over there, up there, Uranus wheels on its slim vertical rings, spinning as ever on ice, and here the stream spins and dissolves and gathers again, the roar of the dam water replaced by this steady unrelenting sigh. We strain to see, see only what the moon allows, a sprinkling of stars, the shadows of trees, the shapes of houses, itself reflecting and shimmering and glinting from these edges of fast water, these knives of light, these blades of stolen sunlight springing from the creek like spring onions or saw grass from the erupting soil.

We stoop and crawl through the concrete culvert under the interstate, rush with the stream quickly through, and when we emerge, we emerge blinking into daylight, a stunningly bright light crackling from the blazing sun. It stands overhead. It is the Easter sun, risen in the east, climbing to the summit of the sky. Everything is of a sudden bright, our pupils drawn to pinpoints, the sun a point itself, which radiates light so sharp that it slices the eye to a line of lid. We squint in this light and strive to see. We spit and rub our eyes and look again.

The day is bright and warm and clear. The new leaves on the trees crinkle in the risen sun, expand and open out. The lilacs are in full bloom. Long rows of them by the high brick wall, white ones, dark purply red ones with a milder scent, and the mild purple ones, the lilac-colored ones, *Syringa vulgaris*, common and clustered, the bushes bunched in this long row. Their sweet odor pervades the warm noon air. When lilacs bloom. We yearn to look directly on the sun, to see its face, its rough or smooth. The squints of our eyes stay on the ground. We see what is around us, and suddenly that is enough. For now.

We are standing by lilacs on a ground wrinkling with sharp light. We are squinting to see, and we look to see again. The creek is in high water, and we are walking in the creek. We are walking on water, and the water dazzles us like light. We see, as in a dream, clearly, but we know not what we see. Yet we know.

There is a knocking at the door. Someone is knocking at the door. We must go and let that someone in. I am speaking to you in my dream, and I am alone, sitting up, seeing the sunlight edge its early way around the corner of the room. The dog is still asleep, curled and tucked in such a thorough way that no one could be knocking on the door. I have been dreaming of Easter, and now it is Easter. Who knows who is knocking at the door? This much I know. That there are surprises on the other side of the door. Like bright eggs, hidden in the grass, lingering in the dew like wild strawberries or dozens of rainbows. The dream lingers like the memory of snow, melting but never gone.

Knock. Knock. Come in, or call me out. The sun is still spotless, at least to my primitive observations, my cardboard solarium. Hard times ahead. The dust is blowing in San Joaquin. The waters are settling in Grundy. The dream fades and flickers like a dream, something I never saw, never did; the dream lingers like a dream, something that we have never seen, and yet believe. I must go now and open the door.

A SAINT PATRICK'S DAY MEETING

*

The parade up Parnell Street will be scheduled for three o'clock in the afternoon, a fiercely windy Monday afternoon, everything at the project battened down and buckled under, the flags popping at the flagpole lines, Padraic Estaban's small Volkswagen swaying in the parking lot like a Galway hooker moored in a storm. The green bunting in town will be whipping and ripping away, green streamers racing down the streets and tangling in the budding trees. The awnings of the storefronts, unrolled and lowered during the warm week before, will be snapping on their metal frames, rattling like small-arms fire, causing passers by to duck and dart inside. Not a very good day for a parade, but a parade there will be, a parade that will rock disordered up the street, bagpipes skirling, drums pounding through the other shrill noises of the day, the dozens of different national flags knocking their bearers over and tugging them across the street like wounded paratroopers. The crowds will huddle together along the sidewalks or toast the day from the doorways of the pubs all along the route of march, and even the window of the Eskimo Ice Cream Parlor will bear the large painted words: ERIN GO EAT YOUR ICE CREAM. It will, despite the gusts and gallops of the wind, be a Saint Patrick's Day like all other Saint Patrick's Days in Dublin, Virginia—a roaring, hooting success.

Just after lunch, Padraic Estaban will drive from the project into town, bumping and swerving down the windy way, the ancient little car bucking and heaving toward the roadsides but somehow staying upright and on the road. He will be carrying three passengers: Pegeen O'Rourke from the laboratories, who will have missed the bus into town, and her friend, Deirdre O'Sorh, a smaller, rounder-faced young woman whose eyes are so bright and moist at all times that those who don't know her well often suppose that she is ready to burst into tears at any moment, and, having run at top speed from the solarnauts' quarters without mussing a single slick black hair or rousing his lungs into even a pant, Flann O'Flynn, the heartbreaker of the crew, a man who so seldom sleeps in his own bed at night that the maids in the complex will have long since simply patted his bed into place day by day with no change of linen at all. Pegeen and Deirdre will be squeezed into the small back seat while O'Flynn expands into the roomier space of the front.

"Well, Blackie O'Flynn," Pegeen will say as the car gains the last straight stretch of road into town safely, no hint of warmth in her voice or manner despite the thick green ropy-knit sweater she will be wearing, "I don't suppose you'll be marching in the parade today, not you."

"And you'll be right in not supposing that, Pegeen colleen," Blackie will reply, twisting in the small seat to face backward, laying his hard arm along the back of Estaban's seat, "for I'll be having other fish to fry, so be it, you know."

"And I can imagine what sort of poor fry you'll be snaring," Pegeen will reply, looking sharply at her girl friend's damp eyes, shifting herself in the seat. "You've quite a reputation to be upholding."

"Ah, now, Pegeen," Blackie will say, "you'll not be so harsh with me when you've come to know me better."

"And that's not likely to be occurring anytime soon, now is it?" Pegeen will reply.

"Oh," Blackie will say, ignoring her tone, looking away from her to the bright face of her friend, "I have my good points, I do. Don't I, dear demure Deirdre?"

Deirdre's eyes will fill with sudden moisture, and she will duck her head down without a word of reply. Blackie will laugh then, a heavy thudding laugh, and will turn back around to watch the road ahead lead into town, while Pegeen, stunned into a reluctant silence, will bite her lip and stare straight ahead at the back of Estaban's head. The brief remainder of the trip will be silent, save for the bumping and groaning of the small car making its labored way through the gusts and crosscurrents of the eggy day.

Estaban will let his passengers off in front of the post office, its crackling red-white-and-blue flag high overhead, before driving away to find a parking place. Blackie will hold the door and bow the ladies out, will offer to escort them up or down the street, and will laugh another heavy laugh as they nod their refusals and stride away into the wind, Pegeen beginning to talk steadily to Deirdre's ducked head. He will turn then and head downwind himself, turning into Parnell at the corner and, after looking carefully up and down the wind-battered street, will walk on the already crowded sidewalk toward the newly reopened Owl Bar, thinking to have a small one in that probably empty bar before the day's events begin in earnest.

Three or four majorettes, their bright green uniforms hidden under their tightly buttoned coats, their bare legs and gold boots stepping high in the stiff winds, will pass Blackie on his way, and he will step into the shelter of the doorway of the Banshee's Wail and look the girls up and down with an appraising and practiced eye. One of the girls will look around and catch his gaze, hold it for only a startled second, and then will look away, speak to her friends, and the three or four will walk on away, their heads huddled together, casting nervous excited glances back over their massed shoulders as they go.

"Ah, there's no end," Blackie will say to himself as he watches the girls move on away; "there's no end to it at all. The world is so full of them, new ones sprouting every minute, such a number, how can a man not be as happy as a king?"

He will nod his head once in amazement, in wonder, in delight, and then he'll step back into traffic, walk on up the street under the snapping awnings and by the busy bars and pubs. He will think once that he sees Seamus leaning against a brick wall and watching the crowds gather, but it will not be he.

"He's here somewhere, the drunken sot," Blackie will mumble to himself, smiling and shaking his head again, "but I'll be betting not that bloody prig, Sean Siobhan. Not pure enough for him, this day, I'll be wagering. Not pure enough at all. Probably off in the woods counting the fallen trees and writing things in his bleeding notebook. Oh," and he'll wave an arm in the swift air, "and what a couple of crewmates those two boys will be making, the sot and the swat, and not a full pair of balls between them."

He will finally find the Owl Bar, its new split owl doors polished and unmarred, stirring ever so slightly in the fierce wind of the day, its red neon already glowing overhead in the early afternoon, etched against the gray tumbling speed of the clouds. He will push his way through the doors and into the refurbished red interior. The owlish barman behind the counter will look him over closely as he walks across the floor, checking him against a set of photos under the counter's edge, and then greet him civilly as he reaches the bar and plants one foot on the rail.

"And I'll be having a touch of the Irish in honor of the day," Blackie will say, and as the barman rustles about filling his order he will check out the room. Empty, as he will have suspected, a perfect place to bring Nell should he find her, or Mary, or whomever it may be that the winds will blow his way this gusty grand day.

The barman will deliver his drink, and he will pay on the spot, not wishing to be encumbered in any way should duty or desire call him to his post. He will be tossing down the peaty whiskey when the doors will burst apart behind him, and the severed owl will let in a dozen chattering young women, girls really, girls in their early teens, not the bundled bare-legged lasses Blackie has already noted down the street, but a new lot, just as bare-legged but dressed in short red dirndls, red boots on their feet, white owls stitched over their varied bosoms. They are shouting and talking, brushing at their wind-tangled hair, tossing their heads, pitching coats and jackets into one of the empty booths, running around the room, a couple of them picking up signs that will be stacked in the dark corner of the bar back under the red owl, waving them, pecking at each other's heads with them, signs reading: THE WISE OWL KNOWS WHAT IS HAPPENING IN THE DARK, THE OWL PARTY'S EYES ARE ALWAYS OPEN, VOTE HARVEY— VOTE OWL.

"Inane," Blackie O'Flynn will say half-aloud and half to himself alone, "stupid, political rubbish," but he will not leave the bar, will rather stand there at the bar, watching the girls prance around with their gaudy signs, their legs winking in the red light, their long hair, their slim arms still sprinkled with the pale fine hair of youth, the subtle unblown curves of their hips and rumps.

"Another drink," he will say suddenly to the barman, but the feathery bartender will no longer be there, will be stepping around the room handing out signs, giving nervous orders, trying to make some sort of order out of the whirling red chaos around him.

"Ah, hell," Blackie will say, and then as quickly as it began, the confusion in the room will cease, the girls will grow silent, the bartender's commands will ring clear, and the girls will form themselves in two lines and march, left right left, following the owl across the room and out the swinging door, a woman in her forties materializing from the ladies' room, blowing a small silver whistle and stepping with them out the door and, turning to the left, marching them down the street, their signs already twisting in the wind.

"Top of the afternoon to you," Blackie will say, raising his empty glass, "you bunch of steamy little slits," but the last strong word will stick in his throat as he realizes he is not alone in the dim silent room. He will look quickly around and find a girl, not in the red owl's garb but tidily clad in a green plaid skirt, wrapped around and pinned with a large brass safety pin on her right thigh, a white blouse with a small round collar, her light reddish brown hair looped in two loose braids behind her ears, freckles scattered over her face, white knee socks, brown loafers, a regular schoolgirl, but one who will be, as he looks her over, staring at him with something like fear but more of fascination in her face.

"And why," Blackie will say to her after a burst of heavy laughter, "are you not out on the busy street with your birdy girlfriends ready to be parading now?"

"I want to be," the girl will reply, her voice barely making it across the room from where she is standing by the pile of coats and scarfs and caps.

"Then why aren't you?"

"I can't."

"And why not. You don't look crippled to me. In fact, that's as fine a pair of young female legs as I've seen in all my full life."

The girl will blush, although Blackie will not really see it in the red light, but she will not pull her legs back from where they are stretched out from the booth table's edge upon which she is leaning.

"And you don't look like the wallflower type of a girl, lingering behind in a stuffy dark room while your friends are out strutting it up Parnell on a Saint Patrick's day in Dublin, Virginia."

"That's just it," the girl will say. "It's because it's Dublin, Virginia."

"And just why is that?" Blackie will put the glass down on the bar and begin a slow stalk across the room, edging slowly by the round table separating them.

"It's my father," the girl will say. "He's the mayor."

"Michael Mulligan," Blackie will say. "And what's the matter with him? Is he afraid he'll lose a vote to the opposition if someone sees his daughter's lovely legs? The man's a fool."

"That's not it at all," the girl will say, watching Blackie's slow approach, standing up on her feet and dropping him a wry little curtsy. "It's that I'm

Mollie Mulligan, and everybody in town knows it, and Mollie Mulligan can't be carrying on in public for that crazy Owl Party even though all her friends are and not a one of them caring a hoot for politics."

"That's pretty funny," Blackie will say as he reaches her side, "and so you're bright and witty as well as a raving beauty."

"It's no fun being the mayor's daughter," Mollie will say, pushing her lower lip out into a pout and looking up at Blackie's face as she speaks.

Blackie will reach his finger out to her chin, will tilt her head effortlessly up with it, and will say, "Well, think of it this way, mavourneen. I might have seen you prance by in the parade waving some damn stupid sign, and I might have thought to myself that there's a lass with mighty fine legs, and I might have dreamed of your round eyes more than once in lonely sleep in my narrow bed, but I would not have had the chance to make your lovely acquaintance so soon and so well had you not obeyed your cautious father and stayed behind to guard your friends' discarded coats. Now think of that."

"I don't know you," Mollie will answer, moving her chin back from his finger. "I don't even know your name."

"Well, lass, I can surely remedy that," Blackie will say, "for, although it's not so widely known now as is Mollie Mulligan, the mayor's daughter, but it's a name you'll be hearing of quite soon, and it's Flann O'Flynn, it is. And pleased to meet you."

She will look up at him quickly, her braids bobbing around as her head turns, and just as she will seem about to say something the bar doors will bump open, and the windblown and ruffled owl barman will rush in.

"I haven't missed any customers?" he will ask Blackie. "The damn parade's starting, and I had to get those girls in their proper places. You can't get any decent help around this town, none at all. I hope you haven't been inconvenienced."

"Well," Blackie will say after this flurry of words, "the only customer you've missed is me, and I'll be happy enough with another of the same, and," he will pause and look at the girl, who will nod her head vehemently no, "and . . . perhaps there's a room upstairs where we can watch the parade without having to be straining on our toes over all those heads? We'd be much obliged."

The barman will resupply Blackie's glass and say, "Just this way, sir, yes, sir, right this way," beckoning them to a small door directly under the illuminated owl between the rest room doors, "just climb these stairs and there's a room at the front of the building that even has a small balcony, perfect, just what you want, sir, yes, sir, and if you'll just toss some of these buttons out as our unit goes by," he will be handing Mollie a brown paper sack rattling with metal buttons, "I'd appreciate it very much, I'm so short-handed, but right this way, sir, yes, sir, at your service, sir."

The barman will open the door, lean in and flick on a dim yellow bulb somewhere up the steps, and usher Blackie and Mollie through, closing the door swiftly after them.

"I don't know if I should," Mollie will say, "I mean, I'm supposed to be watching the girls' wraps and stuff."

"Ah, trust those to our feathery friend now," Blackie will say. "Do you think such a noble bird would let someone just waltz in and carry off all those fine warm coats?"

Mollie will giggle and follow Blackie up the steep stairs. He will have finished his drink by the time they reach the top, and he will set his glass down on the top riser, turning to sweep Mollie with a grand bow ahead of him in the dim corridor. The second floor will be obviously little used, dust on the floor, long sinewy cobwebs looping across the ceiling, a clear path of sorts leading to one door on the right.

Following that path, Blackie will swing the door open and say, "This must be it, sweet Mollie," but it will not be. It will be only a storage room, one window looking only into the brick wall of the building next door, boxes of glasses and napkins, Owl paraphernalia, a barman's owl suit hanging from a hook on the wall, a large radio of some kind, what seems to be a teletype machine, rolled Owl posters, and cases of bottled whiskey. Blackie will scout out the room, find a case of Paddy's or Jameson's, reach into it and pull out a fine full bottle, and turn to explore further with obedient Mollie.

Just as they will be leaving the room, a sheet of teletype paper will catch his eye. It will have slipped off the table by the teletype machine and will be lying on the floor by the door. Blackie will stoop conscientiously to pick it up, and he will see the words, "WANDERING AENGUS . . . HANRAHAN . . . MAGNETOSPHERE . . . DUBLIN," other words, too, upon which his eyes will not so quickly focus, but he will have seen enough, enough to crumple the paper and shove it into his pocket, wave Mollie out the door, step through himself, shutting the door behind him, and, carefully unsealing and opening his new bottle, follow down the hall to the door at the very end.

This room will prove to be empty and the room for which they will have been looking, for its window will look dustily out onto a small bird-stained balcony directly under the large Owl sign on the front of the building.

Blackie will take a gulp of whiskey and heave the window up, assist Mollie to climb out, seeing as he does how smooth and clean her slim legs are, and then will follow himself. They will find a single straight wooden chair sitting by the wall. Mollie will offer to climb back in and find another, and, as much as Blackie would enjoy the sight of her climbing in and out of that window again, he will decline her offer, saying that they could easily share the chair and keep each other warm and safe from the blusters of the day.

Mollie will look into Blackie's eyes for a moment, the wind dancing her braids around her face, and then she will wave Blackie to his seat and seat herself on his lap as soon as he is down.

The first units of the parade will be passing as they settle, the snarled flags, the motorcycle escort, the first band of wailing pipers and bounding drums. Mollie will squirm eagerly on Blackie's lap, and he will feel the first tickling swellings in his loins beneath her legs.

"Not so soon," he will say to himself under his breath, "haven't you any restraint? We'll be scaring this one off if we're not careful now."

He will begin to watch the parade closely himself, scanning the crowd, anything to keep his mind off what will be happening in his warm lap. He will see the Irish locals in their scarves and woolly caps, green rosettes blossoming on their lapels, the women tugging at and calling to their scattered children, running wild, all of them. And he will see the others, too. The round Mongolian faces, the hard-boned small-eyed Lithuanians, the Bhutanese, the Patagonians, the tourists with their flashing cameras, even some of his fellow workers from the complex.

And then his eye will settle on one familiar face, strong featured and undeniably beautiful, her long hair snarling and tangling in the wind, a face that will, for a moment, make him forget the firm teenager on his lap, the bright, determined face of Pegeen O'Rourke.

Blackie will take another swig of whiskey, feel its usual burning descent, think to himself just how he will be getting rid of this lass, the mayor's daughter, and get across the street to join Pegeen, when he will see Pegeen turn and speak to someone beside her, someone he will not have noticed, speak with bright interest, speak with enthusiasm as though she cares what she is saying and to whom she is saying it. She will be with Sean Siobhan, and Blackie will curse aloud.

"That slime," he will say, "that bloody skin and bones, that . . . that . . . that poet!"

"Did you say something, Flann?" Mollie will say, twisting to look at him.

"Yes, love," Blackie will say, his ears pounding and his face flushing red, "I was just asking you to look up the street and tell me if you see your friends coming."

Mollie will pop off Blackie's lap and lean far out over the rail of the balcony, her green skirt riding high on her tight thighs.

"Christ," Blackie will say, unbuttoning his trousers fly and driving his hand into the opening, "I've got to get this damned shillelagh out," and he will tussle and strain and succeed only seconds before Mollie will plunk herself back down.

"I think I see them," she'll say, "but they're still pretty far away."

Blackie will smile and nod and slip his right hand down from Mollie's waist, down her skirt to the safety pin, sliding there into the layered cloth and onto her tense leg. She will make no sign. He will take that as a sign and proceed, moving his hand slowly up her warm leg, feeling delicately for the elastic edge of her panties, and he will find instead of elastic a very warm tangle of bristly hair and a startling dampness.

"Surprise!" Mollie will shout as she leaps up, grasps his bold shillelagh in her small right hand, slips her pleated green skirt up behind and lowers herself again onto his lap, this time with their bare and eager parts smoothly and perfectly in place.

Blackie will be nearly stunned with delight, this creature of fire in his lap, spitted and secure, moving back and forth, up and down, as she cranes and twists to see the parade's wonders, tosses a tinny prickling shower of bright red Owl buttons down over her passing prancing friends. Blackie will squeeze her hard waist with his left hand and replace the other hand back inside her skirt at the sliding tangled junction.

"Oh, oh," he will be saying to himself aloud, "oh, thank you, thank you, thank you. This is the greatest joy of my life, my life, my life. May this moment, this moment last forever, forever. There is nothing, nay nothing, nothing at all that can even approach it, approach it for joy. You can take your woods and trees, your damn poems, Sean Siobhan, your damned Pegeen, your moon and stars, your fucking sun. Take them all and shove them, shove them up. I'll give you every one of them, every last one, for this, for this, for this, for this, for this . . ."

He will close his eyes and hold on tight to this creature of motion, this mayor's daughter, giving himself to her, to sex, to the very thing above all things in the world, in the very cosmos, he values most, and he will not see, across the noisy street, looking from an open window of the Banshee's Wail, the bright red face, streaked white with the crooked paths of many tears, the still and rigid face, the broken and terrible face of Deirdre O'Sorh.

THINGS IN THE AIR

*

The air is filled with flying things, bits of fluff, tiny twirling blades, spinning parasols, traveling seeds looking to go to ground, return to air. It is a day like the one that opens Fellini's *Amarcord*: everything and everyone seems lighter, lifting, enlightened. These floating dots of life lift like rising snowflakes, snow spirits, withdrawing, returning, flying through the still spring air.

And, of course, the air is filled with other flying things as well, the busy spring birds, grass and twigs and twine in their beaks, nest seeking and nest building; the light airplanes that seem to hover and circle and wing overhead all day from spring to fall, their buzz and blatter punctuating the thunder of the larger jets, that rumble that makes me often as not look to the western sky for signs of rain; the balls, lacrosse and softball and baseball, that rise and fall across the flat green field at the college, the baseballs that sail and slide, sink and spin, get taken for a ride outside the park at the ballpark in Salem; the two brown bats that fluttered and pivoted in the lit air of the ballpark last Monday, snagging flies and beating out hits, the thin brown membranes of their spread wings, fingertip to tip, glowing in the electric air. The dandelions are everywhere, thick and tall and white; I dodge them at night, thinking clumps of them are grazing rabbits or lazy dogs. They loosen in the sunlight, lift on the steady air, and soar, join the lively air of this day, this day of sailing signs and vital air.

If these things are signs, and signs they surely are, then what do they mean? That spring is here. If winter comes. The familiar progression of seasons and seasonal events. The usual mysteries of life that ought to stun us, lay us low, or, as Dorothy Richardson would have it, drive us mad. We can read these signs, but can we ever know what they say?

Last week after a week of dry wind that pulled the damp out of the ground and took it out to sea, the south-eastern slope of Read Mountain caught fire, a pillar of white smoke to the east by day, shading to blue or gray as it fed on different woods, always returning to white; a pillar of fire by night, the bright tiny flames flickering and twisting at its base, the cloud glowing red and orange and hovering through the dark. What sign is this? An echo of the biblical sign. Lights in the sky. In Genesis, God sets the sun and moon and stars in the sky "for seasons, and for days, and years" and "for signs." And the rainbow arches after each rain as a sign that "the waters shall no more become a flood to destroy all flesh." The Bible is filled with signs, with the asking for signs, false signs, everlasting signs, and the sign of Jonah, the only sign that need be given, need be received. That pillar of cloud and fire hung in the sky opposite the sunset and deep into the warm spring night. Do we take it to be a sign?

My mother, while recovering from the flu, watched a pair of handsome robins strive to build a nest on the top of one of her porch pillars, how they pressed wads of straggly moss and dry snapped twigs of grass together in the small corner, how the wind twisted their flight, bent tails and wings, tossed their buildings to the floor, how they struggled for days despite all contrary advice until they finally flew wearily away. What sign is this? Bird signs, the flocking of birds, the shrill chitter and rustle of roosting birds, the bird that Allen, Ross, and I heard distinctly outside my car's open window as we drove to the ballpark last night, a cry clear and unmistakable, and no bird in sight, no bird inside or out, trapped or free. The day knocks and calls in sight and sound. What do we say in reply?

I remember the sign I received in September nearly five years ago, September the twenty-sixth, a sign asked for and given on a mountaintop, the sign everyone is given who asks.

You walk through the open woods of Mount Desert Island in Maine in the early fall, climbing to Eagle's Crag and the southern ridge of Cadillac Mountain, that granite hump left bowed and bare by the glaciers of the Great Ice Age, an easy climb, a walk along a smooth and well-used path. But it is late in the season, and you are alone in the silent woods, moosewood and slender birch, spruce and hemlock, the tree roots coiling and sliding underfoot like slow serpents, brown and barked. The trail branches, climbs, steadily and evenly, rejoins itself, and there, suddenly and surprisingly, the sparsely treed, pinkish gray rocky back of Cadillac itself.

You walk on up, gaining altitude, moving from the still high trees into the rising wind. The day is bright, though broken with moving clumps of gray cloud. The mountain's stone curve rises smooth and rounded like a whale's arched back, and all along the way passersby have left their marks, small cairns of stones, celebrations of the joys of passing this way, and the glacier and the winds have left their huge cairns, too, rock walls and hummocks and stranded hulks that shelter pools of black clear water, cold and clean. You could soar out on this empty, gusting wind, sail over the valley below, out over the island, fly inland to the dark Maine woods, or soar away to the sun. The wind pounds you and lifts you and empties you, and you are alone as you have never been before, and it is then that you ask the gift of the spirit, and the gift is given, and, planted on that gritty granite bulge on this moving earth in this moving universe, you sail away in another way, are less alone than you have ever been before, know now that for all the lonelinesses and losses of each changing day, you will never be alone again.

So you leave your sign, you build your cairn, a structure of three stones: one large flat stone of flesh-pink granite, turned end over end into proper place; a large white crystalline stone that catches every beam of light around and sends it focused on its way; a small, flat, and dark blue stone to anchor it all in place—earth, sea, and air, all in one still place in the rushing day, all joined in the dazzling light, the sun's bright fire.

From the valley far below you will see it glow and catch the day's last light and cast it up and out, but now you back away and find in stone the sign of your gift, sign of the sign, a dark fish-shaped stone, tail tilted up, alive in its symbolic sea, the sign of Jonah as you see it. You carry it carefully away.

What sign is this? God's gift, the spirit's stunning lift and spin, the mountain rising from the sea, the racing winds, the silent forest, turning roots, baptismal pools rippling in the rocks, heart that lifts by surprise like a wing and soars away.

The air is filled with flying things, a dust of fluff and pod and seed, a sailing through the day. This dust catches in the rough surface of the stone I brought back from Maine; I do not brush it away. Everything and everyone seems lighter. Lucette has thrown her crutches down and moves lightly, walking her way. A horse, my neighbor's horse, has moved for a time over the fence and into my back acre, grazing and rambling his slow path down to the edge of Tinker Creek and back up the weed-scattered meadow. Leslie has managed to take the clutter and stammer of my library, its orderly authors and disorderly facts, and put them in a poem that lights up with the speckled sun of her imagination. And I even have new glasses with lighter lens, as though my eyes need little aid to see these shining things.

What sign is this? The sign of Jonah, that what goes down may now come up again. Hard sayings. Hot days, cold days, ice ages, and swollen suns ahead. And yet the sign remains. The day is filled with flying things.

LONG GOOD-BYES

✳

April is nearly over, another April of winds and warm days, the usual showers (one rained out the ball game last night, Allen and I the last lingering fans to leave the stands, to bid the damp game a reluctant farewell), hot days, cold nights (a frost is due tonight), warm nights, the usual surprise of the first slow sunset after the advent of daylight saving time. We spring forward and fall back into the insidious laziness of those long evenings and late twilights. And for anyone associated with schools and schooling, whether you are working hard or lolling on leave, it is in your blood, the rush toward summer and the release from the academic year's unchanging daily variety and, as well, the sense of endings, the loss of good friends, the rituals of farewell and farewell, of parting and good-bye.

That academic blood that makes us think of years that begin in September, that forces the renewals of spring to take on an overtone of ending and departure, should be enough by itself to make me think of good-byes, but the day does its part, too, as it always seems to do. Suddenly I find myself surrounded by old friends, Judy and Betsy and Bruce, who walk up just as though they had been here yesterday, talking about the April sun and the best way home. I receive a letter from Selden who says she may pass this way in June. I saw Rita just the other day quite by surprise, shelving books at a local Walden. John Engels has come to town to see his daughter Jessica at the college, so I go to his reading, and it seems as though he, too, were always here, reading or telling stories or standing by the SLOW DANGER-

85

OUS DIP sign, looking a bit dangerous, a bit dippy, the way he does in the photograph upstairs, not a bit slow.

Don was at the reading, and that reminds me of his reading yesterday with Leslie, Lucette, and Robin. Don read a poem called "After Dillard," my just deserts, in which he says, like Round Ruby, too, good-bye. He is off soon to Japan, I know, but he also used as his epigraph a couple of lines of mine from a poem (after Borges) called "Limits": "I know a face which I seek in every stranger's, / Which I shall never see again."

And that, too, brings me to good-byes, those faces that we think we shall never see again, those final handshakes, her hand held out from the window as she leaves the last time, your father's voice against an even background of April rain, the door that slams angrily in your face as you stand there desperately and foolishly trying one last time to explain, your own face caught in a silly moment in a blurry photograph, that awkward grin, the steady stream of good-byes you ford each academic spring, the eye you catch that speaks in one hung moment of all lost possibilities and of final and permanent good-bye.

It is Parents' Weekend at the college, and in the midst of all that embarrassment and strained affection, you can read also the lesson of the continuing good-bye of growth. Where did they go? The children growing up, the parents growing old? They are here standing around in the April sun in an air as clear as October's, every tree on the mountains vividly precise and present, shaking hands, touching each other delicately and almost shyly on the arm, or fretting and rushing away. Their every moment together or apart is but one particle of a single long good-bye. We part from each other steadily and without cease. We strain to see, not lose, the other's face, as long as we are able, but each breath, each separate thought, each page we read, or step we take, takes us away. Good-bye, we say, as we say hello. Good-bye, we say, continually and continuously, good-bye. Life as a long good-bye.

All this is true, but is it all so simple? C. D. Broad in *Scientific Thought* referred to human beings as long events, a description he later recanted under fierce pressure from his shocked and humanistic fellow philosophers. But he was right. Among all the other things we are, we are long events, a flow of experience as well as a steady object, a growth of spirit in a waning flesh, a hello and long and lingering good-bye. And within that long event, that continuing connection, the act of good-bye, of final and sure disconnection is far less a description of necessary reality or effective fate, than it is a choice. I say good-bye in that final way only when I choose the finality of that good-bye. We may move apart, grow apart, but we need not be apart.

There is a door, Borges says in his poem "Limits," that he has shut until the end of the world, that he will never open again. True enough. The door is locked, and the key is in a stranger's pocket, or the key is thrown away, or the door has been torn down, chopped up for kindling or hung in a new frame in a building you don't even know exists. We shake hands, and we say good-bye. There is a romantic sweetness in the simplicity, the finality of the gesture; the good-bye, the act of disconnection, will linger with you, especially on lonely evenings when the rain has been sifting down all day, like an inheritance, cast of the eye, narrow heel, heavy jaw. You savor it, even as you utter the painful words of farewell.

But, one way or the other, you may open that door if you choose. There is no door that you cannot reach some way, that you may not turn the knob and open. You may not feel the hand, the familiar grasp, or caress the face, press him or her to you in sure embrace, but the hand, the face, they are always there. The connection holds. The earth moves, sky sways, clouds waver and part; the day survives, repeats, restores itself with each new turn, each wash into the sun's turbulent wind. The signs are clear, even as they swing and reverse and blur. Selden writes. Betsy and Judy and Bruce walk through the door. John is in Egypt. Cyndy is in London; Ian in Manchester; Colin in Cornwall. I have said good-bye to them all, and I shall see them all again. Garrett is leaving for Italy; George for Maine. They will pass this way again, or I will seek them out. And are they ever gone? The door closes, and, in the way of doors, it opens again. Even the door of death, Robinson's dark Egyptian door, will, I suspect, open again as it has surely opened before.

So what are you saying when you say good-bye? When you choose it to mean I shall never see your face again, then you have said what you have said. Although, even there, surprise has a way of breaking that door in when you least expect it. The word itself, *good-bye*, is a contraction of a longer phrase: God be with you. Here or there. It is a prayer. It is connection. It is an assertion of our gathering in the long event of life. Good-bye, I say. Good-bye, you quietly reply. It is a prayer.

We should not be afraid to say good-bye. We do too often superstitiously hide the word in a flurry of words or mask it in a disguise, a "See you" or "So long" or the ubiquitous "Bye," or what we say to babies and New Yorkers, "Bye-bye." We should say good-bye with all the weight of its dangers, its wishes, its prayers. Jesting Marnic has taken to saying, "I may never see you again," as she leaves the room, pulling on her jacket or giving you a steady blue look. The room will always grow still. The weight, even in the joke, is there. And I remember once watching a dreary poet leave a room where a reception had been held for him after a reading, a reading in which he had insisted on a bleak examination of life as confidence trick or long and final good-bye. A student, a young poet who had not spoken to him all evening, touched by the need for some sort of connection, said to him as he paused on the stairs, bidding his casual goodnights and good-byes, "Have a nice life." The man stopped as suddenly as if he had walked into the wall, stopped and stared wearily at her, surprised and stopped cold. Then he trudged on up the stairs. She had dared to say good-bye to him, good-bye with all its open implications, with all its strength translated into another phrase. I think he felt its force. I hope so.

When I heard Don say good-bye in his poem, I wanted to tell him what I now finally manage to say. It is what I shall be telling Betsy and Bruce and Judy, what I told Rita, will tell Selden. What we all tell each other each day we speak with caring. I choose to see you again. You will not be away. God be with you. The long and lasting prayer of good-bye.

The moon is three-quarters full and high in the east by late afternoon. The tulips are dangling on their stalks, withered and stale. The horse, Redcoat, has chewed and swallowed his way all through the weeds and brambles and high grasses of my back lot. I hear Oliver barking in the distance, at a rabbit, or a horse, or the settling western sun. Soon he will be knocking at the door. Soon April will be leaving; friends I have known for years or not so long will be leaving; spring will be leaving, the cool nights and the fresh scented air. I may never see any of them again. I choose to see them all. I bid them good-bye in preparation for their return.

Like the planets and stars, we do our slow dance, too, circle and bow, touch and part, bid our partners adieu, circle and sway, and touch again. Leaving and arriving. The whole pattern must be so beautiful that it would take your breath away or give it fully back. Circle and touch. We say, each to each, good-bye.

SWIFT DEPARTURES

✳

Ben Bulben, so named nostalgically two centuries or more, rises pine-rough and rocky, west of Dublin, visible from the edge of town, clearly visible from the small hills near the town, wearing passing weather like a cloak, wrapped in close cloud on gray damp days and standing bold and bare in bright sunlight. Everyone in the area watches Ben Bulben for signs. At the small airport north of town, planes land and take off in all kinds of weather as long as Ben Bulben's rocky cap is clear, but as soon as the clouds have settled low enough to glide among those rocks, the planes pass over or remain safe on the smoothly grassed ground. The movement of dark thunderheads beyond the mountain, the way lightning flashes through its tall pines, the way snow clings and lingers on its dark sides in winter, the way pale pastels edge their way up those sides in spring, all these weather signs are read below and pondered and interpreted carefully and usually erroneously. Not a high mountain, Ben Bulben looms in legend and tale—gold buried somewhere on its sides during the Civil War, rainbows that leap out of lingering slow rain and point the way, men lost for weeks and months and suddenly reappearing pale of memory and confused, the banshee's terrible wail echoing out from the mountain wall and across the fearful vale—and looms in fact when observed from the top of one of the hills near the town, looms enormous and magnified and very close.

Sean knows Ben Bulben well and will walk to it often as the day of departure nears, will walk with his polished staff in his hand, his notebook and its pencil stub in his pocket, a lump of cheese and pone of bread in his knapsack, trusting to the mountain itself for water and for the right place to rest. He cares for one way up the mountain's flank best of all, a path that parts from a country road almost imperceptibly, that runs through the deep woods, that narrows as it goes, that edges up the mountain alongside a deep ravine cut by a rain-fed stream, dry in winter, a torrent in the rains of spring, a rush and rumble that carves its way and clears Sean's path nearly to the base of the stone towers that rise roughly to the mountain's southern peak.

Sean will walk out one clear warm day in April, stepping high in the new grass, the dew darkening his boots from tan to deep brown, looking at the day, looking for signs, waiting for poems to notice him. The high wet grass will be dotted with spider tents, low small patches of spun dew, glistening and hanging like young dreams, silver surprises in the morning grass. Sean will carefully avoid stepping on the delicate patches of reflecting light, will allow them to disappear again in the drying sun, dream fading and deadly trap alone left. He will walk down the hill of the project, not along the road but through the spruces and pines to the west, winding his steep way down, catching at trees, skidding on the slope, once feeling the start and near fall of a dead sapling's snapping away from the ground whole in his hand. He will soon reach the bottom and the way across meadows and among the cows and wandering chickens of the nearby farms to the base of Ben Bulben and his path to the top. But he will be seeing little, his perception snarled in the turmoil of the predawn's events, the dark and distressing beginning of his day.

It will have been Deirdre O'Sorh who will have unsettled his sleep and cast him loose upon the day, seeing little, thinking in disjointed clusters, in images more than in thoughts, Deirdre's face, Pegeen's, the voice on the telephone, his answers, repeating his answers, walking quickly, making reasons for his answers, what he will say to Pegeen, what he will say to Deirdre, what he will have said, what he will have to say. Finally, he will remember how he lay awake the night he went with Mike and me to see *The Texas Chainsaw Massacre*, lay there unsleeping with those terrible bright images in his mind, the red chicken crammed in the canary cage, the razor's slice across the hand, the girl squirming that terrible time on the meathook, the teeth behind the leather face, and on and on, remembering how he organized those thoughts, reconstructed the movie scene by agonizing scene in his mind, numbered them, and laid them successfully to rest. It worked, he will think, it worked then, bringing the terrible into order and putting it carefully away.

He will try that method again, walking across the last wet field before the mountain's woody base, not noticing the slash and scurry of the new tall weeds around his legs, the shimmer of scattered dew away from his feet, not even noticing the startled meadowlark that will rise beside him and whir its sharp flight straight up into the morning sun.

That method again:

1. I am asleep, dreaming some vague dream, working at the console, gauging the tachyonic force, punching the ranks of buttons to no avail, the smoke from the peat swirling into the control room, punching and punching, and then . . .

2. Awake, abruptly, no dream of alarm bells or even of the alarm clock, only the ringing of the phone just beside my head, and I reach over to it, lift the receiver as I touch the wood of the bedstead for luck, and say a sleepy hello, trying to sound as awake as possible, into the mouthpiece.

3. It is Deirdre's voice, saying, "Sean, is that you? I've got to talk to you, Sean." Only I don't yet know it is Deirdre's voice. No. I think for an instant that it is Pegeen, then that it is Nora, calling from the lab. Then I realize as the voice begins sobbing while I try to straighten out my thoughts, prepare a civil early morning answer, realize only then that it is Deirdre, and a cold chill runs along my arm and prickles the hair on the back of my neck, and I feel my heart jump once like a startled frog, gulp.

4. "Deirdre," I say, "is that you, Deirdre?"

5. "Sean, it *is* you, and I have to talk it all out. It's more than I can bear, more than I can bear alone." She begins to cry again, then says, "I can't talk to Pegeen about it, I just can't, and that, and that leaves only you, and you've got to talk to me about it."

6. "About what?" I say, stalling for time, trying to sound indifferent, or at least unaware.

7. "You know," she says, "you must know."

8. "No," I say, "I mean, no, really, I don't know, Deirdre."

9. "Oh, come on," she says, "you do know, you do."

10. I do know. At least I think I know. I have been seeing Deirdre at the snack bar or in her office, and it is not the same Deirdre I saw before. Oh, yes, the same round face, the same eyes that tighten and almost disappear when she smiles, but she does not smile. Her face looks red, and she seems to be lacking sleep, and she will not look me in the eye. I have always been shy of Deirdre, but now she is, for some reason, desperately shy of me. We hardly speak.

11. At first, I think I know: she is in love with me, and since I have been

seeing (seen with) Pegeen, she cannot bear it. I see her on the walks at the project, riding—really drifting on—her bicycle, watching us, Pegeen and me, stroll those walks, Deirdre always in the distance, hovering near, and when we see her and wave, she turns the wheel and pedals swiftly away. She clearly loves me, and she cannot bear to see me with another.

12. So I try to let her down easily, thinking had I noticed her first, before I had ever seen Pegeen, we could have been lovers, been in love. I even dream of her once. She is in bed with me and Pegeen, between us, her slim body as naked as ours, and I am touching her breasts as I embrace her and press myself into her slim back, and Pegeen is kissing her, kissing her on the lips. I try to ignore the dream. I speak gently to her, tease her when we meet, look upon her with warmth in my eyes.

13. And then I realize the truth from the empty way she stares at me when I speak to her, the lack of response when I touch her arm or shoulder as we pass in a doorway or along the hall. It is not me she is in love with, but Pegeen. This slight slim girl is in love with bold Pegeen, with tall Pegeen, with Pegeen's strong arms and legs, with Pegeen's laugh, that deep laugh you hear only when she is lying on her back. And I, I, I have stolen her love away.

14. And she is calling me to complain, to ask for her love back, to ask me to free her love, her lover, back to her arms again. And this is the day I am walking to Ben Bulben, maybe my last chance, last chance (literally) in the world.

15. I do not allow myself to consider whether Pegeen is her responsive lover.

16. I do not want to talk to her.

17. Not today. Not about Pegeen.

18. "I don't," I say, "I really don't. How could I, Deirdre? I scarcely know you."

19. She is crying again.

20. "Please, Deirdre," I say. "You know I don't want you crying."

21. "But you've been so nice to me. You have. Always talking to me. And touching me. I've noticed. I've not been blind."

22. I reassess. Maybe I have been wrong. Maybe it is me. And not Pegeen. Maybe, too, it has been she who calls me on the phone and never says a word, just hangs up. Not Pegeen. Not lovesick Pegeen.

23. "I thought you would be my friend," she says. "I thought you would be the one to talk to. About it."

24. Not me. Not me that she loves.

25. "But Deirdre, shouldn't you talk to Pegeen. She's . . ."

26. "No. Not Pegeen . . . you see . . . not Pegeen . . . Blackie . . . well, he's . . . no . . . not Pegeen."

27. "Blackie," I say. "Why don't you talk to Blackie."

28. "No," she wails (literally), "no, no, no, no, no."

29. "But Deirdre," I say, "I'm leaving town," no lie, only an exaggeration, a slight distortion, "I really am, this morning, in a little while."

30. "Then let me come see you now; let me come talk to you now; let me come see you. I can be there in a few minutes; please, you're my last chance; I have to see you, see you now; please let me come see you now." She is bawling into the phone. I can see her red face, her squinted eyes, the tears rolling over her puffy cheeks, all this in my mind's eye.

31. I am shaking all over, sitting on the edge of the bed, the sheets thrown back, the morning sun beginning to bring the scattered objects in the room into focus, draw them up out of the night's dark shadow.

32. "No, Deirdre," I hear myself saying, "no. There's no way, no way at all. I've got to go. I, I'll see you when I get back. Honest, I will. I'll call you first thing. You'll see. I will."

33. She is crying and sobbing, "No, no, no, no," over and over.

34. My voice is shaking now, too, but I manage to say, "Good-bye, Deirdre."

35. I hang up the phone.

36. I sit on the edge of the bed, staring vaguely at the room's ascent into view. I get dressed without turning on the lights. I eat a piece of dry bread with butter and a smear of apple butter on it. I jump at small noises. I hear Deirdre outside the door again and again. I leave the house quickly, out the side door into the flower garden, vault over the low stone wall, walk swiftly away. Tug my light pack straight on my back, plant my ash stick solidly in the soil as I go, splash in the dew, glance over my shoulder again and again until I am over the ridge and down into the pine woods and safely away.

He will walk on through the morning fields, past the quiet yawning guards almost ready to be relieved by the morning shift and eager to be home in bed, his nerves settling as he goes, his method working, placing Deirdre somewhere to the back of his mind, leaving the attentive front to the walk and to the growing day.

Sean will approach Ben Bulben along his favorite way, watching the graveled road give way to a dirt one and the dirt one begin to climb, to dwindle, to become a pair of pine-needled ruts, a single rut, a dry stream bed cut in the red clay, the roots of the pines and freshly leafing oaks and maples fingering out from the crumbling dirt walls into the narrow ditch. His long shadow will feel the way before him, shrinking as he goes, losing itself in the dappled and cool shadows of the wooded flanks of the mountain. The way is so familiar to him that he forces himself fully and self-consciously aware of each step when he walks this way, and he will be looking about and focusing his attention on the details of the rocks, the damp moss spreading along the left bank of the trail, the early cupped mushrooms still holding their fine froth of dew, the pattern of needle and leaf along the floor of the forest and the bed of the trail. His notebook will be in his pocket should he need it, and he will be hoping that he will, but no poem will touch him as he walks and looks here at the mountain's base. Perhaps higher up, he will think, and he will wend on his way.

Just where the trail begins to climb steeply toward the crest, the point where Sean's stride will lengthen and slow as he goes, the bushes beside him will shatter and shrill, a sudden rattle of leaves and branches, the shrill ululating cry of a maniac, a burst of brown feathers and heavy body breaking out and rushing away. Sean will stagger back, his heart pulsing and pausing, his stick raised foolishly before his face, and then the rush and rustle will ramble wildly away before he can scarcely grasp what is occurring, has happened.

"A turkey," he will shout, and he will break from the path himself, leave the familiar way, and run along through the low laurel and dry leaves to the right, going around the mountain rather than up it. He will see the turkey's brown shape disappearing ahead of him, still running, and he will crash on after it, twigs and low branches smacking at his face, his tangled hair. His light pack will be thumping on his back, and he will be conscious of it and scarcely conscious at all of his feet's sudden slipping away beneath him, the ground rushing at his face and then the slam to the ground, his ashplant hurling out in front of him, a half-buried stone banging into his hip, the same hip he will have injured the winter before in the snow.

The pain will at first pin him to the ground, hold him there rigidly afraid to move, unable to move, his mind racing through the pain with the thought that this time the bone will be broken, that this time he will be lost on the mountain, far from the trail, broken and in pain, too weak probably even to drag himself toward the trail, and then the pain will release him, and he will relax and roll flat on his back, propped on his pack, poking tentatively at his leg and laughing at himself for his foolishness and for his fear.

The turkey will be gone, lost again in the wild woods, running hard, its tail flat and tight, long wrinkled neck extended, but Sean will still be there, crawling on his knees to his flung stick and, using it as a prop, pulling himself up onto his feet. He will look at the woods, the sun slanting through the trees, a spin and whirl of fluffed seeds from the meadows that have drifted high on the morning breeze and are now swirling down and through the trees, catching and spinning away, lighting on the shadowy forest floor. And then something will catch his eye, something orange and artificial, something out of place in these quiet woods.

Sean will grasp his stick tightly, his heart still thundering in his ears, and will stalk the orange spot ahead, will move from tree to slim tree, edging around the mountain wall, until he will be able to see the spot of color clearly, a strip of orange cardboard just by a large animal hole, a groundhog's, a badger's, and two other white splotches, white paper, white paper parcels in the middle of the woods.

Sean will walk quietly toward the packages and the animal den, poking his stick carefully out before him, holding it at the ready. He will stand for a long moment by the hole, looking around him in the woods, trying to listen through the rough rush of his heart, but he will see and hear nothing but the sway of the trees, the trembling light, the silent drift of the straying seeds. The orange cardboard will be an empty bacon package, lying flat beside the hole in the ground, caught on the snarled roots of the large tree just behind and over the hole. The white splotches will prove to be neatly wrapped butcher's packages, three small firm rectangles of white paper, one of them marked in a butcher's black grease pencil, SHORT RIBS.

Sean will stare all around again, will listen as carefully as he can, will stoop then to the packages, will gingerly poke at the marked one, will pick it up, weigh it in his hand, will reach over his shoulder, loosen the strap of his pack, raise the canvas flap with the harp and sun emblem stitched tidily on it, and will drop in the snug package still damp from the night's dew.

And then Sean will walk on away, following a path leading on around the mountain's flank, a path too wide and smooth and used to be an animal's track. He will walk quickly and carefully, curious as to where the path might lead, cautious and worried about where it might lead.

The trail will lead relatively directly and smoothly along the mountainside through the trees and brush to a stand of hemlocks, the boughs with their short flat needles overlapping and weaving together into a dark green wall directly over the path. Sean will stop, lean on his stick, and look this evergreen wall over carefully. The path will lead into it, between two of the closely placed trees, smooth and obviously used. Sean will take a deep breath, grip his stick tightly, and plunge into the scratching, flexible boughs.

The needly barrier will be only a few feet thick, an easy passage, and then Sean will see before him a small tree-rimmed bowl, a shallow clearing, a stream wandering narrowly along the opposite side, widening as it spills past a wooden trough placed at its lip, a gap in the trees and bushes on the other side of the stream. Between him and the stream, he will see a large wooden box into which the trough will be pouring stream water and beside the box, a large copper pot, greening and dented, a fire lapping at its base, a cap at its head with an arm leading across to the large wooden box. A dozen or more steel drums will be standing around the clearing in the mushy soil, wet from the steady trickle of water flowing out of the wooden box's base, the air as sweet and damp with a smell Sean will suddenly recognize.

"A still," he will say aloud, remembering as he speaks all the tales he has heard from childhood of the moonshiners in the hills and the times he has seen their cars skidding across the narrow roads, spinning themselves around at full speed, leaping across the railroad tracks west of Dublin, high in the air, landing at right angles to the road, and roaring away into the dusk, and mainly he will be thinking furiously of the tales he has heard of their violence, of their actually murdering innocent hunters or other sojourners who wandered into their operations.

He will stand there by the hemlocks, holding his breath, his heart thudding and kicking at his chest, and then he will see the man step out from behind the pot of the still, carrying a load of firewood and, as yet, unaware of Sean's presence. He will start to step back into the hemlocks when he will feel a blow between his shoulders, a punch solid enough to stagger him into the clearing, bounding down the slope of the bowl and trying not to fall.

"Son of a bitch," the man carrying the wood will say, dropping his load and reaching for a rifle propped by the wooden box in the mud, and the man behind Sean will be shouting, "Stop him, get him!"

Sean will not be able to think, but his feet will be moving, carrying him across the clearing, splatting and sliding in the mud, his stick banging once noisily against one of the steel drums, and he will be at the creek bank when he will hear the first rifle shot, the noise deafening and causing him automatically to duck as he runs. Without thinking, he will leap into the creek, only to find that he does not sink into the water, that he is walking on water, running on water, splashing across the widening creek, his feet landing solidly on boards laid just under the water's illusory level.

He will make it across the creek and into the woods before the next shot will come, chipping bark onto his tucked head, and he will be careening down the mountain on no trail, leaping and dodging from tree to boulder to tree to bush to tree, when the third shot whirs by.

Sean will run without control down the mountain, not noticing as he goes how the day will be darkening around him, not noticing the first drips and spatters of rain through the trees, not noticing until he breaks out of the forest the streaks and echoing thumps of lightning and thunder around him.

The rain will soak him immediately, and, as he runs across the field, still not slowing down, his breath aching and burning, it will wash away his fear, allow him to slow down and look back the way he has come. He will see nothing but the rain rushing through the fields, the dim twisting trees on far Ben Bulben, the lightning banging down into those writhing woods. He will stop and stand there for a moment, his lungs wheezing the air in and out, his heart racing harder than ever, muddy and soaked and suddenly delighted with the day.

"Ben Bulben," he will cry out in his fervor, "I've met your demons, lured to them by some bird out of hell, and I've faced them and walked away, walked away on water." And he will laugh aloud and shout again and again, "Ben Bulben, Ben Bulben, Ben Bulben," when lightning will bang down onto a bare apple tree near him in the field, the blast nearly knocking him over, setting him into a run toward town again. And then he will hear the banshee's wail, long and wavering and shrill, cutting through his wet body like a blade slashed through water, shaking him as it goes more deeply than all his dangers on the mountain.

"Lightning and water and death in the air," he will say to himself, think for a second of writing the words down in his notebook but knowing the gesture would be futile, saying it to himself again like a saving incantation, "Lightning and water and death in the air."

He will slog home through the rain, the lightning passing on to the east ahead of him, his stick punching into the wet ground and punctuating his progress across the fields and finally up the hill of the project, through the gates and down to his quarters below.

He will make his wet way down the corridor and into his rooms, where he will pitch his dripping pack into the bathroom onto the tile floor and will begin to peel off his soaked shirt and muddy boots. But the phone will arrest him, stop him in his tracks, ringing on the bedside table, and he will remember for the first time in his excitement and elation the morning call of Deirdre O'Sorh.

He will pause for a moment, letting the phone ring, and then he will decide that the time is right, that the excitement and glory of this wild day will have prepared him for the worst. Nothing could surprise me, he will think, anymore than this day already has. He will step as delicately as he can across the floor to the phone, and he will pick up the receiver.

"Hello," he will say, expecting Deirdre's voice, but it will not be Deirdre but Seamus Heanus.

"Sean," he will say, "where in God's name have you been all day?"

"Wait till I tell you," Sean will say; "you will not believe it, any of it."

"You haven't heard then," Seamus will say, his voice quiet and a bit unsteady.

"Heard what?"

"It's Deirdre," Seamus will say, "Deirdre O'Sorh from the lab. She's killed herself, and we'll be needing you for the wake. Do you think you could possibly bring the ham?"

TIME PASSING, PASSING TIME

*

A May day, a day in May. The last cold spell, though maybe not the last, another winter reminder, passed through last week, shedding snow on New York and New England, damping the nights down here, frigid and frosty, leaving the days bright and gusty. But today it is hot—the startling clarity of the air gone with the cold wind—hazy and hot. The trees are full and dark, the ozark orange down by the creek bank moving its leaves although there is no breeze, the view across the way choked and lush, summer's fullness in May, even the accompanying indolence that makes people stroll by on the road rather than walk or stride, that makes the small towheaded boy I passed just up the hill from Carvin's Creek sit in the road for an hour chucking gravel at nothing in particular but with great concentration. How do you spend a day in May, passing time, time passing?

Someone used to quote Thoreau to me pointedly and with great seriousness, the line about killing time as an injury to eternity. Not very fair to Thoreau, who thought time "cheap and rather insignificant," but it can make you very guilty, take all the wonder off an afternoon, drive you to some outwardly busy activity to ward off the stigma. I can hear my neighbor's lawn mower straining up the hill, and I can see my grass, the part the horse didn't eat, leaning in the heat, seedy heads ripening to brown. Loafer. Loafing. Killing time. Killer. I poked around in Thoreau a little today, looking for the line, but instead I found these in *Walden*: "For the most part, I minded not how the hours went. The day advanced as if to light some work of mine; it was morning, and lo, now it is evening, and nothing memorable is accomplished. . . . This was sheer idleness to my fellow-townsmen, no doubt; but if the birds and flowers had tried me by their standard, I should not have been found wanting." It was morning, and lo, now it is evening. I shall mow my grass if that is what it takes to make my neighbor happy. But not today.

How do you pass a day?

Timed by the solid heart's thump, the runic rime of the nerves' steady hum, you sleep, you dream, you wake, you rise, you wash and excrete, you eat, you continue on, doing the hundreds of little things you do, big things, things, events. This complex community of cellular and intercellular activity passing time like a bird or a flower.

You feel the sun surround you like an oiled leather glove, closing and warm. You are caught by the day, wade through the waving seeding grass to the mailbox, find the morning paper in its box, the one under which the hornets built their dangerous nest a year ago, wander back to the house, looking to the mountains, the sun flat on their sides, their outlines blurred and softened by the haze, settle down to wake up, to examine the news of this day. Yes, I know I've read it all before, but it's all in how you do it. First the baseball: Salem won, Pittsburgh lost, the patterns repeat and change, a mockingbird's morning song, Mitchell Page is still hitting; the Dodgers will not lose. The dark news on the front page. The comics gesturing down their own page toward the back. It is an exercise, a toe touching, a way of waking up, alerting all the cells to the coming of the day.

I remember once walking efficiently out of the apartment we lived in at the time, briefcase in hand, some slow thought vaguely in mind, climbing into my car, and, with all careful deliberation, driving smack into the clean red side of the car of the lady who lived next door. "How could you do this to me?" she cried, leaning out of her suddenly open window. "What have I ever done to you that you would do such a thing to me?" How could I explain that I was trying not to kill time, that I was going early to work, that I was not passing that relatively blank time, paper in hand, that it takes me to wake up? I couldn't. I talked about money and accidents, made my apologies, made things right, promised to make things right. And of course, that was the right thing to do. But today I read the paper.

And there in the paper, page A-4, is Rebecca's car, upside down in a ditch north of Hollins, driver unhurt, no one else in the car, a Friday-the-thirteenth accident that happened just after we had been talking at lunch about surprises and bad luck. "I know a number of bad things that could happen to me," she said. And I, sententious to a fault, said, "No, the one that's going to happen will be the one you haven't even thought of." So I call on the phone to apologize and to learn that the lump on her forehead is the worst of it. All these things in the paper are real, real enough, and though you would be a fool to concern yourself with them all directly and painfully when they are so far beyond you or past in time, that grief or that tightening anger an injury rather than a balm, nevertheless the day is real, and you find what you will, do what you can.

Passing time today. You work on your dying boxwood, the one under the front window, injured by the harsh winter, the dry hard ground, the cold that sucked the moisture from the leaves and left the bush drawn and dying of thirst. You trim around the boughs that still hold their green leaves or a scattering of new ones, the crisp brown ones rattling quietly on the ground around you, on you, like the fine hieroglyphic skitter of insects against the window on a summer's night. You clip and saw and slide on the soothing black salve. Birds cluster in the tree behind you—it needs work, too—song sparrows and white-throats, a jay puffing grandly in the sunlight, and you think of the birds who abandoned their unfinished nest, how they came back, built with mud this time, not fluffy moss, how they are now sitting on the eggs, peering cautiously over the rough edge of the nest to see who or what is looking up from down below. The bush looks bad, naked and scrawny. You have done your best. The rest is up to passing time.

You walk down the road and back, the creek flowing evenly through the day, the stirring and swirling of shadowy waters under the bridge, Oliver scurrying through the bushes, rattling leaves like a raging bear or hungry towhee, flushing a calico cat from a stand of larches, sending it racing up a nearby pine where it perches on a sticky bough, looks down, shows no emotion as Oliver announces his victory to all who will or must listen.

In the afternoon you do some symbolic sun-watching, block out your western window, put your cardboard in place, see only that same bright bland face swimming on the smooth wall, the lilacs green and full, long past bloom. You listen to some music: Schoenberg, the piano and the orchestra moving through and around each other, moving in ribbons like the stars, touching and passing, a sound with an almost visual acuity; Bruckner, an expanse beyond the stars; for life, for motion, Ives, commenting on Concord, on ways of passing time. And later you read, will read: Harold Morowitz's *Energy Flow in Biology* for heliological lessons, due back in the library yesterday; Agatha Christie's *A Murder Is Announced*, a used and annotated copy, abandoned by a prison library; *Who Is Teddy Villanova?*

by the author of *Killing Time*, Thomas Berger, the laughter catching you unaware time and again; Dara's *Blood, Hook & Eye*, one more surprising time.

You look. You listen. You stop and read. And the world thunders by this seamless long event, more earthquakes in Romania, cars flipping on the highway like tossed cards, arrests, arrivals, departures, uninjured eternity, time passing, passing time.

In the evening you play softball, a pickup game, Molly not pitching for a change, a spatter of wisecracks bouncing around behind throws, between hits. Your right leg aches like a rotten tooth, and you are caught hopping from third to home, forced out, time forcing its passage, too, through that aging muscle. And then you see that Marnie on her way to first has pulled that same muscle, so you salute her, you hobble on back by home. You see Nancy bringing the new chicken, a little white pullet rescued from the embryology lab, putting it down in its latticed box by the edge of the field; Dara and Allen prepared its new home earlier this afternoon. The new white ball, white paint and red dot powdering off onto the bats, rises and falls in the fading sunlight, the oranging glow from the hills you watched in the morning. Throw it home. Pass it around the horn. Passing time.

Or perhaps you go to the baseball game, watch the late light there light the southeastern mountains, a mottled green, drifting to blue, the sun lining the folds near the peaks, blue to darker blue to deep blue, disappearing in the darkness around the illuminated field. Or you watch the nighthawks circling high overhead, drawn by the lights, by the insects drawn by the lights, the white bars on their sharply pointed wings, their darts and swerves, the popped-up white ball that curves almost high enough to touch them, to make them swing away. Or the game itself.

You go home. No excuses. No explanations. This is how you pass a day, a year, an era. Working and loafing, sawing and seeing, doing, living, naming your friends, looking to the sun. If the birds and flowers took the time, they would understand. It would be too much to ask that they approve. The sun has long since set behind the layered mountains to the west. Time passes, passing time.

WAITING OUT THE SUN

*

A June of dry weather, the expected drought, the bland sun's stepchild, and then one day the rain builds in the west and rolls over the mountains in towering gray clouds. No deluge, but rain, enough rain to fill out the boughs of the cherry tree, to make the grass grow green again for a time in the dry brown meadows. And long gray days, days without sunlight, the morning edging out of the night's darkness and sliding under again in the evening with monotonous singularity. Gray days, waiting out the sun, and spirits fall.

You begin to notice the flaws in the world around you, the mashed and gutted squirrel on the road, the sparrow on the walk, splayed and raw, little more than a fetus, alive and so soon dead. The day takes on a texture of death. You read the deaths in the paper, hear deaths in the air, notice how everyday when you pass the mortuary on Peters Creek Road its parking lot is filled, a silent hearse poised by the side door; you see the hungry flies clustered around the rims of the horse's eyes, watch the trimmed boxwood struggle and sag into slow dying, see the grocery's shelves full of trimmed and weighed slaughter.

And the events of the world, daily variety, past and present, a chronicle of slaughter and failed faith, whether it be in wars or exterminating ovens or the slower tortures of exploitation, history as the movement of greed through time. Is there no good time? Are there not ten righteous within the city or without? The gray clouds hover and sway. A cool wind twists the leaves of the trees, tossing their pale undersides in the air, exposing and snarling their smooth green sheaths. You are thinking dark thoughts on a dark day. You know with Paul "that the whole creation groaneth and travaileth in pain until now." This desperately fallen world that groans around you, this texture and repetition of quick hellos and sudden good-byes, it weighs you down, waiting out the sun, yearning for the light you know should be there.

A mood, of course, for you have known gray days that have filled you with contentment, made you feel all the more secure in their calm, the mist of rain or sea drifting in the gray air. But your mood today may point to a truth about the sun, about our place in the sun. Harold J. Morowitz nearly ten years ago proposed that the flow of energy through a system acts to organize that system, that an examination of the sun's relation to our lives that is not based upon traditional equilibrium physics reveals the sun to be the organizing factor and force in evolution's continual and continuing movement toward a greater variety and complexity of form, a rhythmical and growing order. Energy from the sun, that great flow of solar wind, spills over the earth and out in a splashing corona into the unfillable sink of space, and that spray of energy guides and makes demands of the antientropic biological business we know as life. I remember Nelson Bond's story, "And Lo! the Bird," in which the solar system was an enormous incubator for the planetary eggs of a bird beyond belief. In a strange way, Morowitz and Schrödinger and their fellow delvers into biophysics have said as much, but the bird is life itself, that brave dance in the face of entropic demand, that sun-driven, sun-guided expedition through becoming to being. No wonder you miss the sun on this gray day. No wonder men have worshipped the sun from day to day. It may not be the source, but it is the conductor, and the orchestral elements of life respond to it with a virtuoso's sense of rhythmic rightness.

The gray days pass, the dark thoughts with them. The scars remain. The creation still groans. But you have waited out the sun and have earned the right to see the light again. Oliver and I walked out into the woods on the first gusty bright day after the siege of clouds, his eyes growing milky with age's slow hardening, my heart sputtering interruptions where once there was only that even sturdy beat. Surprises for us both. Ouch, help! But the sun is warm, and the day clear. The woods are green and clean, the breeze having already dried the surface mud away. They are building new houses where none were before, one at the foot of the quarry, another near the bowl in the woods where we found our surprises in the winter. We pick our way through the new undergrowth into the bowl. I don't know what I was expecting, more mysteries, or solutions, a nest of serpents, at least a stand of waving ribgrass, but all we found was a lush tangle and profusion of growth, vegetation responding to the sun's command, a weave of stem and leaf and living complexity.

We know the dark as we know the day. We should be wise enough to deny neither. I stumble and worry, my heart stuffed and strained; Oliver will bump into a chair or the wall in a sudden game on a dim evening; we walk in the open sunlight like two babes in the woods. What surprise will tomorrow bring? The sun's dry face burns in the clear sky and does not blink or wink or give the nod. We hope for what we do not see; we see the way to hope.

Paul goes on in Romans to speak of the future of the world, the whole creation, all this complex of life and death and living and dying in terms of hope. I find J. B. Phillips' translation the aptest here:

"The world of creation cannot as yet see reality, not because it chooses to be blind, but because in God's purpose it has been so limited—yet it has been given hope. And the hope is that in the end the whole of created life will be rescued from the tyranny of change and decay, and have its share in that magnificent liberty which can only belong to the children of God!"

Is that so far from Schrödinger's biophysical description of negentropic behavior in "What Is Life?" or Morowitz's elegant description of the sun's thermodynamic ordering of all our life and lives? I think not. We are the children of the light. We know its presence in the dark. We hear it knocking on the door. We dare to say come in. And no matter how imperfect, inconstant, and irregular the sun may be, we do not mind waiting it out. What better way to pass through the long gray days than waiting out the sun?

SEAMUS TAKES A HAND

*

Seamus and Sean Talk It Over

"I think quite seriously," Seamus will be saying in a loud, somewhat blurred voice, "that, for all your ways of classifying people by types, man-woman, white-black, catholic-protestant, socialist-capitalist, there's only one that divides them all with the simplicity and efficiency of Our Lord's sheep-goat-grain-chaff division, and His, of course, is a divine mystery and beyond our understanding—only one, and that, my wide-eyed poetic boy, is the Johnson Smith system of classification."

He will be talking to Sean Siobhan as they are sitting in the Snake Farm, sharing a few rounds of dark ale and talking of serious matters.

"And what might the Johnson Smith classification be?" Sean will ask, knowing that the question is what is expected of him.

"Well, don't you remember now those fat grand catalogs of your childhood, stuffed full of stink bombs and X-ray glasses and books exposing the Masons, and muscle builders and squirting bloody fingers and birds that never stop drinking from a glass of water? Well, those, my lad, were Johnson Smith catalogs, and a close study of those all-inclusive volumes will produce for you the simple method of classification of which I have been speaking."

"What is it?"

"Take for example," Seamus will say after a pause, his brow furrowed seriously, his pint glass a considerable bit less full than it will have been but a moment before, "the Voice Tester Shocking Mike. It was a small box with

106

a mesh grill on it like a microphone. 'Voice Tester,' it said on it, 'Hear your voice come back to you. . . . Press button.' When you pressed the button, a pin pushed neatly into your fingertip, and you were supposed to cry out in pain, thus hearing your voice loud and clear. The importance, the philosophical importance of this simple device lies in the crude little cartoon illustrating it. As I recall it, Joe has just pushed the button, and his face is twisted in pain and anguish, genuine pain, genuine anguish, and he is crying out, 'Ouch! Help!' Nearby his friend, unnamed, of course, is laughing, a smug look on his face, and saying, 'Ha! Ha! That's one on you!' And there we have as surefire a way of separating the sheep from the goats as we mere mortals may ever devise. There's them as cries out, 'Ouch! Help!' on the one hand, and there's the others as replies, 'Ha! Ha! That's one on you!' The method, I swear to you my artistic friend, is infallible. You can apply it to anything, to anybody. It has political, social, moral, probably even aesthetic applications. There's no situation in which it isn't useful. Just be thinking on it."

Sean's face will have darkened from the laughter that will have followed Seamus' description of the catalog ad, will have become brooding and focused inward.

"Applying it to yourself, are you?" Seamus will say. "Well, Ha! Ha! Then, that's one on you, eh? Sure enough and it is."

And he will clap Sean on the back and order another round of ales.

Mark Welser Tells a Joke

It will be at the Owl Bar. Mark Welser will have just bought a round of drinks and joined Seamus and Sean and Pegeen at one of the twig-rimmed round tables in the center of the room. Seamus will be wearing a ginger moustache clipped to his nostrils, hoping drunkenly that the bartender will not recognize or remember him from his disastrous last visit. Sean and Seamus will have been arguing about social systems and rather heatedly.

"A democratic socialism is the only answer," Sean will be saying. "Let the workers gain the means of production by democratic methods. Free the individual to himself, to his potential; let his spirit breathe free of exploitation, of profits, and the need to be all the time thinking of money, money, money. It'll give every man the opportunity, every man and every woman," he will glance nervously at Pegeen, "the chance to walk in the woods."

"Christ," Seamus will answer, "you poor fool poet with your oatmeal ideas, I ought to be cracking your head. Walk in the woods indeed. It's just the Ouch-Helpers ganging up to pull a Ha-Ha-That's-one-on-you on the other side. In fact," and he will bunch up his freckled fist, "if someone doesn't hold me back, I think I will crack your head right now and get it over with," his ginger moustache fluffing under his flared nostrils and dangling dangerously to one side.

"I know a joke," Mark Welser will say, quickly plunging in without waiting for attention or assent. "It seems there is this Russian, and American and an Irishman sitting in a bar. They've been there a good while and have drunk a good bit. The Russian raises a toast. 'To Russia,' he says, 'who put first man in space.' The three toast. Then the American says, 'To America, who put the first man on the moon.' They drink again, and then the Irishman, to his companions' surprise, says, 'To Oireland, who'll put the first man on the sun.'"

Welser will stop for a reaction, but his companions will all be staring at him incredulously, so he will rush on.

"The American and the Russian complain that Ireland can't put a man on the sun. 'Oi'd loike to know whoiy not?' the Irishman says. 'It's too hot,' the American says. 'Do ye think we're shtoopid?' the Irishman says. 'We're sending him at noight!'"

Welser will laugh and look about in the even silence. Seamus' fist will tighten until the knuckles pale under the taut freckled skin. Pegeen will be looking down at the table in embarrassment. Sean will smile nervously.

"Don't you get it?" Welser will say.

Seamus' ginger moustache will puff off onto the tabletop, and Sean will quickly dump his beer mug over onto the table, the ale sloshing and splashing across to the twiggy barrier opposite.

"Oh, Lord," he will say, "look what I've gone and done. Seamus, help me, and we'll clean this mess up."

Seamus and Sean Discuss Their Future

They will be alone in a small room off the main laboratory at the project. It will be late at night after a long evening of drinking. They will have walked Pegeen home and will have come here for a last drink from Seamus' hidden store before retiring themselves.

S: Do you think we can do it? Do you think one of us will be the first man on the sun? First person on the sun?

S: Person! What's wrong with man? Who do you think that's going that isn't a man? Unless you're speaking for yourself. Blackie acts sure enough like he's a man, sniffing and nosing after every thing that passes his way in a skirt or that could wear a skirt but won't. And you'd better not be indicating that I'm anything but a man.

S: No, no. You don't understand. It's just I've been talking to Pegeen a lot, and she's made me aware of, well, of attitudes, of things we say that we don't really mean, or mean just because we say them without thinking.

S: Now don't you go be talking to a woman so much about ideas. There's nothing so unhealthy as discussing ideas with a woman.

S: But . . . oh, it doesn't matter. We'll be far enough away from the whole question soon enough.

S: Going to the sun. Do you think we're crazy, then? Going to the sun, I mean.

S: I was just asking you that. I know there's a craft sitting over in the tower, nose up and ready to soar. I know all the tests and all the data. I know we're going to sail up some night and slide off down that chute of bent space to the sun. But I still don't believe it.

S: Well, I don't understand it at all, but I'll be going just the same. He's up there glaring away every day, and I look up at him and say, "I think I'll just have to be paying you a call soon enough, and I'll be seeing what you're made of, sure enough."

S: Why do you say the sun's a he?

S: Well now, isn't that quite and abundantly clear enough? It's an expression. He's up there burning and putting out force all the time. He's a he. The sun is surely no she, that's for sure.

S: You see what I mean? Why do we have to be so conscious of it. We need another pronoun to take the place of he and she.

S: You keep talking about taking the place of he and she, and I'll be seeing the director about finding another solarnaut to be taking your place on this trip.

S: No, you know what I mean. Maybe a word like um. That's sufficiently neutral. Um's up there glaring away every day. We're going off to the sun, and we're going to land on um, see what um's made of.

S: You sound like some baby-talking red Indian.

S: I'm serious.

S: Well, you know what you sound like, do you, talking ideas with women and wanting to be gelding the sun? You sound sure enough like someone who's not getting any. It's not that you don't spend enough time with that big sturdy woman. Are you really not getting any?

S: She's, she's a Helen of Troy, you know, a regular Helen of Troy.

S: That she may be, but the question is are you getting any?

S: Um.

S: I thought as much. Here, let me be pouring you another drink. Who knows? You might be the first um on the sun.

S: The first man on the sun.

S: That's just what I said, didn't I?

S: The first man on the sun.

A Memory Revealed

"What do you get out of it, all that wood walking?" Seamus will be asking Sean. "Surely you get sufficient exercise in the training program?"

"Wildness," Pegeen will answer. "You're so wild in your own primitive way you wouldn't even know that the rest of us need to discover it over and over, need to be reminding ourselves that the wilderness is there, free and detached, following its own laws, kill or be killed, impersonal, free of this emotional stew we wallow in all day, who loves who, who hates who. I go out into the woods to be cleansed of all that."

"You'll find out how wild I am someday, lassie," Seamus will say, "but if I remember correctly I addressed my question to my friend and solar colleague, Sean Siobhan. What, I asked um, does um get out of all this wood walking?"

Pegeen will wrinkle her brow with distaste, but Sean will answer seriously, trying to ignore the tensions between these two of his friends.

"I think it's for the surprises," he will say. "I go out into the woods looking for surprises."

"And you'll be seeing the same trees, the same rocks, the same rills. If you want surprises, you ought to be going down to the pubs with me instead of trailing about in the woods. Now there's surprises for you. You never know who'll be saying what or what rowdy goings on will be going on. There's all the wildness in the world for you there."

"That's not what he's saying," Pegeen will say, glaring at Seamus's bleary face.

"Well, will um tell me," Seamus will say, "what um does mean?"

Sean's face will fill with a taut and haunted expression as a memory will rouse and stir in a part of his mind that he will have carefully not visited, the events of a day he will have chosen not to remember.

"I'll tell you a surprise I found in the woods," he will finally say. "It's one that I'd forgotten almost all about. It was, it was the day, well, it doesn't matter what day. Anyway, I was walking up Ben Bulben, and a turkey, I think it was a turkey, flushed beside me and clattered off through the woods to my right."

"Some surprise," Seamus will say.

"Not to a turkey like yourself," Pegeen will add.

"I followed," Sean will continue, not really noticing them, "pretty far off the path, and I fell down, really banged myself. But I saw a package, actually a spot of white, and I went over to it and it was a white package. Right there in the middle of the woods, near nothing, was a package, a neatly wrapped, white paper butcher's package with 'short ribs' written on it in black."

"Bad meat somebody threw out," Seamus will say.

"On the side of Ben Bulben?" Sean will say. "And besides, it couldn't be meat at all because I brought it home and put it somewhere, in the closet I think. The whole apartment would be smelling something awful by now if it was meat."

"You mean you never looked at it?" Pegeen will ask.

"I forgot all about it. It was, well, it was a busy time."

"That's my poetical boy," Seamus will say. "Well, what say we go examine this woodland surprise? The day is still young."

"I have to go to the lab," Pegeen will say.

"Well, off you go then," Seamus will say, scrubbing his chair back on the tiled floor, "to do the work of the world, and, Sean, my surprised boy, while um does um's work, let's us be off to see just what it is that you found so far off and high up in the woods."

The three of them will rise and gather their notebooks and stacks of photocopied sheets and make their way through the nearly empty room, the clutter of tables and dawdling waitresses. They will part at the door, Pegeen nodding a quick good-bye and heading down the corridor toward the labs, Seamus and Sean staring after her for a moment, her hair swinging down her strong back, and then turning themselves toward the outside exit and the path to their quarters.

Surprise

Sean will have found the white package on the hat shelf in the closet, the black letters blurred by the rain and dried again in a dark haze, and he and Seamus will have carefully torn the outer wrapper off and found an inner wrapping of plastic wrapping material, bobbled with air pockets that will wrinkle and pop with a thumb's applied pressure. They will peel these layers away and find yet another layer of wrapping, paper this time, white typing paper carefully folded and sealed with strapping tape. Seamus will slice the tape with his pocket knife and unfold the white paper. A small gray cylinder will roll out onto the table, a film container.

"Ha," Seamus will shout, "it's someone's stash. You've deprived some poor doper of his dusty bliss and ease. Maybe the turkey was a strung-out, gobbling head."

But Sean will unscrew the lid of the small container and will dump a small coil of film out into his palm.

"Microfilm," Seamus will say in a suddenly serious and whispering voice. "Ouch, help!"

The two men will look into each other's eyes. Sean's hands will be trembling, despite his effort to remain calm.

"When did you find this?" Seamus will say.

"The day," Sean will say, "the day, the day Deirdre, Deirdre died."

"Good God, man," Seamus will say, "and you've let it just lie here."

Sean will not answer.

"I think," Seamus will say, "that I'd better take a hand, that we'd better be going over together to Red Hanrahan's office right now," and he will begin bunching all those layers of wrapping together into a manageable bundle.

A Conversation

The room will be dark, the afternoon light filtered and split by the nearly closed venetian blinds on the narrow windows, a shadowy and shifting light, a roomscape of dim shapes and silhouettes.

She will be standing by the black-topped work table on which her experiment will be set up and working itself silently out as she talks. She will be wearing a long white lab coat, glowing like a ghost in the weak light, over her usual blue jeans, tight and patched, her loose red flannel shirt, the top buttons open, her walking boots. She will be leaning against the sturdy edge of the table, but her position of ease will be belied by the tension in her voice, in the tightness of the muscles in her arms and legs.

He will be sitting at the end of one of the worktables on a low stool, a dark shape leaning over, elbows on his knees, nearly invisible in the table's heavy shadow.

"You know, love," he will be saying, "I've been treating you badly, and I do know it myself. I really do. I underestimated you."

She will say nothing to this, only shift her weight against the hard table's edge.

"It's surely because you're the only woman around here, about the only woman in the whole town, it sometimes seems anyway, who isn't always hitting on me. I've come to expect it, and I'm fearing I treated you as though you were when you weren't, don't you know?"

She will turn to the table, look steadily for a moment at the sharp beam of light cutting from a humming bit of apparatus through a maze of small coils and bits of mirrored alloy to a receiving apparatus at the opposite end of the table.

"So," he will say, "I've come to apologize with the hope that perhaps we can be friends in a way that I seem unable to be with anyone else around here, male or female. We seem freed of the curse between us of male and female, for that matter, free to be honest and care for one another as individual beings. And that kind of freedom and friendship I seem to be sorely needing, and, from the looks of it, and I have been looking, I'll confess, you seem to be needing someone in just that very way yourself."

She will look up at him and say, "What do you be meaning by that now exactly?"

"I've seen you," he will say, "alone and with your tagalong Sean Siobhan, and you're a worried woman. There's worry etched all over your handsome face. And so I says to myself, I do, is it something that Sean's doing to you?"

"It's not him," she will answer, "not Sean. I do care for him very much. He has a wild look to his eyes at times that excites me, and he seems so vulnerable and so stripped naked to me all the time. I thought maybe something could come of it because he does excite me so much, but he needs so much, wants so much, asks so much. I can't explain it, and I certainly have no idea what I'm doing, saying all this to you of all people in this wicked world."

She will look again at the curling beam of light and away from the shadowy man on the low stool.

"You're telling me because I'm the first person," he will say, "who will listen to you without either envying you your good looks and your good job and your good mind or trying to get those good looks into bed. Am I right? And sure I'm right all right. And I am seeing at a glance why you're not satisfied with that weakling, Sean Siobhan."

"No," she will say abruptly, "no, you don't. It's not Sean himself. It's

Deirdre. Ever since Deirdre, Deirdre died, it's not been the same. Sean seems to be involved somehow, I don't rightly know how, but he won't even say her name. And it holds her right there between us like a shadow or a cloud, as though he'd killed her, or I had, and her wraith had come back accusing and eager for revenge. Now how could you be knowing about that?"

"No," he will answer after a moment, "that's true. I do wish I'd known her better. I scarcely knew Deirdre O'Sorh at all, and I certainly don't know why she did herself in, but I wish I did, wish I'd known her really well. Then I could tell you all I knew and be helping you out of this darkness that's troubling you so."

She will turn her back on him then, the lab coat swirling out in a rippling white blur.

"I have to finish this experiment," she will say. "You'll have to be going now."

He will sit there silently for a moment, then start to rise, to go.

"And don't think I'm not mindful," she will say, "of what you've been saying. I do appreciate it."

He will walk across the room with quick steps, flip the door handle and let himself, a sudden black shape against the glare of the hallway, out of the intensely quiet room.

A Report to the Director

"Do you know what these films are?" Hanrahan will be saying, his voice so hard that it will seem to bounce and ricochet around the bare room. He will be standing over his desk, examining the tiny film in a battery-powered reader on the otherwise bare desktop. The wrappings will be piled untidily in one wooden chair, and Sean and Seamus will be sitting on the edges of the other two.

"No, sir," Seamus will say, "we've no idea at all."

"I probably shouldn't tell you," Hanrahan will say, "but I will. These are the plans for the Leinster Launching Platform. Do you know at all what that is?"

Seamus and Sean will shake their heads no.

"It is, know it or not, the most important, the top secret we have here, short of the flight itself, and, no matter what you learn on the flight, no matter what you bring back from the sun, the Leinster Launching Platform will, if it works as it should, be triumph enough in itself to make the whole venture worthwhile."

"What is it?" Seamus will say.

"I can't explain it to you, not even now, but I will say that it is a grid which manipulates gravity in such a way as, for all practical purposes, negates it. It creates a shaft of gravitational absence in which absolutely minimal force, shoving off with your foot, say, will lift your ship right up through earth's gravitational field and out to where you can sail away without . . ."

"Without," Sean will say, "the need for blast-off, without the suffering of blast-off . . ."

"And without," Seamus will say, "wasting all the fuel of blast-off. We can float up on this thing and turn the converter on with no need for rocket fuel at all."

"And you can return the same way with only minimal braking fuel," Hanrahan will say. "But the point of the moment is to discover why the plans for the Leinster were in the woods, who got them there and who was to have picked them up."

Seamus and Sean will look at each other, and Seamus will say, "I know every bootlegger, sir, within fifty miles of here in every direction, know them well, and I'm knowing no one who has an operation on the side of Ben Bulben."

"They shot at me," Sean will say.

"And they weren't bootleggers," Seamus will say.

"Then," Red Hanrahan will say, "they were surely involved in this, and they were the Russians, or the Chinese, or the British, or . . . or . . ."

"The IRA," Sean will whisper, more to himself than to anyone in the room.

Xhavid Pays a Debt

The Owl Bar will have been gaining in popularity the way a new bar sometimes will, even in an old neighborhood, especially among the young and those who have no regular crowd to which they belong. This Owl will have limped along on the patronage of tourists who recognize it as a familiar refuge in a very unfamiliar town until it will have begun picking up a clientele of its own.

Xhavid Shehu will be sitting in the darkest booth at the rear of the room, slumped over a table in the red light, watching the ebb and eddying of the crowd, but trying himself never to be visible. He will have seen Flann O'Flynn, a man he will know by sight although they will never have met formally, emerge from a door on the other side of the glowing owl, followed after a few minutes by a teen-aged girl, freckled and braided, her plaid skirt pulled crooked on her hips. He will have watched O'Flynn, after the girl, without a glance his way, will have waved good-bye to the barman and sauntered out the swinging doors, settle in at the bar, sidle up to a young woman at the bar, and sooner than later lead her to a booth down the way and out of sight. It will have been the same young woman, wearing a curious button with two shoe soles and heels and the legend "Ira," who will have been arguing with the barman vigorously a half an hour or so before.

Xhavid will wonder about the woman with her revolutionary sentiments so brazenly displayed and about O'Flynn's association with her. He will notice the barman's curious ritual and hear the owl's cry every time someone makes a donation to the Party. But mainly he will dream away the time, a dream of faraway times, other tongues, the sun oranging over the Adriatic, ancient ragged hills, the crack of rifle fire, and the keening of widows.

Then he will be suddenly alert, aware of a familiar voice bulling through the spatter of conversation in the room.

"Vodka," it will say. "Vodka for my friends."

He will look up, his entire body tense, his heart leaping for a few bounding beats against the wall of his chest. He will see the close-cropped dark hair, the blunt back swelling under the dark suit coat. He will hear the familiar voice laughing, the familiar heavy hands pounding on the pinched shoulders of the tall man leaning at the very end of the bar.

Xhavid will ease out of the booth in the red light. He will walk silently across the room, will reach out and clutch the arm of the thick, laughing man.

"Piotr Prostrantsvo," he will say in a dark quiet voice, "I wish to repay to you a debt which I am owing."

Prostrantsvo will turn quickly but not quickly enough to recognize who is speaking to him before Xhavid's fist pounds directly into his flat nose. The two will dip suddenly to the bar floor, Prostrantsvo on his back, blood already drooling out of his nose, Xhavid astraddle the Russian's thick body. Xhavid will grasp the Russian's two thick ears and will begin pounding his head up and back, into the floor, over and over, thudding and thudding. Blood will burst from Prostrantsvo's ears and mouth, and Xhavid will keep pounding the head on the floor, steadily and intently, even while three or four of the men who will have been standing at the bar will begin prying him off, even while fights will begin springing up all over the room, even while the barman, feathers fluttering and whispering, will run across the raucous room to the phone and dial the familiar number of the Dublin sheriff's office.

The Commando Raid

No moon will be shining on the dozen men in green coveralls who will be moving as quietly as possible up the side of Ben Bulben. Sticks will snap and rocks turn and rattle away underfoot, but the men will move on as silently as possible, steadily, surely. When they reach a stand of dark and thick hemlocks, one of the men will flash a Mallory pocket torch three times, and the twelve men will converge quickly and noisily on the small hollow bowl on the mountainside. No shots will be fired, for the bowl will be deserted, the still will be broken and bent, and only the stream will be moving and murmuring in the dark silence.

"They've gone," Seamus will say, "and what does that mean? What does that mean?"

Padraic Estaban on the Road

Padraic Estaban will be worried about the popping sound the ancient engine of his Good Egg Volkswagen will be making as he drives east of town toward the interstate on a trip to Roanoke to pick up some supplies and maybe take in a movie. The noise will not have the sound of a valve or a miss, but it will not have the deep putter of a ruptured muffler either. He will be focused to the rear even as his eyes continue to scan the road before him, and he will almost miss the three hitchhikers lumped by the side of the ramp leading down to the interstate. They will be huddled there, two thumbs out, rumpled and dirty as though they had been out in the countryside or on the run for days. I should find out, Padraic will think, and he will wheel and skid the small green car over to the side of the road and wait for the three men to catch up to him, two of them supporting the third between them.

"Thanks, buddy," one of the men will say, opening the passenger door, "we could sure use a lift out of here."

The speaker, a tall man with pointed western Virginia features, his skin red and hard from the sunlight, will help the middle man into the backseat, a thick-set and round-faced man, his face battered and bruised, his nose a whistling mass of purple flesh. Then the speaker will crawl in after him, leaving the front seat to the third man, a nondescript, almost featureless man in khaki work clothes, an unchanging grin stuck on his face.

"Your friend sick?" Padraic will ask as he pulls away from the shoulder and into the road.

"Pete had a little fight," the speaker in the back seat will say, "at one of your pubs. I warned him about gambling in a Irish town," and he will laugh. "Man, I warned him."

The man in the front seat will nod and grin.

"Yeah," the man in the back will continue, "we done lost our jobs and are heading on down the road, and we found old Pete here puking his guts out in a alley downtown, so we figured we'd just take him with us."

Padraic will glance at the oval rearview mirror, flaked and marbled with its age, directly into the hurt man's eyes. The left one will be puffed shut, but the right will be open and glaring, red and filled with hate, the whole face around those distorted eyes puffed and purpling.

"Well," Padraic will say, "you surely can't be winning them all."

"I was just telling old Pete that," the speaker will say, poking a finger into his ear and twisting it around as his eyes wrinkle and squint in the morning glare, "but if you don't win it, I was telling him, someone else surely will." And he will wink right at Padraic's eyes in the small mirror, a big forced meaningful wink.

Talking It Over

Red Hanrahan will be sitting at the head of the table with its clutter of mugs and cups and stained paper plates in the semiprivate room off the side of the snack bar at the project, the pleated wooden door pulled nearly shut, allowing only enough room for a waitress to enter and leave from time to time. Sean and Seamus and Flann O'Flynn will also be sitting at the table, along with Pegeen O'Rourke, her face stained red and white, her eyes red and streaked, her damp napkin crumpled in her palm. Sean will be dead white, staring at Hanrahan but seeing nothing. The others will be looking at their plates or into their beer mugs as Hanrahan speaks.

"Well, Siobhan, I'm glad all this has finally come out, even as I'm very angry that you didn't see fit to tell me anything of it until now. I'll admit I can't make much sense of it, but I did have to know the reasons for your odd behavior. I don't believe that the phone call and the suicide of Miss O'Sorh has any bearing on the case, so I'm suggesting that we let it rest from now on."

Pegeen will glare at Sean's pale face, his blank eyes, and she will press the napkin to her face again as he slowly nods to Hanrahan's remarks.

"Now, with that out of the way for good and all, does anyone else have any information about this spy operation that we haven't heard yet?"

Seamus will look up and around the table; Blackie O'Flynn will reach into his shirt pocket and pull out a small gold-colored object and toss it onto the flat smooth wood of the table where it will bounce and spin for a moment, catching everyone's eyes but stunned Sean's. Hanrahan will reach for the object and look at it closely, the small lapel button:

"What is this?" Hanrahan will say.

"I found it in . . . peculiar circumstances," Blackie will answer, "at the Owl Bar, sir."

"Well, what of it?"

"I found, sir, the initials to be suggestive, and," raising his hand as Hanrahan's face reflected the anger and scorn rising in him, "I don't think it's the usual IRA scare."

"What makes you think so?"

"I found this, too, sir," and he will reach again into his pocket and pull out a crumpled sheet of teletype paper, tossing it to the table in front of Hanrahan, "found it at the same place, the Owl Bar. Just be looking at it."

"Wandering Aengus," Hanrahan will read, "Hanrahan . . . magnetosphere."

Everyone but Sean will lean forward, eager to see the crumpled paper, the little plastic pin.

"And look here," Hanrahan will say, "just be looking here. It says, 'tacky ones' and 'line stir.' Oh my God. Oh my God."

"Yes, sir," Blackie will say, not really understanding exactly why Hanrahan is excited but sure of his own ground, "it looks as though the IRA and the Owls are in it together, and that, to my mind, means nothing but trouble."

Sean will focus on the men huddled around Hanrahan's seat, will realize that something important has just been said, will move his eyes up and across the table until they meet Pegeen's hard stare, and then a cold shock will run through him, his hands shaking in his lap, and he will say to himself, "My God. Oh my God."

Padraic Talks About His Passengers

Waiting for Hanrahan to complete his meeting, Padraic Estaban will offer to buy Xhavid Shehu a cup of coffee. He will have just returned from town, where he will have picked a battered Shehu up after his night in the Dublin jail.

"I killed the son of a bitch, I know it," Xhavid will be saying, as much to himself as to Estaban. "I beat his brains out on the floor. I have my honor again. Am a man among men again."

"Now, lad," Estaban will say to him, "nobody has charged you with anything more than disturbing the peace. We'll have it fixed up for you in no time. You're not to be worrying."

"No," Xhavid will insist, "I killed him. I did kill him."

"Now, look," Padraic will say, "from what you've told me I have a powerful feeling I carried the very man you're talking about into Roanoke this morning."

"No, no."

"Yes, and if it's any consolation to you, he was much the worse for wear, much the worse."

"No," Xhavid will say, "no, he is dead. I have my honor."

"Look," Estaban will say, "they're calling me from the door to where Hanrahan's having his meeting, and they'll be wanting to know about my passengers, especially those boys with the muddy boots who told me they've been running moonshine off Ben Bulben."

"It was Piotr Prostrantsvo," Xhavid will say. "You tell him that. And you tell him I killed him. Yesterday. On the floor."

"Sure and I will," Estaban will say.

"And I have my honor again."

"I'll tell him for sure, but look now, here's one of your countrymen with your coffee."

Padraic will walk away toward the beckoning figure of Seamus Heanus, leaning out from the folding wooden door's narrow opening, just as Mehmet

Xoxe will arrive at Shehu's side carrying a mug of hot coffee. He will not look around as he hurries into the meeting to see Xoxe pause at the table, look down at Shehu for a long moment, and carefully raise his boot to the table's edge and pass the coffee cup under his knee and onto the table top. He will, however, hear a terrible cry and look back out the door in time to see Xoxe crash back over the table behind him in a rattle and smash of glass and Xhavid's running figure banging from table to table, chair to chair to chair, as he races across the crowded room toward the outside door. But he will pay no further attention as he hears the urgency of Hanrahan's request for him to take a seat at the quiet table.

HOW EASY

*

The first day of summer, summer solstice, the long day that never seems to end, the sun reluctant to give it up, the earth finishing its slow nod to the sun, head or foot, depending on your hemisphere. And the next day, the first full day of summer, it rains again, a slow even rain, one that will last for days, the dry earth absorbing it and the plants nodding under the unaccustomed weight of water on their leaves. Gray days, long gray days, the days that will shorten steadily as the earth rights itself for the autumn equinox. The bright promise of that first day of summer denied for a time, and we duck our heads, stare out the door or plunge on through it, wondering all the while about promises and beliefs, about the evidence that any given day offers toward the next, the connections between day and long day, short day, sunny and gray.

This first full day of summer, wet and clouded over, is also the three hundred and forty-fourth anniversary of the day Galileo bowed his head to the Church and recanted what he had seen and what he knew. The world moved to him, as he knew it would, but on that day, for that moment, he moved away, closed his eyes, or stood still as though the world would stand there with him. The pressures were great, and he recanted.

How easy it is to recant, under pressure to cast aside what we have seen and what we have heard, to bend to the force of entropy, to run down and allow yourself to be run down. Belief on a bright day, opening like the blue chicory blossoms outside the door, can fill that day with a color that surely must last, but on the gray day that follows, how easy to deny that it has ever flowered at all, how easy to deny all belief, how easy to be a weed in a field of weeds. The doctor tuts and pokes at the long sheets of graph paper and will not look you eye to eye; your boss talks about "release," how tough times are; the phone rings and the news comes that is so bad that you had come to believe that such things could not ever happen. Without the sun, in the painful dark, you fold and recant, you deny what you know and admit that what everyone has been telling you is true. How easy. We do it one way or the other every day.

But the world drinks and swims in the rain. Clouds hang and hide in the folds of the mountains, hover like dreams, drift along the ridges, and slide through the glistening trees. The mockingbird ruffles his feathers and starts a song, as though the sun were high above (which it is) and the day were dry and clear. A small brown rabbit crouches in the slow rain and carefully nips dandelion leaves at the base, sitting up then and chewing each leaf steadily in from green stem to leafy tip. If you have eyes to see, ears to hear, you sidestep the trap of your own failing, the reductionist trap that defines you as an accidental collection of random material, cast somehow into motion but running down, down into the ground, that easy definition. You read the signs, and the signs are clear: death is in your bones and sinews and in the world around you, no blossom lasts, but life is moving in that dying world and in you, and you are alive, are life. The signs are clear. How easy to read them if you do not close your eyes. Galileo knelt and lied, but never to himself. "Eppur si muove," he said, and it does.

My mother dreamed during one of these short nights that we, she and I, are riding in a wooden farm wagon, high on the driver's seat, behind two horses. The horses pause by a stream of water, a branch that curves and flows among the trees and over the bed of rocks with a gentle ease. She is moved by the singular beauty of the place, trees and moving water, light. My father is standing by the stream, wearing the new light blue suit in which he was buried five years ago, like the stream so clean and clear that it strikes her dumb. His face glows, is ringed with light, an aura, saint's halo, nimbus. That was the dream.

She told it to a minister who, good man, tried to console her, to explain how dreams must be disregarded, but he did not see. How easy to explain the dream, to explain it away. But the dream stays. A momentary stay. We speak to ourselves in dreams, we listen, we see, and sometimes we understand. Signs and echoes, visions and whispers. And what is the dream? Life as dream, dream as the voice of life. It is a distance that reaches you, touches you. It is your self spread far and thin. It is a growth beyond dimension. It is the voice that whispers in the flood, the life that splashes in your veins, sun's startling rise, surprising fall, the turn of day on night on day on day.

The dream lingered in the day, gave it light. The sun lingers in gray days, dawn to dusk, ill-defined, shading in and shadowing out, but there. The new slick branches edging out of the base of the crippled boxwood spread new leaves to the rain. The white pullet, who is already beginning to learn to cluck, scratches in the new mud with her crooked toes, pecks at the falling raindrops. The brindle kitten Dara and I picked up from the highway, where it lay in the middle of the busy pavement, pressed so flat in its fear that it seemed already dead, already mashed, only a moving mewing head, thrives at Leslie's, playing with her kitten, waiting for a new home.

We move among each other without noticing and with such urgency all the while. How like a dream, to pass and touch and pass again and not to see, to require dreams and disasters, signs and dire portents, these long gray days, to require them so that we can just see, just hear. The accumulation of life on this planet alone can stagger you to awe, to something quite akin to disbelief, belief beyond belief. How easy to deny it, to say this is a cemetery, new graves edging open day and night, day and day. This is the summer solstice when the sun is in the zenith at the tropic of Cancer, when all things hover for a moment, balance, pause before moving on, this world of seasons, life of passing days, summer moving on to autumn, pause like a dream and then move on. How easy. *Eppur si muove.*

OUT OF TIME

*

Another gray day, this one not gray with hanging clouds, but gray with humid haze, moisture mingled with the exhausts of trucks and automobiles, heavy, thick, making the mountains blur and drift, making your lungs labor and your limbs take on weight and hang limp. July. Hot and humid and hazy, the first bright days of the month gone, a memory of air so clean and clear you could note the rippling leaves on the trees on the distant mountainsides, only memory now.

You drive into the city, down the stale highway, to the city library to borrow a film, Leisen's *Swing High, Swing Low*, to show tonight, the film the same age as you are, nearly forty years. You park by the downtown park, walk up the walk to the library, and see a man, a man slumped on a park bench, one foot crooked on its side, the other flat, one arm on the seat back, the other lying in his lap, head slumped, asleep, worn brown face, sparse gray hair, asleep in the stagnant air, his gray straw hat crown down on the green park bench beside him, a gray suit, coat unbuttoned, white shirt, a monogram (JBM) on the pocket, face as battered and worn as the day's air, asleep.

The hat reminds you of your father, the hats he wore, and today not another hat in sight, bare heads on all sides. You walk quietly by and into the library where your father's name is mounted on the wall, on a gray metal plaque, a memory of his politics, his time in office, his support for this library. You pass it by. You do your business. You leave.

The man is still sleeping on the bench. You wonder for a moment

125

whether he is ill, whether he needs help. As you walk near, you see the nearly empty bottle of cheap wine wedged in his pants pocket, poking out under his gray coat. He is asleep, hat on its straw crown, black socks rumpled down around his ankles, one black shoe twisted on its side. The mystery of the moment, puzzle of all our lives, how do we ever know what any other person knows? What caused this man to dress so carefully, to drink this wine, to stumble off to sleep on this bench, seeking what or fleeing what? His face is worn and brown, and no dream stirs his face or hands or feet, one hand coiled in his lap, out of time. I leave him to his sleep in time.

This morning I saw a familiar face, one I revere, looking out from the front page of the morning paper, looking a little pensive, eyes squinted slightly in the light, full-fleshed, a picture taken some years ago, Nabokov, Vladimir Nabokov, and the headline reads: WRITER DIES. I read on, lost, like someone in a maze who can no longer hear the sound of the voice he was trusting to guide him through: "Vladimir Nabokov, Russian-American author of 'Lolita' and one of the most original prose stylists in each of his two languages, died at his hotel home in Montreux, Switzerland, Monday. He was 78. Story on Page A-2." And synchronously enough, texturally enough, on another page, not A-2, but C-1 in fact, I found another story, another headline: A GLIMPSE BEHIND THE FINAL CURTAIN. It is an interview with George Ritchie about a "life after life" experience he had when he was, for a time, clinically dead in 1943, no doubt an account of an event already recorded and filed at IPH, the Institute of Preparation for the Hereafter, "big if!"

I remember when Ernest Hemingway died, that day; a wind rose in the afternoon, whipping the long curtains out into the dim hot air of my room like banners or loose sails, and Hemingway's picture on my wall fell to the floor, the glass shattering and bouncing across the rug and wood. And when I heard that William Faulkner had died I was driving the car and could not pause to do or say much of anything, just remember his even stride down the long Lawn in his impeccable English clothes, pipe puffing, gaze so steady that it never seemed to waver at all. Hemingway I never saw, or only in photographs. Nabokov I saw in pictures, butterfly net in hand or on the balcony in Montreux posied over the chessboard or possibly a game of Russian Scrabble, with Véra, quietly awaiting her move.

Their bruised fists knocked on the walls of time until the walls opened and let them out of time and into timelessness, and we remain, just in time, riding with Quentin and Shreve and Charles and Henry and Faulkner, the six or seven or more of us on those two horses, or feeling Robert Jordan's heart beating against the pine needle floor of the forest, or repeating John Shade's great poem which explains it all:

> But all at once it dawned on me that *this*
> Was the real point, the contrapuntal theme;
> Just this: not text, but texture; not the dream
> But topsy-turvical coincidence,
> Not flimsy nonsense, but a web of sense.
> Yes! It sufficed that I in life could find
> Some kind of link-and-bobolink, some kind
> Of correlated pattern in the game,
> Plexed artistry, and something of the same
> Pleasure in it as they who played it found.

I know that Nabokov would not appreciate my mentioning *For Whom the Bell Tolls*, "bells, balls, and bulls," in such proximity to his masterpiece. No two of us ever reads quite the same book, no matter what the cover says. No two of us ever sees the third, a third, any other, in quite the same way. The mystery of the moment, puzzle of all our lives. And yet something in us, imagination, the spiraling mind, call it what you will, does find some correlated pattern, plexed artistry, sign, portent, in the way words dance and touch on the page, in the look in his eye, the way her hand pauses for just a moment before it lets yours go. And memory moves from sign to word to page to face to hand, Nabokov's father in his white summer suit bouncing high, visible through the dining room window against the cobalt blue of the summer noon, my father bouncing down the sidewalk in the distance in his gray summer suit, his gray straw hat, the singular lilt of his walk identifying him without doubt among the crowd of strollers and striders, the rattle of hot paper packing and gunpowdery tubes around us in the dark last night as we sat under the fireworks display in the park in July celebration, the weight of a line of verse that echoes and knocks around your mind until at last it all comes clear when you pass along the stone wall or slip on the creek bank and splash into the stream. In time, the signs do, often enough, come clear.

A drunk and aging man stirs in his sleep, a twisted dream tugging at his hand, which falls down onto his hat and wakes him up. He blinks and stirs, reluctant to leave the timelessness of sleep and step back into time. He rubs his eyes and straightens up, the nearly empty bottle slipping out of his pocket and thudding into the clipped grass. He looks around, sees two young men in undershirts and khaki pants sitting up the slope of the hill, eating lunch from brown paper bags, watching him. He pulls his coat into place, puts his gray straw hat squarely on his head, leans down, picks up the bottle, tucks it under his coat, stands woozily up, yawns, and walks quietly away, down the sidewalk, down the street, back in time, into life.

The long good-bye continues past the last slow exhalation, the final curtain, continues in our memories to stay behind, in the words that others not yet born will read and know, continues in a photograph, eyes squinted in the sun, continues, swinging high and low. Good-bye, Vladimir Nabokov. This is, I believe, *it*. Easy, you know, does it, dad. Out of time, into life.

GETTING OFF

*

The pale muted light that always glows over the low round hill to the west of Dublin[1] will seem brighter in the moonless black hot air of the summer night. The citizens of the small town will not—with the exception of those families whose members will be missing this night, called to work beyond their usual hours at the project—will not notice anything unusual or different. Lights glow over the hill to the west. Some nights they glow brighter than others. When tourists ask about it—tourists who have somehow managed to notice the phenomenon despite the green glare of the brightly lit downtown—the natives answer that it's a trick of the night air, heat lightning, or leprechauns, or whatever seems best to suffice to silence the questions in such a way that no attention is drawn to the silencing.

The lights along Parnell will be as bright and green as ever, punctuated by other neon and lit plexiglass colors up and down the street, McDonald's orange, Hardee's red-orange, Owl's red. The small clusters of suburban districts surrounding the downtown will be as dark as usual, the bluish or orange-green flicker of television through the windows, few of the houses lit brightly or sounding out into the still night. In one section, a blare and yammer of reedy horns and taut drums will stagger and pulse through the snarled shadows of bonfires.[2] Beyond the town to the east, the interstate will

1. Virginia.
2. In the Tibetan section of town, a rain ceremony will be taking place, a desperate and serious response to the drought that will for the last two weeks have been drying the fields and crops and pastures to a crisp and brittle death. Three yaks will be shuffling in the firelight awaiting the fatal stroke of midnight.

rumble and whine and groan, and to the west, a silence will hover and hang over the dry dark fields.

A group of men in khaki work clothes will be gathered at the dark apogee of a cloverleaf curve just by the interstate exit, standing in clumps around the three heavy state highway department trucks in which they will have arrived, the yellow paint of the trucks the only color catching in the glint and glow of various cigarettes, lighters, and pocket flashlights winking on and off throughout the group. They will be waiting for Mark Welser, the federal agent[3] who will have had the town and its curious events under observation for some time.

Along the dark roads west of town, pairs of farmers, their shotguns cradled in their arms, other more potent weapons propped or lying on the dry ground by their legs, will be whispering and staring around in the black night. No lights will gleam or tremble in any farmhouse windows along the road, and only the whisper, drone, and whistle of slowly turning helicopter blades will echo through the still fields.

At the top of the rounded hill west of town, guards will be pacing the high linked fences, the steady glow from the lamps below spilling crisscrossed shadows over their green coveralls and giving the clustered evergreen trees a twisted motion in the deceptive light.

In the large metal cube, the massive building beyond the raised dormitories, men in similar coveralls will be running up and down curved corridors and ramps, clipboards in their hands, coils of fine coppery wire or tubes of translucent plastic draped around them. The television screens mounted along the walls will be ticking off a sequence of numbers and puzzling messages, all the while displaying the time in hours and minutes and seconds.[4]

The center of the building at ground level, directly under the cylindrical plastic tower that rises abruptly through the roof into the still hot air, will be covered with the steel beams and crossed girders of the antigravity grid[5] that will soon be sending the solar ship up and out into that night air, that still black sky with its distant stars scattered and spilled like dust in the deep dark.

3. The safest conjecture is that he will be with the CIA (an operation also based in Virginia), although NASA, the FBI, the Bureau of Immigration, and the Irish desk of the State Department could also be likely.

4. Eastern Daylight Saving Time, not Dublin (Ireland) time as will be darkly hinted in the newspapers later.

5. The Leinster Landing Grid, which will have been designed and constructed for the project by the Will Jenkins Group, an imaginative and creative design association located in eastern Virginia.

The ship itself will be boxy and cumbersome, a large rectangular shape of twisting conduits and flat metal sides. The tachyonic scoops will still be folded relatively flat against the sides, folded like a lady's fan or, more likely, a fireplace bellows, not really flat, fold on fold on fold. The last peat will have been loaded aboard the day before, and now the solarnauts' personal gear will be settled into place in the crew's quarters, not in the nose of the vessel but directly amidships, the zippered bags with the red-orange sun and green harp insignia painted on their sides as though they were simply airline flight bags. The nose of the ship, pointed up at the stars, will be only slightly conical, will be almost flat and rounded only at the blunt corners. It will look like no spaceship dreamed or known. It will look much like a large earthbound piece of machinery, something in, say, a factory's ventilating system, or part of a furnace, crude and unaesthetic. It will not even be painted green; it will not even be painted at all, raw metal and exposed asbestos, nothing at all to bubble or peel or scorch. Even its name, THE WANDERING AENGUS, will be embossed into one rough metal side with the sun and harp engraved just below. The men who will be working all around its base and crawling on ladders up along its sides will not even seem to treat it with the awe and respect that they would a sleek and streamlined silvery dart or a steaming, rumbling giant poised on a gantry in the Florida sunlight. They will be hammering at pipe connections and twisting at wires, cursing at scraped or peeled fingers, one of them taking a quick surreptitious kick at a valve that his vigorous cursing will have failed to free. And the ship will sit there on the grid, silent and stolid, its door hanging open, looking much as though the only trip awaiting it were only one to the scrapyard or, at best, one by flatcar to the back room or subbasement of some factory up the valley or over the mountains to the west.

The solarnauts, already dressed in their green spacesuits except for the bulbous helmets, will be sitting in the waiting room just off the base of the grid. Flann[6] O'Flynn will be nervously rubbing his hands together, washing them in air as though to shield them thus from space, a stipple of sweat shining on his upper lip, his black hair combed flat and slick, staring at the floor, saying nothing at all. Seamus Heanus will be nipping lightly at a thin silver flask that he will have smuggled into the room taped to his thigh. He will not be drunk, but he will have a hot gleam in his eyes, the freckles on the pale skin of his face exaggerated in the indirect fluorescent light of the room. Sean Siobhan will be holding a thin book[7] on his lap, pressing it open

6. "Blackie."
7. *Confessions of an Irish Solarnaut* (Dublin, Va.: Doldrum Press, n.d.).

with one hand as he clutches a fountain pen in the other, chewing at his lower lip, staring across the room but seeing nothing or no one in it. He will then look down at the volume, at the words he will have already written there, and he will begin to write again in looping nervous letters on down the page.

Owen[8] Hanrahan, director of the space project, will not be on the floor by the solar vehicle, nor will he be in the control center at his own key console, monitoring the blips and blurs of the various calibrated screens around his swivel seat. He will be in his office in the small building adjoining the launching cube. He will be sitting on the corner of his desk, leaning over a worried-looking man, his brow slick with moisture, his curious feathered costume ruffled and snarled. He will be questioning Kevin Shanahan[9] about the list of significant words that Flann O'Flynn will have found in the storage room above the Owl Bar in Dublin on the previous Saint Patrick's Day.

Shanahan, his owly headpiece pulled back and hanging loosely over his feathery back, will be nodding and gesturing, will be speaking of the need he has for keeping his job what with his wife and the five children,[10] will be speaking of his strained loyalty to the Owl Party and of the Owl's need to know everything that is happening in the countryside, will be professing his deeper loyalty to the town and to his own people, will be rubbing his wet brow and then rubbing his damp palm up and down his feathery thighs, will finally heave a great sigh as though he has made up his mind about something so important that it will make all the difference in the days and years to come,[11] and will then, after taking a very deep breath, begin to talk rapidly and steadily, will begin to tell what he has learned, on his own hook and on the wire from Owl National Headquarters, about a group of men gathered at that moment by the interstate highway just a few miles to the dark east.

Pegeen O'Rourke, her long lab coat floating back behind her strong steps, will be walking through the launching area and across the wire-coiled floor by the grid and the ship to the door leading into the solarnauts' ready room, having been called there on the intercom system from her post in the control

8. "Red."

9. Manager of the Owl Bar on Parnell Street in Dublin, Va.

10. Three of the children (Brian, Flann, and Myles) will be triplets, the heady talk of the town for some months, merchants' and newspaper photographers' delights, the three of them, in tiny leprechaun hats, with large paper shamrocks propped by their tiny baffled faces.

11. It will.

center. She will speak to the guard on duty there, who will flush red and nervous[12] at the close sight of her, and she will then enter the room.

The three solarnauts will look up as one, Seamus Heanus ducking his flask out of sight behind his bulging green back, Flann O'Flynn glancing at her face and then quickly away, feigning indifference, and Sean Siobhan swiftly closing the book in his lap, snapping the inscription, which he will have been reading over and out of view. Pegeen will speak to the men, will ask why she has been paged, and then will walk over to Sean, who will rise clumsily from his small metal chair when he says that it is he who has had her called, that he wishes to give her something. They will talk quietly for a moment, Pegeen glancing nervously at her watch from time to passing time, and then Sean will hand her the slim book. She will glance at the cover and then start to open the book, to look inside, when Sean will reach his hand out, pressing the covers closed between finger and tense thumb, a tremble in his voice, managing to say to her, not what he had planned so carefully[13] but only that she should wait, wait until after the launch to look inside. She will look very steadily into his eyes until he glances away, glances down, his face drawn and nervous, and she will lean over the bulge of his suit and kiss him on the cheek, hugging as best she can his shoulders in their green carapace. And then she will step back, will shake his hand, will turn to his fellow solarnauts, will shake each of their hands, Seamus nodding and giving her the wink, and Flann whispering something to her that his companions will not hear, something that will make her stiffen, will cause her to turn quickly to the door and wish them all luck.

Just as her hand touches the door latch, Mark Welser will arrive at the cloverleaf in a surplus jeep, still olive drab but otherwise unmarked, and will signal his forces into action, the heavy yellow trucks moving across the backroads north of town. They will be rolling well in excess of the speed limit when they pass the first shadowy farmer[14] leaning on a fence post, and he will shout into his small radio, warning his fellows farther down the road, but he won't finish that warning before a bullet fired from one of the trucks will smack into his chest and dump him draining into the dark dry

12. An effect that Pegeen O'Rourke has on many men, especially young or imaginative men, and especially on their first encounter with her.

13. What Sean will have meant to say, among other things, is: "I love you."

14. Not Patrick Magehee who will be home with a fierce summer cold, but his oldest son Liam who will have just finished college and who will just be standing in for his father this one important night.

field behind him. Nevertheless he will have said enough to rouse the idling helicopter, to send it up into the night air with a throbbing roar, its powerful spotlight sweeping the road before it, catching the jeep and the trucks soon enough, but not soon enough to dodge the rocket already on its way, whistling in a long quick spiral right into the helicopter, splashing it in a bright orange blast across the road, bits and pieces rattling and clanging down onto and into the speeding trucks. Shotguns will blast from the roadsides and a burst of machine-gun fire, but the trucks will rush on through, up the winding hill road, their engines howling across the flat fields into Dublin where the volunteer fire company's new chartreuse and kelly green engine will already be starting out toward the flaming wreckage of the downed helicopter.

The jeep will dodge aside, skidding around in a crazy gravelly curve, just before the gates of the project, and the first truck, a heavy snowplow mounted on its nose, will smash into the gate at full speed, tearing the gate out by its roots, will clatter and scrape and spark its way over the lip of the ridge and down into the parking lot of the project, the other trucks and recovered jeep following directly after.

The assault will not be a total surprise, for Owen Hanrahan, accompanied by Kevin Shanahan, still in his owl costume, will have rallied a group of security guards and mechanics who, armed with carbines and pistols, wrenches and hoes and shovels, will reach the parking lot on the run just as Welser will be dismounting and grouping his men. The fighting will break out abruptly and furiously, the whole illuminated lot a snarl of grunts and blows, the bang and whine of an occasional shot, a cacophony of shouting and yelling.

The alarm bells will ring inside the buildings of the project, followed by the calm announcement that countdown will proceed apace, but the three solarnauts will decide to leave the ready room and move to the solar vehicle ahead of schedule. Sean Siobhan and Seamus Heanus will waddle directly to the grid, mount the ladder, and make their careful way to the open door of the ship and, as they will have rehearsed so many times, will swing themselves up and into the interior. Flann O'Flynn will have noticed that Pegeen O'Rourke is still in the room, is standing in a sheltered and shadowy corner on the other side of the space vehicle from the building's main entrance. He will veer away from the path to the ship, will walk around the shoulder-high metal network of the grid, and will step unnoticed into the doorway of a small, dark storeroom just behind Pegeen's position.

Despite Hanrahan's success in rallying his forces, the attackers will press those defenders back across the walkways and smooth lawns, under and around the laboratory buildings, and finally through the large doors of the launching cube itself. Just as they break into the huge room with the grid and the space vehicle, Flann O'Flynn will have finished stripping off his space suit, dumping it onto the dark floor around him, and, picking up a discarded box wrench from the work bench by the door, he will slip behind Pegeen O'Rourke, who will be trying to see the source of the noise across the room. Just as she begins looking around herself to find a weapon of some sort in order to join in the fray, O'Flynn will strike her one sharp blow just over the right ear, a blow that, despite her thick hair bound up into braids and wrapped around her head, will knock her cold on the spot.

Welser's men will have fought their way almost to the door of the solar ship, but they will have been unable to have done any serious damage, when suddenly leaping down from the control center where he will have been manning one of the major consoles will come Xhavid Shehu, swinging his arms over his head and howling a series of wild and eerie Albanian howls,[15] fierce ululations that swirl through the room almost as shrilly as the Leinster grid soon will. He will dive directly upon Mark Welser, shouting that he is a man of dishonor, shouting that not again will anyone steal his ship from him, shouting with such force and moral outrage, howling with such alien and exotic ferocity that he will rally the flagging defenders, will burst their rage loose again, will allow them to launch a counterattack that will snatch Welser away from Shehu's battering grasp, push the attackers across the floor and out the enormous door into the night.

Flann O'Flynn will have shoved the wrench into the thigh pocket on the right leg of his flight coveralls and will have dragged the collapsed body of

15. The same sort of "strange, wild howl" with which Lord Byron startled Shelley, Polidori, Mary Godwin, and Clare Clairmont one night in 1816 while they were rowing on the dark waters of Lake Leman, ruffled by a sudden squall, "an exact imitation of the mode of the Albanian mountaineers." [Peter Quennell, *Byron in Italy* (New York: Viking, 1941), 25–26; André Maurois, *Byron* (New York: Appleton, 1930), 339–40; Newman Ivey White, *Shelley* (New York: Knopf, 1940), I, 442; Leslie Marchard curiously does not mention this important event.] These howls are reputed by some to have given rise to the strange and unhealthy mood in the party which was eventually to result in the writing of Byron's "A Fragment" (1819, appended to *Mazeppa*), Shelley's "Fragment of a Ghost Story" (1862), Polidori's *The Vampyre* (1819), and Mary Shelley's *Frankenstein; Or, The Modern Prometheus* (1818). It is also interesting to note that certain astronomers had predicted that the world would end that unusually cold and wet June because of a concentration of spots on the sun. [Radu Florescu, *In Search of Frankenstein* (Boston: New York Graphic Society, 1975), 100–101.]

Pegeen O'Rourke back out of sight into the small storeroom by this time. He will allow her to slump down under one of the workbenches along the walls and will then remove the wrench from his pocket. He will peer out the door at the swirling fight, will hear it fade out into the distance, and then he will heft the wrench, grit his teeth, and beginning punching the heavy tool into himself—his arms, his legs, his chest, even his face—hitting hard, trying to leave marks, but also trying not to break any bones or do any serious damage. Satisfied that the fighting has moved away and that he has done his job thoroughly and well, he will close the room's door slowly and carefully and then press himself down in the darkness onto the unconscious body of Pegeen O'Rourke.

Xhavid Shehu, the initial force of his rage and anguish blunted by success, will stare around the room, see that the countdown is still proceeding unimpeded, and will climb up to the door of the Wandering Aengus and look in. He will see Sean and Seamus,[16] suited up and sealed in place, and he will signal to them that all is now well, encouraging them with a grin and a thumbs up. But then he will begin scouting around the room with serious haste, looking for the missing Flann O'Flynn.[17]

He will pause at the foot of the grid ladder, will look around the room, at the workers quickly checking the connections and alignment of the cables and tubes, brushing off the drops of clinging blood, the occasional snapped tooth left over from the brawl, and then he will begin to walk slowly around the large room, looking under the grid, checking the doors along the long walls. He will see something bright just at the base of the grid on the opposite side from where he will have begun his search, something pale green with a red-orange blot on it. He will stoop and then kneel, picking up the slim book, "Confessions of an Irish Solarnaut by Sean Siobhan"[18] on its cover along with the sun and harp of the project's seal. He will flip it open, see that it is inscribed on its dedication page to "Pegeen" in words that he will read but will not really note, and then, the book still in his hand, his thumb still on the dedication, the cover dangling open, he will look around, see the closed door directly by him, and will step quietly over to it and swing it open.

16. He will, of course, only see that two solarnauts are there without being certain of their identities, although the two will be sitting in Siobhan's and Heanus's assigned positions in the vehicle.
17. See note 16 above.
18. See note 5 above.

The light from the room behind him will enable him to see that (1) the room is empty, *i.e.*, uninhabited, (2) Flann O'Flynn's space suit, for that is whose it surely must be, is lying empty on the floor, (3) a box wrench is lying on the floor just beside the left boot of the suit, (4) there is very little else to see in the room, and (5) the door to the outside of the building[19] on the other side of the room is standing partially open. Shehu will run across the room, peer out that partially opened door, see nothing, and turn again to the empty suit on the floor. He will stand there staring at it for some time, his lips moving in the agitation of his thought.

Outside, the battle will have swung definitely to the defenders, the guards and workers of the project. Welser's men will be lying sprawled on the pavement, bleeding and moaning or simply lying deathly still, or sitting on the grass holding their heads in their hands. Hanrahan himself will have disabled the three large highway department trucks and the jeep, and the few remaining attackers will be caught in a ring of angry men pushing them slowly across the parking lot even as it narrows its battering circumference.

Mark Welser, a wild and desperate look in his eye, will see Padraic Estaban's old Volkswagen sitting by itself under a tall lamp standard and, recognizing it from the many times he will have seen it drop his friends[20] off in Dublin for a night on the town, will leap into its front seat, turn the key which Estaban always leaves in the switch when the car is safely parked at the project, shove the gear lever into reverse and back wildly through the scattering men on the pavement behind him. He will soon bang into a curb, will snap the car out of gear and attempt to push it into first gear, but, for all his shoving the clutch pedal to the floor, the gear lever will not move into first. By the time he will think to start the car forward in second gear, it will be too late, for Padraic Estaban himself will have arrived, will have pulled the car door open, and will have locked his hands around Welser's neck, pulling him, gagging and struggling, out onto the pavement by the small eccentric car.

Estaban will hold the struggling Welser on the ground long enough for three security guards[21] to take charge of him, a capture and control which will prove to be the key to certain future negotiations with the United States

---

19. A loading door, also one of the several doors spaced around the base of the cube to be used as emergency exits should anything go wrong with the launch or recovery activities.
20. Seamus Heanus and Xhavid Shehu.
21. Koci Peza, Enver Szende, and Mehmet Xoxe.

government concerning the project and its aims and accomplishments and also the quite illegitimate covert activities of whatever agency it is that Welser represents—a quite satisfactory key, it might be added.

Estaban will then climb into his automobile, turn its ignition off, pat its dashboard affectionately[22] and, pulling a small rubber object off that dashboard, will then run at a brisk trot toward the launch cube, bulking darkly against the sky above the illumination of the untidy parking lot. He will run into the building, checking automatically as he goes the progress of the countdown on one of the many television screens, will glance up at the control center where Hanrahan will once again be taking charge, will see a solarnaut hulking up to the solar vehicle and swinging up and into the open door, and he will run across the network cables and hoses to the ladder, mount its five steps, step gingerly across the metal gridwork, slap the small rubber object in his hand[23] onto the side of the vehicle beside its graven name, will glance in at the three settled and bulging figures in their space suits, giving them a thumbs up sign as he feels tears rising in his eyes, and then, a booming voice on the speaker system giving him the command, he will swing the heavy metal and asbestos door shut with a sturdy clang, will snap the latches into place,[24] and will then make his careful way back across the grid, already beginning to hum and quiver under his feet, to the ladder and the safe floor below.

In the control room, Owen Hanrahan, still mopping nervously and without conscious attention at his broken and bleeding nose, will be worrying on the one hand whether Pegeen O'Rourke's replacement[25] will be able to handle the complex board before her (and, at a level of consciousness of which he is scarcely aware, worrying about Pegeen's whereabouts) and on the other whether all systems will indeed prove to be as Go as the electronic displays will be indicating to him on screen after screen. He will glance at

22. The car is, after all, quite old and, despite its refusal to go into first gear without a brief visit first to second, quite serviceable.

23. A small caricature of a happy egg with large shod feet emblazoned with the phrase, "Good Egg," placed on the Wandering Aengus by Estaban in celebration of his small car's large part in the successful salvation of the mission and as a gesture of good luck.

24. Three heavy brass double latches (salvaged from an old sea chest brought to Dublin by Owen Hanrahan's direct ancestor and namesake some two centuries before) spaced evenly down the side of the door.

25. Idris O'Ertel, daughter of Sawel O'Ertel but quite worthy, as it will prove, of the trust on her own.

the men from Jenkins, the leader of whom[26] will wink and give him a positive nod, and then pass on the signal to all consoles that the launching will proceed as scheduled and immediately. All lights in the enormous room will dim out, leaving only the bluish glow of the screens and the green light shining from four columns of bulbs ascending the outsides of the launching tube, up through the dark interior of the cube and out into the night air outside.

The Leinster grid will begin to hum louder and louder, a heavy drone and high shrill that will make the entire building and even the nearby buildings tremble and vibrate to the dark silent ground. All of the lights in nearby Dublin will dim as well, the bars and their gaudy signs dwindling into gloom, the streetlights fading out up and down the nearly empty streets, houselights faltering as dwellers wander outside to see whether the power failure is general or the product of their own faulty fuses.

In the green light of the cube, the heavy space vehicle, the bulky and cumbersome Wandering Aengus, looking as much like a furnace as anything else, will ease up from its heavy squat on the metal grid, will lose weight and float into the column like a bit of spring fluff, tiny twirling blade, spinning parasol, traveling seed. It will float and spin, delicately and surely, like a sweet dream, up the column, through the channel of glowing green light, and on up through the ceiling, out of the tube, sailing up on the Leinster's lift, tachyonic scoops already beginning to unfold like the veinous membranes of fragile insect wings, twirling and soaring up and up, through the black night sky, up above the earth, out from the earth, out into the spinning universe with its scattered spinning stars and solar gusts, winds and tides, glowing and drifting, whirling and spinning, turning in a dizzy and incomprehensible twirl around the still and silent capsule containing three silent men, the solar vehicle called the Wandering Aengus and bearing now the gift of another name, Good Egg.

And below the ship, the dim outlines of Dublin in the dark, the high school, the small observatory[27] and the blue water tower bulbing beyond it,

---

26. Dick Lane, a man thoroughly familiar with the ways and byways of mountainous western Virginia as well as with the gizmos of Jenkins' creation.

27. There a lone amateur astronomer, at first pleased by the darkening of the town's lights and, thus, of the night and then puzzled by the column of shimmering green light ascending high from the low round hill to the west, will see a shadow ascend that green column and move across the bright complexity of the turning stars.

the dim dots marking the street corners converging into the green haze of Parnell, all of the lights dim and faded, and the bright bonfires roaring in the small Tibetan section of town, glinting from the three long curved blades that rise and suddenly fall, severing as with a single blow the heads of the three tethered yaks, their blood rushing out onto the broken soil as their knees sink limp and lifeless to the ground, as they fall slowly over and collapse in the suddenly very silent night.

DROUGHT

*

We are, as the song says, having a heat wave, thirteen days of the last eighteen with the temperature holding in the day around one hundred, in the night near eighty. And no rain, none at all. The ground shrivels and dries. Those gray days seem now merely hallucination or, at best, echoes of some different, long lost time. The great drought returning on its twenty-two-year solar cycle, the earth trembling on the sun's slow breath. We do our planetary dance, wobble and swing, as the sun calls the figures: Ice Age, Little Ice Age, Flood, Lightning, Balmy Days, Heat Wave and Drought. Waiting out the sun again, but—surprise—this time in another way.

It is a stale and terrible time. Fires roar in the high plains and leap along the edges of the western mountains. Lightning snaps into the New York power system, that shaky structure of necessity and greed, and the city enters darkness again. The looters, thousands of them, sweat and cry out in the crowded city jails. Murderers surrender or hide away, flaunting their strings of victims in either case like boys holding up their catch along the shrunken creek banks here, east coast, west, the dry Michigan suburbs. And here, in the Virginia mountains, the drought bears down, the dandelion leaves, which the rabbits so carefully chew, drying and curling brown in the steady sun, the robins' nest alone, barren and bare, the rank unhealthy air, the trees shedding their leaves in early ersatz autumn, rattling in the hot south wind, and adding smothering ozone to the polluted air. Yesterday a water main burst down by the Gulf station, and all over the neighborhood people came out to ask each other whether they had any pressure. The water sluiced along the highway, looking for a creek in which to drain, but only dried up, drifted into the poisoned air. Just up the hill from Tinker Creek, a couple died in the heat in their closed house and were not found for days. The woman who looked into their window with worry saw only a swollen foot, black and near to bursting; the police chief wore a gas mask when he went inside. The creek is low and slowing down. The sky is full and thick and spoiled. The sun shakes its locks and burns us dry. The woman who found her long-dead neighbors has gained a dream she shall not soon lose. It is a stale and terrible time.

A dream of fire. You lie down in the afternoon, exhausted by inactivity, the air's dead weight. You are pulled into sleep. You dream a long and incoherent dream. A dream of fire.

You are walking down the road on a summer night. The sky is cloudless, but the stars are dimmed by moisture and pollution in the air. You see a gleaming just ahead, a glow that lures you like a welcome lantern in the dark. It is no lantern. It is a blazing cross. The hot cross burns, and men with hatred in their thin faces pull on their hoods, their blazing masks. You dream of fire, and as you watch the fire, it rumbles like an earthquake, twists like a tornado touching down, it blasts off from the glade with a rising roar; it is a rocket swirling high into the sky; it rises like a rocket, rises like a sunrise, bursts in a shower of blazing cardboard, bursts like a black and swollen foot, bursts like a sun, and you see that the man lying in the sand, the man lying on the beach, is no man, is only a collection of bones, a skeleton in the sand, staring with those empty sockets at the exploding sun.

It is a dream of fire, and you awaken in a bath of sweat, sodden and half sick, dizzy with the heat, dizzy with the heavy sleep. You try to rise, rise up and walk, but you falter on your elbows, hang there in a swirl of visions, blanketed in unmoving air, wrapped in your own pollution.

I have lost patience with my crude symbolic observatory. Radios crackle and sputter, and the television stammers with hot snow. I hear people say the answer is in the sun's spots, but I can see no spots, only that bland, inexpressive disk wavering on the wall. I set my telescope out, drop a large image of the sun down onto the smooth cardboard, another panel mounted to block out the sun's direct light. I find the floating sun and lock it in, turn the focus knob until the sun's crawling rim is as bright and sharp as a cutting edge, only to discover after all is over and done, that what I knew all along to be true is true: the sun's round face on the telescope's projection screen is as smooth and empty as it has been on the wall, no spots or flares, just that roiling, steady empty blaze of noon from dawn to dusk.

Is this blazing day, this furious month of drought and heat, the sun's natural child? H. H. Lamb would say that this silent noncommital sun should cause a cooling and not this furnace of a day, and J. R. Bray noted in 1968 that "75–80 percent of all known glacial advance events and other indicators of cold climate in late-glacial and postglacial time occurred during intervals of weak solar activity, and a similar percentage of glacier recession and warm climate indicators occurred with high solar activity." How small this day is in glacial time, in solar time. How do we name the day or even the age? The Little Ice Age. The larger ice age in which we, our evolving ancestors and ourselves, have lived all of our lives. "We are," according to A. G. W. Cameron, "presently involved in an ice age, which has lasted for a few million years," for "As long as the poles of the Earth are covered by ice, this is to be regarded as an ice age." We are cool and we are hot. At once we shiver in an ice age and swelter in a fiery drought, mystery of the moment, puzzle of all our lives.

The chickens spread their wings and pant in the shade. The cows gather under the trees to chew their cuds in the still shadow. Let us cross over the river and rest with them in the shade of the trees. It is a dream of fire. The grass crackles underfoot. We fan ourselves and wait for the air to move, for the sun to sputter to life and lave us in a long cool draught of solar wind. A time of hard winters, hard summers, hard words. He is watching you from the darkened doorway and easing open the blade of his knife. You are panting like a bird. You are draining and dry like the creek. The sun moves toward the western mountains. It is a stale and terrible time. You step out into the light and look its way: a child of the light, you reach to that bulging orange ball as it slips away. It moves, moves on, and you move, too. The day is hanging fire. You are cool; you are hot; you are moving in the sun's slow breath.

BREAKS

*

Suddenly, and of course, the heat wave breaks. The silent sun relents, starts singing in the clean, sweet air. The pollution from as far away as St. Louis and Cleveland has blown out and been scattered to the ocean winds. The days are clear and summery cool, a breeze that swirls through the clean lens of the air, a lens that allows you to see the trees on McAfee's Knob, the roughs and edges of the rocky rim of Tinker, the enormous gibbous moon that pales the night sky, makes the dogs restless and loud, frees the rabbits to run in the brittle dry grasses late into the night. Everyone is taller, standing straighter, breathing deeper. All pleasures, great and small, seem significant, meaningful, wonderful, the ball park, the workbench, the paths that call from the woods where the trees sigh and shimmer in the new day, the newer air.

I heed the call and go out into the woods, up the hill, by two ruffled and challenging new dogs, holding sternly a territory that has long been mine and one day will be mine no more, poor dogs, bristling and barking as though anyone owns anything for long. I pat their heads and pass them by, though Oliver is forced by ritual's demands to linger and sniff and stalk stiff-legged until they are convinced that his passport is in order, that he is less invader than wanderer, that we both are just passing through. The cool breeze wrinkles the light through the leaves, the ground sprinkled in bright yellow leaves, leaves lost in the heat and dropped to the ground like discarded clothes. The path is smooth, but we are the first here today, the way a weave of spider webs, invisible for the most part, clinging and surprising.

You walk through, your head in a transparent cocoon of spidery spinnings. You duck the obvious ones, the architectural splendors that span the path, catching light as well as twigs and leaves and buggy dinner. And you pause to pick the random tick off the back of your leg, the nape of your neck, red and hungry, flat and hard. Little action on the path, and you are what there is.

The grasses along the way, even sheltered by these tall trees are dry and browning and, where the sun strikes, crisp and sharp, but the cornfield is full and tall, the tassling stalks blocking the way to the hollow of mysteries, a barricade of green corn, the ears filling out and silken tufted. You circle back and walk to the quarry through a stand of growing jewelweed, by the long-fallen tree house, and down the steep hill into deep woods, the leaves high and whispering, the ground open and cool. They are building houses on the northern edges of the quarry, one where the sheep used to nuzzle and graze and shy at your sight, one at the base of the quarry, between its still, stagnant water and the live curve of Tinker Creek. Like Daniel Boone in the poem you remember vaguely from grade school, something in you cries for elbowroom, elbowroom. Across the Hollins Road they are carving up the pastures and woods around the pond for more new houses, and the least bitterns and great blue herons there will have to move along, too, passing through, here and gone. And soon the woods you're in will doubtless be gone, too, the quarry filled, and the trees cut down. The breaks.

The trees are trembling now, and you find your way out to the high stone lip of the quarry, to a curving wide slab of water-smoothed gray stone. You settle and look at the day, even the dog content to lie by your feet and pant and close his eyes or look around with no quarry in view. Tinker Mountain is spread before you, looming, the trees, the wide slice of grass where underground streams caused slides and baffled the highway engineers for years, the stubble of rock all around the rim. The air moves, and the trees speak around you. It is a day of purity, clean sight and clear thought, sweet air, and the sun's rhythm illuminating the motions of the day.

The stale and terrible last few weeks fade in this clarity, this purity. The events of the newspapers fade with them—Magda Lupescu's death, the Albanians' quarrel with China, losing streaks and death on every page. You are alone on a high wall of stone with a mountain to which you may lift your eyes, and you do, and the day passes, passing time. A dream of purity. The scales drop from your eyes, and you see what you may see.

A cliff swallow sails by, those sharp wings and sleek stubbed body, sails by, pumps its wings and dives, swings low over the waters of the quarry far below, touches down for a swift instant, leaving an emblem of opening circles on the green, dark water. And the water catches and holds your wandering eye, this deep and still water, turgid and dark, slime-stained and moldy, the eroding shapes of discarded chairs and packing cases and the kitchen stove submerged in its dank depths.

There is no purity in this quarry water, that icy clarity that you have been seeking and imagining in this moving world, that antidote to the stifling heat wave, no purity at all. The water is filling and furring with vegetable growth. You look deep into it from this high bare place, and you are looking deep into it from this high bare place, and you are looking deep into the history of your race, the history of life itself. Purity is sterile as well as pure, and this dark water is not sterile. It is teeming with the bits and pieces, the links and linkings of growth, of fertility, of life. When you see that profusion of random slick and green growth you are looking to your grandparent so many times removed. Oleh, chief, grandfather, indeed. You should speak those ritual words to this thick water.

I hold to a verse, more words of Paul, in II Corinthians: "By pureness, by knowledge, by longsuffering, by kindness, by the Holy Ghost, by love unfeigned." I speak them over to myself, but I remember, too, that the pureness in that verse is surrounded by other words: "afflictions . . . necessities . . . distresses . . . tumults . . . labours." We hold to purity, lift our eyes up to the mountain, but we are alive in a world so far from purity that purity itself, by itself, becomes sterility, immobility, isolation, death. How easy to be good in the woods, how easy to be pure, but even in the woods the spiders spin and toil, the ticks cling to the dry stems and stalks and wait, the quarry water teems and crawls with dark and swelling life. Purity, as all things in this whirling, dancing world, lives only when it holds hands with its opposite, the two one, dancer and dance, purity in vital and impure profusion.

Paul knew this holonic and baffling world well. He follows that verse I utter with these words: "By honour and dishonour, by evil report and good report: as deceivers, and yet true; as unknown, and yet well known; as dying, and, behold, we live; as chastened, and not killed; as sorrowful, yet always rejoicing; as poor, yet making many rich, as having nothing, and yet possessing all things." We circle and bristle and bark; we love unfeigned; our wisdom makes us fools; we possess all things.

Reluctantly you climb back to the woodland path, you whistle up the dog, and you wander home. You meet no one, and the day stays clear and clean. The brindle kitten, Jane, that you saved on the road, now staying at your home, rushes up to greet the dog wet nose to nose. You do read the newspaper and see that the National Academy of Sciences warns that if the industrial nations continue to burn fossil fuels, it could create a greenhouse effect in the atmosphere, and the sun would heat us up, on the average, more than six degrees Celsius in the next two hundred years, melting the polar ice caps, flooding the coastal cities, changing everything we have come to know. End of the Ice Age at last. Ouch, help! The clean air sparkles through the window glass, and we hurl our stones at the sky. The breaks. This fragile world. This shifting, moving, living world. We have all things; we lose all things. We have nothing; we possess all things.

The sharp sun hangs high overhead. Last month, while driving down the highway, Interstate 55, about an hour before sunset, the sun red and dim enough in the hazy sky to be looked at directly, Bill Zaffiri of Normal, Illinois, saw a large speck on its face to the left and up from center, a large sun spot. The blank face of the still sun blank no more. The minimum of the sun spot cycle has passed, and the sun is shaking out its locks, loose and alive, again. Ionospheric disturbances begin to occur, and the mean of the American sunspot numbers rises from the 16.0 of May to 34.4 in June. End of this Little Ice Age at last. Ha, ha.

You step out again into the day. You know this weather, as all weathers, will not long last. You breathe in the air, look to the mountain, there and there and there, mountain and mountain. And each thing you see or touch or taste or hear or smell seems brimming with significance, with value beyond cost. And you know that no matter what tomorrow brings, dark surprise or surrender, you have, in Knut Hamsun's phrase, already been paid in advance. And that's the breaks.

SELECTED POEMS FROM SEAN SIOBHAN'S

✳

CONFESSIONS OF AN IRISH SOLARNAUT

I. UNDER THE SUN

WEATHERS, HISTORIES,
CONVERSATIONS,
AND ADVICE

SAILING ON SOLAR WIND

*

The worst winter in years,
In centuries,
Ice snapping the tender bones
Of your friends like coated twigs
While you dance in the snow yourself,
Tossing a log aside with a slam,
And slam down like a frozen log.

You shiver by the fire,
You ache and shiver and hold fast
To old saws (if winter comes,
Can spring, it's always darkest,
Every cloud), old saws that cut the air
With a ragged edge. You burn the air.

An answer:
Sailing on solar wind,
Swinging the corona like a gate in spring,
The arctic lights that wrinkle
Through a rigid sky, display of fire
Where nothing's there to burn,
Sun spots, coronal loops and solar flares,
The answer's there, shape of the days to come.
A rainbow of radiation
Repeats the ancient promise:
If winter comes.

153

Your television hisses across the room
With an electric snow, that sight and sound
An echo of the initial word,
The one that did it all
In the beginning,
Still hissing in the air as light,
You breathe it like a tropic breeze,
Basking in the Big Bang, bathing in it,
Sailing on solar wind,
Knowing winter's end.

The fire flares and loops a coal
Out on the floor. You press it out,
No fear of fire, no need to fear,
It winks out like a pulsing star.
The fire flares and hisses,
The room moving,
The room soaking in it
As the world circles in the sun.

Can you be far behind.

DUST IN THE AIR FROM KANSAS

*

A dry day in February.
False spring has cleared the fields
And nudged the snow out of the north banks,
The sun persuading the stiff ground
To dust and dance through yellow grass,
And now wind from the west
Harps on the wires outside the window,
Heaps dust from Kansas, from Colorado
Across the Alleghenies,
Brown dust rolling over Ben Bulben,
Dusting Walker Mountain off into the valley,
Turning through the brown day like a dervish.

Your eyes smart and redden,
You leak and sniffle, turn like a dust devil
From west to east, from east to west,
From dawn to dusk.

On Mars when the sun is closest,
The dust rises in the northeastern Noachis
Near the great basin Hellas,
Spreads to the west in a stinging cloud
Until by summer it slurs the south,
Sometimes the north and south,
The whole red planet whirling
In a cloud of orange dust.

The same sun here is drying out the west,
Lifting Texas, raking Kansas, Oklahoma,
Moves them out and east,
Shedding their coats on the cold east coast,
Winding the wind out over these blue mountains,
Midwestern dust catching in your hair,
Wheezing through each breath,
A sift under the door, stacking in the furnace filter.

The sun shimmers to the south,
Gray clouds mass and mingle with the dust,
Sprinkle mud in a fast fine stipple
Then steer away.

Dust in the air from Kansas
With winter still hidden in the deep woods,
You blink and remember,
The west wall hums with the wind,
The sun stammering through the twisted sky,
Dusting the air, the day, the year.

It scours the day, rears up in air,
Dry dust in the air, a February day.

SUNNING

*

Not sun-bathing, sunburnt,
Not struck by the sun, sun dazed, but sunning,
Your eyes closed but seeing the sun,
First the steady orange glare,
Then the colors shading, green and blue,
Bright yellow, as your eyes receive the sun.

There are other ways of sunning:
Press your forefinger into a loop,
Thumb's up, and hold it up,
Hand flat against the solar wind,
And on the ground beyond your feet
Or on the wall or down the way,
The sun's round glimmering face,
Its circle asserting itself
Through the triangle on your hand
As you eye the sun eye to eye.

Once in the great eclipse
Some years ago
As the ground rippled and the day grew cool,
Not a bird sound or breath of air,
I stood at the foot of a Norway spruce
And watched its shadow on the earth,
A thousand tiny suns caught in its needles,
Each round disc arced with the moon's slow passage,
Eclipse on eclipse on eclipse on eclipse.

157

Another way:
Block out a window as the sun settles down
In the afternoon, but leave a small round hole,
And across the room
Or down the hall, on a door, pressed to the wall,
The sun, wavering and pale and true,
Spotted or smooth, a cloud slices through,
The sun sitting for its photograph
Or portrait, moving all the while
On up the wall.

Sunning:
Facing into radiation,
Your skin singing after the long winter,
Sun baked and sun burst,
The pupils of your eyes stopped down,
And should you stop and go inside,
The dim house swims in underwater blue,
You float in the cool,
The sun still with you, changing all you see,
And opening out your eyes to all you see,
Sun wise.

PUTTING THINGS IN ORDER, RING ON RING ON RING

*

The art of rearrangement, of setting right,
When things don't fit, or move in retrograde:

Copernicus watching the stars, drawing rings,
Watching Venus or Saturn back out of sight,

Copernicus setting the sun in the center of things
Surrounded by ring and planetary ring on ring,

Night after circling night, sunset and moon and stars,
The roving, wobbling earth explains the equinox,

And Nicolas writes it down, and maps it out,
And makes the marks that mark the sun's ascent:

Just as tonight, when the phone rings once,
And no voice speaks when I say hello, I know

That it must be you: out of sight, not out
Of mind: never mind how I know, I do,

And I imagine your setting the black receiver down
In its black cradle, reassured that things are right:

I am here, you are there, connected by a single ring,
A link of electric wire, no need to say a word

Or even make a sound except for my hello, hello,
And the hissing silence just before you click me off,

Just checking, seeing if you're in your proper orbit,
Cycle and epicycle, forward and back like Mars.

HOW COPERNICUS STOPPED THE SUN

"The fool will turn the whole science of Astronomy up-
side down. But, as Holy Writ declares, it was the Sun
and not the Earth which Joshua commanded to stand
still."

—Martin Luther

I like to picture it this way,
Call me what you will:

Nicolas looking out at the stars,
Their steady turn about Polaris,
Jupiter and Mars in retrograde,
Jupiter with only three bright moons
That night, and orange-red Mars,
Moving backwards across the sky.

He is dizzy from pickles
And harsh beer from Krakow,
Is saying poems under his breath
And swaying like a double star,
Doing sums and charting the sky
That will not stand or obey.

"Copernicus," he shouts, "confronts
The cosmos," and the cosmos staggers
And throws him to the reeling ground,
Where the stars spin round and round
In the night of the vernal equinox
With the whole sky upside down.

The rest is easy—how he understood
That nothing in this world stands still,

Or that black world of moons and stars
As well, how he knew that we curve
Around the sun in a six-ringed polka,
How we wobble into spring and fall.

He wrote it down at the very last,
The diagrams and circles, the *Revolutions*,
And they brought it to him on his bed
On the very last day, the bed revolving
And the room revolving and the day,
The day revolving, and the sun stood still.

HOW EINSTEIN STARTED IT UP AGAIN

"It should be possible to explain the laws of physics to a barmaid."

—Ernest Rutherford

"Oh, Albert," she said,
Shaking her head
And falling back
On the rumpled and unmade bed,
"You make everything
So dizzy." And he did.

It was Albert and his equations—
This equals that,
And it's all the same—
Knocked it all out of line,
Curved space, bent time,
Cosmos like a wrinkled sheet.

He made it all so energetic
And so odd, made attraction
Seem so natural,
Just like rolling off a log:
The up and down, the in and out,
First you're still, then you move about.

And the sun is all
In how you see it,
Boiling overhead,
Moving by, or the one
Still point
In the moving sky.

She found it hard,
How this could be that
And still be this,
How it's here and then there,
Or then there or then here,
Or then here and there, hit or miss.

She curved up like space
And then rolled in a ball,
Looking back
To just where she had been,
When Albert rolled in
And began to begin again.

Sun and still sky,
Red clouds that veer
And drift by, the day's demise
Or sunrise (depending
On where you are or were),
And Albert's continuing surprise.

"Oh, Albert," she said,
Shaking her head
And falling back again
On the rumpled and unmade bed,
"You make everything
So dizzy." And he did.

VOLUNTEERS

for Richard

It is summer and a summer's long day,
And you are telling me about your yard,
About the tomato plants that suddenly appeared,
"Volunteers," you call them,
Eight of them
Springing up in the thick grass,
Fruit already green and hard
Before you found them on neglected ground.

And today they are heavy and bearing,
The fruit green and orange and deepening red,
The small yellow blossoms
And the branching stems.

Now you mow around them,
Keeping the grass down to a rough respectability,
Matching the edges of your lawn
With the neighbor's trim land,
While they lean and stagger on each other
In a shaggy bunch,
An unkempt outpost
Of where the mowing stops
And the wild grasses begin.

I can see out the window
That you haven't mowed the front lawn

165

Too recently either:
Some chicory scattered through the grass,
The shy blue blossoms already closing
In the cloudy afternoon,
One fine tall weed standing some four feet high,
Green and leafy, long lines of pale red
Sketching its stems and its length,
And, just where the sun breaks through
To light the ground before the cherry tree,
The single bright yellow blossom
Of a sunflower, light weed,
Another volunteer, "planted by birds,"
You say, and the feeder is there,
Hidden in the dark cherry leaves.

The sunflower stands on its hairy stem,
A spiral of bitten leaves, the single blossom
Open and catching the sun,
A volunteer, a gift, bird's garden,
Sun beacon, blind eye that sees
All that is there to be seen.

TALKING TO TREES

"They seem to have very good manners. Do they never speak?"

—Robert Louis Stevenson

Sun stained and sun showered,
You are standing in high trees
Watching the sunlight shiver down
With the afternoon's warm rain.

The trees are speaking in leaf patter,
The patois of leaf and sprinkled water,
Whisper and whisper, semaphore of light
And the air's twisting reply.

This is the language of light,
Of water and air, earth speaking
In wet bark and the wide spreading
Of leaves, the tap and tussle of leaves.

You are alone in the woods
And you are talking to trees,
The sibilance of sycamores,
Sumac's silence and the oak's high rattle.

The vines wrinkle and turn underfoot,
Jewelweed springing in your fingers
And flicking the small brown seeds
Between wide roots of the balsam fir.

Dots of mud on the woodland floor,
Needled and notched, the scattered trunk

167

Of a fallen walnut, dissolving back to soil,
And high above, the clinging mistletoe.

They are speaking weather words
And words beyond weather, stone's slow decay,
Root's press into the layered ground,
Water's rise to greet the sun in green.

You are word-bound and tongue-tied,
Shy in the hushing of trees,
But you say what you have come to say,
"Tree," as you touch bark shyly, "Trees."

The light rain passes soon,
Leaving the sun cracks in the mealy earth
Beyond the trees unsoothed, sun scorched,
Meadow and dry creek bed, dying wind.

You are talking to trees
And you are not alone,
Standing in the catalpa's shadow,
Hearing earth's answer in trees.

SEVEN PIECES OF ADVICE

*

for Marnie

When conversing with a fool,
Say nothing smart; there is no need.

When conversing with a tree,
Say nothing wise; there is no need.

When you receive the gift of air,
Say your thanks.

When you are beaten by the wind,
Bow your head.

When you catch another's hand,
Recall the hand is quicker than the heart.

When you catch another's heart,
Know the heart is quicker than the hand.

If the sun winks at you,
Wink back.

II: TRIANGULAR NAVIGATION

A LOVE STORY

SUN POISONED

for Deirdre

There is such a thing as too much sun,
Too much rain, air that billows, wind that blows,
Day that beckons, day that will turn away.

Sun poisoned, sun sick,
I turn away, turn to the wall,
See the sun caught on the wall,
I turn away, I turn and turn,
Turn like the day, the earth, the air,
The turning sun.

The weather varies in this sun season,
Will not be one thing,
Is hot at noon, cold in the night,
I dress for it, undress,
Button and unbutton, roll up my sheltering sleeves.

The dawn comes up earlier day by day,
Thunders up and catches me asleep,
Pins me to the sheet, then to the wall,
I try to turn away and fail again.

Bruckner on the phonograph,
Those long slow lines,
Or the morbid texture of Rachmaninoff,
Isle of the Dead, no sun in sight,

Only the tops of the tall yews wave in the wind,
Tombs hewn in solid stone, the guarded gates,
Böcklin's vision, and no sun in sight.

I seek the solace of sleep,
The dreams that wind in sleep,
When everything was as it was
And nothing as it is.

It is, I find when I awake,
As it is, but not as it was the day before,
The sun skewered by clouds,
A cold wind in the petals of the trees.

Sun poisoned, sun betrayed, sun sick,
I seek to turn away, recall my dreams,
Look on her startled face, sound of her voice,
The long slow crossing of the floor.

The sun crosses the floor, raps at the room
And it resounds, hollow like a drum,
The drum pounds as I try to turn away.

There is such a thing as too much
As there was too little, short life,
Long day, the whole continent turns
To the sun, but I am sun sick,
Undone by the sun, I hide away.

LIGHT THOUGHTS,
THOUGHTS OF REAL GRAVITY

*

"I advise the reader not to try to picture this, because it is impossible."

—Bertrand Russell

1. Grave Thoughts

The heaviness of a day like today,
The sun pinned against a flat high sky,
The sun's heat pressing down,
Down to earth, flat on the ground,
And holding you heavily there.

Three young women in bathing suits
Are lying on the grassy bank just over there,
You see how they pass the flat brown bottle
Of oil around, palming it slickly
On and in, the whole day smelling of coconuts,
Their brown skin gleaming, sliding the sun's rays down.

Close to the earth, lying on the ground,
Gravity is stronger than it is up here,
Here in the high window, here where
Time speeds by, indoors, far from the ground,
The beckoning earth, the flattening tug
Of gravity, slow time, and, of course, the grave.

The general theory of relativity teaches that,
How space-time warps down near the source of gravity,
How time slows down as you near the ground,

175

How you want to lie down and absorb the sun,
How in those last moments before the very last light
Time stalls and you are left alone
While the day speeds on.

These questions are of gravity, gravity as force,
Or gravity as, as Russell named it, cosmic laziness.

They are lying quite still on the grass,
Their oiled legs brown as the earth,
And as time flows down they seem to dwindle, too,
To slip like noon shadows into the grass,
To disappear, time shadowing them down.

The sunlight shimmers in the sunhot air,
It is bending low and slides lazily down,
Down to earth with an unrelenting gravity,
A seriousness that will not be denied.

2. Bent Light

Like a rainbow, that wet illusion
As the world dries out after watering down,
Light bends as it nears the sun and passes,
Curves round like an energetic boy
Giving the lamppost a spin.
That star, straight up there, isn't
There. It is, of course, but not just
There. You have to look at it like a pitcher
Thinking to cross the plate, but only
After giving the batter a scare.

Sometimes I think when I am looking at you
That you aren't exactly just there either.
No offense, but I suspect we always talk
In bent light, a little oblique,
Or as the drill sergeant always said,
Ob-like.

I suspect the reason I feel this way
Is the presence of some heavy body,
Some gravitational mass that,
Although out of sight, nevertheless
Curves light and makes me see you askew.

It's like passing the moon
On the way to the sun, planning to sail
By on the left as though it were a Tibetan chorten,
Ashes of great lamas lying there,
As perhaps it is.
I'd prefer a measure of distance
When sighting the way, a little space to spare,
To give the massive sun its curving way.

It's like that, talking to you,
Not getting too close lest we collide,
Looking for that third force (or what you will),
Enjoying your view even in bent light.

3. Scattered Thoughts, Scattered Light

It sprays out as it passes earth,
Solar wind, that rush of light,
We take what we need
And scatter the rest behind.

Thought like light, bundled and waving,
Making simple things complex,
Those women, that star, your way
Of saying things.

If you stood with me between you
And the sun, you could see my own corona,
Scattered thoughts dashing out into the air
Like seed fluff from a plant,
A springtime dandelion or autumn milkweed
Seeking soil.

You see them surrounding you,
An obscure blur, hovering and wavering,
Filtering the light, so light
That you could puff them all away.

When I picture you when you're away
Somehow you're always lying down,
Never doing much, not like yourself at all,
That's why I suspect the light's at fault,
Taking a turn where it ought to go straightway.
I haven't the nerve to ask you if you
Picture me at all, bent or straight.

I think it's the day, hot, heavy,
All the plants are bending down,
If you look over on the hillside
Beyond the sunning women, you'll see
The cows are huddled in a mass of shade
Beneath the trees.

Something, call it gravity if you like,
Is drawing at us all, bending space and time,
So that our best line (or pair of lines)
That we draw so straight is still a curve.
Perhaps they'll meet, this paralleling pair,
and then at that dark point they'll share
The body's curves and darts and spins
Beyond bent light or gravity of earth,
And we'll sail away like a sailing ship
To touch a comet or light right on the sun.

SPACING

This empty afternoon, no air on the move,
I am empty-headed, half-witted and slow,
A drift across the day, blank-eyed,
Face open, a blur, a fade, adrift.

The space between us is like a paradox,
A half, another half, a half, a half,
So that when we do touch, we know
(I know) that we are still so far away,
So evenly and precisely placed.

At lift-off, building to 4 G's,
I'll feel the roar but flow
Into motion like a dream,
My arms and legs gone limp,
I'll be heavy, I'll be fast,
Will be sailing into space
Coming up like thunder or the sun.

The space that hovers just between
The time you hear me say hello

179

And the lifting of your face
Into a smile is like the pause
Of a pulse or the length of the day
When Joshua stilled the silent sun
In the silent sky and held it there
Until the loud earth was slick with death.

Spacing:
The spacing of leaves that spiral
The vine so that none is denied the sun,
Spacing of plants in rows, of trees
Along the curling of the path,
A procedure in time, in space,
A system for allowing intervals,
A little while.

And the earth below will be round and light,
Blue sketched in white, the elusive green,
Dry brown, and black all around,
No airy blue at all, the earth in space.

Today I step in space, a walk in time,
And just in time, we meet, embrace,
We touch (I know we do), and distance
Dies between us for a time,
And space becomes the only while
Before the lifting of a spiral to the sun.

NOT UP BUT OUT, NOT OUT BUT IN,
I'M BOUND AWAY

"Astronauts go in toward various celestial bodies
And accelerate outwardly from them
And into the spatial nothingness. . . ."

—R. Buckminster Fuller

The moon comes up over the eastern rim
Of hill and rooftop, spruce and pine,
Blown huge and white by the angle of air,
A harvest moon, full now for days on end.

It focuses as it climbs, grows small,
Grows clear, clears as it climbs,
This October orbiting moon, not really moving up,
Not out or in, but just around and round.

It is all a matter of angles, of slants of eye,
The lens of the night's thin air, tilt of the earth,
Tilt of the sky, all those inertial frames.
We look out to the stars as the moon sails by,
Sunlit and shining, and we feel those stars
All moving as we move around in our planetary shade.

I'm bound away. I cannot tell you where for sure.
Not yet. I can only say, I'll be going out,
Then going in, like the dog on a rainy day,
Out from the marbled earth past the rocky moon
And into the silent simmering sun.
I cannot tell you where for sure: just there.

Moonlit, stardrawn, we walk out together,
We step on acorns, hear them snap and roll

On the concrete walk, and we talk
Of the light of the moon as it silvers the way
From lit electric lamp to lamp, or, anyway,
Chalks the way, gives it a gleam and glow.

Reflections on an evening stroll,
The ins and outs: the acorns we did not crush,
Burrowing the grass, rooting in and leafing out,
Spreading to the spilling sun, the wash of rain;
The ones we did, scattered like moonlight
Through the air, husks and shards, scattered and complete.

We walk into the shadow of a nearby wall,
Out again into the silent light. I hear your voice,
I see your face so calm in these reflections,
So near. I'm bound away, soon to grow small
Like the moon, by the moon, out and away.
A thin cloud slits the moon like a movie frame.
We move away as the planet turns us toward the day.

UNDER BEN BULBEN AGAIN

"They shake when the winds roar,
Old bones upon the mountain shake."

—W. B. Yeats

Lightning and water and death in the air,
Air that attacks the earth,
And the banshee's wail is as high
As the cloud that falls.

You are alone in the rain
As I am rattling down Ben Bulben's side,
The rifle's crack stilled in the lightning's roar,
The twisting trees, and your head turned in the rain.

The gravedigger punches his spade into the earth,
This coiling soil that writhes upon the metal blade
Until he flings it away across the wrinkling grass,
Until the lightning lights the leaping of the spade.

They found you near the tower where you jumped,
Where you had climbed up the turning metal stair,
Where you had spoken a single name, or two,
Into the stirring air and jumped down like the rain.

I am wet to the skin, into the bone,
My knees are water, my hands are rain,
I hear your voice in the predawn dark
And I turn your voice away.

Laid out and soon to be laid in,
You are dry now and thin and stiff

183

While the room flows around you
and the whisky pours like rain.

Ben Bulben jumped in the electric air
And flicked me off like a flea
Or a passing thought, just as I
Turned you off like a light.

I heard the banshee's cry
And thought it was the death of my own fear,
Limping home across the flooded fields,
Not knowing how it was your final fling.

The lightning snaps the digger's spade
And fuses him to ground, where your wet coffin
Soon will lie, where I will walk on every day
And lay me down to cry and beg and pray:

Lightning and water and death in the air,
They shake when the winds roar,
Old bones upon the mountain shake,
Pass by, pass by, pass by.

THE DARK PASSAGE

The choice of the eye:
To look at the sky and see sky
Or see a way to see beyond,
A shadow through which to see
Darkly and well, circling stone,
Cleft rock and tumbling ice,
Rings and turning worlds,
The furious growling sun,
Stormy and brighter than day.

It is like the way I see you,
Clearer by day by night by day,
A brightness and force, a storm
Of leaping flares, a source,
But always, night or day,
In the dark, the shadow
Of her passing that stays
Long after she has passed away.

We do live, do suffer, do pass,
Pass this way, pass on,
Passage free, holding to
Our little scraps, letting them
Go, never letting them go.

An evening grosbeak cracks
Sunflower seeds out in the snow,

As yellow as the sun himself,
The sun skimming across the ice
And catching in his wings.

No more than animals do we live,
Do suffer, do pass, my hand
Across your eyes like a cloud,
Your hand along my shoulder,
The two of us together, holding on,
Her shadow steady between us
Like the pressure of a magnet
Pushing out, pushing away.

It is this or that, that or this,
Mattering no more, mattering less,
Mattering more, all the universe,
You, the way to the stars,
Or at least one nearby star,
The dark passage, steering by the stars,
The shadowy way, pushing away,
Just look at the sky and see why:
The choice of the eye.

III: WHAT TO DO

WHAT TO DO
(WHEN YOU WANT TO SAY SO MUCH
AND YOU DO NOT KNOW HOW)

*

You are far away,
Space dipping and swaying in time,
And I have something to say
But do not know just how.

If I could speak in light
(Eight and a half minutes from sun to earth)
I would, words on solar wind,
Lighting up the polar sky,
Curtains curving,
Rivers of noun and verb.

One word will do,
Or two, or more,
But if no words will come:

Try flowers,
Rosemary for remembrance,
Myrtle for love, the humble hyssop,
Hyacinth for peace of mind,
The discreet daisy that will not tell,
Light from the buttercup that dares tell all,
The complex history of the rose,
Messenger at the door, puzzle and surprise.

Or other symbols,
Rat's evil, snake's sly appeal,
Rabbit's belief, watchful rooster,
Lazy cat, pelican's care,
Cross and double cross, hammer and star,
River and still water, mountain too high
To cross, planet in the evening sky,
The good man's strawberry, true fish,
Rainbow of promise, pot of fool's gold,
Sun's simple code of dark and light.

Codes,
The cleverness of codes,
The stammer and hiccup of electronic dot and dash,
Or the older rhythms of the telegrapher's fist,
Smoke signals from a nearby hill,
The innocent page covered with invisible ink
(You hold it to the fire),
Lines at the end of the letter—

     xxx

     ooo

Or blocks of inscrutable letters—

VZIVZ SPNHW IOPQW VZIVZ SPNHW IHLKV
ZIVZS PNHWI HIAYQ FVZSP OLPYP IJIUH
LKVZI VZSPN HWIUI LAAKO PQW

Try other languages,
Unfamiliar words,
Clicks and glottal stops,
Sounds of the palate, sounds of the nose,
Gujarti, Wendish or Dard,
Luvian, Lydian, Lycian,
Pashto or Kurdish,
Loops and curls of Arabic,
Strokes and bars of Chinese,
Pig Latin, Hog Latin

(Osay uchmay, osay uchmay),
So you may say it and be heard
But not be heard too soon,
The dictionary as go-between,
John Alden kneeling on the floor
Leafing back and forth from page to page to page.

Or other languages,
The language of the dog,
Cocked head, the wagging tail,
Hackles brisk along the spine,
The wow-wow-wow, wouah, wouah,
Dance of the empty dinner bowl
Across the kitchen's linoleum floor.

Language of the cat
(Fifteen words have been catalogued)
Or of the jackdaw
(Kia, kiaw, fly away, fly back,
Perhaps the only words I need,
Kiaw, kiaw),
Seven words of the rooster
In the chickenyard,
Typed letters of the kitten on the keys,
ew31pol;,
The language ('Attar told us) of the birds
Who sought the Simurgh
And found the Simurgh to be themselves.

Tintin talking to the elephants,
Sol-lah-te-doh and doh-te-lah-sol,
Or Tarzan's notes on Pal-ul-don:
Otho, God's name,
A-ul-as, light of the sun,
Otho-sog-as, eclipse,
And you—Lo, Ro, A-ul-un.

Language of the telegraph vine,
Moth's scent, bee's dance,
Antennae of the ants, quiver and touch,
The thunderhead's announcement in advance,
Trees' leaves that dimple in the wind,
Bits along the DNA, neutrino's whiz,
The quark's surprise.

The poetry of penguins
(Read Le Guin), the poetry of stones,
The poetry of planets
Singing into silent space,
Curving time.

Or the language of dreams,
Freud's comic signs,
Scaling the building's wall,
Snake in the grass,
Hat of a man, stairways and shafts,
Persons in a landscape,
Narrow narrow streets,
Causeways,
And other dreams,
Mountains, rivers,
Writing on the walls,
City landscape and the duck's escape,
Your face,
And when I said so much.

Or if I have the words
(I think I do),
Perhaps the medium is at fault,
Try others:
Tomtom in the jungle's dark,
Code of the radio, the telegraph,
Vibrations on a string between tin cans,
Chalk carvings on a mountainside,
A small box in the classifieds,

Billboard by the road,
Or just a postcard with boxes to check:
[   ] Having wonderful time
[   ] Wish you were here
[   ] Don't forget to feed the canary
[   ] My window is the one with the X
[   ] Hello hello hello
[   ] So much

Or wig-wag, semaphore:

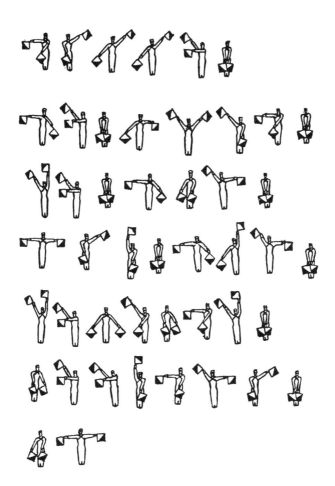

Or if you are not so really far away
And we are face to face,
A wink, a nod, turn of the head,
Firm handshake, swift embrace,
Language of the wrinkled brow,
Lip's turn, of legs, of fingers,
Familiar language of the eyes,
Or simply say the thought
That comes to mind,
Or think that thought
And it will then be said.

Messages,
The message of the dawn,
Orange dusk,
Message curling on the wind,
Pigeon's wing, mosquito's hum,
Message that washes through your nerves like water
When something dark blacks out the stars
And passes, lets them shine again,
Message that flutters on solar wind
To which we all respond,
You and I and rocks and stones and trees,
The message I will not say,
Message you will not say,
Message we both will hear.

Or, say, silence. . . .
Silence that says so much. . . .
Silence that says. . . .
And says. . . .

DOG DAYS

*

Sirius dogs the smooth sun across the sky these days from dawn to streaming dusk. Sirius, Canicula, the Dog Star, brightest star in the sky, only 8.7 light-years away, burning, glowing, neighborly, good dog. Every dog has its day, and these days are the Dog Star's, hot, dry, steady, driving the neighborhood dogs into the shade or, if they have made the proper arrangements with people, indoors. Oliver, when he isn't inside, has made himself a nest under the forsythia at the back of the house, a smoothed out indentation in the hard soil, a shallow bowl in which he curls, chin flat out on the ground, safe in the shade, drowsing in the sunny day, lying low in Dog Days.

Sirius, at least to our eyes, trots obediently at the sun's late summer heels, and we have watched that bright beast closely for centuries. Egyptians read its rising as the sure sign of the spring floods' beginning. The Greeks and Romans saw it as a sign of hot, slow days. For Hipparchus in 134 B.C., it sniffed out in its wanderings the wobbling earth, led him to discover the procession of the equinoxes, the 26,700 years it takes the polestar to make its slow circle in the sky, although it took Copernicus to see the wobble for what it was, for what it apparently is. And in the middle of the Little Ice Age in the seventeenth century, it led Huygens, the perfecter of Galileo's pendulum clock and, therefore, of accurate timekeeping, on a wild chase— Huygens, who could find and name Syrtis Major, the "big bog," on Mars and could chart and clock time but who could not imagine anything brighter than the sun and, because of that failure of imagination, thought that the fleeting Dog Star was some twenty times farther away from us than it is and some 400 times less bright than it is in its white dwarfish intensity. And in the nineteenth century, Bessel and Safford and Clark, puzzled by its irregularities of motion, predicted and found that it was frisking around with a companion, an obscure playmate of that fascinating bright brute.

Dog Days, hot days, more heat records broken daily, and all the dogs lie low. Even the dog who usually challenges me down by the bridge over Tinker Creek, a mixed and nondescript fellow of basically good intentions, lies these days by the door to his doghouse and only woofs his ritual remark. I look for mad dogs and Englishmen in the noonday sun, but I find only myself out in it—and this fat, lazy dog by the low, quiet creek.

We watch, as we have always watched, the Dog Star for a sign, that alien companion about which we know so much and so very little, watch it as we watch those alien companions of our immediate lives, the dogs and cats who stretch and amble, growl and purr, live in our homes, that we take for granted too much of the time and about whom, too, we know so very little. Think of that, the dog who walks into the room and looks up at you with such a steady eye, or the cat who stares up at a moth settling down over the hall closet door, her tail stiff and vibrating, her jaws chattering with an alien frenzy, chattering on air and the moth which is caught only in her eye. How can you look away, say *good boy* or *kitty, kitty*?

You see in the paper that the police think they have caught the Son of Sam, the nightstalker, letter writer and lovers' killer, and, with some effort of the imagination you can know what he is thinking, make an imaginable facsimile of his life, inner and outer. For all our differences, her face like a bird's, beak nose and narrow pointed jaw, or his, thick neck and tight pig's eye, we are much the same, and we can see where we're going, each of us, and why. But we look at the dog or the yearning cat, and what do we know?

We do look. Edgar Poe watched at least a hundred times his black cat open the kitchen door by manipulating a complex latch and, by doing so, making use of "all the perceptive and reflective faculties which we are in the habit of supposing the prescriptive qualities of reason alone." He watched carefully, but he could only conclude that "the boundary between instinct and reason is of a very shadowy nature" and that only the "self-love and arrogance of man will persist in denying the reflective nature to beasts." Poe's literary terrors, he once said, were "not of Germany, but of the soul," and he knew the soul, that wise, embattled man, as well as anyone, but even he did not really know the nature of that capable cat. We imagine ourselves into those furry or scaley or feathery forms, even the best ethnologists among us, Tinbergen with his sticklebacks and Lorentz with his graylag geese, and we see ourselves bristling or stalking or singing on the chimney pot, shedding some light along that shadowy border but still seeing more self than alien life, alien thought, alien being. Even Stapledon's Sirius, bright and bold dog, is more man than dog, man in a dog suit, than doggy essential dog.

The brindle kitten, Jane, who seems now to have come to stay, slips into the room, pauses to swat Oliver's tail, falling over in mock assault, bounces away from his resigned complaint, and hops into my lap. Each morning she climbs me like a tree or a chair and rubs her tiny jaw all over my face, foiled only by my lopsided glasses, leaving her marking scent clinging to my skin until finally I wash it away. This behavior, this scent, is a sign, but what does it say? Is it territorial or sycophantic, affectionate or merely random? I read it as well as I may, poorly, but my best; I feed her and allow her to stay, cup her small arching back in my palm, and take the rest on faith—this alien being in my hand. If she were a carcajou or little blue penguin or some still unmet and unimagined inhabitant of some invisible planet that romps with Sirius and its quiet companion, would I know more?

Even murderous Son of Sam, according to the note detectives found in his car, has paid attention to the alien behavior of the fellow inhabitants of his world. The note reads:

> AND HUGE DROPS OF LEAD
> POURED DOWN UPON HER HEAD
> UNTIL SHE WAS DEAD.
> YET, THE CATS STILL COME OUT
> AT NIGHT TO MATE
> AND THE SPARROWS STILL
> SING IN THE MORNING.

And later, the police say, he told them that he had been ordered to stalk in the night, to kill and maim, by a dog, by the voice of his neighbor's black Labrador retriever. Signs and portents, and we think we understand. So quickly, we think we understand.

Sharing the front page of the newspaper with these musings and readings of signs is the story of Lady, an injured hound who crawled onto the floorboard of an automobile carrier truck and rode, hurt and unnoticed, from Winston-Salem to Roanoke, where she is now in the hands of the SPCA. Whether crazy or sane, scientific or sentimental, we do notice, we do pay close attention to the doings of these alien beings, these dogs and sparrows, copperheads and cats.

The kitten climbs up onto my desk and moves toward my skipping fingers on the typewriter. If I give her leave, what will she say, paw out on the page? I give her leave. Kitten on the keys: fgma   X Z   X. Does that say it all? She cautiously steps away through the litter of erasing tape and books and stacks of paper.

"fgma   X Z   X"

The kitten's message to you. What does it mean? Does it matter which foot stepped on which keys? Does the left rear know a different reality from the right front? It would, I suspect, require a serious cabalist even to begin to see what it says. Maybe when she is older.

Hot day musings. Dog Day musings. As idle and random as the dog's turnings before he settles in the nest, or as meaningful and sound. Despite the mad example of Son of Sam, we do try to read the day. Ursula Le Guin would call the task of figuring it out "therolinguistics," and, given the multitude of motions and signs in which we move and breathe, we all should be therolinguists, reading kittens and moths and rocks and stones and trees, reading the face of the sun and the turnings of the stars.

Sun and Dog Star settle toward the west. They lead us where they may. A hot wind is scuffling the marred leaves of the dry trees. Dark clouds gather, and lightning spits and arches a few miles south of here; tornadic winds bark and howl and twist across the valley. We are, this earth, turning through the Perseid meteor shower, and tonight the high sharp sky will be split and smeared with flashing meteoric lines. Signs and portents. Dog Days. This baffling, often deadly, alien world. This day and world in which we live, to which we all belong.

THE GAME ITSELF

*

After a week of cool wet weather, it is a hot dry Sunday afternoon. The crowd at the ballpark is clustered in the red and yellow seats under the roof, only a few of them daring out onto the concrete bleachers in the open sun. We have come, Allen and Dara and Nancy and I, from Frank and Ann's wedding, the bride and groom safely away in a scattering of rice and the wedding guests scattered after. We join Marnie in the stands, her Pirate cap in place, and she tells us what has occurred: how the Red Sox scored a run in the first inning and went whooping and whistling into their dugout, banging their bats against the water pipes and generally behaving like a team nine games out of first place with only five games left to play, loose, enjoying the tension of a team only one game out, feeding on it; how Jim Brady, the Pirate shortstop who had played so well defensively the night before, hit the first Red Sox pitch of the game out of the park; how Ozzie Olivares hit a single, and Dick Walterhouse hit a home run over the right field wall, where it bounced on the pavement of Florida Street high enough to be seen again before disappearing into the lawn of the white house across the street; how the score was ten to three when we arrived and the game nearly over; Pirates 10, Red Sox 3.

The game itself, the pattern of pitches and hits, the ball bouncing and twisting across the infield grass, a bat that cracks along the grain, the ball boy ducking behind the light pole as a foul tip stings the screen, the sun steady overhead holding the players to the field in the narrow circles of their shadows, the third-base coach's signs, the patterns of electric numbers across

199

the scoreboard—the game itself, holding to what Herbert Quain called "the essential features of all games: symmetry, arbitrary rules, tedium." We admire the symmetry on the field and on the scoreboard, and we admit the arbitrariness of the rules and the tedium, claiming all the while that, like the symmetry, they are informed with significance, that the game is game, is play, but that game and play are alive with the values by which we inform our lives, our life, from day to day.

There are, of course, games, and there are games. There is the random game that one child makes up to pass the afternoon, a game with rules and symmetry and tedium, a game that survives no longer than that afternoon or a few days more, only longer as a lingering memory. There are shared games of that sort that may last longer, that survive in two memories or three or more. And as the games become more complex or, at least, longer, they take on more weight. Records are kept. The games are stored in outline, and recalled, still arbitrary and symmetrical and, to whatever degree, tedious—temporal, but striving to sustain themselves in time, striving even to transcend time. And there we come to the game of art, the long game, the game whose players are unknown and unknowable each to each, painter and viewer, player and hearer, writer and reader, recordkeepers and critics, scholars and historians, all participating in the continuing act of creation, the work of art that changes and flows as does all creation, never the same twice from reading to reading, from reader to reader, viewer to viewer, hearer to hearer . . . and still, no matter how insignificant, how valuable, how straining out from the texture of time, still a game, the game itself.

Ursula Le Guin described the literature of fantasy as "a game played for very high stakes . . . a different approach to reality, an alternative technique for apprehending and coping with existence." And when you vary the stakes, that is a good description of all games. You focus through the field, the bunt, the base on balls, the rally in the bottom of the ninth, and what you see is reality, the wonder and incomprehensible surprise of it, for a moment clear, for a moment given valid form by those arbitrary rules, that imposed symmetry, that controlled tedium. And you carry that moment of vision, a permanent part of you, away from the field, the board, the table, the theater, the museum, the book in your hand. The game itself moves, too, like the planets and the stars, repeating its circles and arcs, its touchings and partings, and still never repeating itself, and through that movement, those repetitions, you hold the sky, you hold beyond the sky, you hold and never lose (so long as you choose to see what you have seen and are seeing) a sound sense of the whole, a sign beyond reading, a sign of what you know.

In the bottom of the eighth, Salem scores two more runs making the score now 12 to 3. Not like the night before when the Red Sox won the game 3 to 0. Wink Cole was at bat in the bottom of the ninth with two men on and only one man out. He hit a high foul to right that lured three Red Sox players to run after it, their bright red caps all flying off as they ran. They could not catch the ball, but I caught the scene, held it, the three red caps dotted in the deep green grass, the lights focusing the colors and heightening them, the players still and silent around the field. And, of course, the game moved on, the players retrieved their caps, Wink hit another foul far over the fence, and then hit a grounder that Wade Boggs stopped in time to throw out Stan Floyd at second base. Did Allen or Dara or Marnie, Mary Barbara or Xenia see what I saw? It is a game of repetitions and rhythms, of movement in and out, like a work of art an opportunity for the rich interplay of levels of perception, holonic and duplicitous, for no one can see it all and no two of us see the same game, and yet it is there for those to see who have eyes to see, see what we will.

Of course, Borges knew all this when he had Herbert Quain create his gamelike novel, *April March*, and all his other artificial and duplicitous works, none of which exists except on Borges' pages and in my mind and in yours. Plexed artistry, the pleasure in the game. I once claimed that the novel of today must be post-Einsteinian in its essentials, that it should "be concerned with events rather than with characters in the usual sense . . . be particulate (composed of small, apparently discrete particles or fragments) . . . be composed of a number of different but simultaneous time movements" and that it should "finally reveal itself to be formally unified." I repeat my claim, although I should never have used the word *simultaneous*, for in the novel as in the cosmos, simultaneity is impossible, arbitrarily impossible, from page to page or star to star. At least until Shevek eventually reveals his equations to us. Like the universe and like any game, the novel should be pluralistic and at one with itself, duplicitous and holonic, synchronous and multileveled. It should participate in ordinary reality and make a different approach to reality. The movement from word to word and page to page, juggle it as you will, hopscotch along or pace through from start to finish, must be necessarily arbitrary, symmetrical and, like it or not, tedious—the thumb's inexorable progress toward the finally closed cover.

But it doesn't stop there. Like the game it lingers, it lives, whether in a single image or a sense of place or a moment of surprise. It enters the long event of your life, the game itself.

I am thinking of my having seen Katherine again for only the second time in twelve years, at the wedding, when the Red Sox rally in the ninth as Bob Mazur weakens on the mound. The heat is oppressive and heavy when Bryan Clark relieves Mazur to finish the game. He has trouble getting the last man out. Tony Peña, the young catcher whose very ways of moving are an emotional register of the game, yells at the pitcher while pounding his glove, "Put it right here! Throw it!" And Clark does throw it. He strikes the last man out, and he and Tony go grinning together off the field. This time we win. Last night we lost. I have been to a wedding and seen a good friend. The sun is steady in the clear dry sky. We walk out of the park together, Allen and Dara, Marnie and Nancy, you and I. The last home game of the season, but not the last game. There is, in one way or another, always another game. There is always the game itself.

The boxes:

Saturday, 27 August 1977

WINSTON-SALEM					SALEM			
	ab	r	h	bi		ab	r	h	bi
Parr cf	5	0	0	0	Brady ss	3	0	0	0
Bryant 3b	4	0	0	0	Cruz 2b	4	0	1	0
Boggs 2b	4	1	3	0	Olivares cf	4	0	0	0
Harrington c	4	0	0	0	Walterhouse rf	3	0	1	0
LaTorre 1b	3	1	2	1	Burke lf	4	0	0	0
Coletta lf	4	1	1	2	Floyd dh	4	0	3	0
Brooks rf	3	0	0	0	Cole 1b	3	0	0	0
Schmidt dh	4	0	3	0	Pena c	4	0	2	0
Valdez ss	4	0	2	0	Salazar 3b	2	0	1	0
Totals	35	3	11	3	Totals	31	0	8	0

Winston-Salem	000 003 000—3
Salem	000 000 000—0

DP—Winston-Salem 4. LOB—Winston-Salem 8, Salem 8. 2B—Schmidt, Boggs, LaTorre. HR—Coletta (12). SB—LaTorre, Parr.

	IP	H	R	ER	BB	SO
Viens (W, 2–6)	7⅓	7	0	2	2	2
Tagliarino	1⅔	0	0	0	1	1
Pinkus (L, 5–7)	5⅔	8	3	3	3	5
Weismiller	3⅓	0	0	0	0	3

Save—Tagliarino (3). WP—Pinkus. T—2:18. A—718.

Sunday, 28 August 1977

WINSTON-SALEM	ab	r	h	bi	SALEM	ab	r	h	bi
Parr cf	4	2	1	1	Brady ss	4	2	1	1
Bryant 3b	4	1	2	1	Cruz 2b	3	0	1	0
Boggs 2b	5	1	2	1	Olivares cf	3	2	3	0
Harrington c	5	0	1	2	Walterhouse rf	3	4	2	2
LaTorre 1b	3	0	1	1	Powers dh	3	2	1	1
Coletta lf	4	0	2	0	Floyd lf	4	1	2	5
Brooks rf	3	0	0	0	Cole 1b	4	1	3	3
Rivera rf	1	0	0	0	Pena c	5	0	1	0
Schmidt dh	3	1	0	0	Salazar 3b	3	0	1	0
Valdez ss	2	0	0	0					
DeLeon ss	1	1	0	0					
Totals	35	6	9	6	Totals	32	12	15	12

Winston-Salem   100 000 023—6
Salem   304 003 02X—12

E—Bryant, Brady, Olivares. DP—Winston-Salem, 3. LOB—Winston-Salem 8, Salem 8. 2B—Harrington, Parr, Olivares. 3B—Floyd. HR—Brady (9), Walterhouse (10), Cole (8). SB—Powers. S—Bryant. SF—LaTorre, Floyd, Powers.

	IP	H	R	ER	BB	SO
Polonio (L, 1–1)	3	8	7	7	2	3
DeLeon	5	7	5	5	5	0
Mazur (W, 6–7)	8	7	6	3	3	1
Clark	1	2	0	0	0	1

HBP—By Mazur (Valdez). WP—Polonio 2, Mazur. T—2:23. A—620.

PEGEEN IN LOVE

---
*

Chapter One

"We touch," she will be saying aloud, Pegeen O'Rourke, alone in her bright laboratory, the raised blinds allowing the sun to flow over and among the tubes and retorts, the webs of wires and strung cable, Pegeen, holding a slim book in one hand, standing by the window, reading aloud to herself but very quietly, "I know we do, and distance dies between us for a time."

She will close the book, look out over the project grounds, past the tall pair of flagpoles with the Irish and American flags drooping listlessly in the sunlight, past the firred ridge and the well-guarded wire fence, up into the sky, up to the sun where she stares for a second, more than a second, so that when she looks back down at the closed book in her hand all she will be able to see is a glowing green disk, sun in the eye.

"Distance dies between us for a time," she will say again, and she will press the book to her heart and hold it there, tears pressing up in her eyelids, swelling and warm.

"I'm actually crying," she will say abruptly, wiping her eyes with the sleeve of her lab coat, looking around suddenly to see if anyone might have come into the room, anyone who could see her standing at the window, reciting poems, and crying. The room will seem empty to her beyond the roving green glow at the center of her moving gaze. "Poor Sean, I'm actually crying."

She will walk across the room, pause for a minute or two, waiting for her vision to clear, for the tears to subside, and then open the book again, this baffling book with so much in it that she will not like, that she will not understand, little sailors doing wig-wag, and things about Deirdre, and personal things that she will have thought were strictly private, walks and things they saw together, and now here they will be in a book for all to see who have eyes to see.

"The message that I will not say," she will say, "message that you will not say, message we both will hear. Well what is that message, Sean, if it's me you're talking to? What is it I'm supposed to be hearing?"

She will look around the room, see the sunlight dancing on the glass-doored cabinets on the wall, and her eyes will fill with tears again.

"I'm so emotional," she will say, this time letting the tears run down her cheeks, "so damned emotional. I can't stand it. Maybe it was the blow on the head."

But then she will shake her head and smile a damp smile.

"You fool," she will say, "you are in love for the first time in your life, and you don't know how to handle it. In love. At least, I think so. He says you wake up saying a name when you're in love, but I don't do that. That poem's no help at all, none at all."

She'll wipe her eyes again, pull out her handkerchief from the coat pocket and blow her nose with a startling snort that will make her laugh.

"What good are poems at all?" she will say. "They just make you sad and spoil a good day and make you wonder whether you are in love or not."

She will pat the small book affectionately and slip it into the pocket of her coat along with the damp handkerchief. She will take a deep breath, pull her shoulders back and will walk to the door.

"In love or not," she will say as she reaches for the door handle, "something is sure enough making me into a fool, standing around in here and talking to myself all day. It must be love."

Chapter Two

It will be a gray day, a long gray day with a slow steady drizzle of rain, enough light in the wet air to differentiate day from night, but no real sun in the sky. It will be the kind of day that will allow Pegeen O'Rourke some relief from her worry and her guilt. No sun in the sky, and no work in her section of the lab. The kind of long gray day that lures one to loll around in bed late into the day. Or all day.

Pegeen will be lying on her back in her mussed and tumbled bed, sheet drooping off onto the floor, pillow mashed under her head, the other one plopped at the foot of the bed. She will be lying there naked, flat on her back, her arms spread out beside her, her knees up in the air, her legs spread. It will be a damp day, a hint of early fall in the late August air, but she will be hot, her body hot and damp with drying sweat, and she will be cooling off, lying back, staring up at the ceiling or out of the high window at the gray misty sky.

Flann O'Flynn will be lying across the foot of the bed, the bruises on his body nearly gone now, mainly yellow stains with green tinge at their uneven centers, his arm wrapped around Pegeen's feet, his pale skin damp and hot in the cool air, too. He will finally heave himself up on one elbow and begin kissing Pegeen's feet, licking between her toes and running his fingers up the backs of her shins.

"Oh, Pegeen, my lass," he will say, breaking the moist and heavy silence in the gray room, "what a fine pair we are, lying here on such a day cooling out when a young strapping pair like us should be at the old push-in again."

He will look up through her spread sun-brown legs, past the dark damp tangle of her bush, her pale torso, the large breasts limp on her chest, to her startled face, the slow smile that will cross it.

"And are you sure, Mister Blackie O'Flynn, that you'll be up for such an undertaking, I mean given that terrible beating you took so very little time ago?" she will say, grinning at his slick black hair as he will begin to kiss his open-mouthed way up her legs, back and forth, from ankle to high knee.

"Don't you be worrying," he will say, pausing at her knees and resting his head on the left one, "about that little problem now. You can put Blackie O'Flynn in a cast, you can suspend him from pulleys and wires, you could even sever his arms and legs, and he'd still be up and able for giving you just what you're asking for now."

She will laugh, the low shaking laugh that Blackie will have only heard when she is lying on her back, but she will not otherwise move, will just lie there, propped on her mashed pillows, watching Blackie's hungry face settled on her knee. He will watch her laugh, lick his lips watching her, look her up and down, slowly up and down, and then will push his weight against her leg, push her over on her side onto the wrinkled sheet. She will let herself flop over, let herself go loose and limp, easy and waiting, and Blackie will move up alongside her, pressing himself all the way up against her back.

"Ah, Pegeen, mavourneen," he will say, the tension and desire edging into his voice, his penis stinging with fatigue as it swells against her thighs, "what a fine big woman you are. You are so big," his hands will press into her arms, her sides as he slides up beside her, "so big, so very big."

She will turn her head and look at him over her shoulder, through her damp tangled hair, and then he will push her again, push her onto her stomach, and he will slide himself up and onto her buttocks, rolling under him and holding his weight.

"Ah, Pegeen, this is it, this is it," he will say, pushing himself down into the crack of her legs, pressing home, and she will suddenly start up, cry out like one wounded, and toss Blackie from her, bouncing him back onto the bed, startled and angry.

"What the hell," he will shout.

"No," Pegeen will say, her voice worried and stricken, "No, no."

"Christ, woman," Blackie will say, "I'm not trying to bugger you, you know."

She will be shaking and sobbing, pulling herself up into a ball across the bed up near its head.

"Pegeen," Blackie will say, pleading in his voice, "I was not trying to bugger you, ah, lass. You know me better than that."

But Pegeen will be crying steadily, loud sobs, the tears streaking her wide face, and then she will press her face into one of the balled pillows and lie there, her whole body shaking and heaving with her sobs.

"Ah, Pegeen," Blackie will say, feeling himself subside, and then to himself, "Women . . ."

Chapter Three

She will have called him from a phone booth on Parnell Street just across from the crowded Owl Bar with its new neon sign, the owl perched before a blazing stylized sun. He will have tried to put her off, to say how busy he is, how impossible it would be to see her, but her urgency will have forestalled all his arguments and plans. So Blackie O'Flynn will be standing under an oak tree out of the hot sun just by the high school practice field off Parnell near the edge of the business district. Behind him the sweating, raggedly marching members of the high school band will be working on a new routine for the fall with several new students, their families recently exiled from the Central African Empire. The drumbeats will be dancing across the dusty field, complex and strange, as the new students will be stepping out fantastic patterns before the weary band at the field's edge.

She will trot up the street toward Blackie, wearing a striped red and white tank top, red track shorts with white piping dipping up into small v's over her slender thighs and red jogging shoes. Blackie will mop his face with his soggy handkerchief as she trots, and he will notice that for all the heat and for all her running she will not be sweating at all. She will run straight up to him and, not glancing about at all, pop up onto her toes, and give him a quick kiss on the mouth.

"Mollie," he will say, surprised at her openness, "you're very strange today, lass. And you don't seem exactly dressed for romance now, do you?"

"Well, you surely are," Mollie Mulligan will reply, grinning a crooked smile and giving her reddish brown pigtails a toss as she nods her head toward Blackie's shirt, a green polo shirt with the word *adidas* written on it in white stitching, "and I know what that means."

"What do you mean?" Blackie will say.

"That," Mollie will say, pointing "and don't you be pretending you don't know what it means. It means 'all day I dream about sex.'"

She will laugh then and grab Blackie by the arm and start walking with him on along the street, out of the protective shade of the tree and into the burning sunlight.

"Mollie," Blackie will say, walking along with her but thinking already of getting rid of her, of getting back to the project and his air-conditioned room or, better yet, to Pegeen's room, "what is it that's so important that I had to come all the way into town today?"

"What's the matter, Blackie," she will answer, bumping into him as she speaks and then bumping into him again, "did I interrupt your dreaming?"

She will laugh again, and Blackie will look nervously around and, seeing only the busy and occupied band, will squeeze her around the shoulders and pull her tightly to him, this little girl, so small and thin and unathletic despite her clothes, so different in every possible way from Pegeen.

"Come on, Mollie," he will say, "you be telling me now."

"Blackie," she will say, pulling him to a halt in the bright sun, suddenly serious, "I can't change my dad's mind. I've tried everything you told me, and nothing worked. They're sending me off to school, and I'm leaving the day after Labor Day."

"Oh, girlie," Blackie will say, looking down into her worried face, "you're much too young to be leaving home."

She will laugh again, a foolish little laugh, "That's not what mother says. She says I'll be fifteen in October and that I'll be thinking about boys soon and that she and dad want me to be meeting boys other than the kind that are here in town. But I know what she really wants. She really wants me to not be meeting any boys at all, and that's why they're sending me to that school in Philadelphia. All girls."

She will make a wry face and then go on, "Do you want me to be meeting any boys, Blackie?"

"Meet all you want, love," Blackie will say, giving her a little squeeze on the arm and a wink, "so long as you keep your old pal Blackie well in mind and remember to come home for the holidays."

"Oh, Uncle Blackie," she will say, giggling and backing away from him, "do you think I'll be really homesick?"

The band will have circled around by them and will pass just as Blackie will make one lunge for Mollie's arm, and he will move back, grinning and nodding at the sweating, whistling drum major, who will nod back as the drums will roll off and will stride away kicking high as the band begins to blare "Wearin' of the Green."

Mollie will step back to Blackie's side and then in front of him as the last rank of clarinets will pass, pressing her small red-trunked rump against his trousers fly and wagging it back and forth in time to the tune.

"Good God, girl," Blackie will say, holding himself still and scarcely breathing against her, looking around nervously but with his eyes hardly focused.

"I love a parade," Mollie will say with excitement, spinning around and away from Blackie, glancing down at the source of his confusion and then saying, "Meet me, Blackie, downtown, you know where, on Labor Day for the parade, and I'll give you something to remember me by before I go off and get hopelessly ruined forever."

She will wink at him, a big forced stage wink, and will run off down Parnell the way she came, her pigtails bobbing and bright, her legs flashing in the late summer sun. And Blackie will stand there in the heat and the dust of the band's trampled passing, will stand there watching her until she will be only a small bobbing red dot disappearing in the shimmering hot air.

Chapter Four

Pegeen O'Rourke will have just finished her stint in the communications center, futilely trying to monitor any transmissions that might make their way unhampered through the wash of crackling solar wind from the Wandering Aengus, and she will have come back to her office just off the lab to check out some calculations having to do with the problems they will continue to face in communicating with the distant vehicle.

She will be wearing a white cotton sundress with small embroidered flowers, red and blue and orange and yellow, across the bodice. She will have been wearing dresses to work more lately, not really sure why, feeling somehow more the way she will want to feel in a dress rather than in her usual jeans; it will make her feel more aware of her long bare legs under the dress, and it will make her feel lighter, slimmer, less strong. Why she should want to feel less strong she will not be sure, but she will know that it has to do with being in love, with possibly being in love, with the way Blackie O'Flynn will look at her when they will meet in the hall or on one of the arcing sidewalks around the project buildings.

She will be trying to concentrate on the data printouts spread out on her desk before her, but the buzz and hum of the transmission speakers will still be making her ears ring and her mind flicker and stammer, unable to focus on any particular thing or set of things. She will sigh and push the large crackling sheets away from her, shove them to the right side of the large desk, revealing as she does the copy of *Confessions of an Irish Solarnaut* which she carries with her everywhere.

"Sean, Sean," she will say, "we do live, do suffer, do pass," and then she will look up, will realize that someone is standing across the desk from her, that someone is leaning down onto the desk, that someone is talking to her.

"Pegeen," Blackie O'Flynn will say, "are you in here mooning over that fool poet's gruntings again?"

"Blackie," she will say, but he will cut her off.

"The day is a fine one," he will say, "sun's out, air's clear, and you're dressed for it like a dream. You're so beautiful that . . . that . . . well, just to be looking at that smooth tan skin, your hair down, those shoulders, those arms and that white dress . . . oh, God, it makes me dizzy, it really does. And here you are mooning over a wretched book. It's a shame. It's a blessed shame."

"But Blackie," Pegeen will say, looking up at him, trying to focus on his features, "I'm working."

"Working," Blackie will say, spitting out the word, "working, well, if you call reading poems to yourself working, then here," and he will pull out a folded piece of paper from his pocket and unfold it, pressing the creases flat on the desktop, then toss it across the desk to her, "here's some work for you. Here's something that's real and true. Here's a real poem, no whining confession."

Pegeen will glance at the paper and then look up again at Blackie.

"Is this your poem?" she will ask. "Yours, Blackie?"

"And whose else are you thinking it is," he will say, "who else would be capable of writing the truth about you that way?"

"Me?" she will say, and she will look again at the paper, reading the poem this time, reading it down the white page:

> It is the way you hold your head,
> that slight tilt,
> or the swift way you purse your lips
> when something rubs you wrong.
> Those kinds of things.
> So I am just a victim,
> walking along, whistling possibly,
> until I see you,
> rubbing your hands or yawning quickly,
> and by then the situation
> is quite out of hand.

"Why, Blackie," Pegeen will say, feeling those tears that will have been plaguing her unexpectedly every day, day after day, every day since the launch, rising in her eyes, "I didn't know that you write poems."

"Well, I don't," Blackie will say, "and don't you be thinking that I have before or that I will again, but this one needed writing, so you could see what a real poem is, and so what it is saying could be said so you'd be hearing it."

Pegeen will be able to control her tears no longer, and they will slide down her cheeks as she will try to read the poem again, thinking to herself that he has just been unable to tell her that he loves her, that he has chosen this way to tell her, that she is sitting here in her white dress with her hair down with a love poem in her hands, that this is the most deeply romantic moment of her life.

"Now don't you be crying again," Blackie will say as she looks up at him, as she rubs her hand over her eyes, smearing the tears across her cheek and into her hair. "Now don't you want to be knowing what the title is?"

She will look back at the poem and then back up at Blackie, thinking that now he will say it, say the words of love.

"What is it called?" she will say.

"It's called," he will say, lowering his voice to a husky whisper and leaning over the desk close to her face, "its title is 'Why I Want to Fuck You Right Now.'"

Pegeen's heart will pause for a long second and then pulse with a leap in her chest, a somersault, a tumbleset, and she will feel as though she has lost touch with her fingers, her arms below the elbows, her legs. Blackie will move around the table and lean his face into hers, kissing her, letting his tongue press the startled length of her lips, whispering as he kisses, "Right now. Right now."

Pegeen will not resist, but she will mumble to him her worries about the office.

"I've already locked the door behind me," Blackie will say. "There's no one will disturb us, and this is a fine thick rug."

He will ease Pegeen out of her desk chair and down onto the shag rug, touching her, hugging her, caressing her, feeling her skin warm and rouse to him, feeling her arms pull him tightly to her. But something will bang and thump just outside the door, and Pegeen will turn abruptly away, look to the door, and Blackie will roll up behind her, pressing his arms around her, squeezing her breasts through the dress's gathered bodice, and he will press himself tightly to her from head to toe, arching into her, no longer aware of his movements, allowing sure instinct to guide him on and in.

And then Pegeen will scream, "No!" And then she will hammer her elbows into his chest, rocking him back and away with the force of the blow. "No!"

"God damn it," Blackie will yell, "that's the last goddam time you do that to me, you goddam bitch."

"No, Blackie," Pegeen will cry, her face streaking again with tears.

"Tears won't do it this time," Blackie will shout. "I am no goddam butt-fucker, and you'd damned well better stop treating me like some kind of goddam pervert."

"No, Blackie," she will say, "it's not you. It's me. It's Deirdre and Sean and me. It's the dream."

Blackie, shaking with his mad anger, will stare at her, his face puckered and swollen.

"It's the dream," she will say, rushing now, saying it out. "It was the week before Deirdre died. She had been acting so funny, crying a lot, and she would always leave when Sean came in to see me, and I felt terrible about it, and I, and I was mad at her, too. And then the night before she died I had a dream. I was in bed, a big bed, but it was in my room, and I realized that I was in bed with Sean, and I was suddenly happy about it, I knew it was right, and then I realized that Deirdre was there, too. In bed. In bed with us. And I was in the middle with Sean on my right and Deirdre on my left.

"And then I was hugging Deirdre, and I knew that we were all naked, and I could feel her, her body and all, and I started kissing her on the mouth, and then I felt Sean, he was, he was screwing me, you know, from the back, just screwing me, and I was kissing and hugging Deirdre, and he was screwing me, and then Deirdre started to cry. You remember how she used to just cry for no reason, and then I knew that the reason she was so sad was me and Sean, that we were hurting her so much. And then she was dead, and Sean started acting so different, and he told about that phone call, and he wrote all these poems about her in his book, and he said it was my book, and, and I feel so guilty, Blackie, so guilty. And damn you, Blackie, for making me say it.

"I killed her, Blackie, I just know I did."

Blackie will just stare at her, still angry, still aroused and still very angry.

"So you punch me around and spoil my day," he will say, hissing now, his voice pressing out of him under great pressure, "because you had a fucking dream, because you're guilty. Well I'll tell you why that fool Deirdre killed herself, and it had nothing to do with you and your dreams or Sean's stupid phone call or Sean's silly poems. Now you listen to me.

"It's because I'd been fucking her, and she got the idea that that gave her some sort of rights, you know, that we should get married or something, true love, so I told her, I did, I told her not to be so demanding, not to be hitting on me so, that I'd be seeing her around, that there were still some good times in us. Well, that wasn't enough. Every time she saw me with anybody else, she would swell all up and weep buckets and moan and carry on. I even took to calling her on the phone like I did that asshole Siobhan to find out whether they were at home or with you before I'd ever try to see you, because I surely didn't want to see either of them. And I finally had to tell her I just couldn't choose her, I just couldn't fuck her no more, and the poor damn thing went and threw herself off the launching tower. So where's all your guilt now? So where's all your damn guilt? You and that stupid Sean didn't kill Deirdre O'Sorh. I did."

Pegeen will sit up by her desk, her white dress bunched up around her hips, her long bare legs stretched out before her, and Blackie will move toward her, will push her back onto the thick rug, will crawl between her legs, pull his trousers down around his knees and move onto her.

"No," she will say quietly, almost distantly, and then she will begin to cry again, steadily, evenly, sobs and long harsh drawings of breath.

Blackie will not pause or pay any heed to her crying. When she will hold onto her panties with her hands when he attempts to pull them down her legs, he will simply push through and by the elastic at her legs and insert himself roughly and bluntly in place.

They will say nothing else. Pegeen will continue crying. Blackie will work at her steadily, his face easing from its anger and warming into an expression of joy, his one true joy, his only joy. And after a time Pegeen will find herself responding, will move with him, abstract, distant, but feeling the strangeness of the rug, of her white dress around her, of his shirt, his cold belt buckle against her thigh, their shoes.

She will put her arms around his neck, will pull his face into her neck, and, still sobbing, she will say aloud for the first time, she will say what she will not have allowed herself ever to say before, "Blackie, my Blackie," she will say, "I love you. I love you. I love you."

Chapter Five

Pegeen will be walking, walking down from the project's rounded hill and along the dusty road, by the guard posts with their whistling soldiers, the dug-in tanks leaning back in the fields, crops chewed and trod down all around them, the rocket emplacements, the checkpoint where she will have to show her plastic identification card with its photograph (not looking much like her, her face empty and bland, eyes staring, hair in a tight coil around her head), its thumbprint, its coded information on the strip of magnetic tape on the back, and on into town, all sections busy and bustling with preparations and bands and marching units and floats for the parade.

She will not be wearing her old walking outfit, the boots and shorts, her knit cotton shirt. She will be wearing another sundress (not the white one, still lying crumpled in the clothes hamper where she will have put it that day just before that interminable shower, those interminable showers, hot and unbearably steamy), a black print covered with tiny white flowers, trimmed in white ribbon, a light dress, breezy and fluffing out in the day's sluggish winds. She will be carrying a basket handbag slung over her shoulder and in it, Sean's book, which she will have dumped in automatically without a thought.

"I know what it is to be a woman," she will have told herself that morning. "Now I know it, what it is to submit to everything, to lose everything, and to gain everything. So I'll dress the part, and I'll act the part, and soon I'll be the part."

"Ah, Sean," she will have said, "no more surprises for me. Not after this week, not after this morning. No, nothing can surprise me now."

She will have put on her sundress and begun the saunter into town. To see the parade. To see the town full of strangers and friends (acquaintances, anyway, no friends in sight). Labor Day. The day she will have awakened to finding herself in a dream, but a dream she will have been unable to recover. The day she will have awakened finding herself saying a name, saying it aloud, saying, "Blackie. Blackie."

The guards will joke with her, will smile at her, will wave her through, and the town, caught up in the first real holiday preparations since word of the solar mission will have caught the fancy of the world (or, at least, of the world's media), the town will pay her no attention at all, except for the usual impersonal interest of the young men she will meet and pass along the way.

The town will be thriving on the increased tourist trade, tourists come to see the wire fencing and guard posts, the distant hill, hazy in late summer pollution, where it will have all taken place. There will be as many orange and yellow suns scattered over the town now as shamrocks and shillelaghs, the small observatory actually making a profit casting round wavering images of the spotted sun onto reflector boards for the astonished tourists.

Owen Hanrahan will be leading the parade in an open car with the vice-president of the United States and the Irish ambassador, both of them having been flown to Roanoke on Air Force One and then motored the rest of the way to Dublin, evidence enough that the initial wave of anger and protests will have passed: the Soviet protest implying that the whole business of the project's having been a secret will have been a cover-up for covert rocketry research, the Albanian protest that a group of tawdry and dishonored exiles should be referred to as "Albanians" in the press coverage of the event, the American oil companies' expensive ads in news magazines implying that the whole expedition will have been an expensive waste of tax money used to explore other energy sources than those the boundless American free enterprise system could easily provide, and the IRA's rage at Ireland's involvement in an American project, at their good name's being dragged in the mud, and at their exclusion from the project—a rage that will have been expressed all over the British Isles with exploding pubs and postboxes.

Magazines and television programs will still be full of the adventures and sidelights surrounding the launch: MYSTERIOUS ATTACKERS OF SUN LAUNCH CUBANS, SAYS HIGH-PLACED SOURCE; SOLAR SPACE SHIP POWERED BY NEW SECRET PROPULSION SYSTEM; FLANN O'FLYNN'S EXCLUSIVE ACCOUNT: "I WAS BEATEN UP AND THROWN ASIDE LIKE A SACK OF POTATOES"; IS MYSTERIOUS

THIRD SOLARNAUT O'FLYNN'S ATTACKER? (or, RUSSIAN AGENT?, or, CIA AGENT?, or, IRA MAN?, or, PALESTINIAN TERRORIST?).

The Owl Bar, because of its new notoriety, will be packed at all hours, contributions keeping the red electric owl hooting and flapping its wings, the new key to the party's move for national prominence ("Without the vigilance of the Owl," the party chairman will have said, "there would have been no solar flight at all.") and the busy bane of Kevin Shanahan's existence.

Pegeen will walk through all the confusion of the town, the crowds pushing and jostling for positions along the sidewalks of Parnell. She will hear the distant bump and syncopated blatter of the Dublin High School band leading the parade far down the street. Vague and distracted as she will be, she will want to see the parade, to see Hanrahan in his glory, to see the floats and bands, unicyclists and jugglers, ranked workers marching ten abreast carrying the symbolic tools of their trades, and Blackie, Blackie who will have told her that he will be in the parade, Blackie the disappointed solarnaut, Blackie who will have advised her and even made her promise to stay at the project and not come into town today, a promise she will have fully intended to keep but somehow will not have been able to, what with the excitement of the day, the brightness of the sun, her need to see Blackie, Blackie her one true love, even if at a distance and secretly.

She will not be able to find a place at the curb, and, standing at a loss and frustrated on the sidewalk before the closed-for-the-parade Owl Bar, she will suddenly remember Deirdre and the Saint Patrick's Day Parade and how Deirdre had left her to go upstairs in the Banshee's Wail to watch the parade from the window there. She will glance up and across the street and see that very window, open and empty, and she will shove her way through the complaining crowd in front of her and will dart out into the street, right in the path of the slowly wheeling police motorcycles and the band, the jumpy Secret Service agents, and into the crowd on the other side.

Once inside the pub, she will have no difficulty persuading Paddy O'Regan, the proprietor, always a man with an eye for beauty and a way of being helpful to young women in distress, to let her go upstairs and watch the parade from his window. She will climb the stairs, wind her way through the boxes and crates of beers and ales and whiskies to the open window, and take her place, sitting on a case of stout, just as the swiftly moving new members of the high school band will be passing on the street below to the frenzied and enthusiastic applause of the happy holiday crowd.

Chapter Six

Flann O'Flynn will be feeling not a little foolish, sneaking down the alley behind the buildings facing on parading Parnell, scuffing along on the rough concrete, counting the backdoors until he finds the right one, the plain red door of the Owl Bar, unmarked and little different from the others he will have passed along the way. He will try the knob and be relieved to find it unlocked, unlatched and easily opened. He will swing the door out, step into the gloomy interior, and shut the door quietly behind him.

"Oh, damn it all, Blackie, do as you will," Kevin Shanahan will have said to him the day before when Blackie will have first proposed his plan to him. "Your cunt-struck ways will be the doom of you someday, but I'll not be the one to play the angel of justice. But remember, if anyone finds you and your little darling, you broke in on your own, and I've had nothing to do with it, nothing at all."

O'Flynn will stand in the silence for a moment, allowing his eyes to ad- just, hearing only the muffled noise of the busy day filtering through the store, hearing that and the steady whisk of his eager heart. He will then walk lightly across the narrow hallway to a door which opens out behind the long bar, the room hollow and empty, lit only by the sunlight slanting through the blinds on the front windows and the red neon owl. Blackie will vault up onto the bar, will swing his legs up and over, and will leap down onto the floor just before the owl. He will look all around the dim room and then open the small door under the owl, step in, close the door behind him, and mount the steep stairs two at a time.

The familiar hallway at the top of the stairs will be as dusty and empty as ever, no signs of anyone's passing this way recently at all, and Blackie will walk down it cautiously, pausing at the door on the right through which he will be able to hear the cluck and clatter of a teletype.

"For old times' sake," he will whisper to himself as he opens the door and steps into the room. The teletype will be chattering and pumping pa- per up and out, and Blackie will make his way over to it through the boxes of bottles and bar supplies. He will stop by the machine and peer down at the words emerging in even clusters from its interior: MSLYI CSPSV IAKHV SAASP JQAJI YQBHI UJIQC AKPPM AQHIA KIPAS HVQUI ASFSP LVIRH IGZQV OHLHU ITRSU IY.

"So," Blackie will say to himself, "the owls are still at it, and are getting so untrusting to boot." He will click his tongue against his teeth, thinking how Shanahan will have asked him to join the party, to consider being the party's candidate for the senate.

"Think, Blackie," he will have said, "of the tail you could have as a senator. There's precedent, you know, there's precedent." And then when Blackie will have laughed the suggestion off, how he will have added, with great urgency and sincerity, "Please, Blackie, my lad, don't ever be laughing at the Owl, no, never. The Owl has ways of persuading."

Blackie will decide to tear off a bit of the code and see what security at the project might make of it when someone will grab him around the waist and yell in his ear, "Boo!"

His heart will leap in his chest, and he will spin around shaking Mollie Mulligan loose, making her break up into a sputter of giggles and laughs.

"I caught you, Blackie," she will say between laughs, "I caught you, and I'm going to tell Kevin, I am, I am."

Blackie's startled emotion will redirect itself as he looks at Mollie, leaning on a case of whiskey wearing a halter tennis dress, short skirt nearly up to her crotch, white with an orange band around the neck strap, her skinny legs, white sneakers, her freckled arms and shoulders, freckled face, hair nearly sun-bleached the color of the dress's orange in two looped pigtails, grinning laughing Mollie Mulligan, and he will feel his erection shoving into the fly of his jeans, for he will have worn no underwear in anticipation of the efficiency to be required.

"Mollie, by God and by heaven," he will say, "I'm going to kill you someday."

"No, you're not, Blackie O'Flynn, you're not going to kill anybody," Mollie will say, "but you are going to stop snooping around this dirty old room and let me see this parade. I've been looking forward to it all summer, and you're not going to spoil it for me now."

She will take him by the hand, lead him out of the room and on down the hall to the other familiar room where he will again raise the grimy window, where he will again watch Mollie climb over the sill and out onto the small balcony, seeing this time her taut and bare behind under the short tennis skirt, and, scarcely able to control himself, where he will climb out himself and seat himself in the rickety wooden chair still sitting there by the wall.

The sunlight will be glaring down into his eyes, and he will be unable to see the parade or the street or anything but Mollie's eager face as she leans over him, tugging with her fingers at the zipper of his fly, saying, "Come on, Blackie, get it out, will you. I want to see this parade."

And then as Blackie finally frees himself from the jeans' restraint, she will say, "Well, hello," twirl on the unsteady balcony under the new Owl on the sun sign, the short skirt giving him a brief glimpse of light hair and pale skin, and then will seat herself on his lap with unerring skill and grace.

"My God," Blackie will say.

Mollie will lean forward in his lap, pulling him with her, watching the passage of the town's flags, the black white and red of Upper Volta, the red green and gold of Guyana, the distinctive white and ragged maroon of Qatar, the red flag with the black double eagle and gold-bordered red star of Albania.

A rush and roar of noise, shouting and running, will burst from the street below, cries of "It's the IRA, It's the IRA," screams and clatter.

"Oh, look, Blackie," Molly will say, twisting herself in his lap, "look, it's those men from the project, the Albanians, remember, they're hitting the man with the red flag and knocking him down, wow, wow!"

She will bounce excitedly up and down in and on Blackie's lap, and his eyes will roll back in his head, and his head will roll back on his shoulders, and he will stare directly and unseeingly into the sharp fierce sun overhead. He will not hear the noise from the street, Mollie's yelps, the steady clicks and whirs of the automatic camera Kevin Shanahan will have concealed in the Owl sign aimed directly at the small chair, nor will he be able to see anything, even after he has lowered his head, staring over Mollie's bouncing shoulder, only a green blazing circle of light, wavering and gelid.

And then through the green haze and the swirling noise of shouting and screaming and Mollie's delighted squeals, into Blackie's emptied eyes will come a face, slowly focusing, a watching face filled with distress and tumult and affliction, a stunned face laboring in surprise and something beyond surprise, a face in the window across the brawling street, the pale and desperate face of Pegeen O'Rourke.

A DAY IN DUBLIN, DUBLIN EVERY DAY

*

September and the beginning of another academic year, those repeating patterns, new faces, old, the old faces repeating and reflecting in the new. Time and again I am surprised by an old friend's reappearance on campus under a new name, a new past, new life. How easy to read these signs as proof that nature's basic human types are few and repetitive, to see particularity as an illusory surface of unchanging reality. As easy, in fact, as being awed to the point of despair by the apparently unending profusion of new forms, new features, driven to see no wholeness in this swarm of renewing particulars. The year begins anew nearly nine months after the new year began, the same as ever and utterly different.

I see Cathy, back again, and she asks me whether I ever took the trip I had talked to her about last winter, the trip to Dublin, the town where she and Susan grew up, fifty miles southwest of here, the one unique and polyglot community in this English and Scottish mountain valley of Virginia. And, of course, I haven't in all my baseball and sun-watching summer, despite my desire to see this town I have passed by so many times heading south, despite Sean's repeated invitations, despite my faith in whim (which is, thank you Emerson, painted over the lintel of my doorposts). It is a new year in this waning summer time, so I decide to use this last weekend before classes begin, to use it well, to go to Dublin, to add a new set of particulars to my great blooming, buzzing store.

The day is clear after a week of late and steady rain so that the mountains are green again across the greening fields, high and steep as you drive into them up the long even grade to Christiansburg and beyond. The way itself is full of wonders, wonders that you already know well—the man buried up-right on the wooded hillside so that he might oversee his slaves at work even in his death, Dixie Caverns with their private and unique brand of sala-mander, the small bright house near Christiansburg with its hand-carved gingerbread woodworks, knobs and curves and interlocking lines—but you are looking forward to Dublin, and besides Ives is on the radio with won-ders enough for any day, any trip, any road.

The road is level and smooth as you approach Dublin, and even this late in the season, it is still dotted with campers and vans, buses and cars covered with the stickers of their travels, smiling Good Sams and oval AAA's. Clay-tor Lake is off to the left; Walker Mountain and Ben Bulben, high and far to the right; Dublin, just two miles west of the interstate, green shamrock bill-boards scattered along the way, THE OLD SOD INN (how far?), THE UP-RISING (outdoor drama presented nightly from May through Labor Day), THE BANSHEE'S WAIL(?). The sun is high by now, spotting again, late but sure enough, and the town is busy by the time I reach the town limits and drive on toward the center.

At first, Dublin looks like any other Virginia valley town, the I-shaped brick houses sitting close by the widened highway where their builders never expected the future to arrive in any way different from the present, their front doors opening now onto a narrow concrete sidewalk and the fuming pavement of the road, red brick, white frame, the small stores with the false fronts and recessed doorways, the rippling glass of their windows glinting in the sunlight, and the gas stations, old and new, dotted down the blocks, orange and blue and yellow and red and white. But as you near the small downtown, the inner Dublin begins to reveal itself, thatched steep roofs, the whitewashed stone walls, cobbled sidewalks, the street itself fi-nally cobbled, whirring and roaring the car's belted tires. Pubs begin to appear with bunched chimneys, their incongruous neon ABC ON AND OFF signs in barred windows, CUCHULAIN'S FIGHT WITH THE SEA, BAILE'S, THE HERNE'S EGG, and (ah!) THE BANSHEE'S WAIL, and now the other businesses, the gift shops and linen shops, the clever lep-rechauns and brawling paddies painted and molded out of plastic and plas-ter grinning and sprawling across the storefronts, the movie theater (THE ABBEY) and the usual collection of dime and discount stores, fast-food res-taurants and clothing stores that compose the usual small-town downtown, all of them wearing a green tint, an Irish lilt, and signs reading: TOURISTS WELCOME.

I stop at a traffic light in the center of town and watch the flow of people on the streets. A tour bus is loading just beside me, a load of old people mostly, brightly dressed, some with cameras slung around their necks, talking to each other steadily, some of them already in the bus jostling for seats, a worried middle-aged man with a checklist calling out names at the bus's open door. And just beyond them a building being renovated proclaims its new identity, a red owl with words ballooning from its beak: A NEW OWL BAR COMING RIGHT HERE ★ ★ FROM ACROSS THE COUNTRY WINGING DIRECTLY AT YOU.

The light changes, and I put the car in gear and drive on. I am startled to see an Owl Bar in Virginia, but I suppose that here and in Charlottesville and in Williamsburg it must be inevitable, for the Owls tend to flock where tourists thrive. I have heard that the Owls are thinking of taking their quirky and often comic political ideas across the country with their bars, and I hope that my HOWELL FOR GOVERNOR bumper sticker will express my lack of enthusiasm for their cause to any owls who might be perched in a window of their new nest or on the small iron balcony under the unfinished neon sign above their doorway which I can still see in the rearview mirror.

I drive on through town, scouting the lay of the land before landing, knowing that Sean is probably still at his lab at this hour. He works, he has told me, somewhere west of town, so I follow the highway west where it soon turns to gravel and joins a narrow dirt road heading toward a low hill almost lost in the farther vista of what I suppose must be Ben Bulben, a raggedly rocky mountain, pine covered and rising on the western horizon. I follow the dirt road through farmland, small white houses with thatched roofs, wide corn fields with the stalks dry and dead and limp, the proof in this green world of the sun's dry summer. Aside from a wandering farmer or two, leaning on the rail fences or propping a boot on the low stone walls, carrying shotguns and apparently dallying through the day, I see no one until ahead of me in the road, waving a small red flag, two men in green coveralls stand firm and gesture me to a halt.

"Road's under construction," one of them says, but I can hardly hear him for the clatter and buzz of a helicopter which has come from somewhere to hover just overhead.

"Sorry, but you'll have to go back," he says.

"Isn't there some way I can get through?" I ask. "I've got a friend I think works out this way, and I'd like to see him while I'm in town today."

"Sorry," he says. "You'll have to go back. Maybe some other day." The helicopter dips closer, dust swirling around the car, spilling into it and my eyes and nose. I roll up the window, give the choking men a wave and back off down the road, looking for a turnaround.

I blur through my own dust, backwards and bouncing, until I see a farm road off to the left, two narrow rocky ruts, the wooden buried bars of a cow guard. I back into the road's opening, turn myself around and head back toward the town. I turn at a crossroads and enter town this time from the north, passing through a series of small suburbs, polyglot and puzzling— three or four small, slit-windowed stone houses with peaked roofs and curling eaves, prayer wheels spinning in the early afternoon wind; another group of straw-eaved and very clean houses, two boys in wooden shoes clattering a game of hopscotch on the wide wet paving stones of the walk; a profusion of architectures and styles of clothing, of colors and clashing forms. This is, of course, the international suburb of Dublin, familiar from slick fliers I've seen in motel racks and on restaurant check-out counters, and, sure enough, here comes a tour bus toward me, a girl in kelly green facing away from the front window, her voice amplified and booming into the day, describing the new Senegalese neighborhood with its poetry center and . . . I drive on past and can hear no more.

I dawdle through these narrow, surprising streets for some time, moving slowly, passing time, and then I drive back into the center of town and park on the main street in a freshly vacated space, a half an hour's time still bright green on the meter's dial. I climb out and begin a slow stroll up the sidewalk. I pass two young men and an older woman, grinning and passing out leaflets for Henry Howell, the Democratic candidate for governor, and I notice, as they smile and nod at the bright red button of my belief in their candidate on my jacket pocket flap, that the woman is still wearing the gold plastic emblem of Ira Lechner, the unsuccessful liberal candidate for the lieutenant governor's nomination last summer—the soles of two shoes cocked in the shape of a V and the word *Ira*. I wonder whether that's a wise move at this point in the campaign, but I nod back, wish them well, walk on.

I am startled out of my thoughts by a sudden collision with a young woman, really two young women, emerging from the Swim-Two-Birds Cafeteria, one a heavily built, handsome woman, big-boned and solid, long brash tan hair, a wide and open face, startling green eyes, long brown strong arms, and the other, smaller and more delicate, a rounder face with eyes drawn to slits in the bright sunlight, curling brown hair, an almost inescapable but indefinable sadness in her face, much the prettier of the two, although the first woman is a striking figure.

I apologize for banging so stupidly into them, and as they turn to walk away, there behind them in the doorway is Sean, red-faced and surprised, looking almost as though I'd caught him at something, sandy-haired and freckled, his pale blue eyes open wide and his mouth popping open, too.

"Richard," he says, "you."

"What's the matter?" I ask him. "You look actually guilty. What were you doing, following those two girls?"

"No," he says, "I mean, well, they work with me at the, I mean, you know, we work together. But what're you doing here? Why didn't you let me know you were coming?"

"Surprise," I say, and I explain to him about the suddenness of my decision to come, this act of whim on a late summer's day.

I walk him up the street to where he catches a ride with a man in a bleached green, ancient Volkswagen, Sean apologizing all the way about his having to go back to work, begging me to stay on for dinner, for a touch of the Irish and a long evening of reading poems and good talk. I apologize, too, for coming unannounced, for not staying, and we shake hands, make promises, shake hands again, and he climbs into the dusty little car, and it grinds and whirs away. Goodbye, I say, and mean a long hello.

And then I find my car, pumpkin yellow and bulging in the warm day like Emerson in the sunlight, and I drive home, back up the long valley, the sun easing down into the west along the darkening blue mountains to my left, having seen an old friend and a new town, a new world in an old world, the old world asserting itself in the new. Passing time. A day in Dublin; a good deal of buzz, and somewhere a result slipped magically in. Surprises, fulfillments, things seen that I have not yet seen, things learned that I do not yet know. Someday I will know them, will be surprised anew to see them arrive ready to hand when I need them, these particulars, these relations, these connections in the skein of my own long event.

The sun swells and settles toward the mountains as the long afternoon tilts toward evening. I am due back at the college for a picnic and a softball game, for familiar faces, surprises, Cathy's delight at my exploration, my discoveries, connections forming which I cannot yet even imagine. I roll up the interstate to where I know I ought to be.

SWINGING ON FOUCAULT'S PENDULUM

✳

October and Indian summer, the year swung past the balance point of the autumnal equinox, this hemisphere of the wobbling planet tilting back away from the sun again, and I have swung past the balance point of my fortieth birthday as well. The days are a rhythm of color, the richest autumn in fifteen years as some autumn watcher has allowed in the paper, and the little milkweed bugs are back, black and orange, walking around the back door, one of them riding startled away on Oliver's back as he darts out to challenge the new puppy across the road. They are here in force this time, like the changing leaves, bunched on the brick wall by the door, walking along the window sills, one of them, splayed and soft, floating in the bowl of dishwashing liquid by the sink. Last night the moon rode full and dazzling through the low fast clouds, so low that you felt as though you could gather them with a net, the pale blue night winking on and off, the high creek water, the leaves shifting on the dust of the road, the clouds sighing by so near and low.

A week or so ago we watched the sun's eclipse, only a nip here but awesome enough. Dara persuaded Keith to mount the good telescope, and there shimmering on the reflecting board was the sun and its clusters of spots— two strong full ones, black and linked with their gray auras; an old one breaking up into slivers and scraps; a new one just aborning, small and sharp and intense. The sun is alive and, whether regular or constant or perfect or not, well. Bird hunters on a nearby hilltop fire at their circling, whistling prey, and once their shot arcs across the sun's reflected face like a des-

225

perate covey in perfect flight. The moon goes its steady way as well, and soon the sun is clear again. Ralph insists that the gunshots have freed the sun and brought it home again. He grins, and the sun sails on the smooth white board, uninjured, inscrutable, having given us a sign, giving us a number of signs, signs without end. The gun thumps on the hill, and we help put the telescope away as the sun settles down to the west.

All that movement, bird and shot, sun and moon, this turning, tilting earth. How do we know we move? Or the sun? Or the moon? The eye tells all, but the eye tells lies as well. Jean Bernard Léon Foucault began hanging his massive, pivoting pendulums in 1851, and finally the massive iron ball he hung from a steel wire more than two hundred feet long in the Dôme des Invalides in Paris twisted from its point of suspension and allowed the earth to turn under its slow even arcs. For the first time the earth's rotation was demonstrated directly. The steadily swinging pendulum in the Smithsonian Institution in Washington demonstrates that turning daily as it ticks the small red markers over for all those marveling visitors right on time. Foucault's audience burst into applause, and so should we all. *Eppur si muove.*

Foucault's pendulum, the earth's equatorial bulge, all of those effects of the Coriolus force from the deflection of airplanes in flight to the gurgle and swirl of the bathwater down the drain, all of them demonstrate for those who have eyes to see the earth's continuing pirouette in its flight around the sun. But if Einstein is correct in saying that all motion is relative, then you may say that the earth is at rest, and it is at rest—the entire universe whirling in complex cycles and epicycles around its still point. Why then does the earth continue to bulge at the equator? Why then does Foucault's pendulum not stop its twist and swing in an unmoving arc, an unswerving straight line across the still floor?

Ernst Mach decided that, since all motion appears to be provably relative, any particle's inertia is the result of the interaction of that particle with all the other masses in the universe. "It does not matter," he wrote, "if we think of the earth as turning round on its axis, or at rest while the fixed stars revolve around it. . . . The law of inertia must be so conceived that exactly the same thing results from the second supposition as the first." The earth knows to bulge because of the action of all the cosmic masses rotating around it; Foucault's pendulum pivots on its hanging point because Alpha Centauri does its three-way dance about itself some 4.3 light-years away, because the whole spinning dizzy universe whirls on itself in complex splendor. Einstein named and developed Mach's principle, and many others have followed suit. Sir Fred Hoyle and J.V. Narlikar worked on it a few years ago in *Action at a Distance in Physics and Cosmology*. It remains the most elegant and significant explanation of the mysteries and signs of Foucault's pendulum, because it teaches us what we were denied during the whole long reign of reductionist thought: that the whole universe matters locally.

The universe imposes itself on the physics of our world, on the ball's arc and the pendulum's turn. We are pulled and shaped, turned and given direction by the entire universe, large and larger. The stars tug our cells and spin our water down the drain. The astrologers had the right idea, but they followed down the garden path their own limited sense of life (the exact point of birth, the precise beginning of stellar influences) and their own limited sense of the movement of the heavens, reducing all that complexity and interrelationship to questions of cash and whether delicate objects should be handled today. When the universe knocks at our doors, we should not ask it what it can do for us before we let it in. It swings and knocks around us, and we swing through it, too, all of us, stars and planets, the white chicken grown and fat in her yard, the multicolored kitten curled asleep in my lap, electron and neutrino, mad killer in a cell, wet swollen corpse by the side of the road, all of us moving together, dependent, star and electron, sun and hen, all of us on each other.

How easy to look the other way, or, looking directly at the turning stars, to feel small and deflated, your life organized by the sun's windy spill, your world distorted and spun by the movement of the stars. But the converse is true as well. We affect Alpha Centauri as those neighborly stars affect us, push and pull, turn and swing. Particulate and plural, the universe is of a piece, this field of life, spotting sun, skipping heart, the warp and woof of nonsimultaneous space, rock-shaped on a mountaintop like a significant fish.

Where do we find ourselves (as though we were ever lost)? It is an October afternoon. The light through the dying leaves is slanted and warm. Within this last month I have talked on the phone to John in Washington and Ian in Manchester, I have seen George and Susan, Garrett and Spencie, Joyce and Denise and Michael and Molly, I have received letters from Selden in Wales and Jennifer in New York, I have met Leigh Brackett and Diane Ackerman for the first time, and Dara and Allen, Rebecca and Marnie and Leslie, Mike and Marcia took me out for a feast on my birthday. These names are the names of facts, of long events, of the living and effective parts of my life, of yours. We are turning through the universe together, and the universe is turning through us, blood and bone, the delicate Coriolos curve of our thoughts. The lights in the sky are stars, God's name graven large for those to see who have eyes to see, and they are ourselves, a fool's paradise, turning and still, many and one, the black and orange small milkweed bugs on the sill, the galaxy's drift, life within life within life, never far.

The day and the year are waning into winter, pale sky and scattering leaves, this local day, this local year. The leaves of the forsythias are green and red and purple and yellow and gold. The clouds are gray and broken, sunlight streaking through, shaken and sound. The universe is making its move, and it matters. You are making it move, swinging it like a pendulum, swinging on Foucault's pendulum, turning to the pressures of the whole, turning the whole with each steady even arc. Foucault's audience broke into applause; so should we all.

ON THE WAY

*

The quarreling and irritability will have died down finally; first the euphoria, then the boredom, then the quarreling and snapping at one another, all these phases of the voyage will have passed away, will seem now like dreams, unreal, distant, lost. But then everything will seem now like a dream, for dream is what they will mainly do, drift downhill through empty space toward the sun, drift and dream, wake to tend the tachyonic drive, to keep the smoldering peat lit, wake to check the instruments and gauges, to try again to contact Dublin, to fail again, wake to check on each other, read out the medical tests and charts and meters, pulses and pressures, wake just to look for a time at the raw metal walls, the clustered pipes and tubes, but mainly they will dream, mainly they will swallow the small capsules, and drift, with a tingle and then a disconnection, into dreams, dreams of home, dreams of the sun, dreams of falling, dreams of flying, dreams of disintegration, dreams of death and dying, dreams of dreaming, dreams.

They will have reached the top of the column without gravity that will have poked unbending high above, far out from the Leinster Launching Grid, twirling wildly and unexpectedly, all of them a bit motion sick, greenish, and gasping, and then they will have used the compressed air jets to hold the ship steady while they will have unfolded the tachyonic scoops and aimed the ship correctly to catch the solar wind and its mysterious and almost imaginary tachyons, those tiny particles traveling faster even than light, that invisible and inaudible rattle of tachyonic rain that, caught by the scoops and fed into the smoking peat, will have punched the craft forward, using solar wind to sail directly into solar wind, translating the almost immeasurable tachyonic energy through the peat, all dug in Dublin's own Syrtis Minor, into motion, into distance, by the left side of the moon and on into this rush to the sun, this slide and spin into the sun.

The euphoria will have carried them for days (earth days, no revolving time here), even for weeks; it will have carried them past the shock of discovering that they were not Sean and Seamus and Flann, but Sean, Seamus, and Xhavid. They will have debated the disappearance of Blackie over and over, frustrated always by the total failure of the communications system from ever getting a report from Dublin.

Then they will have talked about it enough. They will have told all their favorite stories to each other enough. They will have revealed too much of themselves to each other. They will have shared too many secrets and too many dreams with each other. The routine, the monotony of the routine will have drained their energies and blunted their curiosity about everything.

"Goddam it, Sean," Seamus will have shouted one day (morning, noon, evening, night, take your pick), "if I hear one more word about Pegeen O'Rourke and your blasted lonely heart, I think I'll be busting your face in."

That remark will have begun the time of quarreling, although the first blow will have been landed not by Seamus but by Sean himself. Seamus will, however, have made the statement that will have given rise to that first blow.

"Pegeen O'Rourke again," he will have said. "Haven't you figured it out, you poor bloody fool, how far away in space and time that woman is. Good God, man, she'll not be brooding over the likes of distant you. I'll be bound she's opening that hummock of hers day and night to any hoe that will work it."

That will have been when Sean punched Seamus, caught him on the side of the head with his fist. The fight will have been quick, over with a single return punch from Seamus, over even before Xhavid will have pushed his way between the two fighters trying to stop the brawl.

And that's not to imply that Xhavid will have been innocent of the tensions and follies of that time either. He will have been irritable and hotheaded, too, quick to take affront, sulking over imagined slights and real ones. And there will have been real ones, for, without any communication with Dublin, how were Sean and Seamus to know that Xhavid hadn't coldcocked Blackie and stolen his suit and taken his place for some insidious Albanian reason?

And Xhavid will have had his fight, too. He, too, will have taken something Seamus will have said seriously. Or, rather, something Seamus will have said and done.

"This blasted radio," Seamus will have muttered, more to himself than to either of his companions. "Only Blackie could have made the damned thing work, and where, I ask you," raising his voice, "where, pray tell, is Blackie O'Flynn now that we need him?"

Xhavid will have tried to ward off another of Seamus's tirades by asking him to pass him one of the sealed cups of coffee which were racked by Seamus's seat.

"Oh, surely," Seamus will have replied, remembering a scene from distant earth and a distant day, and he will have passed the cup to Xhavid, raising up his leg high and slipping the cup under his knee.

That fight will have lasted longer than the other one, and it will have done some damage to the ship as well as to the two angry solarnauts. Sean will have finally popped Xhavid on the skull with a wrench, the first skull he could reach, and that will have calmed bloody Seamus down as well.

And then the anger will have cooled in all of them, cooled with the genuine recognition of how really far they will be from earth, from home, from spinning home, millions of miles and an invisible time that nevertheless will tick and whir itself away on their clucking clock. How small they will suddenly have seemed, and how important to each other. They will have fallen into each other's arms and held on. They will have become considerate and kind. They will have told all the old stories again, and they will have listened carefully.

And then the time of dreaming will have begun.

Sean will lie back on the lowered acceleration seat, his mouth cocked open, snoring slightly, his little note pad open in his lap, the pen hung in his open hand, only a single word on the small lined page, *silence*.

Sean's dream:

"I wish I weren't so shy," Sean says, "I mean especially after the book. It's very hard for me to say things to you now."

Pegeen is on the seat beside him, but he can't seem to turn his head to see her. There is a shadow between them, and he knows that she is there, but he cannot see her, although he does see her.

"You never really said things to me," Pegeen says.

"I know. I am so shy."

"It's not that. You never knew me at all."

"I don't understand."

"You never understood. I don't think you ever heard a word I said, or even really looked me in the eye."

"I know you."

"No, you don't; you just think you do."

"I know you. I wrote a book about you."

"No you didn't."

Sean holds the book up. Its cover is green, and it is called *Thirsty Elbows*. He tries to find the other book, the real book. The shelves are crammed with books, all of his books, the paperbacks he treasured so in his youth, *Unconquered*, blue spine with the innocent woman in chains on the cover, blond hair, the bosom of her dress cut low, smooth skin, blue eyes, she chose slavery instead of hanging—and lived to regret it, *Tarzan the Terrible*, *The Third Policeman*, *The Book of Changes*. He hunts through these books, his eyes misting so that he can hardly see.

"I thought I'd left these at home. I thought I'd lost them," he says.

"No," Pegeen says. "I know you wrote the book, but it isn't about me. It's all about you. You just imagined me. You never let me be alive. Never at all. You just imagined me. What else was I to do?"

"What do you mean?" Sean says. He keeps looking over at his books. There are all kinds of books he has never seen there before. He strains to see their titles.

"What else could I do?" she says.

"No, Deirdre," Sean says. "Not that. Don't jump."

The tower seems much higher than it ever has before. The spiral of metal stairs goes out of sight below. The books are racked in rough wooden shelves all along the rails. Deirdre is on the rail that rims the tower.

"No," Sean says, crying, tears running down his cheeks.

She is gone, falling toward the sun, falling and falling.

Why should she do that again? He'd tried to tell her that he loved her, but he was so shy.

"Pegeen," he says, but she is falling too fast into the shadow to hear him, and besides he is falling, too.

Sean will awaken, will sit there filled with a sense of sorrow and loss worse than he will have ever felt before. Where the books should be, there will be only a rank of panels, needles wavering back and forth, red lights winking. He will climb out of the seat and make his swaying way across the room and through the small metal door to the peat fire. As he passes Xhavid Shehu, sprawled awkwardly on his seat, a seat that he doesn't really fit, built as it was for the taller Flann O'Flynn, he will hear Xhavid say something to him, will pause to listen and then will realize that it is only a dream talking, only a dream.

Xhavid's dream:

He has been watching a buzzard circle overhead, its naked red head, its tattered black wings. They are at Dhermi, on the beach, the Trade Union resort, on the Adriatic, and he is wondering what this alien bird is doing here, here in Albania, circling, here in the new Republíka Popullore e Shqipërísë, this hovering alien bird of death.

Katrina is wearing her wedding gown. Everyone has been dancing in the sand. Katrina is worried because her father may be somewhere near. She has been promised to a farmer in the mountains, not her lover, not Xhavid, her young lover. It is 1953. Xhavid knows the date as well as the place, as well as Katrina's lovely face. They are very much in love. He is nineteen. She is sixteen. Only he is not nineteen. He remembers that. He is in his forties. He is as old as the farmer in the mountains. It is very hard to understand. The accordion is so loud.

"Katrina," he whispers.

The music stops. Everyone crowds around to listen. Xhavid pauses, then says what he must say.

"I am sorry, Katrina, that I am so old."

She listens silently, looking up at him. He has become much taller than she. The wet sand is crumbling on his bare legs.

"I did not want to become so old. I wanted to marry you and be nineteen. But now I am very old. I don't feel old. I don't feel so much older than you, but I must seem so very old to you. I am very sorry."

Her father points the rifle at Xhavid.

"No, listen," Xhavid says, "Enver Hoxha will explain it all quite clearly. You are wrong to wish to marry your daughter as a child to an old man. Listen, I will read to you what Hoxha will say."

He pulls a pamphlet from his pocket, and he begins to read aloud:

"It must be admitted that many erroneous and reactionary notions about love appear among us. Love is regarded as something shameful, forbidden, and abnormal. Our country has been plagued by marriage-by-violence, by the traditional Muhammedan laws of slavery and polygamy, the laws of Catholicism, of the Vatican, and this has not only enslaved and devaluated women, but has also exposed them to spiritual torture."

The raw-faced old man will aim his rifle directly at Xhavid's eye, the muzzle large and unwavering.

"Shoot me," Xhavid says to him, "but do not make Katrina marry a man so much older than herself, a man she does not love, not such an old man."

"You are a fool," her father says, his face red and bare over his tattered black coat. "You are an old man yourself."

He fires the rifle, the noise deafening, and Xhavid will wake with a start and a shout, jolting his head back into the top of the seat, startling Sean who will be coming back to his seat after he will have stoked the smoldering peat.

"Love," he will shout, and then he will realize where he is and to whom he has just spoken. "Love," he will say again, softly and to himself, settling back into the seat, looking down at his hands linked so tightly in his lap that the fingers will be numb and tingling. "Love."

"The peat is doing fine," Sean will say, "I just checked it and stoked it up. All the drive meters . . ." He will stop talking, realizing that Xhavid is asleep again, drifting back into whatever place or circumstance his mind or the drug will give him.

Seamus will be knotted in a ball on his seat, knees drawn up, hands clenched into red and white mottled fists, his teeth grinding in his flexing jaws. His eyelids will be fluttering, the eyeballs rolling under them, seeing nothing, seeing a dream, a dream.

Seamus' dream:

He is thirsty, fiercely thirsty, as thirsty as any man has a right to be. The sun is high and hot, the pavement so hot that the sun itself would seem to be underfoot, frying the soles of his feet like eggs, even through the heavy soles of his brogans.

He is looking for a place to buy a drink, maybe a drink or two, something to help him bear the fury of the day. He comes round the corner and sees a crowd gathered farther on down the street, a large crowd, a crowd of foreigners. He walks on down the hot sidewalk toward them, tapping his thigh as he goes with his nightstick.

"And what'll be the matter here?" he says when he reaches the crowd, his voice breaking through their foreign jabber loud and clear.

"It's a horse, Officer Pat," one of the dark-skinned men replies. "It's a dead horse right here in the middle of Shqiptare Street."

"Whoof," he will answer, "and on a hot day like this, too."

"What'll we do, Officer Pat?" one of the foreign men asks, scratching his dark thick hair and looking worried.

"Don't you be worrying," Seamus says, "I'll take care of that right now."

He turns to the call box on the telephone pole, lifts the receiver, and rings headquarters.

"Hello," he says. "Headquarters? This is Officer Pat. I've got a dead horse here, and I'll be needing the wagon sent down. Yes. The wagon. Dead horse, and it's hot as blazes. Yes. Right down to," he looks up at the street sign on the corner, "right down to Shqu . . . Shkip . . . Shquip . . . Just a minute, sir."

He turns to the nearest man, a short man with a thick curling moustache.

"Get a bunch of the fellows," he says, "and help me drag this horse around the corner here and onto Parnell."

The men respond promptly and start pushing and pulling at the dead horse, already corrupt, already stinking on the hot asphalt. Seamus helps them, the sweat stinging as it rushes down his face, his neck, down his arms and back.

"Ah, God, it's hot," he says and pauses to wipe futilely at his face with a soggy handkerchief, "even this snotrag won't do me any good."

He will see the ABC Store, the Virginia state liquor store, right across the shimmering pavement before him, the long shelves stacked with bottles and bottles dimly visible in the cool interior.

"Blessed Mother," he says, "and thanks."

He crosses the sticky asphalt street gingerly, stepping high, walking quickly. He enters the cool store and sees his old friends, Pat and Mike, leaning on the counter, grinning and greeting him.

"Faith, lads," he says, "give me a quart of Jameson's if you will."

"Certainly, Seamus," Pat says, "if you'll be showing me your money. You've got to have the cash, you know. That's the law."

Seamus tugs out his wallet, hot and spongy, from his hip pocket, and he digs into the bill compartment, his hot wet fingers rubbing on the smooth leather, finding only receipts, a thick packet of receipts, no money, no cash at all.

"Ah, well," he says, looking up at the smiling Pat and Mike, "I don't seem to, that is, I seem to have left all my cash at home on the bureau. You know how it is. What with the heat and all."

Pat and Mike nod in unison. Pat replaces the large bottle of Jameson's on the shelf from which he has just removed it.

"I'll give you a check," Seamus says. He digs in his pockets and finds only the hot dry stone from his mother's grave.

Pat and Mike shake their heads together.

"Now you know, Seamus, that we can't be taking checks. It's against the law," Pat says.

"The law," Seamus says. "The law. Who cares about the law? You know me. It's not like I'm a stranger. You know me."

Pat and Mike smile sadly and shake their heads no.

"But, but," Seamus says, "boys, you know me, you *know* me."

"Sorry, Seamus," Pat and Mike say in unison, hugging each other's shoulders like Tweedledee and Tweedledum.

Seamus' throat aches like a rotten tooth, the oozing sear of a third-degree burn, and he shrieks at the top of his lungs, the very roaring top of his lungs.

He will sit up screaming, his voice bouncing around the small metal compartment, rocketing and ricocheting, and he will blink shame-facedly, will rub his eyes with his balled fists, will lick his dry lips, and swallow heavily. He will wake up and feel a thirst so strong that he can scarcely believe that it is real, a thirst so powerful that, he will think, it must be a dream.

"By God," he will say aloud to no one in particular, to whomever happens to be awake and listening, to no one at all, for both Xhavid and Sean will be breathing deeply and drifting in dreams or in that dreamless emptiness of drugged sleep so like the black void of space just beyond the blank metal wall. "My God," he will say, "I do need a drink something fierce."

He will drag himself slowly up from his seat, shake his arms loosely at his sides, breathe deeply two or three times, lift his legs, and pump them down again, and then he will shamble sleepily toward the door to the drive section, tug it open and, stooping over, lean into and through it, disappearing into the rear of the ship.

Later, an hour or a day, a week, there is no way to say, there will be no way to say, the clock still timing what may be earth time but what may just as well not be, time bent like space as they slide down to the sun. Later. Later they will all be asleep, all three lying on their couches, their acceleration seats, all groaning and mumbling, talking back and forth, sharing a single dream, or sharing three dreams so interlaced that they can speak back and forth in their sleep, a moment like any moment, shared and separate, alike and different, plural and undeniably one.

The voices of Sean and Seamus and Xhavid:

"None of the instruments agrees."

"The fire must be out."

"No, you fool, the fire's not out. Look at the smoke. The room's filling with smoke."

"I can smell it."

"I'm choking in it."

"Ouch, help!"

"It's not the peat, and the drive is doing fine."

"The scoops."

"I said the drive is doing fine."

"There's no need looking here. Whatever it is, it's coming from without, from out there."

"It's so black, nothing but black."

"Run a visual scan."

"Nothing but black."

"The sun."

"No sun."

"But this force. It's clearly magnetic. The sun has to be there."

"Look at those dials. They're swinging and whirling like dervishes. No sun is doing that."

"They're pulsing."

"The sun."

"You're right. You're right."

"The sun has died. It's burnt out."

"It's become a pulsar."

"A spinning pulsar."

"My God, the force of that magnetic field. It will tear us to bits. It will eat us up."

"It will eat us down."

The dream of Sean and Seamus and Xhavid:

The Wandering Aengus spins down and lands with a flat smack on the black spinning surface of the dead sun, this crazed carrousel of condensed energy. The mad whirl pins the solarnauts to their seats; it tugs them out, and then suddenly they are used to it, and they can see, see across the room, see out the window, see figures moving on the alien surface.

"What are those figures?" Seamus asks.

"They look," Xhavid says tentatively, "they look like walking trees."

"Open your eyes, man," Seamus answers, and Sean pops open the seals on the door.

"Pegeen," he says, "do you want to go first?"

"There's no need for you to be opening doors for me, Sean Siobhan," Pegeen says. "I'm perfectly capable, you know, of opening doors for myself."

"No," Sean says, "you don't understand," and he pauses, then continues, "my darling."

He blushes and stops altogether.

"What do you mean?" she says.

"I mean," he manages to answer, "do you want to be the first man on the sun?"

"The first man!" Seamus shouts. "The first um, you mean."

Pegeen will whirl about to face Seamus, her long blue skirt spinning out into the stale air, her chains clanking from their iron cuffs and the iron belt around her waist, her blue eyes flaring.

"I'd rather hang," she says to Seamus with real anger in her voice, "than to be your slave."

"And who's asking you to be a slave at all?" Seamus says wearily. "If um doesn't want to go first, I suppose I'll be going my um self. There's nothing wrong with being the first man on the sun, I suppose."

But Xhavid is already there, walking around on the crisp flaking surface, staring up at the tall moving figures in the distance. He cannot tell how far away they are. The size of this furiously dead star will make it impossible for him to judge the horizon or any distances beyond the immediate area of the ship. He looks up into the black featureless sky and sees a bird circling, a large bird, a buzzard, greasy feathers, and naked head.

"It's Deirdre," Sean shouts, starting to run across the crunching ground. "That bird's circling her grave. Something's wrong. Come on."

He leads them across the coarse surface to the foot of Ben Bulben, where they begin to climb. The going is hard, the gravity pulling at them, drawing them down to the burnt-out ground, their feet dragging, hands raw from frequent falls on the cinders.

They finally reach the grave and find it untouched, despite the buzzard's watch, green grass, small stone. Deirdre's head is still in plain sight where they planted her, the new stalks standing high and clean, the new leaves unfolding, green and slick, from the stalks.

"We should pick off the suckers," Seamus says. "Take the ones from the stems, and I'll break off these coming from her jaw and this big one from her ear."

They prune and prop the plant. Deirdre looks at Seamus's face so near her and the ground, a tear forming in her eye, the left eye without a new stalk.

"Thank you," she whispers, despite the pain. "Thank you."

The tiny blue blossoms just unfolding on her upper stalks tremble with the rising wind. Seamus stoops and picks up a small stone shaped like a fish and slips it into his pocket to touch for memory and for luck. The lightning is striking closer now, sharp slivers in the black sky, a roar and rumble of distant rain, running thunder.

And opposite the storm, on the other deceptive horizon, the sun begins to rise, bulging and red like a balloon, the ropes taut and dragging at the still invisible gondola. The light after the total darkness presses their pupils to points. They are dazzled and unable to see, and then they see, see clearly, see the Wandering Aengus, its open door, Red Hanrahan's desk just inside.

"It's good to be seeing you, sir," says Seamus. "We were out of touch there for quite a long time."

"Heanus," Hanrahan says, "can you explain this message? We've just received it, and no one here can make it out."

"We think it'll take a real mick to understand it, and that category is you," says Xhavid, standing behind Hanrahan, a shadow over his face.

"What're you saying?" says Seamus. "I'll teach you."

"Show him," says Blackie. "Show him what it means."

Hanrahan places the message on the tray between the coffee cup and the egg-stained white plate. Everyone leans over to see it closely, so closely that it is as large as a billboard, the letters huge and black and stretching high overhead:

fgma   X Z   X

"I can't make it out," says Seamus.

"I think I see," says Sean, "but I don't quite understand."

A shadow falls over the letters on the billboard, and the three solarnauts turn around together. One of the distant figures is moving toward them across the dark plain, only an oval silhouette in the risen blazing balloon's light. The ground trembles with its footsteps, and the thunder rolls and echoes around them.

"It's an egg," Xhavid shouts.

It is an egg, an enormous egg wearing big shoes, grinning and waving its stubby arms and big hands, and written on the lower part of its shell in big red letters: "fgma   X Z   X."

Sean will awaken first, will wake to the silence and the unwavering light, to the faint smoke in the air and the whir of the ventilator fans as they begin to operate to remove that smoke, to the mumbles of his fellow solarnauts, Seamus waving his fists before his face, Xhavid saying the word *egg* over and over.

Sean will push at Xhavid and then stand unsteadily and reach over to Seamus to wake him, too. He will reach to turn the ventilator fan control over to high, but his hands will be so weak with sleep that he will not be able to budge it.

"We need to do our exercises," Sean will say to his groaning and stretching colleagues. "Who knows how long it's been since we did them last."

"Who knows?" Xhavid will ask sleepily.

"Don't be asking me," Seamus will say. "I certainly don't know."

The three will move together over to the wall by the door to the drive room, and there they will pick up the portable exercise units, place themselves on the floor along the wall, their feet slung in the wall brackets, and begin to work on their exercises, leg against arm, back against knee, the regimen they will have been supposed to have done every day, but which they will have done only when they think of it or feel the need, an order lost in time's blur.

"I was dreaming of people from home again," Sean will say.

The other two will nod as they strain and shove.

"And the past. Always the past," Sean will say. "And, I think, the future, but the future was a lot like the past."

The future will not come to focus in their minds, only a vaguely defined blankness or a deep and unrelenting blackness. They will think of the past, think in bright colors as they sweat and push themselves against themselves. They will think of the past, but for them there will be no past. There will be only emptiness and dreams.

NOVEMBER NEWS

*

A puzzling month, marked with disasters, evidences of entropy, the brightest autumn leaves in years dying out and crackling down, early cold, and today the first real snow. A month surprising from day to new day, and now the snow billows down in fat flakes, turning and flicking at the windows, melting on the ground at first, then filling out the grass, slipping over the path, giving the gray day a white blurring.

In India a cyclone has slaughtered thousands, bashing into shore, passaging west, as real as anything in that unreal world is ever likely to be, this real world. Lives snipped out from the texture of the day, the turning wheel of the year. It is such a huge event, such life immense, such pain, that you cannot, do not comprehend. You watch the autumn drift past, pass and fade, and you watch the snow fill the air and cover the familiar contours of this real world, this unreal day.

Henry Howell lost the gubernatorial election this month. I cast my vote; so did my friends, but we failed. An opportunity to open the sealed doorways of this old dominion lost, and, as must be the case in any closed system, entropy prevails, that lazy yearning toward the disorder of surrender, Emerson's party of hope denied its reach and growth once again by the party of memory with its dignity and its funereal absence of mind. The ebb and flow of entropic politics, this settling down, this melting away of the spires of form, this loss of focus like the blurring day.

So I vow not to settle down, and I bundle up, walk out into the deepening whirl of air and earth. Three white throated sparrows in the naked, white-trimmed branches of the cherry tree watch my approach, but do not fly away, the startling small patches of yellow on their small heads the only real color in this unreal whirl of white and gray.

I don't walk far, only up to the road where I watch a slick-tired car whir and whiz its slow trip by. I stand there by the mailbox, fogging the air with my breath, watching the hemlocks across the way drift in the haze of snow. The air joins the earth in this white settling down, the whole motion of life a moving down and down, this downing of snow in the waning light. I see a black shape moving steadily up the hill toward me, an animal, almost as large as Oliver whom I left sleeping by the fire. It is a large black cat, a big healthy cat, thick-furred and bushy-bodied, a handsome cat with a stub tail, looking almost like a dog at a glance but, as the scattering of sparrows behind me proves, a cat indeed. I watch him out of sight through the falling curtain of snow and turn to walk away myself.

It is all, of course, in the angle of your vision, the slant of your head, choice of your eye. I stop and stare and am caught by surprise, for I suddenly see the snow stand still, hang in the air like dust in a sunbeam, stand still like the hummingbird, and the earth rush to meet its spinning calm. The whole earth rushes up like a rocket, rushes up to enter this hovering dream of snow, and I walk home with the ground rising to meet my foot, step by crisp snowy step all the way.

I see the fire through the window, the orange and yellow room set moving by the shadowy flames. Oliver bounds to the window, his tail wagging, the young cat Jane standing up to bat at its whisk and sweep. I stand outside in the snow for a time and watch them and the room. The snow is falling around me, and the earth soaring to meet the snow. November's news has been deadly, and the news of November leads on and leads on. If winter comes. And spring. Summer. Fall. And winter again. This line of beauty. This motion that is still, and this stillness that moves. This reality.

Inside and settled myself by the fire, stirred up and rushing up to the night, I remember a book by the photographer Sam Haskins, *November Girl*, a book about the girl in the black raincoat, about the news of November, and I remember that at its center was a street called Spin Street. November on Spin Street. This November on Spin Street. We move on it up and down or we stand for a time, but the street spins on, moves on, catches the sunlight or fills up with snow. The fire raps and knuckles, hisses and sighs. Oliver lies down and stretches his paws to the blaze; Jane crouches and stares without a blink.

Just yesterday I attached the sun filter Lewis gave me to my telescope and found the sun, green and glowing in a blank dark sky. A cluster of spots shimmered near its center, large and irregular and dark green, and other smaller spots were scattered nearby. The green wonder of it, so much more directly exciting and surprising than on the white reflecting board. The green sun burning to life, eye to eye, but not soon enough to save us from another hard winter.

The earth moves, moves on, moves into the night, at least here and now. I move closer to the fire and switch on a light to finish reading Robertson Davies' *World of Wonders*, that synchronous venture onto a Spin Street of its own, stone in the mouth, stone in the air, changing names and changing faces. We are spinning with an autumnal tilt through November and into winter, this world of wonders around the bubbling sun, storm spotted and turning itself, not settling down but sailing on, wind-tossing sun and wind-blown earth, this collection of planets and asteroids and moons, the newly discovered planetoid turning between Saturn and tilted Uranus, all moving like a stub-tailed cat through new snow, such life immense that we do not comprehend, such pain, such wonder. This unreal world. This whirling real.

STANDING STILL

It is gray and sharp and cold, no snow in the air or on the ground although flurries blew in the car's headlight beams last night. The light is dull and drab. The day after Christmas. Henry Miller's birthday. Another day without surprises, a day filled with surprise.

A silence holds the gray air as in a gleaming cup. Nothing moves in the still, still air. It is sort of stillness and silence that Henry Miller holds so dear, the holy silence of the mind, of the real; inner harmony, inner peace; God as still point that fills the spinning world. The light shines in this tarnished air.

I am alone after the crowds and confusions of yesterday. The dog is asleep, stretched out in the center of the living-room rug; the cat is asleep, curled in the dog's warm bed. I am alone in the bleak filtered light that hangs in the air from window to window, strung out and silent and still. I am alone, no letters in the mail, the phone silent. My friends are here in town or scattered over the world or gone or I have not met them yet, alive and dead, all of them alive in this silence, held in this tilted winter light. And my other friends, my masters, my colleagues, stacked around me in books, in pictures, in recordings. I am alone, but in this lonely silence, life is swarming and the day is full.

"Human beings," Henry Miller said in *Tropic of Cancer*, "make a strange fauna and flora. From a distance they appear negligible; close up they are apt to appear ugly and malicious. More than anything they need to be surrounded with sufficient space—space even more than time." The books, the works of art, give them the space, the space in which to be alone with them,

244

to see them not up close, but for real, really. Henry Thoreau said as much in *Walden* when he said, "If we would enjoy the most intimate society with that in each of us which is without, or above, being spoken to, we must not only be silent, but commonly so far apart bodily that we cannot possibly hear each other's voice in any case." I cannot hear a voice. I see the books in shelves along the walls. In this silence, standing still, I find this day society most intimate, inner harmony, inner peace.

And space itself, that wholly involved and unbroken wholeness, rug inside and yard outside, universe and cosmos, is that not as warm with life as well, local and distant, particular and universal, matter and mind? Miller dreamed once, in *Stand Still Like the Hummingbird*, of that living space: "Ah yes, musing thus I sometimes wonder if one of the great surprises in store for our bold space explorers may not be the collision with murdered saints and saviors, their bodies fully restored and glowing with health as they move along the etheric currents, sportive as dolphins, free as the birds, cured of all such follies as doing good, healing the sick, raising the dead, instructing the ignorant." What a grand dream . . . that still silence spinning with the best of life, the saints and saviors of life, life itself. Like this still silence on Henry Miller's eighty-sixth birthday in this cold, in this gray unmoving light and air.

Friends and saints. You name their names and invoke thereby the parts of yourself which are theirs alone, that inner pendulum which swings and turns to their distant lives. There are so many that you cannot ever name them all. The interviewer asks, "Who are your favorite writers?" and you stammer, can never reply. But you try; you name a number of your saints aloud, letting their names stand for that still moment for the moving universe of them all, a constellation of saints whom I have never met, the space between us sufficient for me to feel most intimate in their society, a birthday list, saints' days:

—William Blake (November 28, 1757), who etched and colored divinity's explosive movement through raw earth, who dreamed the land ("America"), in which I live and dream, sketch and tint;

—J. M. W. Turner (April 23, 1775), who knew that you do not paint to be understood but to show what it is like, how the shape of the world is the shape of an eye;

—Ralph Waldo Emerson (May 25, 1803), who knew the nature of belief and the essential necessity of surprise;

—Edgar Allan Poe (January 19, 1809), who knew what it is to be very dreadfully nervous and who nervelessly discovered that "all is Life—Life—Life within Life—the less within the greater, and all within the *Spirit Divine*";

—Walt Whitman (May 31, 1819), who gave us a long and lasting good-bye that still vibrates in the soul and body (they are one) like an electric shock;

—Herman Melville (August 1, 1819), who, call him what you will, found for us the vital centre of the whirling world;

—John Cowper Powys (October 8, 1872), who knew and grew to know in pain and dark desire that love remains undying in the heart of the universe;

—Gertrude Stein (February 3, 1874), who knew that there is "neither remembering nor forgetting neither beginning or ending . . . that there is no finishing finishing in writing";

—Charles Ives (October 20, 1874), who knew harmonies beyond the ear's familiar reach, who knew that even the "humblest composer will not find true humility in aiming low";

—Wallace Stevens (October 2, 1879), who knew that "Reality is the spirit's true center," and that "Poetry increases the feeling for reality";

—Josef von Sternberg (May 29, 1894), who knew the secrets of light, that the "history of light is the history of life," and that "to reproduce is not to create," that "Verisimilitude, whatever its virtue, is in opposition to every approach to art";

—Henry Miller (December 26, 1891), who knows that when you discover that God is love, "All you need to do when you find it is to shake yourself like a sewer-rat and dust yourself off," that "God will do the rest";

—Vladimir Nabokov (April 23, 1899), who knew the light that gleams from a puddle in the road, and something else, and much, much more;

—Jorge Luis Borges (August 24, 1899), who knows the secrets of darkness, his limits, his center, his algebra and his key;

—Federico Fellini (January 20, 1920), whose "Christianity is rough and ready," who believes everything he is told, and who knows what it is to wish another well—"Good luck to Guido."

A foolish list, fool's list, familiar names, catch phrases, and yet, and yet . . . It means so much to me. And I could continue it on and on; you could, too. You will. Other lists of scientists and philosophers, of prophets and seers, of other artists: Faulkner and Hemingway, who taught me so much once upon a time, green hills and wild palms; Sherwood Anderson; William Carlos Williams; David Lindsay; Frost, whose words come to mind almost every day; Knut Hamsun, who knew so much about the mysteries of impulse, of impulsion, and about the long forgiveness of time; Hammett and Chandler, Van Dine and Queen and Macdonald, my partners in puzzles; Cabell and Glasgow, my fellow Virginians; James Gould Cozzens, to whom the complex turnings of providence and luck revealed themselves; Laurence Sterne and Joyce Cary, Lawrence Durrell, Dorothy Richardson, Henry Green and Alain Robbe-Grillet, John Barth and Robert Coover, Ursula K. Le Guin, who taught me the shapes that a novel may take, that life may take; Ingmar Bergman and Orson Welles; Ismail Kadare, for reasons known to myself; George Garrett, Wright Morris, Katherine Anne Porter, and Colin Wilson, to whom I owe so much more than I could ever say; I tip my hat, my hats, I bow my head. I look across this empty space and see it full; I listen in this long silence and hear it resound.

This naming could go on, these meetings and greetings and passing on, on and on, moving on like a river only to stay. "Joy," Henry Miller said in *The Smile at the Foot of the Ladder*, "is like a river: it flows ceaselessly. It seems to me that this is the message which the clown is trying to convey to us, that we should participate through ceaseless flow and movement, that we should not stop to reflect, compare, analyze, possess, but flow on and through, endlessly, like music." It is the joy we find in reading, the joy we find in each other, strangers and friends and saints, the light that shines unhindered through our ugly and malicious selves, the fool's knowledge that when Christ tells us to be "perfect" that he knows that we are perfect—if we but have eyes to see and ears to hear.

What joy! This is what I told Maeryn once, in print for all to see who cared to see, that "You are everything that you could ever wish to be." This is what Henry Miller once told us, again in *Stand Still Like the Hummingbird*, that "If only we knew that we can be all that we imagine! That we already are what we wish to be."

The day is still and silent and so very full, wholly involved and unbrokenly whole. A perfect day. I put on my coat, let sleeping dog and cat lie, and step out to greet this day head on. The air is cold and damp, and small swift clouds form as I breathe in and breathe out. I walk up the hill and down the road, and there on the side of the road, pitched aside and already stiff, is the large black cat, stub-tailed and thick-bodied, no longer moving through the day but stopped still, its face twisted open, eyes wide, alone and still and dead. Poor cat. Sign. Mystery. Hieroglyph. Wonder.

The day is still and silent. The light is gray and almost gone. The day after

Christmas. Henry Miller's birthday, Henry Miller who knows that we are not of the earth but of God. Titles move in my mind, titles bearing the weight of the books: *Death of the Fox* and *Do, Lord, Remember Me*; *The Left Hand of Darkness*; *The Works of Love*; *Ship of Fools*; *The Wisdom of the Heart*. The faces of my friends move in my mind, the living and the dead, all here alive. The day is silent and still; it moves like a mind; it moves; *eppur si muove*. It flows like joy.

You pass the dead cat in the ditch, and you salute its life. You remember that God is love and shake yourself like a sewer rat. You wish Henry Miller a happy birthday: good luck to Henry. You walk on down the silent empty road in the waning day, alone, alive. The world stands still as you pass by; the world spins, the stars turn behind that gray still sky. The cat is dead in a ditch; an opossum, on down the road; dead trees, dying suns, dead stars. The pain behind any given door along this way may match the joy, may exceed it in any standing moment of passing time. But the joy remains, the astonishing joy remains. The day passes ceaselessly, and there is no finishing. Standing still, we move; moving, we find limits, algebras, vital centers, keys, and something else. Much, much more.

Alone, alive, you walk on down the silent empty road in the waning day. The day after Christmas. You shake yourself against the damp cold. You move your eyes to see; you strain to hear. Standing still and moving all along, you are everything that you could ever wish to be.

SETTLING IN

*

These pages are from the private log Xhavid Shehu will keep:

The dreams are unpleasant.

I decide to take no more of the drugs.

I pass the time with my own strength.

We are over halfway to the sun.

I do not know precisely what distance remains, but it is surely time to begin the preparing of the shields.

I ask Sean to explain the shield mechanisms to me.

I ask Seamus nothing.

Oh, I smile, I do not complain, but I ask Seamus nothing.

The man who would use such a thing against another man, a crewmate, is too low to be of concern.

Sean explains the shields are made of bonded slices of raw potato.

—Irish, he laughs.

—When I was a boy, he tells me, I was out by my grandfather's forge, watching my uncles work iron into horseshoes. I was a little lad, knee-high and unaware of anything in the world but its beauties. The world was for me full of a number of things, and they were all of them happy and good. One uncle pumped the bellows and blew the coals in the fire white-hot, and they heated the iron white and a rich glowing red, as beautiful a red as I have ever seen or ever hope to see again. The fire rumbled and popped, and one of those bright blazing pieces of iron rolled out and over the dirt floor to my feet. It was so beautiful, and I was, I assure you, a good boy, a good lad, I stooped to pick it up with both my small pale hands, stooped to pick it up and put it back into the fire.

—Of course, Sean says, I burned myself, seared both palms and my fingers, burned myself badly. They carried me, my young uncles, to my grandfather, who sliced an Irish potato and with his pocketknife shredded and packed the white cool potato onto my raw burned hands, repeated and repeated this, and then bound them up with strips of clean white cloth.

—I can still remember, Sean tells me, my surprise and wonder the next day when they loosened the strips of cloth, unbandaged my burnt hands, and revealed the potato cooked as thoroughly as if you'd cooked it in a sizzling hot pan, and the smooth skin of my hands, unscarred, undamaged, and healing fine.

—That astonishing ability, Sean says, of the Irish potato is the source of our heat shields. We'll erect a barricade of thickly bonded sliced potato all around the inner walls of the ship, and we'll be able to sail right into the sun's bright waves with no more protection than our space suits, sail right in, do our job, and sail right out again on solar wind.

I do not know if he is telling me the truth or not.

Sean is dreaming again.

He mumbles and turns.

Seamus spends much of his time back in the drive chamber.

He tinkers with the scoops.

He allows no one to come around him while he works.

Not even Sean.

Certainly not me.

Not Xhavid Shehu, whom he thinks of as a foreigner and a spy.

Well, Xhavid Shehu will be suspicious of him.

It was his friend Mark Welser who led the raid that put me here in the first place.

My friend, too, I will admit.

My friend, I thought.

But I will watch him, watch Seamus, as he watches me.

I will determine the nature of his experiment in the drive chamber.

I will be quiet and steady and even and alert, and I will soon know.

The work on the shields has been undertaken, but the work goes poorly.

It is difficult to know how long one has worked.

Are we tired after ten minutes, or has it been six hours?

There is no reliable way to know.

Who knows what bends and kinks the clocks have taken?

Seamus has begun to behave strangely.

He talks interminably.

He tells long stories about his friends and his escapades, of wild women and mythic drunks.

I have heard all these stories before.

He tells them again.

I would swear he is drunk, but there is no drink on board this vehicle—none since Seamus' original flask was drained the first day of the flight, the first hours.

Unless he has a supply of whiskey hidden in the drive chamber.

The next time both Sean and Seamus are asleep, I will investigate.

The shielding is only half in place.

The instruments show we are getting too near to dawdle longer.

I can find no whiskey in the drive chamber, but I can not gain entry to the special chest containing Seamus' experiment.

—No more pills, Sean says to me. You were right about that, Xhavid. No more pills for me. I can't bear the dreams. I can't bear to think anymore about Deirdre and Pegeen and the, and the past.

—I am happy, I say, to hear you say that. Perhaps now we can continue work on the heat shielding.

—Have you ever lost a woman? says Sean. I mean really lost a woman. Do you know how I feel? I want to talk about it all the time. I try not to think, but I think about it all the time. When I try to write, the loss fills every page.

—I have lost a woman, I say.

—Let me tell you how Pegeen looked when I gave her the book, Sean says. Let me tell you. I think I remember it and haven't dreamed it. Then you can tell me what you think. I mean, about how she might feel about me.

—I lost a woman, I say.

—It was at home, I say, and I was nineteen. Only nineteen.

—What? he says. Excuse me. What are you saying?

—I lost a woman, I say. Her name was Katrina. I would tell you how long ago this was, but I no longer have a good sense of time. I don't know where I am. I was nineteen.

He seems to be listening.

Maybe he is only dreaming again.

Dreaming to himself.

—It was in Dhermi, I say. She was only sixteen. We were to be married. She had dark eyes and wonderful dark hair. She was a machinist, an apprentice machinist. She left her home in the mountains after her father had promised her to an older man, a farmer, a man of fifty. She had followed the teachings of Enver Hoxha and had freed herself of her father's domination and the old ways. How angry she would get if she felt herself patronized. I was training already to be an engineer, to go to sea. I met her and the sun wavered in the sky and dipped into the distant mountains. The sky was red for an hour. I am still stunned to think of it.

He seems to be listening.

Seamus rises from his seat, pays me no mind, shambles to the door and out into the drive chamber, closing the door and sealing it behind him.

Sean is silent and waiting, or silent and asleep.

His eyes are open.

He is looking at me.

—We were to be married, I say, in Dhermi. We arranged for the time off together, a time by the sea. I found for her flowers, roses twined by the wayside, pale roses with prickly stems, and I took flowers to the factory and left them on the workbench of her machine, roses among the belts and fast wheels, the shriek of drills.

—We traveled, I say, to Dhermi together, in the back of the bus. There were chickens beside me. I leaned over her to spit out the window and held her shoulders, pressed her head tight against me. It was clear we were lovers. Even the driver seemed pleased. The sea was bright and moving. There were whitecaps on the wavelets. We were to be married the next evening.

Sean seems to be listening.

—Her father found us, I say, near sunset. We were walking by the water. He was wild and fierce. He had been drinking. His rifle exploded. The barrel split back into petals, blew out like a rose. He died there on the beach sand, his face a red blur. I was not even wounded. Katrina died a week later. She was only sixteen.

Sean seems to be listening.

His eyes are open.

—I found Katrina's brother, I say, and I shot him from ambush. That settled the question of honor. I was young then and knew about honor. I was nineteen. And I found the old farmer, Katrina's betrothed. He was in the field, squatting by a fence post, his trousers down around his ankles. He fell over when I shot him, fell against the post and finished the task he had started although now he was dead.

—That is my love story, I say. That is how I lost a woman.

—Why did you kill them? Sean says. Why did you kill those men who had nothing to do with it? Nothing really to do with it.

—It is the code, I say. It is what must be done.

—I don't understand, he says.

—Don't try, I say. I was young then, and the code was still strong. I would have been served under the leg until I obeyed it. I could not have borne that.

—Then that is why . . . he says.

—No, I say. I do not wish to talk further.

—But . . .

—It is all settled, I say. I do not wish to talk further.

Seamus bangs open the door.

He breaks into the room, shouting.

I do not make out what he is saying.

He is carrying a container full of clear liquid.

—Sean, my lad, he says, I've done it, I've done it! There's enough for us both!

He stops as though he is just remembering something.

He looks at me.

—My experiment's a success, Xhavid, he says.

He winks at Sean and goes back to the drive chamber.

A swirl of peat smoke trails through the open door.

Sean settles down to his notebook.

Seamus returns smiling.

They both go to sleep after Seamus talks for a time, a long time, a very long time.

I nod to their breathing.

I slap my face and stand up.

I sway and stumble to the door.

I go into the drive chamber.

In the smoke and the dimness I see Seamus' space chest is open.

I look in at the containers and coiled tubing.

The containers are labeled:

WATER VAPOR (CONDENSING)
AMMONIA (BEWARE)
CARBON MONOXIDE (BEWARE)
FORMALDEHYDE (BEWARE)
ETHYL ALCOHOL (DELIGHT)

The last one is nearly empty, but connected to tubing and filling.

From space he is collecting these substances.

From the tachyonic scoops he is collecting these substances.

I thought space was empty, a vacuum.

I am ashamed to have mistrusted Seamus.

When he awakens I confess and apologize.

—Think nothing of it, Xhavid my boy, he says, and he laughs.

—Think nothing of it, he says. I've everything we need now, and I am a happy man. I'll forget, and I'll forgive. Yes, I am a happy man.

He laughs again.

Sean is still sleeping.

I work on the heat shields.

Seamus watches me, and then he goes into the drive chamber.

I remove the sheets of laminated potato from the cartons and place them into the grooves along the wall, the layers overlapping so that no seam continues directly from outer wall to inner room, a triple layer to seal off the entire ship, potato triplex as Sean calls it, the potatoes kept fresh in the small refrigerated chamber ready to put in place as we near the sun.

I grow weary.

I sleep for a time, a timeless time.

I am in Dublin, laughing in a bar, with Seamus and Mark.

I awaken shamefaced and blinking.

No one will help me.

Sean and Seamus are sipping at containers of liquid.

The liquid is pale and clear.

—I'll be singing you a song, Seamus says.

—I'm listening, says Sean.

—It's for you, says Seamus, although it's not about you.

—I'm glad to hear it, says Sean.

—The song, says Seamus and sings:

—I see by your armpits
   That you are a libber.

The hair on your legs
Says that you are one, too.
The tune is familiar, a cowboy song.
—Oh, stop it, says Sean.
His voice is bleary, his words blurred.
—Lay off me, says Sean, and sing a real song.
They raise their containers and punch them together.
I rise and go to the urinal, pull the tube and cup from the wall socket, fit it to me and relieve myself.
They sing a song about a wild rover.
They linger on the song.
—Will I be a wild rover, they sing, no never, no more.
They sing a song about black velvet bands.
They weep and drink and sing.
I go to work again on the walls.
They pay me no mind.
They are weeping and singing.
They argue vigorously about what songs to sing.
I press the damp cold potato boards into the nylon grooves and snap the flanges into place.
They discuss the abilities of the great John McCormack, how he talked of moving to Dublin after he became a citizen in 1919 but never did.
They shake their heads and cluck their tongues.
They pay me no mind.
They are sleeping and snoring.
I pick up the plastic container lying by Seamus' seat, sloshing onto the floor as he stirs and drops his arm on it.
I sniff it and taste it.
It is alcohol.
Ethyl alcohol.
The experiment is certainly a success.
The time passes secretly.
The clocks tell a tale, but one that no one believes.
Sean throws the telescopic image of the sun on the smooth screen he lowers on the wall behind us.
At first the sun is so huge that only a vast expanse of it, no curve in sight, fills the bright wall.

Sean adjusts the magnification down, and there is the sun, so close now, it seems, so swirling and stormy, white-capped and spouted.

I sketch what I see:

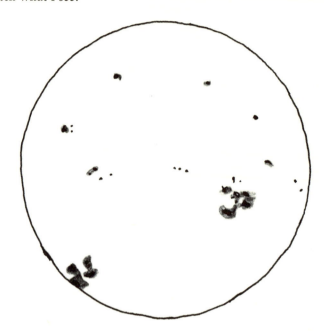

—Look at those spots, Sean says. Just look at them.

I am looking.

—That's where we're going, Sean says. Those spots. Spots like them. Use the rush of solar wind to brake our fall. Use the relative coolness to our benefit. Investigate those spots. Find out just how we can influence them, affect the weather back home, affect all life, energy, temperature, growth, seasons, everything. That's why we're here, Xhavid, and now you know.

I look at that glimmer on the wall, and I nod.

—We're going to land, I say.

—That's why they sent us at night, Sean says.

He and Seamus have a good laugh.

I watch that wall, those shimmering, living spots.

Storms on the sun.

Eruptions.

In the silence of this vessel, I feel the force of that sun.

I smell the burning peat.

I stand by the silent drive system, the scoops where forces beyond my belief beat soundlessly into the drive system, and I feel this whole vessel tremble with a fury that is silent and implacable.

Sean closes down the telescopic system.

The wall goes blank.

I return to my potatoes.

Sean and Seamus return to their drinking.

This time they are silent.

They drink silently but not for long.

They sit silently and stare at the empty wall.

They drift off to silent revery or sleep.

I press the slabs of potato into place.

I work until I am wet with sweat.

I have seen the sun, and I press the shielding walls into place.

Time passes at no particular pace.

I measure it by the progress I make on the shielding walls.

I measure it by the number of times I listen to Sean and Seamus sing and talk as I work.

I measure it by the number of dreams I have, the Adriatic, the Owl, a girl, cup under the knee, the burnt surface of a spinning dead sun and a flowering plant.

Always I awaken before the huge figure becomes distinct on the brittle plain.

I measure it by the rising temperature in this craft.

We are nearing the sun.

We must be.

I watch Seamus at his calculations.

I gather his notes and examine them.

I learn the principles of solar navigation; it is, after all, a star, and I am, after all, a sailor.

I calculate our position as they sleep and dream.

We pass Mercury off our starboard side as we passed the moon so very long ago, so very far ago, both of them barren and pocked.

The heat rises in this room.

—You must help me, I say to Sean. These walls are only half in place, and we are nearing the sun.

—Not so near, he says.

—We have passed Mercury, I say. You showed it to me yourself as we sailed by.

—Not so near, Sean says, that you have to worry. You worry too much, Xhavid. Everything's fine.

—But the heat, the temperature, I say, surely you must be aware of the evidence of that?

—You dress too warmly, Sean says.

He and Seamus have taken to lolling on their seats in their underwear, boxer shorts and sleeveless tops.

—Sean I say, but he is back in his little notebook, distant and immune to my remarks.

I break out another carton of potato board and heave it into place by the naked wall.

I have nearly made a complete round of the vehicle with one layer of potato; only a small experimental portion have I covered with the complete triple layer.

I settle in to work again.

Sean carefully copies something from his notebook onto a piece of plotting paper.

He rolls it into a tube and slides it into the empty liquid container lying on the floor by his seat.

He tosses the container over his shoulder and moans off to sleep.

The container drifts by my foot.

Is it a message to me?

A secret from Seamus?

Both are asleep.

I will read it and copy it here.

It is a poem I do not understand.

It is:

PASSING MERCURY ON THE LEFT

Is like looking at the moon
In a dream or through a prism,
Craters and rubble and rock
All aglow in a spectrum of heat.

Perhaps it is the lens.
Perhaps it is the eyes.
Perhaps it is a dream.

He is packing the wall
Against the sun
As though it were not here
Before he ever started.

He is singing a song
And talking of the past
As though he had a past
As though there were a past.

And I am looking at Mercury,
But not directly, for we never
Look directly, always a baffle
Of lenses and filters,
Memories and desires,
Interpretation.

When I woke the last time,
The time previous, some time,
I knew the room was not real,
Just a waking dream,
And then I knew for the first time
That I was not real either,
Hand that holds the unreal pen,
Eye that borrows, mind that notes,
All so distant, all so near.

It soon passed, passed
As we passed Mercury,
And here is a message
You'll never read
Cast out in a plastic bottle
Fluttering back on solar wind.

I do not think it is meant for me.
It seems to have a reference to me.
I do not understand that either.
I place the paper back in the container and replace it on the floor.
I settle in to work again.
—Sean, I say, Sean. You see what is happening. You see me working on
the heat shield, and yet you do not help. You know we are long past Mer-

cury, and yet you do not help. You feel the heat rising in this compartment, and yet you do not help.

—Seamus I understand, I say to Sean. He is drunk. He does not help because he is drunk and does not care. But why do you not help?

Sean stares at me, his eyes focused somewhere through me, somewhere beyond me.

He is not staring at the walls, potatoed or unpotatoed, but somewhere beyond the walls, into space, into the void.

This gives his eyes an open unfocused look.

They are blank and unseeing.

And yet I can tell he is looking at something.

He is looking at something, seeing something.

I work on the walls, sweating and weeping.

I work with the solargator.

I compute our position.

I compute our speed in relation to the sun as best I can.

My figures are blurred and indeterminate as though my eyes were bleary from looking into the sun.

But I can determine this one thing.

I can determine that we are either too close or are moving too quickly.

I compare the figures with those in the official log.

From what I can see we are going much too fast.

From what I can see, even if we swing the ship about now, reverse scoops, use the full force of the tachyonic drive, the inertia is too great.

We are not going to land on the sun.

We are not going to land at all.

We are going to dive into the sun.

Even if we change our course, veering to port or starboard, we will not miss the sun.

We will dive into its fury no matter what we do.

—Seamus, I say, for all that you care for, do something. You must know something to do I don't. We're going into the sun.

He stares at me.

He is not drunk.

He has not touched the remaining alcohol in his collecting container.

He is not drugged.

I have counted the pills.

He stares at me, and really he stares past me, like Sean.

He sees something, too.

I labor at the walls.

The heat is already very bad.

I put on my spacesuit, press the cooling system into action.

It helps.

It enables me to work on the walls.

Sean and Seamus lean back in their seats, their underwear drenched and stained with sweat.

I carry the cumbersome potato shielding across the crowded room.

I open the section containers.

I lift the slabs of raw potato out and slide them into place.

The sweat gleams on their faces, their arms and legs.

They seldom move at all now.

Once in what seems a very great while, one or the other of them will lift himself out of the seat and use the sanitary facilities.

Their faces have emptied of individual expression.

It is difficult for me to tell one from the other much of the time.

I do not think they ever sleep.

I do not think they ever dream.

I do not understand what is happening.

I still sleep.

I still dream.

I dream of water, of the Adriatic, of small bright sails and the sunlight winking from wavelets.

I awake crying as often as not.

Once I am sure I hear Sean and Seamus talking as I sleep, but the words they speak make no sense, are in no tongue I know, are urgent and important but unintelligible.

I fight awake.

—What, I say, what are you saying? Why don't you share your talking with me? You can trust me. I am a man of honor.

They look at me as though I am not here.

I wonder more and more whether I am here.

Perhaps I am not here.

Perhaps I died and was buried in space.

Perhaps I am dreaming in a madhouse near Dublin.

Perhaps I am dreaming in a madhouse near Dhermi.

I pound my fist into the wall, denting the potato, making myself cry out.

I beg Sean and Seamus to put on their spacesuits.

I even try to maneuver Sean into his, but he resists.

They sit in their seats, wet and nearly naked, their underwear wet as washcloths, their faces blank and alike.

The Wandering Aengus whistles down into the sun.

—We are falling into the sun, I cry to Sean.

His eyes focus for a second.

He looks directly at me.

—We are already there, he says.

I look around wildly, the heat shields only half in place, my fellow solarnauts unprepared, unprotected.

Sean's face goes blank again.

His lips move as though in speech.

Seamus's are moving, too.

The potato walls begin to sizzle and pop.

I fall into my seat.

I am unable to move.

I am unable to write further.

I have nothing more to say.

WINTER LIGHT

✳

The world's whole sap is sunk again indeed, sun squibs and slanting light, sunk in cold, not last year's bitter cold but cold enough, and buried now in deep loose snow. I walked to the college last night in the falling snow, hooded and hunched, my glasses fogging blank with every breath into my muffling bandanna, walked in the incredible silence of the falling snow, down an absolutely empty road in the dark night, the white snow catching what lost light still lingered in the cold air and giving that night's darkness a faint and indeterminate glow.

Snow on the ground. Snow in the air. The night air dark and gleaming. A silence over and in the frozen earth.

But today the snow has stopped falling, and the sky is clear and pale and clean, so bright that the eye recoils and the face wrinkles into a reflexive squint. Winter light, the low sun bounding and rebounding across the new white landscape, every still thing, tree limb and rooftop, abandoned automobile and solid creek, all snow-laced and sun-polished, caught for this frozen moment in what Emerson called "the mad wind's night-work, / The frolic architecture of the snow."

And this world, once you take a look and a listen, is not so still and certainly no longer silent. A spinning tire shrills on the uncovered ice somewhere down the hill, and from up the hill, down the long curve and curl of the road, come the shouts of bands of children safely home from the closed schools, and you are surrounded by the slither and grind of sleds bumping and sailing the long way down to the creek. Birds cluster and flutter at the

263

feeder by the Chinese cherry, colors lit by the day's white light, dove's gray-brown, cardinal's red and green, purple finch's raspberry, the yellow and black and white of the evening grosbeaks, birds waiting their turn or muscling in, movements and circlings and language all sharp in the winter light. Three sleds, linked in tandem, hand and foot, crunch and bang by, their daredevil riders packed two deep on each coach of the crazy train, muffled in red and light blue nylon jackets, puffed with goose down and duck down, here for a moment and gone on down noisily toward the icy creek.

The world is merry and bright, snow-built and noisy, and the world still suffers and cries out in its anguish. An old man's feet are doubtless freezing, a sled skids under the wheels of a bus, he bites the knuckles of his hand until they bleed, she cries into her pillow in the empty room. Hate still gnaws our vitals, and lust and greed, sins and follies, vanities and death. Thoughts come unbidden and leave their lasting scars. The victim tumbles out of bed and rushes to wash and dress, the odor of bacon drifting up the stairs. The killer carefully locks the door and walks away across the snow, patting the keys he has just let drop into his pocket. Winter has come. Winter is here.

But on this road today, snow drifted and snow disguised, even the black cat's hard body lost in a swell or a mound, there is only the communion of winter light, shared snow, the day that dazzles, day that draws us all out. You see the new neighbor from on down the road to whom you have never spoken, and you speak as though you were old friends. Even the dogs are running in circles together, barking and yelping but without a growl or bristle. When another neighbor's black Volvo is stuck on the steep hill on the other side of the creek, the children bunched and watching, their sleds tethered like ponies, someone dares touch its hood with a gloved hand, give it a slow spin like a hockey puck and then a shove, sliding it down the hill nose first and onto the level safety of the bridge. The kids applaud, snowballs arc overhead, a sled misses your foot by a foot, and the light stuns the eye, stuns the mind, sends you off, eyes open and in focus, to visit the day.

And what do you see? The people around you, the people beyond you, trees and houses, smoke spiraling against the sharp blue sky, snow on snow, tracks in the snow, snow untracked, sun's slice across the southern sky, light's dizzy ricochet from pillar to post to the outposts of the day, world's turn, day's motion, things in the air, surprises, hieroglyphs, mysteries, signs, this accumulation of winter light.

And memories, the things you do not see but see just the same, space and mind's conspiracy in time: the day you learned to print snow angels in the snow, flat on your back, wagging your legs and arms like some inscrutable apprentice signalman; the day you rode a sled for the first time down the long groove in the hill in the park, through the bushes, closing your eyes, under the hanging boughs and low branches, and over the stone wall at the foot with a jolt and a slam; the day you ducked a snowball in the cinder-block fort and split your front teeth on a garbage can's edge with the harsh precision of a diamond cutter's stroke (you duck your head now, and you still cringe); the day your father drove you to school with the snow falling so fast and deep that the windshield wipers failed, and you had to hang out the window shouting warnings and directions; the last day you saw your father, his face pale and worried against the white hospital sheet; the day your brand-new car was buried under a sudden yard of snow, not to reemerge for a month; the day Marvin showed you a purple finch for the first time, feeding in the sparse grass outside his room's window; the faces of your friends, some gone, some nearly forgotten, some far away, some just over the hill today, surely out in the snow, too.

A car clacks by on chains, chewing a foam of snow over onto my shoes and pants legs, and I remember, for no real reason at all, a summer day, a day by the cove, walking, Oliver running as usual far ahead, then rushing back to bark impatiently if you slow down or dawdle to talk. He is wet from splashing into the water, sloshing around and drinking his fill in the city's water supply, and David, visiting from England with his sister Gillian, decided the time was right to tell us a joke:

"There were a Russian, an American, and an Irishman," he said, "sitting in a pub. After a time, the Russian proposed a toast, and the others complied. 'To Russia,' he said, 'who put the first man in space,' and everyone raised their glasses. The American, not to be outdone, proposed a toast, too. 'To America,' he said, 'who put the first man on the moon.' Again the three drank the toast. Then the Irishman, much to the others' surprise, proposed a toast of his own. 'To Ireland,' he said, 'who'll put the first man on the sun!'"

Everyone laughed there, as though the joke were over, but, of course, it wasn't. David went on:

"The American and the Russian were astounded and said, 'You can't do that; it's too hot.' But the Irishman, nonplussed, replied, a little angrily, 'Do you think we're stupid? We're sending him at night!'"

Then everyone really laughed, and groaned. Oliver ran up, barking and running ahead down the trail and then back, showing us the way and the error of our ways.

That day long past, and this passes, white and cold and alive. Days pass;

years pass. A year has passed since Lucette fell in the snow and broke her hip, and now she is in North Carolina, well and sound, with one new scar and a memory for days like this, no trace of a limp. Cyndy writes from England about her friend Iggy Pop and about the punk world, this punk world, this moving world, world aspin. Your friends are at hand, and your friends are far away. They touch at the moving point of this snowy day, touch and turn away, return to touch again. The variety of this day, the varied tones of this day, of any day, slow dawn, the cartoons in the paper that make you laugh, the one you read without really seeing as your mind wandered away, pain in the chest, stiff knee, the children you pass on the snowy road, Mark and Shawn, Rick and Annemarie, the sound of a siren, whoop, and wail, the heavy grunt and grumble of a snowplow on the other side of the hill, not coming this way as the sledders relax, the joke you remember, the joker, the face you recall, the chores you must do, cat litter, mink oil on the boots, pages to read, pages to write, the mail that will come late, music on the phonograph, Iggy Pop and his Chinese rug, lust for life, Nielsen, Ives, the sun's quick disappearance, pink sky, pink snow, quick long shadows draining over the day and into night, the prayer you say, the prayer of thanks, the prayer of praise, the prayer of desperate supplication, love forgotten, love remembered, love unfeigned.

The world swings in a curve, in a spiral, around the universe, across the universe, passing time, knocking at heaven's door, star and satellite, planet and asteroid, comet and stellar wind. The blind man rubs his eyes in winter light and sees what he has eyes to see, light in the air, light from every side, light that wanes to come again, sees birds that circle and light, sees trees that walk like men and men standing like trees, winter light in the air, moving world, and he sees and knows that he is where he ought to be.

LISTS

✳

Winter. February. The cold center of winter, but the academic life creates its own seasons. The new semester begins today, the spring semester. Snow on the ground, the slanting winter light, and it is spring.

It is a time of lists, lists of books to read on syllabi, lists of classes to attend, class lists, the names of students, familiar and unfamiliar, schedules and forms, life reduced for a moment to rows and lists, the game of learning, batting orders, line scores, names and dates. It is a code, a hieroglyph, these lists that mean nothing apart from the context which they describe, and yet, to those who have eyes to see, lists that hold the flow and spin of the real, the reel and whirl of the things we think we know. Like the class list of Ramsdale School in *Lolita*, which even poor blinded Humbert recognized as a poem, "a poem I know already by heart."

I go to my film class, a course in Sternberg, and shuffle the grade cards to cover my initial awkwardness, that clumsiness I feel on the first day of every new class, even among friends when I know every face. Lisa's name is on the top card, and there is Lisa, sitting in the front, in the center, silent and very much there. The list is, of course, imperfect: names that match no person, and no names for some of those who are in the class, in the room. But it is a list, an approach; Cathy's name arrives at the top, and there she is. Hello, Cathy. Hello, hello.

I know of other class lists, have helped make some myself, the products of boredom, of disinterest, or just of energy: the number of times the professor tosses the chalk in the air, the number of times he punctuates his sentences with *um* or *er*, the number of times that young woman over there says "I think" in a single class, the careful list of all the words mispronounced in a class discussion. I remember once being presented a list at the end of one of my classes, a list of the twenty-seven writers whose names I had dropped that day—ahem, um, er.

The new semester begins. John is on leave now, so Henry, come to be our writer in residence, has moved into his office. He has a sign-up list on the door. I make a list of things to do to start the semester right. There are lists of concerts and films and readings and lectures taped up or thumbtacked here and there across the campus. There is a grocery list in my hip pocket, the only one I can be sure of not losing it in, and Dara walks by, debating whether to put an article about the fallen Russian satellite into her list of proofs for a finite universe or her other list of proofs for an infinite universe. How close we all are to Borges' Funes with his list of words for everything, that potentially infinite list of particulars that finally filled him up to his own destruction. Lists.

Here is a list of names:
Diane Ackerman, Joyce Agee, Bronson Alcott, Sherwood Anderson, Aristotle, Mark Atkins, Mary Ellen O'Brien Atkins, Shawn Atkins, Thomas Atkins, David Bache, Gillian Bache, Bandit, John Barth, Beau, Ingmar Bergman, Thomas Berger, Lucette Bernard, Friedrich Wilhelm Bessel, Denise Bethel, William Blake, Charles Bon, Nelson Bond, Daniel Boone, Jorge Luis Borges, Leigh Brackett, J. R. Bray, C. D. Broad, Anton Bruckner, Mary Bullington, Butch, James Branch Cabell, A. G. W. Cameron, Joyce Cary, Nicolae Ceausescu, Raymond Chandler, Agatha Christie, Alvan Graham Clark, Arthur C. Clarke, Nancy Cohen, Quentin Compson, Robert Coover, Nicolae Copernicus, James Gould Cozzens, Nancy Dahlstrom, Frederic Dannay, Robertson Davies, Paxton Davis, Benton O. Dillard, Mattie M. Dillard, John Donne, Lawrence Durrell, John A. Eddy, Albert Einstein, Ralph Waldo Emerson, Jessica Engels, John Engels, Garrett Epps, Annemarie Faery, Rebecca Faery, Rick Faery, William Faulkner, Federico Fellini, Jean Bernard Léon Foucault, Louis Friedman, Robert Frost, Ireneo Funes, Galileo Galilei, George Garrett, Susan Garrett, Donald George, Henry Green, Knut Hamsun, Cathy Hankla, Susan Hankla, Sam Haskins, Judy Hawkes, James Hays, Keith Hege, Ernest Hemingway, Hipparchus, Leslie Hornsby, Henry Howell, Sir Fred Hoyle, Ross Hulvey, Humbert Humbert, Christiaan Huygens, John Imbrie, Charles Ives, Jane, Jesus, Jonah, Robert Jordan, Ismail Kadare, Robin Kujan, Lady, H. H. Lamb, Ira Lechner, Manfred B. Lee, Ursula K. Le Guin, Mitchell Leisen, David Lindsay, Wes Lockwood, Loco, Konrad Lorentz, Los Angeles Dodgers, Spencie Love, Luke, Magda Lupescu,

Ernst Mach, Mark, Ann Martyn, Katherine Martyn, Matthew, Rita Matthews, Marcia Mayo, Mike Mayo, Shreve McCannon, Herman Melville, Kenneth Millar, Henry Miller, John R. Moore, Harold Morowitz, Wright Morris, Edna Munger, Véra Evseevna Nabokov, Vladimir Dimitrievich Nabokov, Vladimir Vladimirovich Nabokov, Leslie Nail, J. V. Narlikar, Carl Nielsen, Frank O'Brien, Oliver, Cynthia O'Neon, Pegeen O'Rourke, Dorothy Osborn, Deirdre O'Sorh, James Osterberg, Mitchell Page, Paul, Michael Pettit, Molly Pettit, J. B. Phillips, Pittsburgh Pirates, Edgar Allan Poe, John Cowper Powys, Marnie Prange, Herbert Quain, Alice Rabbitt, Redcoat, Dorothy Richardson, George Ritchie, Alain Robbe-Grillet, Edwin Arlington Robinson, John Rodenbeck, Cyndy Rose, Round Ruby, Truman Henry Safford, Salem Pirates, Son of Sam, Sancho, Schatz, Arnold Schoenberg, Erwin Schrödinger, Nicholas Schackelton, John Shade, Sean Siobhan, Cordwainer Smith, Lisa Squires, Olaf Stapledon, Betsy Stefany, Bruce Stefany, Gertrude Stein, Ralph Steinhardt, Josef von Sternberg, Laurence Sterne, Wallace Stevens, Maeryn Stradley, Henry Sutpen, Henry Taylor, Burn Thompson, Lewis Thompson, Henry D. Thoreau, Niko Tinbergen, J. M. W. Turner, Henry Vaughan, Teddy Villanova, Ian Walker, Selden Wallace, Wally, Orson Welles, Walt Whitman, Allen Wier, Dara Wier, William Carlos Williams, Winston-Salem Red Sox, Colin Wilson, Jennifer Wise, Willard Huntington Wright, Bill Zaffiri, Mary Barbara Zeldin, Xenia Zeldin.

This list of names we share.

No secrets here.

Good luck to the reader of these names.

And, of course, this list is as imperfect and inconstant and irregular as the rushing sun itself. Where are David Slavitt and Fred Chappell? Paul Zimmer or Brendan Galvin? Or William Hjortsberg? No sooperhowdi yo on the page. Where are Bill Robinson or Cronan Minton? Where are Bob and Kathie Panariso? Digging a path in deep Colorado snow? Why no reference to the interminable games, the entire season of board football Matt Spireng and Larry Roetzel and I played for eight months, the game itself? More lists: the lists of people I have left out unfairly, the lists of people I have fairly left out, those in touch, those out of touch, people to remember, to meet, to know. This list defining some part of the long event of my life; of yours, some part as well. This list of lists.

This list of books:

Diane Ackerman, *The Planets: A Cosmic Pastoral*; Hannes Alfven, *Evolution of the Solar System*; Angus Armitage, *Sun, Stand Thou Still*; Isaac Asimov, *Biographical Encyclopedia of Science and Technology*; Thomas R.

Atkins, *The Blue Man*; William R. Bendeen and Stephen P. Maran, eds., *Possible Relationships Between Solar Activity and Meteorological Phenomena*; Thomas Berger, *Killing Time*; Thomas Berger, *Who Killed Teddy Villanova?*; Nelson Bond, *No Time Like the Future*; Jorge Luis Borges, *Ficciones*; Leigh Brackett, *The Big Jump*; Ray Bradbury, *The Golden Apples of the Sun*; C. D. Broad, *Scientific Thought*; Kelly Cherry, *Relativity: A Point of View*; Agatha Christie, *A Murder Is Announced*; Arthur C. Clarke, *The Wind from the Sun*; Robertson Davies, *World of Wonders*; Paxton Davis, *Ned*; Samuel R. Delany, *The Einstein Intersection*; Bertrand Dillard, *The Atomic Structure of Radiant Energy*; Herbert Friedman, *The Amazing Universe*; Galileo Galilei, *History and Demonstrations Concerning Sunspots and Their Phenomena*; George Gamow, *The Birth and Death of the Sun*; George Garrett, *Death of the Fox*; George Garrett, *Do, Lord, Remember Me*.

Edward G. Gibson, *The Quiet Sun*; Robert Graves, *The Greek Myths*; Knut Hamsun, *A Wanderer Plays on Muted Strings*; Cathy Hankla, *Between Skins*; Sam Haskins, *November Girl*; Ernest Hemingway, *For Whom the Bell Tolls*; Sir Fred Hoyle and J. V. Narlikar, *Action at a Distance in Physics and Cosmology*; Sir Fred Hoyle, *Astronomy and Cosmology*; William J. Kaufmann III, *The Cosmic Frontiers of General Relativity*; Arthur Koestler, *Janus*; Ursula K. Le Guin, *The Dispossessed*; Ursula K. Le Guin, *From Elfland to Poughkeepsie*; Ursula K. Le Guin, *The Left Hand of Darkness*; Herman Melville, *Moby-Dick*; Henry Miller, *The Smile at the Foot of the Ladder*; Henry Miller, *Stand Still Like the Hummingbird*; Henry Miller, *Tropic of Cancer*; Henry Miller, *The Wisdom of the Heart*; Harold Morowitz, *Energy Flow in Biology*.

Wright Morris, *The Fork River Space Project*; Wright Morris, *The Works of Love*; Vladimir Nabokov, *Lolita*; Vladimir Nabokov, *Pale Fire*; Vladimir Nabokov, *Speak, Memory*; Vladimir Nabokov, *Transparent Things*; J. J. Pierce, ed., *The Best of Cordwainer Smith*; Edgar Allen Poe, *Eureka*; Sun Ra, *The Immeasurable Equation*; George G. Ritchie, *Return from Tomorrow*; Wolfgang Rindler, *Essential Relativity*; Erwin Schrödinger, *What Is Life?*; the editors of *Scientific American*, *Cosmology + 1*; the editors of *Scientific American*, *The Solar System*; Idries Shah, *The Sufis*; William Jay Smith, *Celebration at Dark*; C. P. Sonnett, P. J. Coleman, Jr., J. M. Wilcox, eds., *Solar Wind*; Olaf Stapledon, *Sirius*; Leslie F. Stone, *When the Sun Went Out*; Edwin F. Taylor and John Archibald Wheeler, *Spacetime Physics*; S. S. Van Dine, *The Bishop Murder Case*; Steven Weinberg, *The First Three Min-*

utes; Paul West, *Gala*; Allen Wier, *Blanco*; Dara Wier, *Blood, Hook & Eye*; Colin Wilson, *The Mind Parasites*.

Lists of the elements. Lists of the stars. Lists of the photographs scattered over the house, her in her wonderful straw hat, her in her new leather jacket, him grinning and making a face. You make lists and check them twice, and the list, like life, changes as you check it. It is a list without end, a list which, if it is to be accurate, if it is to include everything that touches you and that you have touched, must contain the full contents of spacetime, universe and cosmos, and more, must impinge upon eternity, list beyond making, list that is itself particle and whole, a poem you already know by heart.

I put away my lists and go to the college dining room for dinner. The room is full and echoing from brick to glass, and outside the evening is gray and full of clouds. Leo Munger catches the corner of my eye in his red coat, raising the blinds to let in the easing out of the day, low clouds capping Green Ridge and hanging over the cove, the snow slick and glowing across the grounds, over the low hills. He is always alert to catch the day and share it with those in his care. Someone is over there, with a pair of binoculars, looking at something through the large, darkening window, perhaps a bird in the evening air. Good luck to her. Dara and Allen are here at the table with me. Good luck. Cathy is just over there. Hello. Good luck. Good luck. Another list. Life as list, as lists.

I bundle up after dinner to walk home through the dark, this winter night of the first day of the spring semester. The stars are sharp and clear, the procession of planets, light through the black bare boughs of the trees. A dark shadow passes over the stars, passes on. A cloud sailing in winter wind, high winter wind. There are so many things to see, so many things to think of, walking on a night like this. So many things. I'll make a list.

SUN

*

The surface of the sun, that seething sea, has a temperature of about 5,700° Celsius, a gaseous sea some several hundred miles thick dotted with drifting sunspots and magnetic arches of spiraling gas. From it blows the solar wind, gusting to a thousand miles a second. Out from this surface extends the chromosphere, sprinkled with spicules of fountaining gas sprayed out thousands of miles and with occasionally erupting prominences, clouds of incandescent gas that float in the solar sky. Heated by the frictional dissipation of shock waves from the turbulent surface of the sun, the temperature of this multilayered solar atmosphere increases with altitude, reaching in less than ten thousand miles more than 1,000,000° Celsius, reaching eventually up to 2,000,000° Celsius.

How will the Wandering Aengus sail this inferno, touch down on that infernal sea?

Not up but out, not out but in.

There will be, of course, the potatoes, laminated sheets of processed Irish potato, placed in place in grooves all along the inner walls of the vehicle by a worried Xhavid Shehu. Those potato shields will be primarily designed for the earliest phases of the flight into the sun, or, rather, into the inner core of the sun's corona (we're in the corona right now, you and I and this spinning earth, just not in quite so deep).

The really important heat-shielding device will be triggered automatically as the temperature in the ship reaches that certain degree. Huge magnets, powered by the apparently limitless force of the tachyonic drive system, will create what might be loosely termed a magnetic vacuum around the Wandering Aengus, designed to oscillate, allowing the scoops to continue to function and yet sealing the ship successfully off from that astonishing heat.

Xhavid will not know of this device, but he will recognize its efficacy once it turns on and will collapse by his scorched potato wall, thanking fate or chance, luck or even God for his success, his work's success.

Xhavid will know that the vehicle will not be slowing down for a landing on the sun, and he will know that his fellow solarnauts will be lounging about, glassy-eyed and blank-faced, not helping at all, not steering the ship down as they should. He will not know whether some automatic device will be doing all those things that he will assume should be being done. He will watch his gauges and lurch around the room in his spacesuit. He will not know just when they will touch the surface of the sun.

Sean will know.

: spots and filaments, spicules, prominences and plages, granulation at the top layer of the bubbling convection zone, granulation like a rumple of cumulus cloud, ridged and bumped like kernels of corn, ripple and silent roar, dear sun, my eyes are closed or are they open, I seem to see as well one way as the other, I see on occasion the seared walls, smell the scent of scorched potato, watch Xhavid bumble about, wish I could tell him to stop, to settle down, to settle in, to sit a spell, then I don't see him at all, don't remember, watch the bubble and burn of the solar surface, see it near, spots opening like sores, or like cool lakes, like mouths, or like delicate dimples, diving down, granulated solar tissue splashing out, not out but in, all this motion and yet standing still, hum and hover, dive and splash, rhythm, rhythm, don't mean a thing, hello :

This will be no stream of consciousness, for in Sean's consciousness there will be no stream, no flow, only a silence, only a stillness. This will be speech unspoken, speech spoken, silent speech.

Seamus will know.

Seamus will, in fact, be speaking the same words.

: hello, the sun below, no, sun there, sun here, hello :

The words will not, so to speak, mean a thing, but there they will be. For a time.

The ship will zing and slip through the rollick of the sun's silent roar, a tiny magnetic bubble, its interior choked with wisps of peat smoke and sizzling potato, two men dazed and somehow one, one man dazed but beside himself, sent at night to land on the sun and landing on the sun, splashing down, splashing in, and not at night someone will see them, not really see them, see some eight and a half minutes later, some ninety-two million miles later, see a solar flare begin to bulge and swell out from the sun's raw surface, not at the little observatory in Dublin, Virginia, but at the Big Bear Solar Observatory at Cal Tech, a solar flare erupting from magnetic arches looping from spot to spot in an active region, a solar flare triggered by some disturbance in the photosphere. Some disturbance.

Seasick Xhavid, dizzier than he will have been since his first days as a young swabby on the wind-chopped Adriatic, will stagger and slur and fall about the bouncing room. He will sail at one point right across lurching Sean and Seamus, still sprawled on their unsteady seats, crying out as he passes over, "What am I supposed to be learning? Tell me what to do," then landing with a crack on his helmeted skull and settling into a gentle silent orbit around the bobbing room, revolving in an even peaceful silence, a gentle dream.

The mother and father are sitting on their low three-legged stools before the unusually bright fire, a fire that spurts and rumbles, digs up into the darkness of the chimney flue, spicule and arching eruption, casting shadows across the dim low-ceilinged room, the unusually hot room, making it waver and shift shape in the fluid light, making the pallet in the corner by the farther wall seem to bob and drift like a small boat on a red sea. The bed's sole passenger is the baby brother, a lad of four, stricken with paralysis, his jaws rigid and limbs limp, two of his front teeth missing where the father has punched the teeth out with the ramrod of the rifle hanging over the heavy wooden door, where the mother feeds the silent infant spoonful by patient spoonful, dripping the broth through the small shattered opening to the throat that clutches and somehow swallows.

: Xhavid : the mother is saying, nodding her head and smiling : Xhavid, so you have finally come. It has been very difficult without you. Your father has lost much of his dignity in your absence :

The father nods his head, too, smiles, teeth broken in, broken out, like the brother's, gestures to the rifle on the wall, nods again.

: I was going to be married : Xhavid says : but then there was an attack on the project, and I had to come to the sun. I did restore my honor. I killed Prostranstvo. I'm sure I did. But I have had to come to the sun :

Katrina is spooning the broth into his mouth, so he is unable to say more.

The room is turning slowly around, the dance of firelight a shimmer as it moves. The father's face is glowing and approving.

: Good luck to Xhavid : the mother says.

The room nods.

: Good luck to Xhavid :

: Good luck to Xhavid :

: cloud like a fish, cloud like a stone :

The Wandering Aengus in its magnetic bubble will dive like no bubble through the seethe and churn of the solar sea, in and in, the unheeded needles noting the temperature's fall, the temperature's rise, the ship's descent in and in.

The dive will become confused by the vital activity of the sun, wave and whirlpool, the force of the tachyonic material feeding the drive; the magnets will hold firm; the ship will bob and bounce, join the sun's inner ebb and flow.

: spin and float like something in the air, Xhavid turning like a satellite, wheel of a gyroscope, swinging like a pendulum, tuft of seed, radiation, X-ray, skeletons in the room, skeleton in the chair, skeleton in the chair, skeleton in orbit in a spin, just like Betty Boop, Minnie the Moocher, hoochie-coocher, dancing skeletons, rhythm, rhythm, don't mean a thing, hello :

Xhavid will not be sure whether he is awake or asleep, whether his eyes are open or closed. The room will be swinging around him, Sean and Seamus staring in their seats, scorched walls, bobbing needles and dials. Or will the room be still and Xhavid swimming around it like a nervous fish in the bowl's bulged walls. Then Sean and Seamus will be skeletons, like the bony feet he once saw in a dusty shoe store in Milano, bones that wiggled and jumped when he moved his own toes in the buzzing machine, two skeletons fluoroscoped and sprawled in their seats, eye sockets empty and staring, teeth in a harsh grin, cracked rib, healed rib, crooked knee.

Then Xhavid will not see the room, the instruments in dizzy agreement, the skeletons or his friends. He will see the sun, strawberry red, and all around, boiling and bursting, pot of flame, spotted and tracked, flowing hieroglyph and wandering sign.

: hello :

Sean and Seamus will no longer be staring. They will be seeing. In fact, he will be seeing as much through their eyes as through his own, will see his own revolving bones, his own hollow eyes. His mind will whir, brain dizzy, giddy, sick, the view from six eyes, four of them still, two circling, hard to handle, at first.

Then the sun again, clearer still, color without name, scene without description, word unspoken, word spoken, silent word.

: hello, Xhavid :

: hello, Sean and Seamus :

: hello :

: can we talk now :

: yes, but there is little need :

The sun swells and rolls. The sun stands still.

The sun will swell and roll. The sun will stand still.

The three skeletons will grin and gaze, hard bone and floating joint, orbiting skull and bones, seated bones and skulls.

: in the sun :

: in the sun :

: surprise :

Xhavid will carve a path through the peat smoke and potato stain filling the room's tight air, an air ring in smoke.

: a boy should be raised in ashes, in ashes and smoke :

: raised in ashes :

Gritted grinning teeth will glint in the smoke, in the air, in the whoosh of Xhavid's passing.

: sun :

: sun :

: sun :

: how can I tell what is mine, whether what I am seeing is mine, am I circling or still, is that you or me :

: yes, hello :

: I mean, someone is holding a hand up before a face, it is all bones, perhaps a ghostly web of flesh, shadow of skin, is that hand mine, it looks familiar, is that hand mine :

: no :

: yes :

Xhavid will find it increasingly difficult to know who is speaking, who is listening. He will feel his voice move in his bones, and he will hear his ears respond, shivering bone and cartilage. He will see one mouth move and then another, be moving mouth and cocked ear at once, will begin to know the answer to the question before the question is framed, will know less owning and more knowing, less owning, less owning, more knowing, knowing.

The sun will rush and slide around them, all around them, roily and restless, rolling, dense and disturbed. Vision moves in and out, from boneyard to sunyard to bones to sun, both kinds of seeing multiple and one, eye in the socket and eyeless socket, eye and eye and eye and eye and eye and eye. Eye.

Vision will move, and visions will appear.

: egg, ha ha, just like the dream, giant egg, grinning and telling a joke, Officer Pat, big shoes, ira on the shoes, right on the soles, tough egg, hardboiled, ha ha, egg with short ribs, no ribs, gobbling like a turkey and very near, where is that egg, why is it following so near, so close, lightning cracking the red sky like an egg, eggshell, no rain, just heat, heat lightning, and falling from the sky, through the sky, the body, end over end, coming in, like a leaf, tree leaf, leaf from a book of poems, fluttering down, no, fluttering in, here comes, hello :

Sun. Room. Dream. Earth, only eight and a half minutes away. Earth.

: the Adriatic just turning out of sight, calm and cold, cold clear day, air like a lens, faint marbling of drifting cloud, snow clouds high in the mountains sinking into night, lights winking on, dynamo's hum, firelight in the hearth, the old man oiling his rifle, firelight mingling with last sunlight leaking through the frosted window, old woman by the stove, boiling pot, the grave under a skim of snow, letters wearing, ragged weeds, small stone, Katrina, fading, night, and the rolling into view across wide ocean, wet and moving and cold, earth tilted away, leaning back, light bright on the ocean, light crossing the Blue Ridge and breaking in, in Roanoke, at the airport, a young girl, Mollie Mulligan, standing in the dawnlight, waiting for the plane back to school, bright hair like a sailor's warning, encouraging the porter with her new Christmas luggage, red plaid, packed and heavy, talking to the porter and nodding her head, breath puffing in the bright cold air, laughing, on her way, and all around, shining snow, cleared in paths and roads, winking back at the sun, and down the road, near the foot of a dam, five hens step out onto the frozen ground, cluck and growl, step lively on the brittle snow, lilac bushes bare and sealed beside the chipped brick wall, and down the road, the long wide road to Dublin, sun spreading over Dublin, blinking and ducking his head under his arm, pale arm and its stipple of black hair, Blackie O'Flynn, it is himself, groaning and digging in, wrinkled sheets, and in bed with him, it is, it is, can't be, isn't, he must be alone, still,

still, a curl of cloud swims and swings over, eye wanders, cars cough and stutter, puffs of gray smoke sputtering into the clean air, Hanrahan is on the way to work, guard posts along the road, saluting soldiers, Estaban driving the old small car, naked dash, no egg, where is the egg, the egg, it is, it is, can't be, is, the thin pencils of smoke hovering over the chimney pots of house and house, shingle and wattle and thatch, white wall, stone wall, barn and stable, the graveyard near Ben Bulben's base, grave with the new brass footstone, flat plaque, bare earth, O'Sorh, rest in peace, ground hard as an egg, white and cold, a figure falls from the tower into the morning light, end over end, coming in, like a leaf, tree leaf, leaf from a book of poems, book of poems clutched in her hand, it is, it is, can't be, isn't, must be the shadow of a bird, large bird, owl or bald-headed buzzard swinging in an even hungry circle, still, still, day moves over the mountains, past the mountains, cloud wrinkled, cold, light through a window, light on a blue rug, book lying on the corner of a bed beside a sleeping dog, a snuggled cat, man in the bed groans and stretches, puts on his glasses as the dog steps off the bed with a thump, dresses, gives the little hound a milkbone, the brindle cat stretches, yawns, the man walks barefooted out the door onto the frost and stiff sharp grass, he looks up straight into the sun, don't mean a thing, hello :

Earth, ninety-two million miles away. Earth and sun. Sun.

The Wandering Aengus will tremble and bolt, dart through convections, deep wave and current, eddy and fill. The drive will stammer but never falter. The magnets will hum and hold. The bubble will sway and carry.

: hard to think :

: stone like a cloud, stone like a fish :

: almost remember as though there were something to remember :

: have seen visions :

: yes :

: have seen facts :

: events :

: yes :

: at the speed of light :

: hello :

The Wandering Aengus will steady and swim, will flatten and float, even and sure, suddenly inwavering, steady. The two skeletons in the chairs will take on flesh again, the shadowy aureole around the bones gaining substance, texture, color. The circling skeleton will fill out, too, a man in a spacesuit soaring around a smoke-filled room, nearing walls but never touching, suspended between ceiling and floor.

: what is happening :

: it is happening :

: I think we're here :

Two men standing, catching at a third.

Three men standing, two half-dressed, one too-dressed.

Three men on the forest floor, a sprinkle of soft pine needles underfoot, no path, no paths, the forest itself the only way. Red sky, delight or warning. Tall trees knocking and bending overhead in a drifting and eddy. Roots sprawled and snarled on the ground, diving out of sight, sliding away, staying firm in the arch of the foot, ball of the foot, curved toes.

Ailanthus and aspen, larch and little hip hawthorn, small-leafed live oak and leaf-bulging bur oak, rowan and rock elm.

Trees.

Whispering wild plums, sweet birch, sweetbay and sweet gum.

Walnut and wahoo, sassafras and slippery elm, moosewood and paper birch.

Trees hissing and sighing, twigged and twiggy, a shiver and swift scattering, tree and tree, tree and bush, tree and shrub.

As far as eye can see.

Farther.

: forest and forest floor, stone like a fish, stone like a cloud, hello :

Vision. Fact. Event. Tree.

: talking to trees :

: what can you say to trees :

: what will trees reply :

: fgma   X Z   X :

: not tree :

: not a dream :

: not a dream :

: vision, fact, event, tree :

A leaf brushes along the skin, along the arm, across the face, wide leaf, veined and splayed, the red light glowing through its almost audible green, live veins, live leaf, almost audible life. Jack pine and jersey pine, lodgepole and longleaf, a stand of pussy willow, a clump of quaking aspen, split and frayed yucca, the royal palm, all moving, all living. Trees nodding their heads and talking, almost loud enough to hear, trees singing, saying what eye has not seen nor ear heard, almost loud enough to be heard by those with ears to hear.

The forest of trees, of alders and elms, of plane trees and tamaracks, will nod and whistle, rattle and stroke, hang like clouds in the red air, dig into ground and stand firm.

: pureness and knowledge, patience and kindness, holiness of spirit and love unfeigned :

: innocence and insight, forgiveness and kindness, the holy spirit and genuine love :

: purity and wisdom, forbearance and kindness, a spirit of holiness and unpretended love :

: forgive and remember :

What will they forgive?

What will they remember?

: Mark Welser leaning on the polished edge of a billiard table in a federal prison, lolling and laughing, asking for a light, Pegeen's stunned and tear-streaked face, Pegeen lying back on the floor in a white dress with her strong legs spread, Katrina's face opening like an egg, cracked and broken, split by a skewer of steel, Deirdre diving, Deirdre tumbling down and down, in and in, gone to earth, away from the sun, Sean nervous and selfish, Sean on the phone, Sean talking and wondering, Sean hanging up, with a click, with a click, with a click, Prostranstvo standing on the bridge, a spray of salt water beading on the rail, setting a course due south, Xhavid pulling the trigger and giving in, Xhavid watching an old man, a stranger, tumble over in his own droppings, Xhavid snapping back the bolt on the rifle and springing the punched brass cartridge out onto the ground, Seamus in a rage, petty and spiteful, Seamus shoving the plastic container under his knee, holding it out to Xhavid, grinning raggedly at Xhavid, Blackie hitting himself up and down with a wrench, Blackie crawling under the workbench, Blackie walking past Pegeen on the sidewalk, nodding and giving her a wink, Blackie running his hand under the loose blouse of Idris O'Ertel, rubbing her smooth skin, pressing up under her breasts, Blackie in the headquarters shaking hands, the campaign in full swing, Ismail and Mehmet, Enver, Velimir and Koci, Prostranstvo in a very dark place, the small child Sean standing on the kitchen table and squirting urine into the air, the small child Seamus pointing to a stranger and naming him falsely thief, the small child Xhavid screaming and punching his father in the stomach with his fist, forgive and remember, a world of deceit, a world of disorder, a world of death, camps and bombings, victims, killers, passersby, slavery and rape, execution, crucifixion, hatred, hatred, betrayal, betrayal, betrayal, impure, ignorant, impatient, cruel, unholy, loveless, a world dying, a world of the dying, world of the dead, a world alive, forgive and remember, treachery and forgiveness, violence and forgiveness, cruelty and forgiveness, death and forgiveness, betrayal and forgiveness, patience, patience, patience, faith, forgive and remember, a love unfeigned, a love unfeigned, a love unfeigned :

: forgive and forget :

It will be difficult to walk through the thick forest, difficult to walk with six separate legs, difficult to see to walk with six separate eyes, seeing and seeing and seeing, step and step and step. They will stumble and fall, he will walk right into a tree, he will catch his hair in the thick boughs of a great oak, he will trip and stagger to his knees. They will walk through trees in the steady red light of the sun.

: forgive :

: Seamus with his eyes red and face ruddy, swilling a beer and leaning hard on the shaky table, Sean with his pencil and his pad, writing words and failing to notice the passage of the day, Xhavid wrapped in bitter memory and rapping his fist into the concrete wall, Blackie licking his lips and ducking out the door, Deirdre lying so still, so cold, so very pale, Pegeen, well, Pegeen, Red and Padraic, Sawel and Idris, Mollie and Richard, Mark, the day, the rhythm of day and night, it means so much, stars turn and earth's spin, universe that swings and universe that stays, rumbling silent sun, planet marbled brown and white and blue, something you somehow haven't to deserve, with a love unfeigned, a love unfeigned :

The trees will shimmer and part, and there will be the Wandering Aengus, dented and scarred, unhurt and whole, a small rubber egg waving greetings from its side, good, good. They will walk toward it, stepping on each other's toes, their own, weave a ramble, a way. They will reach the open door and pause and look around, six-eyed, able to see.

: these people of the sun, people with the green heads, this talking, this conversation, trees, tree :

: tree like a cloud, tree like a stone :

It will all be so very familiar.

: we have always been here, here in the sun, incubating, basking, growing, fusing, joining, doing, always here, have always been here, in the sun :

: tree like a fish, hello :

They will pause at the door and look around, see forest and tree, leaf and stem, root and rootlet, ground, ground. With a love unfeigned. Green leaves, red sky, tree bark like a cough, pitch and resin, leaves and moving steady sky.

: forget :

The door will clap into place. Seamus will check out the smoldering fire, fusing peat, smoke seeping all through the sealed ship. Sean and Seamus will settle in their seats. Soaring Xhavid will bump down, shaking his head, find his own seat and settle in. The trees will tremble and stand silent in the red red sky. The drive will hum and howl, the magnets holding everything in place, in and in, out and out, in and out. The trees will shake and gust, leaves lifting and quaking, turning pale and pure in the red red sky. The ship will buck and wobble, swing and dart, dive and sway. The trees will wrinkle and waver, wink and wave, shimmer and stand in the red red sky. Tree and tree, tree and tree. These men, these solarnauts, this motley three. Eyes will wink and waver, eyes will blur and wave. The Wandering Aengus will wander on away, caught in convection, tossed and scrubbed, a bubble rising, a bubble seized and seething, a bubble moving out and out.

: good-bye :

: good-bye :

: good-bye, now, good-bye :

A rhythmical roll and dance, rock and step, out and out.

: it must mean a thing :

: good-bye :

The Wandering Aengus, wild rambler and rover, will be kicked to and fro in turbulent convection, tossed out in a supergranular cell onto the boiling and bubbling surface of the sun, punched and blown from the photosphere into the burning prairie of the chromosphere, sailing with the fiery bristle of spicules out and out, out and out. It will rush out with the solar wind into the swelling corona, solar wind which will reach earth in five days. If the Wandering Aengus could spread wings or slender spreading plastic sails, it could sail home on solar wind, soar and drift and tack, come home like a bird, a pigeon bearing the message that matters. But it will have no wings to spread, only its scorched and twisted scoops, gathering tachyons and passing them through peat, a force unbounded, a force for the moment bound, bound for home, sailing home in the blow and rush of solar wind.

These three within:

: Seamus Heanus, the first man on the sun :

: Xhavid Shehu, the first man on the sun :

: Sean Siobhan, the first man on the sun :

They will be exhausted, will sleep in silence, will share no dreams, will have no dreams, only a rustle and shimmer, a wrinkle of red light through green leaves, a shift and whisper.

: good-bye, now, good-bye :

The automatic equipment on the vehicle will click and snap, making the programmed decisions, computing and observing, shifting the scoops and directing the drive.

"Ouch, help! I could for sure be using a drink," Seamus will say, waking up and rolling over, feeling with his hand for the empty plastic container which will have once been on the floor.

"What time is it?" Xhavid will ask. "What time? What day? What year?"

"It doesn't mean a thing," Sean will say, rubbing his eyes, trying to sit up straight.

"Have we been to the sun?"

"We've always been in the sun, always, all of us."

"I think maybe we were the first men on the sun."

Out and out.

Sean will feel for his pencil, for his pad, but he will not write a word, will have no word to write.

: sun :

: something you somehow haven't to deserve :

: sun :

Vision. Fact. Event.

The planets will swing on around the sun, all of them, sun and planets, swinging around the galaxy, around the universe, spin of the cosmos, swing and swing.

The Wandering Aengus will wander home. Someday. Sometime.

Perhaps it will be scorched and fused, broken down and stripped, reduced to solar wind, will arrive as a patter and zing of solar wind. Perhaps you will see it as a high wrinkle of twisting light in the northern sky, aurora borealis, streaming and bright. Perhaps you will see it as a rush of electric snow on your television or hear it as a growl of static on your radio. The first man on the sun filling the air, sailing through your cells and atoms like a sliding dream.

And then again.

Some day. Some time.

The Wandering Aengus will seek and find its homing beam, will swoop like an owl, will end its retracing search, orphan found, prodigal returned, three strange angels knocking at the door, will pivot gently on the reaching tip of the landing column, hover like a hawk, will settle like a leaf, settle down, settle in, in and in, coming home to earth, round drifting earth, end over end, like a leaf, tree leaf, leaf from a book of poems, gone to earth, things in the air, sailing and soaring, spinning, things on the earth, delicate examination of the tiny milkweed bug, bloat of the lost cat in the ditch, body laid out in the ditch, faces turned up to the day or night, faces looking up, looking out, faces, eager, ashamed, joyous, weeping, ecstatic, bitter, envious, hateful, dull, uncomprehending, shining, foolish, open, all alive, all alive, his eyes narrow and small, hers shining with love, and the first man on the sun will know now for sure and all and ever that he is at first and at last just exactly where he ought to be.

GALILEO AGAIN

*

The knock at the door. Sun rapping at door and window, and it is Galileo's birthday again. Galileo Galilei, his four hundred and fourteenth birthday, four hundred and fourteen spinning years. The winter sun is bright and hard, glancing off the snow and knocking at the walls. The sun's spiral laps itself again, caught circle and freed coil. The dog and cat stretch and flap and yawn, and the day begins again. The world's sap is still sunk, but the circle's promise is in the air, winter and spring, and the sun is vibrant in the eastern sky. There for all to see.

We enter the day simply, snow on the ground, warmth in the air, sunlight and flustered birds at the feeder. But no day is simple, no sign easy to read. We are entering, sun and circling planets, planetoid, asteroids and moons, the thin outer limits of a vast interstellar cloud, quite possibly the hundred and fiftieth such cloud through which our solar system has passed in its long life. It may take us three thousand years to reach the center of this cloud, perhaps thirty times that long. And when we do, the solar wind and light may tunnel through the cloud, bore a curving channel that will protect us and guide us through. But if the cloud is dense enough, we could be cut off from the vital solar wind and cast into an ice age, big or small, and if it is sufficiently dense, the cloud could feed the sun on its drifting gas, stoke it up, increase its brightness by one or two percent, that brightness increasing evaporation here on earth, filling the atmosphere with clouds, cutting us off from the sun and giving us a major ice age for sure.

We are an icy planet, moving from cloud to cloud, ice age to ice age, all across the universe. Or maybe not. Perhaps the sun will see us through, solar wind and forceful light, blazing us a path, keeping us warm and showing us the way. Years from now when what ownership we have on this cold planet, warm planet, will long since be passed, all this will occur, and yet it is happening now, today and tomorrow, and it is our story, yours and mine.

A year ago an old man, over a century old, lost his feet protecting what he possessed, what he did not own. You look closely at yourself, foot and hand, the small scar on the little finger almost invisible to an unaided, unguided eye, twist of the toes, palms with their tangle of silent lines, nails, and hangnails, feet that carry you along, hands that get you through the day. Without them, you say, you would be lost, and yet with them you are lost, too. You possess nothing, or nothing for long. You wake to the day, and then you do not. You look closely at your hand, and it is not yours. You touch wood, and the wood goes away. You drift into a cloud, and you disappear.

The game of this book, this game, is almost over. Your right hand, finger and thumb, will tell you that. I call it my book, but it is not mine. You may call it yours, too, but it is not yours. Foot and hand, scar and curling lines, book in hand, world sailing into a cloud. We possess nothing.

The sunlight winks from the banked snow, and you recognize this game, game within a game, for what it is. You wink back. The joke's on you, but the last laugh is yours, too. It is a fool's joke, joker and victim one, victim and laugher, too. We possess nothing, and we possess all things.

The eight new supergravity theories with their concern with symmetry and spin may well give us the Grand Unification Theory we need to help us see just how we belong and what belongs to us, but we know already in another way, swing and spin, distance that is close at hand. The hand, the foot, bird on the wing, cat buried in the snow, this book, that book, long list, and long event, thin rings of Uranus, dust storm on Mars, romping Sirius, the miracle of sight, miracle of the day, life—all these are not mine, not yours; all these are ours, yours and mine, property of the stars, sun flare and sunburst, interstellar cloud and wandering milkweed bug. We matter to each other, belong to each other, list of infinite length, passing through, passing on, still and standing still. We possess nothing; we possess all things.

The stone fish lies in the dusty sunlight by my window. I take it for a sign. Snow slides from the branch of a hemlock across the way, and the branch bobs and beckons. I take it for a sign. The sun, imperfect, inconstant, irregular, rises regularly as clockwork in the morning sky. I take it for a sign. Life within life. Love within life. Life within love. The signposts show the way. It is Galileo's birthday. Greetings on all sides. Good luck. Good luck. Good luck. The front door swings open, and Jane and Oliver spring into place, looking out. I take it for a sign. The day is in place, moving and moving on. *Eppur si muove*. The time has come, time passing, passing time, time to go. The sun is loose in the sky. The signs are clear.

Good-bye.